Sweetwater Blues

Told with the sureness and wit of a modern-day Mark Twain, *Sweetwater Blues* stakes its place among American classics. Thank you, Raymond Atkins, for taking me on a coming-of-age journey every bit as hilarious, honest, bittersweet, and wise as that of Huck Finn on his raft—and from a prison cell, no less.

—Lynn Cullen, national best-selling author of *Mrs. Poe*

Sweetwater Blues is a compassionate novel that asks the reader to go beyond the headlines on the nightly news to the human story. Atkins created a brilliant character in Palmer Cray, who insists the reader suspend his or her judgment and listen to what he has to say.

—Ann Hite, author of award-winning *Ghost On Black Mountain*

Like an Otis Redding tune, *Sweetwater Blues* will seduce the willing. Raymond Atkins is one of Georgia's natural wonders—a crack-wise writer, who invokes laughter and invites imagination. *Sweetwater Blues* is a frolicking good read, sure to be a hit among convict book clubs nationwide.

— Karen Spears Zacharias, author of *Mother of Rain*.

Raymond Atkins is a marvel. As one of Georgia's most talented authors, he magically weaves complex stories from believable characters. You know the people he writes about; they are flawed, complicated, and real. From the first page to the last, *Sweetwater Blues* takes the reader on a journey filled with consequences, courage, and redemption. Using his remarkable wit and masterful gift of storytelling, Atkins brings us full circle. When you close this book you will wonder, what else has he written? Then you will rush out to buy his other award-winning books.

—Renea Winchester, author of
Farming, Friends & Fried Bologna Sandwiches

MERCER
UNIVERSITY PRESS

Endowed by
TOM WATSON BROWN
and
THE WATSON-BROWN FOUNDATION, INC.

Sweetwater Blues

A Novel

Raymond L. Atkins

MERCER UNIVERSITY PRESS | Macon, Georgia
35 Years of Publishing Excellence

MUP/ P495

Published by Mercer University Press, Macon, Georgia 31207

9 8 7 6 5 4 3 2 1

Books published by Mercer University Press are printed on acid-free paper that meets
the requirements of the American National Standard for Information Sciences—
Permanence of Paper for Printed Library Materials.

Library of Congress Cataloging-in-Publication Data

Atkins, Raymond L.
Sweetwater blues: a novel / Raymond L. Atkins.
pages cm
ISBN 978-0-88146-507-5
ISBN 0-88146-507-0
(pbk.: alk. paper)

1. Friendship–Fiction.
I. Title.
PS3602.T4887S94 2014
813'.6–dc23

2014020491

For Marsha, who believes in me. For Anna Jane,
Charlie, and Max with love and hope. And for Ann,
who allowed me the privilege of remembering for her.

Acknowledgments

Thanks to Marsha Atkins, Jeanie Cassity, Linda Nieman, and Melanie Sumner for reading and commenting all along the way. Thanks to Mercer University Press for being everything a press should be. Thanks to Joyce Hutchings and to Iron Will, keepers of the faith. Thanks to my copyeditor, Kelley Land, for minding the p's and q's and for helping make this a better story.

Contents

Sweetwater Blues

Prologue

Morphine is a flat-out bust. On a scale of ten I'd give it a two. Maybe a three if the nurse giving the shot has nice boobs. You know how we always heard that the stuff would really mess you up? Funny thing about that. It does mess you up but it doesn't really make you high. I asked the nurse about it because if I have to lay here for the next ten weeks wearing these two casts, I wouldn't mind having a little buzz on. It would kind of help the time pass. The nurse told me that when a person is in a world of hurt—which is where I am—the morphine kills the pain but the pain burns off the high. That's just bad planning if you ask me. I could stand a trip into the zone right now. It would take my mind off of my troubles.

And man do I have troubles. In case you haven't figured it out yet, you are dead. Or at least that's what they tell me. I didn't actually see you go into the ground, but why would they lie about something like that? It's kind of hard for me to get used to the idea. The last I remember, you had your shirt off and you were wearing your graduation hat. That stupid tassel was hanging down in front of your nose and you kept swatting at it like it was a fly. You were drunk and hollering kick it while I caught another gear in the Camaro. And now you're gone. It's like there's an empty spot right beside me that you should be standing in. You left a big hole in the world when you fell out of it. If I'm not careful,

1

I might fall through it myself. If things don't smooth out soon I might even jump.

I'm probably not going to be able to read this later because the handwriting is wandering all over the page. That's the messed up but not high part of morphine I was telling you about. Remember back in school when Mrs. Williams would smack our hands with a ruler if the writing got outside the lines? I think she wore out two or three rulers on me. She'd be whacking my hand now for sure.

Teachers aren't allowed to hit children with rulers anymore. That's probably why penmanship is going straight to hell. But the reason I'm bringing her up is because of this journal. You are probably wondering why I'm writing it. She always made us keep one and I always thought it was a waste of time. But now I'm a believer. I've been pretty low since the accident, and writing this seems to help. Yeah, yeah, I know, I need to man up and all that. But it was a bad accident. I got busted all to pieces and you got killed and I feel really weird about that. So I'm trying to sort out some stuff. I'm ironing some wrinkles.

I had a couple of false starts with the journal because I felt real stupid just writing whatever was in my head. You wouldn't think it would be that hard to do, but it was like I was talking to myself. Once you start doing that, it's only a matter of time before they take you away. I was about to give up on the whole thing when I got the idea that I would write to you. That has worked out better. It's almost like we're talking to each other. All we need now are a couple of cans of beer, some Slim Jims, a tank of gas, and a stretch of night road.

Since you are dead, you won't be reading this anytime soon, so my handwriting shouldn't matter much anyway. But I'll do my best. Who knows? You could be floating behind me right now, looking over my shoulder and trying to read every word I write. That would be kind of cool. Or at least it would be from my end of things. From your side I guess it all kind of sucks. But give me a heads up if you're there. Tap on the wall or something. Give me goose bumps. Put a sheet over your head and drift by. Hello?

I'm sorry I didn't make it to your funeral. I was busy that day trying to die. They tell me I made two good runs at it. I'll have to take their word for that because I don't remember any of it. Never saw any bright lights or tunnels. I guess if you're going to have near death experiences, sleeping through them is the way to go. Mama went to your funeral though. She said it was standing room only. Poor Mama. This has been hard on her and it's not over by a long shot. Most of the time she doesn't know how to act or what to say. So she just sits and sobs and wipes her eyes with a Kleenex.

I don't know what to do about how I feel about killing you. I never killed anyone before so I don't have anything to compare it to. There's all this stuff running through my head. Check it out. I feel happy because I'm alive and I feel guilty because you're dead and I feel sad that I've lost my best friend but I am truly pissed that you got killed—like it was your fault or something. Plus, I'm really afraid of what's going to happen now. It looks like I'm in for a hard time with the law, and I'm ashamed of being scared of that. All of this is going on at the same time. It's like there's a pack of crazy dogs in my head ripping off little pieces of my brain. I've got to get those dogs chained. I've got to put them down.

When we had the wreck, I took a pretty good knock on the head. You took a bigger one. We hit the Cherokee Oak at the bottom of Bankhead Hill. I remember we climbed that tree back when we were kids and I guess we tried to climb it again in the Camaro. I hope you never felt a thing. I asked the doctor about that because it was bothering me. You always were a little skittish about getting hurt. Well, you were. Anyway, he said he was sure you died so fast you never even knew you were gone. We always said that was the way to go if you had to go. Get it from behind and never see it coming. But I was sort of thinking it might be fifty or sixty more years before the problem came up for either one of

3

us. That's what I get for thinking, I guess. I need to leave that to people who are better at it.

The law has been buzzing around like bees ever since I woke up. They tell me I was the one driving and they are going to make a case against me. That's been hard on the old man, partly because he's my old man and partly because he's a guard at the prison. A cop is a cop I suppose. They had a couple of investigators come in here to question me but my old man ran them off until he hired a lawyer. His name is J. Randall Crane and he's an okay guy. When the cops came back they did the good cop, bad cop thing just like you always see on TV. I asked them if that was what they were doing. J. Randall Crane told me to hush and the bad cop called me a smartass. Then they arrested me in my bed right in front of Mama. That was just plain wrong. The sight of it nearly killed her. My old man was really pissed and if J. Randall Crane hadn't stepped between him and the cops, he probably would have been heading for an arrest too. They could have waited until Mama went to the bathroom or for a cup of coffee before they nailed me. It wasn't like I was going anywhere.

My old man thinks J. Randall Crane is a great lawyer. I hope he is, because if they convict me I'll be gone a long time. I feel bad about wiping you out. But I don't feel bad enough about it to go to jail for it. It won't bring you back. It won't fix a thing, so unless you just want to see me sitting in a cell because you're dead and it was my fault that you got killed, put in a good word for me with the big man. I'll owe you one and you know I'm good for it.

1

Flying the Red-eye

Prison time is comprised of equal parts mindless activity, enforced idleness, and utter boredom, but it does have the advantage of offering a young man plenty of opportunity to consider his shortcomings and reflect upon his transgressions. Anyway, that was Palmer Cray's experience. He had given his measure of sin its full share of contemplation during the long days and longer nights of his incarceration, and the deliberate passage of each slow moment had led him to the conclusion that the biggest problem with killing his best friend was that the one person he really needed to talk to about the whole sad business was dead and planted, so he couldn't strike up a conversation with him, or at least not one that went both ways. Dead men told no tales, according to the generally held view.

This gradual epiphany was completely detached from the physical reality of being imprisoned, which was definitely a problem in its own right and every bit as bad as its reputation implied. And then to be considered was the whole question of maybe going to hell as final penance for his crimes. This was the outcome his mother thought most likely. It was the reason she spent large portions of her days down on her arthritic knees, petitioning the Almighty for mercy and trying to out-pray the inevitable as she sought to strike a deal on her son's behalf. Palmer didn't believe in a literal damnation to an underground destination that included fire, brimstone, and malevolent red demons with affinities for pitchforks and roasted sinners, although he seemed to be in the minority on that particular point among the people in his neck of the woods. Out of respect for his mother's fervor, however, he had to concede that there was at least a fifty-percent chance that he was wrong, and if that should prove to be the case and a postmortem journey to the Baptist hell came to pass, it would no doubt be quite unpleasant, an experience literally never to be forgotten.

Rodney Earwood had been Palmer's best friend for as long as either could remember. They were both the only children their parents had ever produced, and they had grown up together in and around Sweetwater, Georgia. They had attended the same small school, four block buildings and a ramshackle gym that contained all of the school-aged children from Sweetwater and the surrounding countryside. They went to the Baptist church together, marched down there by a pair of mothers who might as well have been twins for all the real difference there was between them. Rodney and Palmer were two peas in a Southern pod, brothers in all but the genetic sense, each born late in the lives of good women who had given up on the dream of motherhood by the time their respective miracles occurred.

The boys wandered the hills of north Georgia, hunted the pine woods, fished the cool, green streams, and camped under the stars. They shared each other's clothing, each other's families, and each other's homes. They even entered the mysterious world of dating together in the company of the Nickel sisters, Tiffany and Kaitlyn, although Rodney was a bit better at the social graces than Palmer was, smoother and more self-assured. They grew into tall, good looking young men, and they excelled at the art of being alive and full of promise. And on a hot May afternoon right after they turned eighteen, they both graduated from Sweetwater High School, numbers seven and eight in the crooked, sweaty line that held a class of thirty of Sweetwater's finest.

Shortly thereafter, Palmer killed Rodney.

It wasn't like he stole his father's vintage service revolver, pulled it from beneath his robe at the reception, and gunned Rodney down, although the outcome of graduation day for both boys was much the same as if he had done just that. When Palmer did what he did, it was an accident, one of those bad turns of the cards. It had only taken one tick of the second hand to happen, a mere blink of the jaded celestial eye, but Palmer knew he would carry it with him like a jagged scar until the end of his earthly time, and perhaps for longer than that. Indeed, as the years had passed since the killing, he had actually come to feel worse rather than better about the episode. Rodney's demise had rubbed Palmer's conscience as raw as a bed sore. Every day that he awakened and drew breath was another day he had stolen away from his friend. His guilt was compounding interest at an extraordinary rate. The debt was staggering in its scope and could never be fully paid.

The fact that Palmer was still unable to remember the particulars of the accident made the entire state of affairs worse in his view. But try as he might, he could not bring the details into focus. He could retrieve a glimpse here and an impression there, but mostly he drew a blank. This was a problem for him because killing a person was a significant event, and having engaged in this activity, he believed he ought to have the good grace to remember at least some of the larger details. It would have been the decent thing to do, and he felt that he was being disrespectful to his friend's memory because he had forgotten. So Palmer Cray felt bad about killing Rodney

Earwood, and he felt worse because he didn't remember doing it. It was the rare day that the subject didn't cross his mind, and some days it was all he thought about.

After receiving their diplomas on that sultry Georgia afternoon, Rodney and Palmer each attended the obligatory rounds of family gatherings that went with such an occasion. The afternoon was a blur of hearty handshakes and warm hugs, crisp twenties and fifties tucked into shirt pockets, and paper plates loaded with potato salad, fried chicken, and sides of well wishes. Once these festivities peaked and waned, the pair struck out on their own to begin their celebration in earnest. In Sweetwater, that meant riding around in the car while drinking beer and listening to the radio. They chose Palmer's 1969 Chevrolet Camaro because he had more gas and because his radio picked up better stations. Plus, Palmer liked to drive, and Rodney had always been more of a passenger, preferring to leave his fate in the hands of his nominal brother while he contentedly watched the features of the North Georgia landscape dash by.

"Kick it," Rodney said as they settled into the bucket seats.

"Kicked," Palmer replied as he dropped the Camaro in gear and popped the clutch.

To complete the celebratory plan, they needed beer. One of the advantages of living in a dry county was that the bootleggers seldom concerned themselves with their customers' exact ages. If drinkers' legs were long enough to reach the pedals and their arms were long enough to reach the cash, then they were old enough to buy alcohol. The pair of graduates took advantage of this liberal sales policy and bought themselves a case of beer and three bottles of cheap, sweet wine for toasting. This wasn't the first alcohol they had ever consumed, not by a long measure, but it seemed the best they had ever tasted, perhaps due to the gaiety of the occasion. They clinked their beer bottles in mutual salute as they sailed down the narrow

8

asphalt in the Camaro. This was their turf. They had run these roads more times than they could count. They knew them like they knew their own names: Rodney Earwood and Palmer Cray, two up-and-coming young men parting the silky dark curtains of the soft Georgia night, curious and eager to see what marvels lay just on the other side.

Eventually they found themselves parked in the graveyard behind Mission Hill Baptist Church. It was an exceptional spot to drink or to take the Nickel sisters because Millard McChesney, the local policeman, never came up there when he was out making his rounds. Millard was a large, rough man with a short left leg, and to his great shame, he was afraid of all manner of dead people, both the freshly departed as well as those who were little more than memories drifting on the gentle breeze. This was admittedly an odd and somewhat limiting trait for a law officer, considering the nature of the work and the eventual likelihood of encountering an individual who had ceased to breathe. But Millard was an odd and somewhat limited man, so it made sense for him. Still, the dead can do no harm. It is only the living who must be watched.

Rodney and Palmer were deep into their celebration and not worried about Millard McChesney or his phobias when they decided that the night was still young enough for another journey to the beer joint. It was a decision that forever altered the small part of the world they knew and called their own. Many times during the ensuing years, Palmer Cray marveled that he was able to recall those moments at the cemetery so well, especially considering that he didn't recollect much at all from the time right after. But the memories were there; all he had to do was close his eyes, and they all came back to him, as welcome as a night terror, as wanted as a hurricane.

The stars that night had been twinkling lights strung randomly against a backdrop of black cloth, blue and white beacons sparkling just out of his reach. The only cloud in the entire sky had wrapped

9

itself tightly around the heavy moon like a cape. A wispy ground fog meandered to and fro among the white tombstones. The gravel road gleamed alabaster in the moonlight, and fireflies danced their careful dance, ever watchful for barefoot children bearing mason jars.

It wasn't just images that came to him. He could breathe the scents of early summer as they lingered on the gentle breeze, the sugary perfume of the blossoms on the fat honeysuckle vines as they hung from the branches overhead, the thick sweetness of the gardenias, and the overripe richness of the magnolias. He could hear the crickets and the tree frogs as they croaked and skreeked, and from a great distance came a long, mournful note as a freight train approached a marked crossing. It was a slow moment in time, a rare glimpse of perfection, a brief calm before the gale descended and the tides surged against the seawall. At that instant, they had all the days of the world before them. Their lives were unblemished canvas, and they could paint just about whatever they wished.

Later in his life, Palmer would sometimes awaken in the cool silence of the night and see in his mind's eye those two young boys as they reclined like sultans upon the hood of the Camaro. They were parked on the dirt road in the Mission Hill graveyard, as carefree as newborns, guzzling beer as they boldly sculpted their tomorrows and shared these plans with each other and with the neighboring dead. If he only knew the spell that would save them, Palmer would chant the syllables and throw the bones. He would rip the seams of the universe and reach across the indifferent years, and his invisible hand would snatch the keys from the ignition switch and hurl the keychain so far that it would be out there still, rusting slowly away, an aging artifact from an unwelcome reality. He would gently settle those young men into a slumber among the headstones, out of harm's way until the morning sun was born in the east and the world was once again safe. But sadly, the pair was well and truly beyond his power to protect. Sleight of hand could not compete with the wiles of destiny.

He only ever had one slim chance to save them, anyway, and when he climbed into the Camaro on that outlandish night, he had let the opportunity slip through his fingers like dry sand on a windy day.

And now Palmer's remembrances of what happened after he and Rodney left the boneyard are preserved like freeze frames from a particular hell. They play over and over for him like a looped tape, but they are jumpy, like the footage from an old eight-millimeter film that has missed a cog on the projector's drive gear. The pictures are grainy and indistinct. The soundtrack is tinny and its volume irregular, as if someone is turning the sound up and down at random. It hisses and crackles like the vintage seventy-eight rpm records that Palmer's grandmother used to play.

The reminiscences rise and fall with the moon and the sun, lapping at him like haphazard waves. First Palmer hears what he has always called the Big Bang. He found out several days after the accident that this noise was produced when his Camaro t-boned the Cherokee Oak at a spot about ten feet up its trunk. Local myth held that the tree was the longtime meeting place for the many Cherokees who had roamed the area in previous centuries. This fable may or may not have been true, but it was a big tree regardless of its heritage, and Palmer's car had folded itself around the venerable hardwood like it was giving a hug to an old friend.

The next thing he pictures is usually a strobed image of flying. He whips past the trees like a runaway rocket while wondering vaguely why he is doing so. There is no discernible up or down until he notices that the full moon has traded its cape for a ghostly ring. It hangs in the sky like a white pumpkin. His head hurts badly, and he hears his grandmother—seven years in the grave—telling him that a ring around the moon predicts the arrival of a storm. He has the impression that he is rotating in a sidereal manner as he sails, like a Frisbee or an aboriginal boomerang. He recalls that he is screaming like a banshee, realizing that he isn't designed for flight at all, and that no good can possibly come of the experience. When they come back to him later in life, these screams have the effect of making him afraid all over again, as if the horror of that night is hardwired in him like an electrical circuit. In his final recollection from the scene, he whooshes feet first into a soft, yielding substance, and the world disappears.

After he was released from the hospital, Palmer borrowed his mother's Oldsmobile and drove out to the place he had taken to calling the scene of the crime. Actually, the sequence of events on the day of his medical discharge included, in order of their occurrence, being released from the hospital, being re-arrested on the charge of homicide by vehicle, being bailed out by his father, who signed a fifty-thousand-dollar property bond secured by the Cray home and his good name, and *then* driving the Olds out to the scene of the crime. The second arrest was necessary due to procedural errors associated with the first. These irregularities mostly revolved around the fact that the district attorney did not wish to have to prosecute a young man who had been arrested in a hospital bed in front of his mama, which was where and how the first arrest had occurred. He had thought, and rightfully so, that it would look bad to the jury.

So Palmer was un-arrested one day and re-arrested the next, but the process of becoming an alleged felon for the second time took a while. Thus it was late in the afternoon before Palmer was able to make his return to the scene of the crime at the bottom of Bankhead Hill. It was morbid curiosity that took him there, a desperate urge to see and remember. He had bits and pieces of graduation night rattling and chattering around in his head like chunks of tramp steel in a bucket, and he needed to see the accident site before he could even begin to believe what he had done. He only went that once, though, because there were one too many ghosts lounging around the Cherokee Oak to suit him. The memory of Rodney hung heavy on the place like a weighted velvet drape in a funeral parlor.

At Palmer's trial, it was revealed that the car had left the road at the bad dip in the pavement at the bottom of Bankhead Hill, and, according to the investigator, the vehicle must have been speeding along in excess of 120 miles per hour when it took flight. As Palmer Cray listened to this testimony, he didn't doubt the assessment, although he was curious about the methodology the expert witness had used to arrive at that number. Perhaps the official had employed some type of arcane algebraic equation taught only at the police academy, a formula in which the known values were the depth of the dip in the road and the height of the impact on the Cherokee Oak, and the variable being solved for—x, as it were—was the speed of the Camaro. Or maybe he had simply guessed. Regardless of how the estimate had been made, however, Palmer was certain of one fact. The Camaro had always run like a wild bat out of hell, and Palmer had always loved to drive it that way. So it was quite likely that he and Rodney had been going at least 120 miles per hour as they shot down Bankhead Hill like a jet on a runway, and the sad fact that he wished that they hadn't been really didn't matter.

Those who do not farm for a living might be surprised to learn that in modern times, it is nearly impossible to locate a haystack. One might be found on a family farmhold in Europe, perhaps, or in an Amish hayfield in Pennsylvania, but in the state of Georgia, hay comes pretty much two ways: in large, round bales or small, square ones. If Palmer had flown into either of those, he would have been as dead as Rodney was, even before the echo of the Big Bang made its way back across the valley from the mountains to the west. But as luck would have it, Mr. W.M. Mitchell, whose hay Palmer had landed in, had once been bitten by a cottonmouth that had wintered inside a bale. When the twine was snipped in spring, the rogue reptile had sunk its fangs deep into W.M.'s left arm. The snake was big and arguably perturbed, the poison was strong and plentiful, and W.M.'s arm drew up like he was afflicted by palsy. Ever since that year long past, W.M. had stored his hay loose. When questioned about this practice, he always noted that he would rather lose a little hay to the wind or the rain than sacrifice his remaining good arm to a hungry snake with a bad attitude due to awakening on the wrong side of the bale.

In his memories, before the world disappears that night, Palmer sees himself lying on his side high atop one of W.M. Mitchell's piles of fescue. It's an odd point of view, as if he were both in the hay and floating above the haystack, looking down upon himself. He can't move his right leg, and his left arm is bent in the wrong direction at the elbow. Blood drips into his eyes, where it clings and burns like sweat. It is quiet except for the crickets chirping and the hiss of his breath as it rasps like sandpaper on a plank of dried hickory. Presently, a white light bobs into view, a will-o'-the-wisp that makes its slow, crazy way through the darkness. Palmer wonders if he should move toward the light. He has heard that this is a crucial step in the dying process, and from the way he feels, he assumes that he must be passing on. Oddly enough, he is not fearful; an unnatural calm has covered him like a down comforter. Then, between one blink and the next, the phantom light turns into a state patrolman with a flashlight. When he spots Palmer, he says, *Oh, shit.* Then he hollers, *Here's another one,* even as he shines the light in Palmer's eyes. From the distance, a voice resembling Millard McChesney's shouts, *Is that one alive?* As the picture dims to black, Palmer Cray strains to hear the answer to that intriguing question.

As she was prone to do with any inexplicable occurrence, Palmer Cray's mother, Laurel, saw the hand of the Almighty at work in her son's nocturnal haystack discovery. "It's one of God's blessings," she said while visiting him in the hospital. This was eight days after the accident and less than twenty-four hours since Palmer had awakened from the blessed oblivion of unconsciousness. Rodney was three days in his grave. Assumedly, Laurel's reference to divine beneficence was directed only at the haystack landing and not toward the entire Big Bang. Palmer later thought that a case could be made that surviving the eighty feet between the windshield and the hay was miraculous in its own right and just as unlikely as the mere fact of the hay.

"The Lord has a plan for you," his mother insisted. "We'll just have to be patient. We can't always know His design for the world." She had spent the morning quietly crying as she straightened and re-straightened his hospital room.

"Yes, ma'am," Palmer had replied, all the while thinking that if the Lord had a design for that particular moment in the world, it wasn't much of one. It was Palmer's view that any plan currently in motion seemed sketchy, bordering on poor. But perhaps the morphine drip plugged into his good arm had dulled his ability to perceive the heavenly hand as it moved the pieces across the board. Possibly, that trip through the windshield had limited his sense of divine intervention when it was occurring right in front of his broken nose. Who knew about the true nature of these things? Palmer certainly didn't claim to, and he kept his doubts to himself because he didn't want to tread upon his mother's beliefs. She needed her faith like she needed food, water, and Marlboro Menthols. It kept her alive, and she was entitled to it.

Despite Laurel Cray's certainty that all was going according to plan, Palmer's father, Trenton, hired his son a lawyer. It was his belief that the good Lord helped those who helped themselves and that young men in trouble with the law should always seek benefit of legal counsel. So Palmer was provided with an attorney. Unfortunately, he wasn't able to offer a great deal of assistance in preparing his own defense. He wasn't trying to be difficult, but since he couldn't remember most of the facts from the critical period between leaving the cemetery in the Camaro and awakening at the hospital, he couldn't recall many that were to his benefit.

15

Part of him wondered, then and since, if one of the reasons for his inability to help with his own case stemmed from some innate psychological need to be guilty as charged and punished accordingly. After he went to prison, Palmer spent hours lying on the bunk in his cell, looking at the mattress above, memorizing the stripes and stains on the fabric while wondering if he had an inner need to make reparation for his deeds and wanted to be held somehow accountable for his friend's demise. He didn't know the answer to that question, and he probably never would. Even the counselor at the prison wasn't much help. His name was Morris Cato, and he was a good-hearted soul just eight years older than his client. A contract worker, he only came to the prison once a week.

"I can't tell you what you think," Morris said when Palmer put the question to him during one of their weekly visits. "Only you know how you feel, and only you can decide what to do about it."

"Then what good are you?" Palmer had replied in a tired voice. He was having a bad day. He was sure that he didn't want to be in prison, but the whole question of whether he deserved to be there remained unanswered in his own mind, even though the State had rendered a more definite and tangible opinion.

One fact was certain. Even if Palmer had wanted to walk away from the charges scot- free, chances were strong from the outset that he would not be able to do so, because he was as guilty as sin itself, and his defense attorney, J. Randall Crane, wasn't a very good lawyer. He wasn't a bad person—quite the opposite, in fact—but he *was* a bad attorney, which can be an almost insurmountable setback when presenting a defense against a charge of vehicular homicide with extenuating circumstance. And perhaps it was even the case that J. Randall Crane wasn't so much a bad attorney as he was simply an inexperienced one. He was fresh out of law school, newly admitted to the bar, and still making payments on his dark blue vested suit. Palmer Cray was his first big criminal defense.

But on J. Randall Crane's behalf, even if he had been an absolutely top-notch barrister with years of courtroom experience, Palmer knew he didn't have much to work with. Palmer had committed the crime, after all, and there is only so much that can be done for a client who finds himself in that unfortunate situation. Furthermore, regardless of his legal competence, J. Randall was the best lawyer that Palmer's parents could afford, and they nearly broke themselves paying for him. The Cray family home was mortgaged not long after the accident, and the portion of proceeds that didn't go toward Palmer's medical bills and recovery eventually went to his defense.

In his role as the captain of the prison guard, Palmer's father had seen a truckload of attorneys come and go over the years, and he had developed the theory that the best of the lot were always the ones who had initials for first names. He also believed that this characteristic signaled the presence of an excellent physician. So after the charges against his son were filed, he went out and found Palmer an initialized lawyer. Once J. Randall Crane was placed on retainer, Trenton Cray stepped back and allowed better legal minds determine his son's fate. He had done what he could. The rest was in the hands of the American legal system and Jesus. Hopefully, neither would fail the Cray family in its hour of need.

J. Randall Crane tried a variety of strategies to defend his client, including an ambitious attempt to use Palmer's spotty memory of the accident to his advantage by arguing that he was suffering from post-traumatic stress syndrome and was thus unable to assist in the preparation of his own defense. It was a novel approach, but it didn't fly with the judge, the prosecuting attorney, or eventually the jury, all of whom seemed more interested in the defendant's state of mind *before* he hit the tree rather than after the collision had occurred. To be frank, the theory had sounded a little thin even to Palmer, though he was definitely invested in having the tactic succeed. But as J.

Randall's worthy legal opponent pointed out during closing arguments, maybe the boy did have post-traumatic stress syndrome, and then again, maybe he didn't, but either way, he had also been drunk as Cooter Brown on the night in question and had gone through a Camaro windshield on top of that, and those two facts no doubt contributed to his sketchy recollection.

J. Randall had also advanced the hypothesis that, since there were no witnesses to the actual accident, who was to say that Palmer was even driving when the car hit the tree? After all, authorities had found what was left of the steering wheel more or less imbedded in the Cherokee Oak, which was the same general vicinity where Rodney had met his maker. On the other hand, the passenger side of the front seat was in a direct line with the haystack where Palmer had landed. It actually wasn't a bad premise, and Palmer, at least, preferred it to the opposing and prevailing assumption, because if it were somehow true that he wasn't the driver that night, then he wasn't guilty of killing his best friend.

Unfortunately, most of the evidence seemed to point in Palmer's direction, and try as he might, J. Randall Crane was unable to plant any seeds of doubt. To begin with, the pair had been in Palmer's car, and a succession of his unwilling peers had testified that no one but Palmer ever drove that Camaro. It was his baby. Additionally, Palmer had been found guilty on one other occasion of operating a vehicle while under the influence of alcohol, back when he was sixteen. The State deemed this piece of information to be quite significant. It was, in fact, presented so many times during the trial that even the judge finally got tired of hearing the story.

"The bench *gets* it," he told the prosecuting attorney. "The boy likes to drink and drive. Move on." The final nail in Palmer's coffin, however, had been the fact that someone had seen him driving the Camaro on that fateful night. Of all the facts presented against Palmer, this last one was particularly troubling.

Probably the most innovative strategy employed by J. Randall Crane was his eleventh-hour decision to call Rodney Earwood's mother, Kathleen, to the stand. She testified in tears in her Sunday dress while her husband, Harris, sat in the gallery and glared at J. Randall Crane, Palmer, the judge, and a goodly number of the rest of the courtroom's occupants as well.

"Do you know this young man?" J. Randall had asked the distraught woman as he pointed toward his client. It was an amazingly stupid question, because just about everyone in the courtroom knew just about everyone else on a first-name basis, but J. Randall was trying to be a thorough lawyer, and Palmer thought that this at least was a good sign.

"Of course I know him. He's Palmer Cray. I've known him since he was a baby." Kathleen turned her gaze to Laurel Cray as she made this statement, and they shared a moment of silent misery.

"Do you think he ever had any intention of harming your son?"

"Objection!" barked the prosecutor as he shot from his chair. "The question calls for speculation on the part of the witness."

"Overruled," replied the judge. "Let Mrs. Earwood talk."

"But your Honor—"

"I said let the woman answer the question," the judge growled. "I want to hear what she has to say."

J. Randall Crane repeated his question.

"No, of course not," Kathleen Earwood replied. "He would have never hurt Rodney. They were like brothers."

"Do you want him to go to prison for what happened to your son?"

"Objection," said the prosecutor.

"Overruled," replied the judge.

It seemed as if everyone in the courtroom held their breath as they awaited this answer. Kathleen was quiet for a moment. Then, once again, she caught the eye of Laurel Cray.

"No. Palmer didn't mean to do it, and sending him to jail won't bring back my boy. I've lost my son. There's no point in Laurel Cray losing hers, too. No point at all."

It was a poignant moment. Kathleen Earwood had spoken with such quiet dignity and bottomless sadness that she left no room for rebuttal, and the prosecution declined the State's right to cross-examine her. He had seen the looks on the faces of several of the jurors, mothers and grandmothers of boys close to the same age as the deceased and the accused, and he wanted Kathleen Earwood and her Sunday dress off the witness stand as soon as possible, before she could harm his case any further.

As the trial unfolded, most of what became the official version of Rodney Earwood's death was filled in by people who were nowhere near Bankhead Hill when the young men took their short, deadly flight, people who did not see the Camaro take wing or hear the Big Bang as it ricocheted through the pines. The agreed-upon sequence of events was deduced from both forensic and circumstantial sources of evidence, and it was deemed to be the truth because that was the way it had to have happened, given the facts as presented. This composite of blame seemed to fit Palmer Cray like a worn and comfortable calfskin glove.

The pair had made it to the bootlegger's that night without incident and had bought another case of beer. Houston Bibb—the bootlegger—testified to this fact, and he further added that they were both as drunk as fish while they were there. After the purchase, they roared off into the night like a pair of bucks running from the hounds of perdition. According to Houston, Palmer was behind the wheel at this time, opening another can of beer as the car fishtailed from the gravel driveway onto the highway. Approximately two hours later—sometime around 2:00 a.m.—the Camaro hit the dip in the road at the bottom of Bankhead Hill and flew into the Cherokee Oak. Rodney Earwood went through the windshield but was unable to penetrate the tree. He left this world and joined the ranks of the departed members of the Earwood family, a long line that extended from the bark of the oak back through time and across the slate-gray seas into the mists of antiquity. Palmer Cray flew feetfirst into a haystack in the dark—an improbability on several levels—after which he spent a week in a coma followed by several long weeks in the hospital, accompanied by his thoughts and his mama while nursing a broken arm, a fractured leg, a concussion, a cracked pelvis, and several bruised internal organs.

J. Randall Crane objected to Houston Bibb's testimony, but to no avail. "This is hearsay evidence," he argued, "and that witness is currently awaiting his own trial for a variety of offenses, including the sale of alcohol to two minors, one of whom is my client. He will say anything to ameliorate his own legal difficulties. Additionally, I don't see how he can possibly offer testimony concerning the defendant's state of inebriation unless he did a blood-alcohol test, which he obviously did not do!"

In Palmer's admittedly biased view, these were all valid points. Maybe J. Randall Crane was coming along after all.

"The man's a bootlegger," the judge replied. "He ought to recognize *drunk* when he sees it."

"But—"

"Overruled." The judge was an equal-opportunity magistrate and overruled each barrister at about the same rate.

During the course of a six-hour trial that concluded just a week shy of his nineteenth birthday, Palmer was convicted of homicide by vehicle and other lesser but still serious crimes, one of which was the possession of an ounce of marijuana at the time of the accident. The cannabis had actually belonged to Rodney Earwood, but Palmer didn't want to impugn his friend's reputation or tarnish his memory in front of his grieving mother, so he didn't mention that fact. Besides, it was in Palmer's car, and that made it his in the eyes of the state of Georgia regardless, so he remained silent. He had taken too much away from Kathleen Earwood already, and he knew that he was going to jail no matter what he said or who had actually paid for the dope. It could just as well have been his, anyway, and there were plenty of times when it had been. So he let it be.

His sentencing hearing came a week later, on the date of his birth. It was a fearful episode, a ghastly moment in time, the permanent low point of Palmer's life. As the subsequent days and years crept past his cell door, each more deliberate than the last, he often drew sad comfort from the knowledge that he had already hit bottom hard and had somehow survived, and that every subsequent sunrise was a bonus of sorts, guaranteed to bring a better day than that dreadful day had been. It was a liberating feeling to know that the worst had come and gone, and that although it had branded him like a steer, it had at least left him still trudging among the living.

On his birthday, he had stood before the judge with J. Randall Crane at his side and heard his fate. Because he had been intoxicated and driving recklessly, and due to the fact that he was in possession of the marijuana when they hit the tree, and in consideration of his thoroughly reported previous DUI conviction, Palmer was sentenced to fifteen years in prison and mandated to serve no fewer than ten. It was a surprisingly stiff sentence, and both Palmer and his attorney stepped back when it was rendered, as if they had been slapped. J. Randall Crane strenuously protested, but Charles "The Hanging Judge" Herrett felt that the punishment fit the crimes, particularly since it was an election year, and he invited the young lawyer to hush unless he wished to join his client.

They took Palmer from the courtroom in shackles, stainless steel manacles that dug into his wrists as they clung tight. For Palmer, the hardest part was hearing his mother's gasp and seeing the sorrowful look on his father's face as the court deputy marched him out the side door. He was surprised that they were taking him straight to jail.

He had supposed he might get a day or two to say his good-byes and make his arrangements, such as they were. Rodney's mother was crying too, but for a different reason. Or maybe her anguish had the same root cause, after all. Both women had lost their sons during the Big Bang, and the only real dissimilarity was that Rodney's departure was quicker and arguably more merciful, his mother's grief more concentrated. Either way, the pain in the courtroom that day was deep enough to pile with a shovel.

Palmer reported in chains to Sweetwater State Correctional Facility and stumbled through a surreal afternoon of procedural matters as if he were trapped in a bad dream. He was stripped, probed, poked, examined, and categorized. He was instructed, questioned, answered, documented, and filed. He was shaved, barbered, deloused, washed, and dried. He was photographed and fingerprinted. Then the jailers issued him underwear, socks, tennis shoes, and denim shirts and trousers—his Sweetwater Blues—and had him dress. He was handed a large cloth sack that resembled a seabag. It contained two changes of clothing and a few toilet articles.

He shouldered the bag, and then he and an escort began a long, slow walk that led through a series of steel doors and sturdy gates. Each was another stage in the journey from freedom to imprisonment. After crossing four of these thresholds, Palmer found himself walking down a broad corridor, following a yellow stripe painted on the floor. Cage after cage of imprisoned men lined each side of this gauntlet. Some were whooping, some were hollering, and some just stood and silently watched as the new man passed. Eventually, Palmer and his silent escort reached his own cell.

The guard swiped the key card and the steel door swung open. Palmer hesitated. He had arrived at the ultimate before-and-after moment. He knew that his entire life would forevermore be divided into two distinct parts. The first would be composed of everything that had occurred right up until that very instant. The second would begin with whatever happened next. His escort gave him a firm shove, and he stepped over the final threshold. The door clicked shut behind him, and he stood there with his bag clutched in his arms, staring at the opposite wall of his new home. It looked to be about twelve feet away.

I need to apologize to the people I've hurt and make up somehow for the pain I've caused. When I made a list of these people, everyone I knew was on it. So it looks like I'll be doing a lot of apologizing. By the way, you're the only dead guy who made the list. You got the number one spot. Since you already know I didn't mean to slam you into the Cherokee Oak, I'm only going to say I'm sorry this one time. But I am sorry. Sorrier than I've ever been about anything. I have wished a hundred times that I hadn't killed you or that I had gone along with you to keep you company. I even wish sometimes that I had gone in your place. But then I get to thinking that if I had died instead of you, then you would be here dealing with all of this, and I wouldn't wish that on anyone.

The way that people look at me drives me crazy, and like the old joke says, that's a pretty short drive these days. Some of them look at me like they feel bad for me but don't really want to be around me. Mama is one of those and she doesn't even know it. To her I'm a walking, talking reminder of how fast everything can go wrong. She comes to see me every visiting day, and she looks sad and numb at the same time. Sometimes we'll be talking and one of us will say something that doesn't even have anything to do with you or the accident or any of it, and out of nowhere she'll start shaking and then she'll go to crying. I know this is killing her but she won't stay away. Maybe she can't. It must be a mama thing.

As bad as Mama is, your mama is worse. She reminds me of a balloon with about half of the air gone out of it. When she looks at me, I can tell that her heart is broken. I know I'm the one who broke it and I wish there was something I could do to fix that. But with her it's like it's been broken twice. Once for you and once for me. When I look at her I get it that sometimes the people who die are the lucky ones. I used to think that was crap. You might still think it is. But I always thought that there was nothing in the world worse than dying. Now I know better. Sometimes living can be the worst thing there is.

You know who else looks at me with sad eyes? The Nickel sisters. Those are two good-hearted girls and that's a fact. They'll make fine wives someday, but not for you and not for me. Tiffany looks the way she does because she misses you. She is working hard at not blaming me for killing you and most of the time she makes it. It's tough for her, though. I guess it is human nature to want an accounting, and I crashed her true love into a tree. That's a hard fact, one of those that won't get better with time.

Poor Kaitlyn knows it's not ever going to be like it was before the accident. Before my trial I told her she needed to find someone else to be her boyfriend, because if I was a betting man I'd be willing to lay odds that jail was in my future. I told her that even if I didn't end up in a cell, the fact that I killed you would always be there. We went for a ride right after I got out of the hospital, and the whole time it was like you were sitting with us in the car. You weren't, were you? I didn't think so. But the memory of you was between us, and that was when I knew we couldn't pick up where we left off. When I told her that it might be better if she didn't see me anymore, she cried and cried. But then she went on away. I think she knew just like I did that it was the only thing to do. Kaitlyn is number two on my apology list, tied with Tiffany I guess, but I can never make it right with either one of them just like I can't make it right with you.

Other folks look at me like I'm a criminal, which I guess is exactly what I am. Your old man is one of those. He hates me. But you know what? He never liked me much, anyway, so he can kiss my country ass, stitches and all. He came to the hospital a little while after I woke up. He was drunk, but where's the news there? He was in my room, hollering *that I was going to hell and that he might just send me himself. It really upset Mama. My old man had stepped down the hall to get a cup of coffee, and when he came back and saw what was going on he snatched your old man up by the collar and backed him on his tiptoes across the room, out the door, and up against the wall in the hall. Then in this quiet voice, he told your old man that the next time he saw him would be the day that he died. I swear it made me shiver. He sounded like Clint Eastwood. It would've done you good to see it.*

I guess I need to get used to people looking at me sideways and treating me different. Not everyone has killed someone, so that singles me out. I'm special, but not in a good way. I didn't mean to do it, and I know you know that, but I need to keep saying it. I'm sorry. I was only going to tell you that once, but here I am saying it again. If I ever get a chance to make it up to you I will. The counselor Morris would say that I am overcompensating, but I won't tell him if you don't.

2

Sloppy Luck

Before Palmer Cray went to jail, about the only notion he had of what doing time might involve came from a song his father liked to sing. It was called "Mama Tried," and it was originally written and performed by Merle Haggard. Merle did a much better job with the song than Trenton Cray did, which was to be expected. In the song, Merle lamented that he "turned twenty-one in prison doing life without parole, and no one could steer him right, but Mama tried." Despite the song's claim, Merle didn't actually do life without parole, and he may not have even turned twenty-one in prison, but there is not much doubt that his mama had indeed tried, as has been the case throughout history with most of her kind. And he did serve time in San Quentin, a somewhat infamous penal facility in California.

As Palmer eventually came to understand from one of his fellow inmates—a middle-aged man called "Pittypat" who had been unsuccessfully combatting the urge to rob convenience stores his entire life—there were prisons and then there were prisons, and he was a con who had acquired his facts the hard way. According to

Pittypat, who *had* turned twenty-one in prison and who was now doing life without parole, sentences at San Quentin or at Reidsville in middle Georgia or at Limestone over in Alabama or, perish the thought, at Mississippi State Prison in Parchman were all much worse than serving a stretch at Sweetwater State Correctional Facility. Palmer took this information on faith and believed every word as if it were gospel, although if the truth were told, Sweetwater was plenty bad enough for him.

Sweetwater State Correctional Facility was built during the 1970s as a means to alleviate the crowding caused by Georgia's prison population, which was growing exponentially at that time due to the state's strict penal code on the one hand and the cocaine epidemic on the other. The prison was originally intended to house 500 inmates, and even though the elected representatives of the state of Georgia insisted on calling it a medium-security detention and correctional facility, it was a prison, pure and simple. There were wicked double coils of razor wire strung around the perimeter, and a kill zone between the inner and outer fences. There were two guard towers—one at the north corner of the compound and the other at the south—and armed guards stood in those towers, some of them looking like they might just know how to shoot and were itching for an opportunity to demonstrate their proficiency with a high-powered rifle and a rubber bullet.

As is often the case with best-laid plans, Sweetwater State Correctional Facility did not turn out to be the ultimate panacea for the surplus of errant Georgians requiring incarceration. It became too small even before its opening day, and less than a year after it was completed, more than 600 prisoners had made the facility their home. That census continued to climb as time passed and as relatively expensive cocaine gave way to cheap and nasty methamphetamine, the growth industry of rural Georgia. The day before Palmer Cray walked the long yellow line, the population at

Sweetwater had swelled to 707. His arrival bumped that number to 708. The prison had originally housed two inmates per cell, but since it was already close to fifty percent over capacity by the time Palmer took residence, some of the cells had acquired a third bunk and occupant.

Luckily for Palmer, his cell was not one of these. Three in a cell had a built-in two-against-one dynamic that could be a problem for a newer or weaker prisoner, and being caged was bad enough without having to worry about maintaining a defense against battery or sexual assault. The cells were claustrophobic with just two people in them— eight feet wide by twelve feet long—and the general consensus on the cellblocks was that the poor souls housed in the three-bunk cells were being subjected to cruel and unusual punishment and that they ought to get a good lawyer and sue the State over this violation of their constitutional rights. The problem with this plan, of course, was that if any of them had been able to afford a good lawyer, they most likely wouldn't have been stacked three-high in Sweetwater State Correctional Facility to begin with. It was a no-win scenario, a catch-22.

Palmer deemed himself lucky to have drawn a two-bunk cell, but it turned out that luck had played a very small role in this, and it had even less to do with the assignment of his cellmate. There was an aphorism around the town of Sweetwater that, one way or another, about half of everyone in the city limits wound up in prison every day. This saying had its roots in the fact that the cotton mill had closed down and emigrated to Mexico back during the mid-eighties, and as a result of this strategic relocation, the detention center had become the single largest employer in the county. One of these employees was Palmer Cray's father, Trenton, who was hired on as a prison guard when the penitentiary was still being built and who had risen to the rank of captain of the guard during the ensuing years. As

Palmer was to discover, having a father on the prison payroll could work to an inmate's benefit.

In addition to the numerous Sweetwater citizens who worked at the facility, there were also some few townsfolk who had strayed from life's straight path and had wound up there as residents. One of these was Palmer's first cousin, Cheddar Cray. His given name was David, and he was the son of Trenton Cray's only brother, Cullen. Cheddar was doing an extended stretch due to his choice of occupation, which was the manufacture and sale of methamphetamine. Unfortunately, Cheddar was the type to take his work home with him, and he had begun to sample his own wares on a regular basis. Besides a double armload of prison time, this habit had also earned him his descriptively accurate nickname, because over the years his teeth had acquired the color and consistency of a wheel of sharp cheese, and for those who found themselves in close proximity to him—a mistake that the majority of the people he encountered did not willingly make twice—there was a definite cheddary odor as well.

As he stood in his new home, the last two things in the wide world that Palmer had on his mind were his father's occupation or his cousin's teeth, so he was quite surprised when this same cousin hopped down from the top bunk and grinned a cheddary grin. He had greasy black hair streaked with gray and a scraggly beard that was little more than salt-and-pepper stubble scattered over a pointed chin. He sported several impressive scars on his forehead, cheeks, and forearms, reminders of a chemical miscalculation that had resulted in a frightful explosion, his second incarceration, and the fiery loss of his mobile home. His shirt gaped open to reveal a tattoo of an extremely limber redheaded woman with an impossibly large bosom. Cheddar looked like hell on a biscuit, but Palmer didn't care. He had never seen such a welcome sight.

"Welcome to paradise," Cheddar said. He took Palmer's hand and gave it a few shakes. "The bottom bunk is yours. I like to be up high, where I can see what's coming."

Palmer was beyond amazed. He just stood there and stared at his cousin. His mouth worked a bit, but the effort, although earnest, produced no words. He had been close to tears since hearing his sentence pronounced, and only the whirlwind of activity since that moment plus maybe a light case of shock had kept him from breaking down on several occasions throughout the day. He had been somewhat ashamed of this strong need to cry. The urge had peaked like a high tide when he was compelled to strip to the skin and change into his Sweetwater Blues in front of an assortment of armed strangers. Luckily, none of them had been particularly interested in their charge, so they hadn't seen him blinking frequently as he kept his tears at bay. Now, however, upon seeing Cheddar Cray in such an unexpected setting, a familiar person with orange, crumbling teeth and an outlandish tattoo miraculously appearing among the first bleak impressions of forced captivity, tears began to stream down his cheeks.

When Cheddar saw this emotional reaction, he grimaced, grabbed Palmer's arm, and pulled him back into the cell, as far away from the door as he could get. He looked alarmed as he positioned himself to block the view from the small window in the door and from the cell across the corridor.

"Shit, man," he whispered loudly. "Don't let anyone see you do that. Not in here. Not ever. They'll eat you alive and then try to have me for dessert."

Palmer made an effort to regain control while trying to apologize to Cheddar for his lapse. The resulting gulps and snorts sounded unusually loud in the small cell. Cheddar held up his hands as if to say that no apology was necessary, that these things happened from time to time.

"If you gotta, you gotta," Cheddar reassured him. "You just can't let anyone know. Listen, man. Drawing your first piece of state time can do this to you, I don't care *who* you are. It hit me the same way. But if you have to do it, do it into your pillow. At night's even better. Quietly." Cheddar looked over both of his shoulders, as if he thought someone may have crept in during Palmer's moment of weakness, but all was well, and they were still the only two people in the locked cell.

Palmer's mouth was dry, and he felt squeezed out, like a sponge. He placed his bag on the bunk and sat beside it. There was not a chair in the cell, so Cheddar sat on the steel toilet opposite Palmer. The bizarre day had caught up with the freshman convict, and he shook with emotion and fatigue. His head pounded, and his heart hurt. He looked at his cousin sitting on the makeshift stool, and it hit him like a thrown brick that for the next ten years, he was not even entitled to privacy while performing the most basic of bodily functions. He shook his head in despair. Tomorrow might be better, but today he wanted to die.

"I'm sorry," he said to Cheddar, who appeared to be trying— unsuccessfully—to look encouraging. "I've been keeping that swallowed down all day. But when I saw you jump down from the bunk, I was so relieved to see someone I knew that it just sort of broke loose. I was dreading meeting my cellmate. I was afraid he was going to be some big, mean dude who hadn't seen a woman in about thirty years."

Cheddar nodded sympathetically. "That happens sometimes," he noted. "There are guys in here who'll try for it." Palmer grimaced. "But I'm not one of them."

"Why are you here?" Palmer asked. He was glad to see his cousin, gladder than he could possibly say, but he didn't believe in happy coincidences, or not anymore, anyway. Recent events had all but cured him of the expectation of serendipity, and the previous week had inoculated him for life against the hope for miracles. He was the newest member of the glass-half-empty club, and as such, he didn't believe that it was just good fortune that his cellmate was his cousin.

"Bad question in here," Cheddar replied. "Don't ask anybody else. Don't ask them how long, either. Some guys don't mind talking about it, but other guys do, and you never know which is which until you're getting your head caved in with a chair leg. But anyway, the state of Georgia wants me to quit making meth, and what I'm doing here is twenty-five years with no chance of parole because I haven't been paying attention to them." Cheddar said this matter-of-factly, as if he had just told Palmer what the weather forecast for tomorrow was, or what was on the supper menu at the dining hall. He shrugged. Cheddar was ten years older than Palmer, and he had been caught manufacturing methamphetamine three times since his seventeenth birthday. He was now a ward of the state under the harsh three-strike law. He would be in his fifties before he drew his next free breath, assuming he kept his nose clean and didn't get any additional years tacked on. "I've already served two years," Cheddar continued. "Just twenty-three more and I'll be walking out that door." He looked off a moment as he spoke, twenty-three years into the future, perhaps, or three years into the past. "Free as a bird."

"I don't know what to say," Palmer said. He had only done about an hour's worth of time, so far, and that was enough to make him cringe at the thought of a quarter of a century behind bars. Twenty-five years was six years longer than he had even been alive. It was a number too large to imagine, a concept drawn from the reaches of infinity. He shuddered as if a ghost had floated through him.

"How long did you get?" Cheddar asked, breaking his own rule.

"Fifteen years," Palmer said quietly. Tears came to his eyes once again. He shook with effort as he tried to blink them away. After a moment, he mostly succeeded and was able to continue. "I have to serve ten." He looked at his cousin with despair. "I can't believe any of this." He gestured at their surroundings. "I'm in prison. I'm only nineteen. I'm nineteen today, for Christ's sake! It's my birthday." The scene was too bizarre. He was sitting in the jail cell that would be his home for ten years, comparing prison terms with his ne'er-do-well cousin, the one his mama had always warned him to steer clear of because the boy just wasn't right. "I'm not a criminal. I was just riding around with Rodney Earwood drinking some beer, like we've done a hundred times before. I don't even remember the wreck. I never wanted any of this to happen, and I don't want to be here." He shook his head in disbelief. Cheddar nodded solemnly. If anyone could appreciate how quickly it could all head south, it was Cheddar Cray.

"Sometimes the world just lands on you hard," he said. "Who was your judge?"

"Herrett."

"Ho-lee shit! The Hanging Judge! You poor bastard. That guy would send his own mama to jail. I had him once, the time before last, and I swear to God I thought he was going to give me the firing squad. It's some kind of bad when he looks at you with those mean eyes over the tops of those black glasses. I'm telling you, that guy ain't normal. You're lucky he didn't make you serve the whole piece."

"I don't feel lucky," Palmer replied, although it was possible that he was not seeing the situation clearly on this day of days. He was forlorn. It felt like the entire Cherokee Oak, the remains of his Camaro, and a fair number of the rest of the weighty objects in the world had fallen on him and bounced twice for good measure. He was nineteen, and he was in prison for ten years. With luck, he would be twenty-nine when he got out. He shook his head. He had participated in each step of the process that had brought him to Sweetwater State Correctional Facility, and he still didn't know how

34

he had arrived at this place. Palmer needed to change the subject. His inclination was to lie back and feel sorry for himself, but even in his emotional state, he realized that this would be a bad idea. He took a deep breath and forced himself to speak. His mama had always told him that the first step was the hardest, and now was the time to test her theory. "When I asked you a while ago why you were here, what I meant was, why are you *in here*? With me. In this cell." He pointed at the floor, just to make sure his point was taken. "I didn't even know you were in Sweetwater." The last he had heard from his Uncle Cullen, Cheddar was in a facility down in Middle Georgia.

"Your old man arranged that. He told me to take you under my wing and show you the ropes. He wanted me to keep you between the ditches and out of trouble."

Palmer had not expected this news and wasn't quite sure how to take it. His father had never struck him as the kind of person who *arranged* things. He didn't come across as a mover and a shaker. At home it had been his mother who ruled the roost, making lists and lining out the other members of the household. He could see her in his mind's eye, sitting at the kitchen table with her legal pad and her pack of Marlboro Menthols, writing out the day's agenda. Trenton Cray was always somewhere out there on the periphery, maybe reading the paper or mowing the lawn, but mostly he just tried to stay out of the way. Laurel Cray was definitely the person in charge. She ran a tight ship.

"My old man is just the captain of the guards," Palmer said.

"No, man. Put that out of your head. Your old man's *the* guard. He runs this place. The warden's the boss, on paper. He wears a coat and tie and takes the VIPs to lunch and all that, but your daddy is the man down here inside the walls. This is his house, and if he says *jump*, guys don't even ask how high. They just start jumping and hope that's good enough. He told me if I did him this solid, he'd keep an eye out for my wife and my kid on the outside. He said

Cheddar, you help me and I'll help you. I told him I wasn't much worried about my wife since the bitch turned me in this last time and all, but I love my kid, and I would surely appreciate him looking in on that boy whenever he got the chance." A shadow of melancholy crossed Cheddar's features. Then he shook his head and looked back at his cellmate. "When I get out of here, that boy will only be a little younger than I am right now. He might be married and have a kid of his own." He pointed to a snapshot taped to the wall that featured a little boy in overalls holding up a fish that might have weighed six ounces. He was named Dakota Blue. "That's him on his first fishing trip. He caught that channel cat all by himself."

"Your wife turned you in?" Palmer asked.

"Oh, man, you didn't hear about that? I figured it would have been all over town. You'll love this. The bitch waited until I was asleep, well, passed out, so I couldn't even try to run when they came for me. Then she turned me in. When I woke up, Millard McChesney was standing there with that big Smith and Wesson revolver pointed right at my head." Cheddar pointed to a spot in the center of his forehead, like it was a target. "The barrel was resting right there. He was so close, I could see the bullets in the cylinder and smell the snuff on his breath." He shook his head and shuddered. "You think *that* won't fuck up your whole day, you just try it sometime."

Cheddar was a born runner, for all the good it had ever done him. When the lawmen came, he went. Sometimes it was out the window. Sometimes it was off the roof. Once he had gotten carried away and jumped into the Echota River, and only after the dive did he recall that he couldn't swim. He had always been swiftly apprehended during these flights from justice, but he felt it was important to his self-respect and perhaps to his reputation as a felonious persona to make the effort. Now, though, his own wife had denied him one last futile sprint from the longish arms of the law.

36

The mother of his only child had deprived him of a final attempt to put the wind at his back and make that mad dash for the high country. By the time he got out of Sweetwater prison, he would be too old to do much serious running, although he might still manage a brisk walk if the need were to present itself. Cheddar being Cheddar, it probably would.

Palmer had to agree with Cheddar on at least one point. His wife was known around town to be a bitch on wheels, and that was the somewhat charitable assessment made by an assortment of people she *hadn't* turned in to Millard McChesney. But upon reflection, Palmer didn't suppose that being married to Cheddar was an easy task, even on the good days, so perhaps she could be forgiven at least some portion of her bitchiness, maybe even as much as half. Her maiden name had been Annette Dewberry, but everyone who knew her simply called her Bay-Annette after the edged military weapon of the same name. Cheddar had sworn with raised right hand on more than one occasion that she was as sharp and deadly as her namesake, and that she was just as prone to kill a man if the circumstances were dire.

Palmer was still mulling over the fact that his father had apparently gone to the trouble to ease his transition into life as a convicted felon. The two had not spoken much about Palmer's predicament, but this behavior wasn't unusual for them, because they never talked about anything else, either. Since the wreck, Trenton had mostly just looked at his son with deep sadness etched upon his features, an expression that caused him to resemble a bloodhound. Since he wasn't a talker to begin with, Trenton likely figured that the impending imprisonment of his only child and heir for the ignominious crime of homicide by vehicle was a poor subject around which to build a new habit of chattiness, so he just skipped the exercise rather than set the bad precedent. His father's taciturn demeanor had suited Palmer, because he really didn't have anything to say about the whole business, anyway. He was ashamed that he had killed Rodney and sad that he was gone. Additionally, he was afraid of what was going to happen next, and he was dealing with several other emotions he couldn't even identify, none of which were good. The last thing he wanted to do was talk to his father about the whole sorry affair. It was bad enough just thinking about it.

"So my old man got me assigned to a cell with my cousin?" This revelation made him feel both better and worse. Palmer was relieved to know that his father had his back. But he was also ashamed that his father had been placed in the position of having to intercede at the very prison where he was not only a guard but the captain of the guard, the kingpin of Sweetwater State Correctional Facility.

"He did more than that," Cheddar continued. "Did you stop and think about the fact that you're even here? At Sweetwater, I mean. Every convict in the state of Georgia gets sent to Jackson first, to the classification prison. That's where they decide if you're dangerous, or crazy, or need detox, or if you're about to kill yourself. After Jackson, most convicts get sent wherever the next open cell is. You hardly ever end up at the prison just down the road from where your mama lives. I didn't. They sent me halfway across the state. Of course, my mama wouldn't visit me anyway, but that's not the point."

Cullen Cray's wife—Cheddar's mama—had been a quiet woman whom Cullen had met, impregnated, and married while he was stationed at Ft. Riley, Kansas. Her Christian name was Dolores, and after being the cornerstone of her little family for more than twenty years, she had decided one dark afternoon that they were no longer worthy of that honor. She was last seen at the rest stop on I-75 just south of Chattanooga as she climbed into the cab of a northbound Kenworth truck, perhaps in the initial stage of making her way back to the high plains.

"This last time, they sent me to Arrendale," Cheddar said. "I was there for two years, and Sweetwater is like the Hilton compared to that place. I wouldn't even send my dog there, if I had one." Cheddar had been dogless since the trailer explosion. "Then out of the blue, I was transferred here about three months ago. I tell you, your old man's been pulling strings all along."

Palmer had to admit that he hadn't really been thinking in terms of which jail he might end up in, because he had assumed that he would be sent to Sweetwater. But now that Cheddar had brought it up, he considered it for a moment. The classification prison was news, and he was grateful that he had been spared that experience. And while he wasn't thankful that he was in Sweetwater, he now realized that it could have been much worse. There were over thirty state prisons in Georgia, and Palmer might have been shipped to any of them. Plus, every county had a jail and some of the bigger cities did, too. Incarceration was a growth industry in the Peach State, and any prisons with room to spare housed state prisoners on a contract basis. Palmer realized that it was fortuitous, indeed, that he had been assigned a bunk in his hometown facility. Here was further proof of Trenton Cray's intervention.

"And the word's out on you and on me," Cheddar said. "We are protected property. Private stock. If anyone even *thinks* about messing with either one of us, your old man will land on them hard."

"What do you mean?"

"Your daddy spread the news that if anyone decides to screw with either of us, he'd have them shipped to Reidsville."

"Can he do that?"

"You're not listening to me! He can do whatever he wants. He said if anyone puts hands on you, they could plan on getting shot while escaping. Maybe they'd get it in the leg. Maybe they'd catch one somewhere else. And don't get the wrong idea just because they use rubber bullets, either. They can hurt real bad. If you get hit in the head or the chest with one, it will kill you just as dead as steel will. If you catch one in the nuts, you just wish you would die, and you can forget about having kids." They both grimaced at the thought of it. "I got hit by a rubber bullet down at Arrendale one day when the yard got rowdy. All I was doing was trying to get out of the way, and the next thing I knew, it felt like someone had run over my knee with a freight train hauling wet coal. The doc down there said it was a ricochet that got me, but I think one of those guards shot me deliberate, even though it was clear to anyone who had eyes that all I wanted to do was get back to my cell. My knee still has a knot on it, right here, and it hurts like a mother on cold mornings."

"My old man said he'd shoot anyone who gives me trouble?" Every time Palmer thought he was beginning to get a handle on the moment, another surreal tidbit would upset his equilibrium. For some reason, this last piece of information brought to mind the time his father had visited Sweetwater's elementary school to talk with the principal about some bullies who were harassing several of the younger boys on the playground, including Palmer and Rodney. Palmer had never learned what had transpired during the meeting, but the bullying ceased to be a problem that very day. Now he wondered if his father had threatened to pepper the playground with rubber bullets or perhaps had sworn to ship the miscreants to Reidsville Elementary School at the next sign of trouble.

"I believe it," Cheddar said. "I can't testify to the getting shot part because I didn't actually hear him say it, but Pittypat and a couple of the other guys all swear he did. But whether he did or not, he's not kidding about you being left alone. He means it, and everyone knows he does. Check this out. We had a guy in here named Mondo. You need to believe me when I tell you that Mondo was bad. If they put me in a cell with him, I'd just hang myself the first night and be done with it. It'd be quicker that way, and I'd suffer less. After your old man put the word out that you were off limits, Mondo said he didn't care who your daddy was or what he said, there wasn't no one gonna tell him what to do. Mondo said he was going to catch you in the shower, and when he did, he was going to break you down like a shotgun. You know what he was talking about, right?"

"Yeah." A vivid image crossed Palmer's mind.

"Well, the next thing anyone knew, Mondo was shackled and on the way to Reidsville. He's in general population down there now, and for a child molester, that's not a good place to be. Mondo's in for a real long next twenty years. I hope someone cuts his throat."

"I always thought the old man was just a regular guy," Palmer said. "He puts in a garden every year. He takes Mama to church on Wednesday night and Sunday morning. He likes to watch baseball on TV. He cooks hamburgers on the grill." Palmer had only even heard his father swear once that he could recall, and that was when he slammed his hand in the car door. But now, Cheddar was describing him in terms quite different. It was like hearing that his mother used to be a table dancer at the Prancing Pony Lounge over in Attalla, or that Reverend Jimmy Paulson, the pastor at Mission Hill Baptist Church, was running a string of girls out of a gentlemen's club by the Memphis Airport. The concepts didn't match the realities. The captions didn't fit the photos.

"See, that's why he put you with me," Cheddar said. "There's a whole lot you have got to learn if you're going to make it out of here in one piece. We might as well have lesson number one. Ready?"

"I think so."

"Everything's different in here. Out in the world, you were just a kid who ran out of luck. It could've happened to anyone. You had a few too many beers, you hit a tree, and a guy died. Bad things happen, and your mama cries. Up until last week, they even pretended like they thought you were innocent until they proved you were guilty. But all that's changed now. In here, you're a convict.

You're a criminal. You're an inmate. You didn't mean to kill Rodney, but that don't matter. He's dead, and you have been convicted just like you meant to do it. And you're in here with all the guys who *did* mean to do what they did. They are *real* criminals. They belong here. Don't forget that, no matter what. You can trust you, you can trust me, and you can trust your old man, but don't turn your back on anyone else, inmate or guard. In here, you're only as good as you are bad. And by good I mean safe. And by bad I mean tough. You can't show any cracks. You've got to be as hard as an iron bar and as sharp as a straight razor. You've got to be as mean as my old lady. At least, you've got to be that way when people are looking. I'm serious about this, now. Do you hear what I'm telling you?"

"I hear you," Palmer said. He knew he would have to toughen up some to rival Bay-Annette, but he was game, and the words that Cheddar spoke rang true.

"The guards will mess you up. They are riding herd on over 700 of us, and there ain't anywhere near that many of them. 'Course, they *do* have the guns, which evens the score some, but you notice they don't wear them in here. And they've got riot sticks and tasers, too. If you don't think they'll use them, you just hide and watch while some con runs his mouth at one of them. They'll beat him 'til he breaks and swear he fell down. Then they'll drag him out and fry him like bacon. Then they'll make him clean up the grease. When you're around a guard, remember what you are, and remember what he is. They train them to put a convict down fast and hard, before things get out of hand. About half of them were mean son of a bitches to start with who didn't need much training. They'd work here for free just for the chance to fuck with someone. The only difference between us and some of them is that our uniform is blue and theirs is gray. So keep away from them when you can. A guard will hurt you."

"I'll keep my distance and make sure my mouth stays shut."

"A short guard's the worst."

"Got it."

"Not all of the guards love your old man, either."

"I'll remember."

"That's good. Now, listen to me. We're in a medium-security jail, and that's supposed to mean that the really *bad* mothers are somewhere else. But you can't count on that. These days they have to put guys wherever there's room. That means that some of these boys in here haven't got anything to lose. They're here for life and a day. A man with nothing to lose is dangerous. He does not care. He'll kill you for your shoes. He'll kill you for your pudding. He'll kill you if he doesn't like the way you look or how your name sounds. On top of having nothing to lose, some of the guys in here are just flat mean, like Mondo was. And some of them are crazy. *Some* of them are all three. Don't make any fast moves around them." He was quiet for a moment. Then he added one final comment, as if it were an afterthought. "And pretty much all of them would take a crack at the Head Bull's boy if they thought they could get away with it." He pointed at Palmer. "And the only reason they don't is because they're afraid of what your old man will do to them if they try it."

"Enough," Palmer said. There was too much information of the wrong sort coming his way.

"You *better* hear me. And you damn well better understand. This is not summer camp. You need to listen to me and do what I say. Your old man will do his part, and I'll do mine. You just be sure that you do yours."

"All right. I hear you."

"That's good. Your old man is the meanest son of a bitch in the valley, but it's a big valley, and he can't be everywhere at once."

"What valley?"

"You've never heard that before? Ha! It's the badass version of the Twenty-third Psalm. *Yea, though I walk through the valley of the shadow of death, I will fear no evil, for I am the meanest son of a bitch in the valley.* That's your old man. I won't say that he has never been screwed with, because he has. Look at Mondo. But no one's ever done it for long, or twice."

While he was digesting this newer version of Scripture and his father's place in it, a thought crossed Palmer's mind. "I only got sentenced today. When did you say you got here?"

"They brought me up about three months ago."

"And when did Mondo get sent to Reidsville?"

"They shipped him down there last week, the prick."

"My father must have known I was going to get prison time."

"Well, that wasn't any big secret. There was no way you were going to get probation, no matter what. I mean, you were driving, and you were loaded, right?"

"So I hear."

"Even if you hadn't drawn the Hanging Judge, you were screwed."

"Looks like."

"Your daddy started putting the word out right after I got here, before your trial even started. He told me that short of Jesus coming back to take the faithful home, it didn't look like there was any way around you catching some time. He said he didn't want to wait until the last minute to take care of the things he needed to take care of. So somehow he got you out of Jackson and into Sweetwater. And he had me moved up here from Arrendale. Then he sent Mondo down below the gnat line, and I don't think anyone was sorry to see him gone. After that, he asked if anybody had any questions. I didn't, and nobody else raised their hand, either."

Palmer sat on his bunk and absorbed all he had been told. A nameless song blared from a radio somewhere along the cellblock. The angry, arguing voices of two men drifted past. Away out of sight, a door slammed shut, and that noise echoed down the main corridor like a lockdown. These were the sounds that Palmer would have to get used to. They were the harsh music of captivity.

"I wish my old man had talked to me about all of this," Palmer said.

"Maybe he thought it was bad luck to talk about it," Cheddar said. "You know, like he was hoping for the best but planning for the worst. Or maybe he didn't want to take away your hope. Hope is a big deal. It can give a man a reason to stay alive. You lose your hope, and you might as well just lay down and die."

Palmer nodded. Maybe that was it. A rueful smile flickered for the briefest of moments. He swallowed loudly. Then he sighed as a small revelation descended upon him. "Do you know what this whole thing is?" he asked, looking at his cousin.

"A cluster fuck?" Cheddar asked.

"Well, yeah. But besides that."

"I don't know, man. What is it?"

"This is Cray sloppy luck."

Cheddar considered this observation for a moment. Then he began to nod. "By God, I hadn't thought of that," he replied. "But you're right. It *is* sloppy luck."

It was Palmer's turn to nod. "Think about it," he said. "I smashed a car into a tree at 120 miles per hour and didn't die."

"That's some sloppy luck," Cheddar said.

"I went through a windshield and flew eighty feet before landing in the dark in the only standing haystack in the southeastern United States, and I landed feetfirst so I didn't break my neck."

"Sloppy," Cheddar said, still nodding.

"I got sent to a prison that was hand-picked for me by my old man, a jail so close to home that my mama can walk over here to see me whenever she wants to."

"I've never heard of sloppier luck in my whole life," Cheddar noted.

45

"And then, when I get to that jail, I find out I have two people watching my back. One of them is a badass guard who is also my father, and the other is my cousin."

"Sloppiest luck I've ever seen. You ought to bottle it and sell it."

If Grandpa Cray's anecdotes were to be believed—and he was generally a truthful man—sloppy luck was a trait that selected members of the Cray family had exhibited for many generations. It was a phenomenon difficult to define and was perhaps best described by example. The first instance of sloppy luck that Palmer had heard of was associated with the family legend of Granny Brown and her wedding. In days long past, Palmer's great-great-grandmother was once engaged to a circuit-riding teacher, a man who rode from small town to small town trading rudimentary knowledge of letters and numbers for his keep. He was a quiet, handsome man who was not particularly known for his luck, sloppy or otherwise, as indicated by the fact that he was struck and killed by lightning on the very day that he and Granny Brown were to be wed. This bolt of white fire came from a clear blue sky as he rode his mule to the church for the ceremony. It was a tragedy of the highest magnitude, and the loss had devastated Granny Brown.

But as the arrangements for the funeral were being made, spare wives began to crawl out of the woodwork like termites from a weathered barn. It was eventually determined that the deceased groom was already married three times, and that Palmer's great-great-grandmother would have been wife number four. Thus, the terrible happenstance of losing her betrothed on the day of her wedding proved to be to her benefit, and that wasn't even considering the fact that the mule had survived the lightning strike. Granny Brown kept him as a souvenir of the time she almost committed inadvertent mortal sin, although he tended to be skittish for the rest of his mulish days. She also developed a taste for sugared whiskey during her period of grief and mourning, and she continued to enjoy this small vice several times daily for the next fifty years or so. Hers was arguably the original case of Cray sloppy luck, the alpha sloppy luck, as it were.

Another example involved Cheddar's father, Uncle Cullen, and the loss of all but limited use of his right leg in the defense of democracy, or at least of a random stretch of jungle in a forgotten part of the world. After he graduated from high school, Cullen Cray was drafted by the United States Army and sent to the Republic of South Vietnam for a year's tour of duty. This was a routine practice at that time and place in the world, and nothing about the experience was commonly associated in any way with the phenomenon of luck. Sometime near the end of his time in-country, Cullen found himself walking the point position on a patrol in the Central Highlands, and it was there that he was accidentally shot in the right leg from behind by one of his own platoon mates, a new trooper who had forgotten to engage the safety on his weapon before stumbling over an arbitrary Asian root. Uncle Cullen cussed Vietnam, the new man, Richard Nixon, and stupid people in general while he was quickly bandaged and choppered out of the jungle and straight into the operating room.

The wounds were severe, and Cullen Cray nearly lost the leg during several hours of surgery. Meanwhile, the rest of his platoon continued patrolling right up until the moment they walked into an ambush, during which they were killed, quickly and to the last man. When Cullen heard this news, he had only two words to say to the solemn chaplain standing before him. "Sloppy luck," he said philosophically, and the chaplain, who had no idea what his wounded lamb was talking about, just nodded and smiled as Cullen drifted back into a drug-induced sleep.

Cray family history was littered with such instances, so when viewed in a certain light, Palmer's current situation was nothing special. He was in prison, but he was alive and not alone and was, in fact, being watched out for by at least two people who had his welfare at heart. He was the latest in a long line. He was the next generation.

"When you think about it, me being in prison is a case of sloppy luck, too," Cheddar said.

"Yeah?"

"You know I can't leave the meth alone," he said. Palmer nodded. Everyone knew that. "When I'm out, I'm using all the time, and that shit is just killing me. If that bitch hadn't turned me in, I'd probably already be dead by now. She did me a favor when she dropped that dime. She saved my life."

Palmer nodded again. Sloppy luck was a matter of perception and generally rested in the eyes of the beholder. It was an imperfect gift.

"Why did Bay-Annette turn you in?" Palmer asked. "You never said." Bay-Annette wasn't an unflawed stone herself, thus her bar for acceptable behavior wasn't set all that high. She had put up with a great deal of scurrilous activity from Cheddar during their turbulent years together, so she was bound to have developed some tolerance for his foibles, and Palmer was curious about what, exactly, had sent her tumbling over the edge. He figured it had to be something major.

"It wasn't much of anything. I had a girlfriend, and my old lady got jealous about it and turned me in."

"Women are that way," Palmer said, but he still didn't get it. Cheddar had attracted several inamoratas over the years—usually girls who would do anything for some meth, as demonstrated by their willingness to sleep with Cheddar—and Bay-Annette had always seemed happier when he had one, like maybe the pressure was off of *her*.

"I still think if she hadn't seen the girl's picture, she might've gotten over it," Cheddar continued. "But you know what they say about *might have.*" Palmer had no idea what they said about might have, but he did have another question for his wayward cousin.

"You showed your wife your girlfriend's picture?" he asked incredulously. Palmer was only nineteen, and aside from the sweet attentions of one the Nickel sisters, his experience with the opposite sex was still somewhat limited and was likely to remain that way for another decade or so. But even though his familiarity with females was scarce and his prospects along those lines curtailed, he still knew better than to show the wife the girlfriend's picture. He may have been born knowing better. It simply wasn't done. Cheddar must have been several miles into the meth zone to have made such a monumental error in judgment. It was almost beyond comprehension, like the theory of relativity or the map of the human genome.

"Well, I didn't exactly mean to. I forgot I had this tattoo, and when I took off my shirt, I was caught like a rat in a trap. Man, was Bay-Annette ever pissed. She beat the hell out of me." He shrugged, as if to say *go figure.*

"*That's* your girlfriend?" Palmer asked, nodding at his cousin's torso.

"That's Amber," Cheddar said, nodding. He looked down with fondness at the likeness inscribed on his skin. "Nice boobs, huh?" There was no denying that they were an exceptional pair, perhaps even bordering on world class.

"Cheddar, I don't know what to say." Sometimes mere words were simply not up to the task at hand, and this was one of those occasions.

"There's nothing to say. It's kind of funny, though. Bay-Annette turned me in when she found out about Amber. Well, that's not quite true. She didn't care about her. She turned me in when she saw the tattoo. It made her mad because I'd never gotten one of her. I tried to tell her that I didn't even know I was getting *this* one until it was already done, because I was passed out when I got it, but by then she was wound up and not listening to a word I said. Anyway, when she turned me in, she probably saved my life. Maybe I'll get straightened out in twenty-five years. Plus, Amber's husband is this big, dumb dude, and he has sent word he's gonna kill me if he ever sees me around her again. Now I've got twenty-five years to get off the meth—well, twenty-three, come next Tuesday—and he's got plenty of time to forget about me." Cheddar had taken the long way around the cell to make his point, but he had finally arrived. "A lot can happen between now and when I get out."

"Sloppy luck," Palmer said. He lay back on his bunk with his hands behind his head. He had a bad headache, and he needed to rest. Perhaps he would sleep until morning, and then there would only be nine years and three hundred sixty-four days to go before his release.

"Sloppy luck," Cheddar agreed. That was all it could have been.

I knew it was coming, and now it's here. The Hanging Judge ran over me like a loaded dump truck with burned out brakes. He gave me fifteen years for killing you, and I have to serve at least ten of them. No one in the courtroom could believe it. Even the prosecutor looked surprised. I guess Herrett decided to make an example out of me. J. Randall Crane told me before the trial began that I needed to prepare myself because I was probably going to get convicted, so it wasn't much of a surprise when I did. He also told me that I'd most likely get sentenced to around three years and maybe have to serve one of them. So that's what I was looking for. It was what I had gotten my mind prepared to hear, and that would have been plenty bad enough. When the man dropped a whole dime on me, I couldn't believe what I was hearing. Ten years? Are you kidding me?

I know that my sentence is not as long as dead, which was what you got, and you didn't even get a trial. But ten years is still a long time. I'll be almost thirty when I get out. Everyone we both know will be married with jobs and kids and houses and such. I'll be an ex-convict, bumming loose change and hoping someone will give me a break for old time's sake. You'll love this. I got sentenced on my birthday. I guarantee you that the Hanging Judge did that on purpose. He's a piece of work, for sure. You know how sometimes you hear about a judge getting shot or blown up or something? I understand the urge. The only thing I don't get is why it doesn't happen more often.

Don't tell Morris, but ever since I got here, I've been thinking that being dead might be better than serving ten years. What do you think? How bad is being dead? Would you rather be wherever you are doing whatever you're doing, or would you rather be in a jail cell for ten years? I'm really thinking about it, and I need your opinion. Send me a sign or something. I don't have many options, but going to take the dirt nap is definitely one of them.

The real problem is that if I decide to come join you, it could be tough to manage. It's harder than you might think to kill yourself in prison. You can't just take a bottle of pills and go to sleep, because there aren't any bottles of pills or at least there are not any that I can afford. And even with some of the other ways, they sort of expect guys to try it so they watch out and try to prevent it. I guess if too many convicts off themselves it makes the guards look bad, and then they don't get their Christmas bonus. But there are ways. The trick is to not let them know you're thinking about it. If they get a clue, they'll lock you down tight in the isolation block. Once that happens, you're sunk. The only way you can kill yourself in there is by holding your breath until you die or by beating yourself to death with your own Bible. There's a guy a few cells down named Booty who swears he almost did that once, but I think he's lying.

To be honest I might've already given it a shot, but both our mamas are about this close to coming apart and I think that me killing myself might be just enough to kill both of them too. They're standing pretty close to the edge, and I don't think either one of them can take much more. I don't want to hurt them any more than I already have. I've got enough bad karma, and I don't need that on there, too. I would probably end up coming back as a possum or one of the Hanging Judge's grandkids.

Mama cried when I got my sentence. Your mama did too, but your old man looked as happy as a fat pig in the sunshine. I was sort of surprised that he even had the balls to show up at the courtroom after his last meeting with my old man. You should have seen the way my old man looked at yours all the way through the trial. It was like he was daring him to say even a single word. Just one. Take it from me. The business between those two isn't over yet. I'll say this for your old man, though. He has learned to keep his mouth shut when he's in the same room with mine. Still, if your old man isn't careful, Trenton Cray is going to hand him his ass in a sack. That is a fight I would pay cash money to see.

They took me to Sweetwater prison, which was good news for Mama, at least, because I'm close enough to home for her to be able to visit every week. I just hope that the next ten years don't finish her off. Keep your fingers crossed that she doesn't worry or smoke herself to death on my account. I wonder if it wouldn't have been better if I had been sent off to a prison she couldn't get to every week. It might be less of a strain on her if she could only see me every now and then. If you had a kid, would you want to see him behind bars and be reminded every week that he was in prison? I wouldn't. I'd want to put it as far out of my mind as I could get it.

So far, the days in prison have not been so bad. What I mean to say is that the daylight hours are not as bad as I thought they'd be. I'd rather be somewhere else, for sure, but at least I can stand it most of the time. There are some scary guys in here, but you learn quick who they are and how to stay away from them. The people who run this place give everyone work to do unless they're sick or going to school. They even pay you to do it, but then they apply what you earned to what it costs the State to keep you up, so you don't actually get any cash. I'm not complaining, though. Money isn't worth as much in here as it is out there, and having something to do does help the time pass.

In prison, that's what it all boils down to. Everything you do is about making the time pass. They can't really make you work, but if you don't they can sure make you wish you had. A few days ago a couple of guys refused to work. Said they were going on a strike. It was laundry duty, too, which is almost as good as it gets. When the guards got through persuading them, they were begging for something to do. They ended up on permanent shower duty, which is about as bad as it gets. But they had it coming, so I don't feel too sorry for them. They broke the first rule of prison, which is to never piss the guards off. Guards carry clubs and guns. Guards can make your life hard. You would have to be crazy to make one mad. So those two guys got what they got.

You'll never guess in a million years who my cellmate is. It's my cousin, Cheddar Cray. He is just as crazy as he ever was, but it's good to be in here with someone I know. I was really worried that I'd have to sleep with one eye open for ten years. Rooming with Cheddar wasn't just good luck, either. My old man arranged for me and Cheddar to be in the cell together. I never would have thought it, but it turns out that the old man is the main man in here. He walks around carrying that big stick, and from what I hear, he doesn't mind swinging it when he needs to. I still have a hard time picturing that. Sometimes you think you know all there is to know about a person, and then it turns out there's a whole other side to them. That's my old man. And since he's my old man, he keeps an eye out for me.

Talking about work, some of the inmates have jobs outside the walls. It's funny how things turn out and how your point of view can change. There's nothing like the sound of the steel door slamming to change the way you look at the world. I used to feel sorry for the state prisoners who were riding on the backs of the garbage trucks or cleaning

53

out the ditches. I used to think, you know, how low can a guy sink? But now I wish I was one of them. It would be pretty sweet to get out into the world every day. I would love to clean out a ditch or pick up a can. It's my bad luck, though, that they won't let me work outside the walls. I'm a flight risk because I'm nineteen, so they keep me behind the razor wire.

According to Cheddar, younger prisoners with long sentences tend to boogie every chance they get. I really don't know if I would run or not, but I might. Cheddar never seemed to have very much luck with running, but that's Cheddar. So maybe I would run if the opportunity came up. I think it might be one of those deals where I won't know until it happens. If I got caught I'd have to serve my full sentence and they'd tack on some more years for the escape on top of that. Cheddar said five years, but I don't know if that's right and it's not like I can check it out with the nearest guard. Anyway, the full fifteen plus something for escaping would add up to more time than I could stand. I don't even know if I can stand the time I've already drawn. I guess we'll find out together. Keep your fingers crossed.

Cheddar and I work in the kitchen. This is considered to be good work among the inmates. I wash dishes, which is not as bad as it sounds. The automatic dishwasher does the washing, but I scrape trays and load the thing, and then I unload and stack the trays when they're done. Also I help serve and clean up. Cheddar is a cook's helper. His main duty is standing around in the kitchen with his hands in his pockets talking to the cooks. Sometimes he opens some cans. Leave it to him to get the sweetest job in here. The cooks aren't prisoners, and most of them are pretty good guys but not pretty good cooks. They feed me and Cheddar in the kitchen on the days we work, and when that happens we eat what the cooks eat, which is better food than the general population gets. So like I said, the days aren't so bad. But the nights are a different story. The nights are long.

3

Milestones Suck

As Palmer Cray settled into his new life with Cheddar, he discovered that the prison clock was not bound by the laws of physics or the rules of men. Rather, time in the slam was a sluggishly fluid substance. It was dark, slow matter that oozed like chilled oil, and its passage was not marked by hours, days, or even years so much as it was by events that occurred outside the normal prison routines, happenings that Palmer came to think of as *milestones*. Ideally, days in prison were notable only for their bland similitude, and in this purest form they would pass in deliberate lockstep like soldiers marching past a fallen comrade, each just like the last, none any more or less remarkable than another. Palmer and Cheddar descended into this routine of sameness, and, barring any disruptive milestones, time passed without much conscious thought concerning the nature of their mean condition.

A comparable experience would be that of the long-distance runner tuned into the rhythm of stride and the cadence of breathing to the exclusion of all else. Ideally, that runner would slip into a reality where no interruption would follow, an alternate universe devoid of cramps and blisters where thirst and hunger could not intrude and fatigue and pain did not exist. Once in this state, the runner's world would become breaths, steps, and heartbeats, and the next conscious thought would be that the finish line had been crossed and the race was done.

This was the existential state that Palmer and Cheddar sought when they settled into their daily routines at Sweetwater State Correctional Facility and began to pile their respective mountains of time. Just like the marathon runner, they strove to enter a mindless world, a fugue state from which they would emerge weeks, months, or even years later, marveling at how fast the days of captivity had passed. Cheddar had told Palmer that this was the way the old-timers did it, and it was the time-honored method that the two of them would employ as well. They would simply dig in and stack days. There was no use reinventing the wheel when the wheel already rolled well enough for their purposes.

"Don't even *think* about being in here ten years," Cheddar said. "And I won't think about all that time I have to do. It's too long. The numbers are too big. You can't get your head around them. Even a year is too much to imagine. I knew a guy at Arrendale who only had to do two years. Two years! I could serve two years and not even have to sit down. But this guy wouldn't listen to me. He was counting down every day. He had a calendar taped to the wall, and the last thing he did before he went to sleep was cross off another box. Do you know what happened to him?"

"What happened to him?"

"He went nuts and tried to hang himself with his T-shirt. *That's* what happened to him. Over a little two-year stretch. There's no telling what ten years would have done to the boy. Twenty-five would have blown him up on the spot. But the point is, he was thinking about tomorrow. You can't do that, and neither can I. It'll make both of us crazy if we do. The only thing you and me need to worry about is *today*. Just today, and that's all. We get up. We go eat. We work in the kitchen. We eat again. We work in the kitchen some more. We eat one last time. We come back here and maybe read a book or play a game of checkers or some cards. Then we go to bed. That's all we need to think about. If you keep your mind on today for enough days in a row, it'll be time for you to go home. And if I do it long enough, it'll be my time, too."

When an event occurred that broke the mindless routine prescribed by Cheddar—when a milestone intruded upon their lives—it was always a bit of a shock to both of them, like they had been doused by a bucket of cold water or slapped in the face. And because prison routines weren't grand in scale, it didn't take much to interrupt them. A troubling letter from home could smash an inmate's protective psychological wall like a bulldozer. An unsettling comment from a visitor could slice through a con's layer of mental insulation like a wicked knife. A honey bun or a cigarette missing from a locker could shatter a prisoner's composure like vintage glass. And as a general rule, the bigger the milestone, the larger the ripple it produced, like a chunk of mountain stone tossed into a pool.

Such was the case the day that Bay-Annette came to ask Cheddar for money. Bay-Annette hadn't been to see her husband since the day she turned him and his tattoo over to the unforgiving arms of the law. This lack of companionship was perhaps more understandable when he was down at Arrendale, a long six-hour ride away. But Cheddar had been back in town for months, so he was suspicious of Bay-Annette's motives when the guard informed him that his wife was there that Sunday to visit.

"I wonder what she wants," he muttered as he slipped on his shoes and buttoned his denim shirt to the very top button, just to be on the safe side.

"Maybe she brought your boy to visit," Palmer replied. Usually Cheddar's father brought him, but maybe the plan had changed.

"Not likely. I guarantee the bitch is up to no good."

"Well, she can't do much more to you than she already has," Palmer noted.

"If you say so." Cheddar, it seemed, wasn't so sure.

Their visit lasted about thirty minutes, and when Cheddar returned to the cell, he was visibly upset. His eyes had a dangerous gleam, and his fingers opened and closed, as if he were performing hand exercises or trying to snatch invisible weapons from the ether. He was as beside himself as Palmer had ever seen him and appeared to be agitated enough to remain that way for days.

"Trouble?" Palmer asked, looking up from his copy of *Rolling Stone*. Each inmate was allowed subscriptions to five magazines, and his mother had subscribed her son his limit. Of the five periodicals, he enjoyed every page of *Rolling Stone*, *National Geographic*, and *Nature*. He was less enthusiastic about *Ladies Home Journal* and *Guideposts*, but he read them anyway out of a sense of obligation and to have something to do.

"Shit," Cheddar said. He seemed to be speaking to himself more than to Palmer. He sat on the toilet and stared at his son's picture taped to the wall. Occasionally he repeated his initial comment, and these were the only sounds he made for a long time. Palmer went back to his magazine. He figured his cousin would talk when he got ready. Later, just as he finished reading every bit of text—including the ads in the back, which were sometimes the best part—Cheddar spoke again.

"I know she's lying." Again, this was addressed to no one in particular, even though Palmer was sitting right there. "I know it like I know my name is Cheddar Cray. She asked me for money for some kind of special doctor for the kid, but I know she just wants it so she can buy some drugs and some booze. I swear to God, I don't know why I married her." This observation was not quite the gospel truth, although in his defense, Cheddar may have forgotten the details of the whirlwind courtship. He had proposed to Bay-Annette on the very day she informed him that he had inadvertently burdened her with child, and that she would kill him in his sleep if he didn't do the right thing by her and do it quickly. "But what if she's not lying?" Cheddar continued, addressing Palmer for the first time. "That's the hell of it. What if for one time in her sorry life she's telling the truth and the boy's really sick?" It was a conundrum. Cheddar's features were etched with anguish and indecision.

"What did she say was wrong with him?"

"Something called pernicious anemia. I may be saying it wrong. She said she needed to take him to Emory. He didn't look sick when my old man brought him last week, but how do I know what a kid with pernicious anemia is supposed to look like?"

"I've heard of that disease," Palmer said. "A guy I went to school with had it, I think. He looked sort of normal."

"Maybe she's not making it up, then."

"Well, whether he's really sick or whether it's just Bay-Annette scamming you, there's not much you can do about it either way. You're in jail. What little money you earn goes to the State. I have a few bucks hidden in my socks that you can have, but it's not enough for a trip to Emory."

Cheddar looked at his cousin with an expression akin to pity, and he sighed. Palmer had a lot to learn, and he was a slow learner.

"Palmer, *I'm* in jail, man. My money isn't." Upon further explanation, it turned out that Cheddar's methamphetamine enterprise had been successful even after the normal write-offs for attorneys, bail, and burned mobile homes. Over the years, he had buried more than a few coffee cans full of profit at strategic locations around the county, good hard cash on which no tax had been paid. He called these containers his retirement fund, and barring torrential rain, excessive rust, or unfortunate gravesite selection by strangers, they would comfort him like a warm blanket during his waning years. As he discussed his business affairs with Palmer, however, Cheddar suddenly became quiet.

"What's wrong?" Palmer asked.

"I was a meth dealer. I hurt a lot of people. What do you think about that?"

It was a decent question. Palmer was no saint himself, but neither was he a former meth dealer with several dozen coffee cans full of twenties, fifties, and c-spots that spoke to his success at that profession. Given that methamphetamine was more addictive than life and nearly as fatal, it followed that Cheddar had been a bad man in his heyday, a purveyor of misery and slow death. Palmer didn't care for the man that Cheddar had been, but surprisingly, he had no issue with the person that Cheddar was now. That individual was his cellmate and friend. That man, like Palmer, had been tried and found guilty by a jury of peers and was now making restitution for his past sins. That man, like Palmer, was earning his second chance one slow day at a time. He was rehabilitated for at least the next twenty-three years.

"Cheddar, everyone in the county knew you were a meth dealer. Probably everyone in North Georgia knew it. You were on the state news twice that I remember. I think you made the networks when your trailer blew up. Even the cops knew what you were up to." Palmer gestured at the cell's bars to illustrate this final point. If Cheddar's occupation was supposed to have been a secret, it had been a poorly kept one, for sure.

"I just want us to be cool," Cheddar said.

"We're cool. Of course, I killed my best friend, so the bar's not set that high with me. You might need to pile on a few more years before you try to join the church choir. Can we get back to the story? Did you give Bay-Annette some of your retirement money?" Palmer was betting that his cousin had, because when it came to family, his heart was even softer than his teeth.

"Yeah," Cheddar said. He shook his head in self-disgust. "She said she had to have it right away. I told her where a small coffee can was buried, a Sanka can." Apparently, Sanka cans were used for reluctant disbursements. "There was just five grand in it. That ought to take care of any doctor bills in case the boy really is sick. I still think she's lying, but I can't take the chance that Dakota Blue needs help and I wouldn't give her the money. If I didn't let her have it and he got worse, I couldn't stand it."

"That would be bad," Palmer agreed. "If I were you, though, I'd have Uncle Cullen check the story out, just to keep Bay-Annette honest."

"I will."

"Maybe he can get some of the money back if it turns out that she lied to you."

"Nah," Cheddar said. "Let her keep it. I can't take it with me." He looked at Palmer. "What is pernicious anemia?"

"I think it's got something to do with low blood," Palmer replied. "Like maybe he needs more iron. There might be something about it in the library." Sweetwater State Correctional Facility boasted a library that contained over five thousand volumes. The warden believed in keeping his charges occupied.

"That doesn't sound too bad."

"I'm sure they can fix him up down at Emory."

"You know," Cheddar said, "if it was just Bay-Annette needing some money, she could hook for it. It wouldn't be the first time. Hell, that's how we met." His eyes got a faraway, dreamy look for a moment as the pleasant memory came to him. "Man, that girl was magic back then. She could make you talk in tongues. She still can, if you can catch her in the mood and she doesn't turn you in to the law."

"Maybe she'll be in the mood by the time you get out," Palmer offered helpfully. He didn't know what else to say.

"Forget that! I got all the way over her while I was staring up the barrel of Millard McChesney's Smith and Wesson."

"Time heals all wounds," Palmer noted. "Or most of them, anyway."

A death on the cellblock, whether from natural causes or otherwise, was another event that qualified as a milestone every time it happened, and it was more common than Palmer would have ever dreamed. One morning as he and Cheddar lined up in front of their cell for breakfast call, they noticed a vacancy in the line ahead of them, a gap where an old man should have been. A con named Glass had stepped from his cell into formation on schedule, but his cellmate, Pittypat, did not appear behind him. At the command from the guard, they all began to march to the dining hall, and as they passed the cell, Palmer looked to the right. A sheet-shrouded body lay on the bottom bunk. Talking was forbidden in the chow line, so he nudged Cheddar and nodded toward the deceased. Cheddar grimaced and looked away. Cheddar, like Millard McChesney, did not care for the departed. Later, while they worked in the kitchen, they discussed Pittypat's final roll call.

"I liked that old man," Palmer said as he scraped and rinsed trays. "He was a nice guy. I was just talking to him a couple of days ago. We had oatmeal that morning, and he was telling me about how bad the oatmeal was over at Limestone. He told me it tasted like warm sawdust and glue." The oatmeal at Limestone was infamous among the prisons of the Southeast. No one who had ever consumed the lumpy, bland substance was ever again able to put it completely from mind. In that respect, it held much in common with the rest of the Limestone experience.

"I heard they had bad oatmeal over there," Cheddar said. "They say the oatmeal at Limestone is even worse than the Salisbury steak at

Arrendale. I know for a fact that *that* would gag a maggot. I talked to Glass at breakfast, and he told me that Pittypat died in the middle of the night. He said he felt the bunk shaking. Then he heard him start to make a strangling noise, and when he checked him out, Pittypat's eyes were all bugged out, and he was choking and turning blue. Glass hollered for the guard, but by the time he got there, Pittypat was dead. They just covered him up with his sheet and left him in the cell all night. Said there wasn't anything that could be done for him now, and no use waking up the doctor. That's creepy, right there. Glass said he didn't sleep a wink. I wouldn't either, not with a dead guy in with me." Cheddar shuddered. The idea was all over him like a bad rash.

"I wonder what he died from," Palmer said.

"He died from being an old man in Sweetwater prison," Cheddar said. "It's a terminal condition."

"That's not a disease."

"It's the worst disease there is."

"Pittypat wasn't a bad guy," Palmer said. He felt that someone ought to be feeling low about the ancient inmate's relocation to that halfway house in the sky, but he wasn't getting any takers in the prison kitchen. Perhaps they weren't the mourning type, or maybe they wished to grieve later, during the quiet time after the meatloaf pans were slid into the cavernous ovens and the large tubs of potatoes were mashed. In Palmer's view, Pittypat hadn't been much, but he had been theirs, part of their odd, extended family. He had been a human being, and now he was just as gone as if he had never even been there at all. According to Cheddar, Glass was already assigned a new cellmate, a car thief from Summerville, and time was marching on. Palmer hoped that someone had at least remembered to change the sheets, but he supposed that was the new man's problem.

Cheddar, for his part, noticed that his cellmate was having philosophical issues with the passing of their colleague.

"When you said that Pittypat wasn't a bad guy, did you mean to say that he wasn't a bad guy for someone who liked to rob 7-Elevens at gunpoint and who had spent most of his life in prison?" Cheddar asked, providing a succinct summation of Pittypat's life.

"Well, yeah, I guess that's what I meant to say. Maybe you shouldn't be the one to get up and say a few words at his service."

"What service?"

"His funeral service."

"That'll be six guys from the yard detail and the chaplain, unless it's the chaplain's day off," Cheddar said. "In that case, it'll just be the six guys. I think one of them used to be a preacher, though."

"That doesn't seem right."

"Remember what I told you about most of these guys belonging in here?"

"I remember."

"Pittypat stuck people up with guns. He was good at it, and he liked to do it. He told me once that he liked to see the fear in their eyes. He belonged in here."

"Well, he never held a gun on me," Palmer said.

"That's because they don't let us have guns," Cheddar replied. Palmer had to concede the point. "Otherwise, he might have taken a run at you. He shot a guy once, you know. A store clerk. The guy had a wife and some kids. Pittypat shot him in the chest, too, up there where all the important stuff is. It didn't kill him, but that was just his good luck, and you can bet that Pittypat didn't stop to check. He was old and pitiful in here, but back when he was running wild, he was a bad man. He was the kind of guy you didn't want knowing where you lived."

"That was a long time ago, though," Palmer said. "Ever since I've known him, he's just been an old man. He was over eighty. He died in prison, alone." Technically, he had been with Glass when he went. Glass was an arsonist by trade who was in for first-degree manslaughter due to a slight miscommunication about the location of the night watchman during the commission of an insurance job, and Palmer felt sure that he hadn't been much of a comfort to Pittypat during his final moments, laying there breathing his last while contemplating the great mystery of what was to come next.

"A lot of people die in prison alone," Cheddar said. "He was serving life and a day, and today was the day. It was his time. That's how it works. They don't hand out those life-plus sentences to shoplifters or jaywalkers, you know. You have to screw up pretty hard to get one. Pittypat did that his whole life."

"I just realized I don't know his real name."

"Lee. His name was Bryson Lee. Glass told me."

"What'll happen to him now?"

"If someone claims him, they'll hold him until the next of kin picks him up. If no one steps up, they'll bury him in the field behind the prison. Dead cons are the reason our garden grows so good." Palmer hoped he was kidding about the fertilizer. With Cheddar, it was sometimes hard to tell.

"No one will claim him," Palmer said. "He didn't have any family at all. No kids, no wife, all his people dead. He told me that he had spent over fifty-five years in prison, one way or another. The first time he drew time was back during the 1940s. He's been at Sweetwater since it opened."

"Well, there you go, then. Everyone he knew on the outside is dead and gone, and now he's dead too. Eighty is a good long run, even if most of it was spent in a jail cell. I'd sign a deal for eighty years right now, no questions asked. That'd give me over twenty-five years as a free man after I get out of here. I could do some damage in twenty-five years. Here. Scrape these trays. You're thinking, and that's a bad thing. Pittypat might be in a better place, or he might even be in a worse one, if you believe in that. Hell, maybe he's nowhere at all, which is my take. But one thing's for sure. Wherever he is, at least he's in a *different* place, and that means he's not *here* anymore. That's gotta be worth something." Palmer had to agree. Pittypat would finally get his set of civilian clothes, and he would leave Sweetwater State Correctional Facility behind. He had been released.

Holidays were among the worst milestones, and Palmer came to dread them because of their disruptive effect on his normal day and because they made it impossible not to think about what all the free people were doing to celebrate the occasion, all those lucky souls who weren't living in a cell with Cheddar Cray. He first noticed this phenomenon on the Fourth of July immediately following his incarceration, when he had only been in prison for a little over a month. He and Cheddar had both gone to great lengths to avoid knowing the date—even to the point of averting their eyes around calendars and humming loudly when they overheard conversations that seemed to refer to the topic—because it was their belief that time passed more swiftly when it was unmeasured. They had been so successful in their enterprise that they were a bit surprised when Independence Day presented itself like an unwelcome visitor at the door of their cell.

"I hate holidays," Cheddar said morosely. They were back from their breakfast trip to the dining hall, during which they had learned from a well-meaning and patriotic felon that it was the anniversary of the signing of the Declaration of Independence. On the outside, it was a day of parades, fireworks, picnics, and cookouts. For Cheddar and Palmer, the day was an unwelcome milestone marked by a scoop of Neapolitan ice cream with their supper. "I knew the Fourth was close," he continued, "but I was trying to keep it out of my mind."

"You know," said Palmer, "the Fourth of July has never been one of my favorite holidays. For one thing, it's too hot outside. I remember once the temperature showed 106 degrees on the thermometer under the kitchen window. Every year, my old man burns the ribs. Unless we're having hot dogs. Then he burns those. You'd think after all this time he would have figured that he just doesn't have the knack for grilling." Cheddar nodded in agreement as Palmer finished his thought. "Then, even though the meat is burnt, we eat it anyway."

"The ribs suck," Cheddar agreed. "The hot dogs are not that bad. The trick is to put plenty of mustard and onions on them."

"Your old man always gets depressed," Palmer said. "When that happens, he starts hitting the beer, and then he gets drunk. Then he gets mean and wants to fight. When no one will fight with him, he gets even more depressed. Then he passes out."

Cheddar nodded. He had missed a few of the family Fourth of July celebrations over the years due to conflicting commitments at various penal institutions, but the ones he had attended were all pretty much like Palmer had just described. The only thing he would have added would be that some years his old man threw up before passing out, usually on someone.

"Daddy's leg hurts," Cheddar said with a shrug, even though an explanation was not necessary. Not to Palmer, anyway, and not to the rest of the Cray family, either. It was understandable that Cullen Cray would lament his bad leg, and no one faulted him for his occasional excesses, particularly on patriotic holidays such as the Fourth of July. He had lost the full use of that leg in defense of his country, more or less, and the loss weighed heaviest when the trappings of democracy were on full display, when the flags snapped in the brisk breeze and the fireworks burst in the night sky. "It still hurts him after all these years. He says it feels like it's full of bullets."

Palmer sighed. "But even though the Cray family Fourth of July sucks, I'm really going to miss not being there with the folks, eating burned ribs and potato salad, maybe helping you load Uncle Cullen into the car after he passes out. Now that I can't be there, I want to be there. It's kind of like wishing I could work on the garbage truck. You always want what you can't have. Human nature, I guess."

"I could go for some of your mama's pineapple upside down cake right now," Cheddar said.

Palmer nodded. His mama's upside down cake was good stuff. He could almost taste the tart fruit and the caramelized sugar. "The year before last after the family cookout was over," he told Cheddar, "me and Rodney took the Nickel sisters down to the lake. I guess you were at Arrendale. We shot fireworks and drank cold beer. Later, we skinny-dipped and drank more cold beer. We stayed all night, just looking at the stars and talking. Well, not just talking. That was the first time I made love with Kaitlyn. That was the best night of my life." He was quiet for a moment. Then he tried to laugh, but it had a bitter sound, shrill and hollow. "I should have died the next morning and gone out on a high note." Sitting in a prison cell talking about it with Cheddar was a definite anti-climax.

"You're killing me," Cheddar said. "You've got to quit talking about skinny-dipping, cold beer, and women."

"You talk about Bay-Annette," Palmer pointed out.

"I am wrong for that."

"I'm just saying."

"This is why I hate holidays," Cheddar said. "You can keep your mind off of what it's like on the outside most of the time. But you can't do it on a holiday. That's when prison really gets on top of you, because you're not out there with everyone else, having a fine old time. If you think today is bad, just wait for Thanksgiving and Christmas. Guys are wandering around like zombies then, especially the ones with kids. About half the cells have to be put on suicide watch. The guards come through picking up belts and shoelaces, and they won't let anyone shave."

"Well, I hate it today."

"I do too, buddy. I do too. Tomorrow will be better."

Such were the milestones, the departures from the normal flow that were setbacks for Cheddar and Palmer and for the majority of their peers at Sweetwater State Correctional Facility. There was a certain irony to the fact that this discomfiture was the same regardless of the nature of the interruption. Whether they were presented with good news or bad, they felt as if they had been shaken by a temblor or jarred by a collision, and it took hours and sometimes days before they regained equilibrium. It required willpower and work to reestablish the mindless routine of the professional prisoner and to reenter the prison zone. It was like trying to forget about a pink elephant. The harder they tried, the bigger it became.

Many small milestones marked Palmer's incarceration, little signposts along the way that served to remind him that he was not deemed fit company for a world that was moving on without him. In addition to these, there were milestones of the monumental variety, guaranteed life-changers that molded him into a different Palmer from the one he had once been. They were evolutionary steps on the road from the present to the future, flagstones on the path from here to there. The first of these large milestones may have in fact been the largest, and it occurred on a cold day in hell just nine months into his sentence.

It was a frigid February afternoon, a Sunday, and Palmer had been summoned to the visiting area, where he expected to meet his mother. She had come to see him every Sunday since the first week of his imprisonment. Each time, she brought reading materials and sweets, which was not strictly legal but was allowed due to her status as Captain Cray's wife. She always stayed as long as they would let her, but even then, more times than not she had to be given a second reminder that her time was up. Again in deference to her status as the captain's wife, she was spared the customary search to which all other visitors were subjected, and Palmer appreciated this consideration. His mother was a private woman, and it would have been difficult for her to tolerate strange hands patting her down, although Palmer believed she would have done it willingly if that had been the price of admittance.

But this week, it was not his mother sitting on the other side of the bulletproof glass. It was Trenton Cray, whom Palmer had not seen since that fateful day in the courtroom close to a year past when he was marched in chains to his new life. He had wondered more than once about the paucity of visits from his father and had puzzled on the nature of this isolation. Trenton Cray had always been a quiet and undemonstrative man, perhaps even a bit aloof, but even so, Palmer was a little surprised not to receive a single visit from him since being jailed. He had discussed the matter with his cousin, and Cheddar had explained his view on the dynamics of the situation.

"He's still protecting you, man, just like he has been since even before they slammed the door shut behind you. He's staying away from you so it's not up in everyone's face all the time that he's your daddy and that he's keeping an eye out for you."

Palmer hadn't considered this possibility, but now that he did, it made sense to him. "He wants everyone to sort of forget that he's my father."

"You've got it, man."

"Still, it'd be nice to see him," Palmer said.

"Yeah, well, would you rather see your daddy, or would you rather not get stabbed some morning out in the yard? That's kind of what it boils down to. Me, I'd rather avoid the shank." Cheddar had a way with words. He had made his point quite clearly, and Palmer decided to let the matter drop. He could see his old man when he got out. It wasn't like he didn't know where the man lived.

That Sunday in the visiting room, Palmer sat down with a premonition of dread. Because he was still considered a flight risk, he met all of his visitors in the isolation area, where they sat on the opposite side of a pane of unbreakable glass. He picked up the receiver, and his father did the same. Neither spoke for a long moment. Then Trenton Cray took a deep breath and began talking in a quiet monotone, the same voice he used for all communications. Palmer had to strain to hear the words above the subtle background of white noise issuing from the telephone earpiece.

"Your mama's dead," Trenton said to his son. "She died last night in her sleep. The doctor says it was a stroke. She didn't suffer. She never even woke up." He looked away for a moment, gathering himself. Then he continued. "She twitched a few times, and I thought she might be having a bad dream. You know how she always had those nightmares." Palmer nodded. He felt like he was in the middle of one of those nightmares right now. "I tried to wake her up, but she wouldn't budge. I shook harder, but she still wouldn't open her eyes. That's when I figured something was bad wrong. I called the ambulance. Then I did CPR until they got there. But it was no good. She was already gone. I think she was dead when I made the call."

There was a long silence punctuated only by the slight hiss of their breathing on the telephone line. This news was totally unexpected, and Palmer didn't know what to say. It seemed as if his life had become a series of unpleasant firsts, and the loss of his mother was another of these: the first time he killed someone, the first time he went to prison, the first time his mother died. When his father said the word *dead*, Palmer felt a sharp pain in his chest, like he had been shot.

"I just saw her last Sunday," he said, mostly to himself. His father nodded.

"I know."

"She looked fine." Truth be told, she had looked tired around the eyes, and her features were puffy. Palmer had told her then that she needed to go home and take a nap, and she had promised she would. Now he wondered if she had, as if a Sunday afternoon snooze could have changed her destiny. He looked at his father. "How can she be gone?" he asked.

"She'd been going downhill since you came inside," Trenton said. He wasn't being intentionally cruel, but the words carried blame. "Longer than that, really, but it got worse when they sent you here. I could see it, but I couldn't stop it. You know your mama. Kind of stubborn. She didn't want you to know that she was sliding. She was afraid you would worry about her and blame yourself."

"She was right."

"It's not like that, Palmer. You know she had bad high blood pressure and a touch of sugar, and she was always forgetting to take her medicine. Plus, she loved her Marlboro Menthols. She smoked two packs a day since before we married. She knew she needed to quit, or at least slow up, but some people just can't. She was one of those."

Palmer took a deep, ragged breath.

"I never really understood all the details about what her doctor said," Trenton continued, "but she also had some kind of heart ailment going on. Something to do with one of her valves murmuring. And she never slept anymore. I'd hear her wandering around the house at all hours, fixing up care packages for you or talking to herself like she was speaking to you and Rodney."

He ceased his monologue for a moment and took some deep breaths of his own, as if he had been shoveling sand or chopping wood and needed to catch his breath. He had the habit of inhaling through his mouth and exhaling through his nose, and the cadence of his breathing was pronounced. The room was cool, but sweat beaded on his forehead. "The doctor at the emergency room said that all these things led up to her having a stroke."

Palmer folded his arms on the table and laid his head on them. He couldn't believe it. His mother was dead, and he felt that he was to blame. Sure, the Marlboro Menthols had helped, and there was no getting around the genetic component, but he had contributed significantly to his own mother's demise. Now the count stood at two: Rodney Earwood and Laurel Cray. He raised his head and placed the receiver back to his ear.

"When is the funeral?" he asked. He was speaking from inside a tunnel, his voice reverberating in his ears as if he had shouted.

"It's in a couple of days. I asked the doctor to do an autopsy. Once that's done, I'm going to bury her at Sweetwater Cemetery. We sat down last year and talked about...things, and that's where she said she wanted to go when her time came. I'll put her in next to her sister."

Palmer nodded. The family plot was at the northern edge of that cemetery, edged by trees on two sides and a tangle of rhododendrons on a third. It was a pretty spot to spend eternity.

"Will they let me come?" he asked.

"No."

"They won't even let me out for one hour to come to my mother's funeral? What about...what do they call it...a compassionate furlough?" He had felt the harshness of captivity many times during the preceding nine months, but never so keenly as at this moment. The full weight of his loss of freedom pressed down on him like a slab of granite.

"The warden thinks you'll run," Palmer's father said simply. He looked down when he spoke. Palmer mulled over this statement. Then he smiled sadly.

"Do you remember when I was a kid and we used to watch *Cool Hand Luke* every time it came on?"

"I do. That was a good show. I always liked Paul Newman."

"Remember when Luke's mama died, and Strother Martin made that speech? He said something like *when a boy's Ma dies, he gets rabbity.*"

"I remember it."

"This reminds me of that," Palmer said. He looked at his father. "I'm not rabbity. Tell him I won't run. He respects you, and he'll listen to you. You're the captain of the guard."

"He thinks I'll *let* you run." Trenton Cray looked back at his son through the smudged pane of reinforced glass. He shrugged, and his features were marked with sheepishness, or perhaps full-blown shame, as if he had been caught doing something wrong.

"He said that?" Palmer asked.

"No, he didn't say it. But that's what he thinks. I could see it in his eyes when I asked him."

"That's just crazy. You wouldn't do that."

There was a long break in the conversation. Trenton Cray caught his son's gaze and held it.

"I *would* do it," he said.

"What?" This was the last thing Palmer expected to hear.

"I wish I'd made you leave before the trial even started. Your mama and I talked about it, and she was all for the idea. She wanted you to go to Canada. But I thought you would only get a year or two, and I didn't want you to have to live your life looking back over your shoulder, which is the way it would've been if you had run. If I had it to do again, though, that's what I'd tell you to do. I'd put some money in your pocket and some gas in the pickup, and I'd send you to Canada."

"You would have lost the house," Palmer said. The Cray home had been pledged to secure his bond.

"I never liked that house much, anyway. Hot in the summer and cold in the winter. But that's water under the bridge now. You're here. And the warden's just being careful. That's what they pay him for. He's a smart man, and he's right about this. I would let you run if I thought you might get away. So I suppose it's better this way. That you don't go to the funeral, I mean. It'll keep us both out of trouble. Your mama knows you want to be there, and she knows you love her. That's what counts."

Palmer was caught short, both with respect to his mother's death and in consideration of his father's admission. It was quite uncharacteristic of Trenton Cray to admit doubt or show weakness, and, being a prison guard, he had certainly never been ambiguous about his feelings concerning escape. He was normally as solid as an oak bench, a man with a firm and abiding respect for the law not generally prone to entertaining notions of jailbreaks and the like.

"I know this is all my fault," Palmer said. "Rodney dead, Mama dead, you bending and breaking the rules. All my fault." It was what was on his mind, and he felt that it needed to be aired. The burden he had carried since Rodney's death had more than doubled now. It was like a pile of boulders that threatened to crush him to the floor.

"It's not your fault, son."

"I feel like I killed Mama. I'm sorry."

"Mama didn't take care of herself like she should have. That's what killed her."

"I had a hand in it."

"No, you didn't. People die every day, and we're all going to ride that train sooner or later. It was just your mama's time, bless her heart. Her people have all died young, mostly with strokes or heart attacks. All except your Aunt Midge, anyway, who got hit by that tree branch. It's in their makeup. As you get older, you'll need to watch out for that yourself, because there's some of her in you. I know you can't see it now, but you won't be in here forever. Someday this will be over, and then you'll just be a regular man out here in the world, making your way the best you can, just like everyone else. These days will pass, and someday they'll be like a bad dream. You'll see. The day you get out, we'll go to Mama's grave together. In the meantime, you go on back to your cell. If you want me to, I'll see to it that you're let off of kitchen duty for a few days."

"I'd rather keep busy."

"All right, then. I'll leave the work schedule alone. I've got to go now. I've got a lot to do. I'll tell Mama you love her and that you wished you could come. But she already knows that. She's here with us now. I can feel it. You know, she never had any doubt that you were a good son. She loved you more than she loved anything else in this world. You just keep that in your mind, and you'll get through this all right."

"Can I ask you a question?"

"Yes."

"Why did you tell me like this?" He gestured to their surroundings.

"I'm trying real hard to treat you like everyone else."

"Are you in trouble for bringing me to Sweetwater and putting me in with Cheddar?"

"I'm trying real hard to treat you like everyone else for your sake, not mine."

"I know that. But you didn't answer my question."

"Let's just say I won't be making major any time soon." He hung up his phone, stood, and slowly walked away. Palmer watched him until he was out of sight. Then he placed his own receiver on the cradle, arose, and waited to be escorted back to his cell. It seemed a longer way back than it ever had before, and it felt like he had been walking for hours when he finally arrived.

Palmer went in, sat on his bunk, and stared unseeing at the opposite wall. There wasn't that much to see there: two lockers, a Madonna poster, a picture of a Harley Softail, a few pictures painted by Cheddar's son, some birthday and Christmas cards still taped up long past their respective occasions. Palmer saw none of it as he stared through the cracks in the world. Occasionally he would wipe one eye or the other, but otherwise he was motionless and silent. After about an hour of this, with Cheddar trying to engage him the whole time, he finally broke his gaze and his silence and looked at his cellmate.

"My mother's dead," he said. It was the first time he had said it out loud, and the words were like hot gravel on his tongue. "She died last night in her sleep."

"Ah, man. I'm sorry." He sat beside his cousin on the bunk. "Aunt Laurel was a good woman. I'll miss her. She didn't judge like a lot of Christian folks do. I'll tell you one thing, though. In your sleep's the way to go. I hope when my time comes, I'm either asleep or messed up." He considered this a moment. "Being messed up *and* asleep would be better still."

"Mama wasn't much of one to get messed up," Palmer noted. He knew that Cheddar was just nattering to fill the silence. He meant well, but he had definitely strayed from the main trail.

"Sorry, man," Cheddar said. "Sure she wasn't. I didn't mean it that way. I was just running my mouth."

"They won't let me go to her funeral," Palmer said.

"They ought to let a guy go to his mama's funeral."

"The old man says the warden's afraid I'll run."

"That's tough, man. They should let you go. But it don't surprise me that they won't. A lot of times they end up having to chase a guy down when he goes to take a leak and then crawls out the bathroom window and just keeps on going. That's what I'd do. By the time they knew I was gone, I'd be in the next county, moving fast for Mexico."

"Not Canada?"

"Too cold up there."

"Well, anyway, I'd like to say good-bye to her."

"Sure you would, man. She's your mama. Like I said, Aunt Laurel was a good woman. But don't let this thing get you bowed up. Remember that we are in a whole other world. Weddings and funerals and baptisms and things like that are not for the likes of us, not while we're in here. You've got to pretend like your mama's funeral is on the moon. There is no way that you can even get there, no matter how hard you try. It's impossible to go. You'd do it if you could, but you can't, just like you can't fly through the air or breathe under the ocean." He thought a moment before adding a codicil. "Well, you can't breathe under the ocean, anyway. You seem to fly okay."

"Thanks."

"It's impossible to go," Cheddar said.

"It's impossible to go," Palmer echoed.

"Now you've got it right. So why feel bad about something you can't help? She won't even know if you're at the funeral or not. And just between you and me, there's not a lot of good to be had by spending time around dead folks. Close your eyes and think about her like she was back when she was alive. That's how you want to remember her. Hold her in your mind and talk to her like she was here on a Sunday to see you. That's what you've got to do. It's a better memory of her for you to keep than one of her in a casket, anyway. I hate seeing people in their coffins. The undertakers always try to make them look real peaceful, like they're just asleep. But they're not asleep. They're dead, and they look like wax dolls to me." Cheddar shivered. "It's just creepy. Sometimes people even kiss them." He shivered again.

"Cheddar, I know you're trying to make me feel better."

"Not a problem."

"And I appreciate it. But it's not working. I'm not feeling better."

"It was just her time, man."

"That's what my father said. I know she wasn't in the best health and that she smoked too much, but I feel like it's my fault she's gone. I think she mostly fretted herself to death. She worried herself into an early grave over me. The old man said she'd wander the house at night, talking to me and Rodney like we were there with her."

"That's some crazy shit," Cheddar said in a sympathetic tone.

"I put her into that coffin."

"No you didn't. You didn't kill her."

"I can't help how I feel, and I feel like that's what I did. I pushed her in that direction, for sure."

"You know, she was a grown woman before she ever had you. She just died, that's all. She didn't want to die, and she didn't kill herself, and you didn't kill her. She just died. People do."

"Maybe you're right," Palmer said. He wanted his cousin's words to be true, but he wasn't convinced by a long shot that they were.

As a postscript to the passing of Laurel Cray, the week following her funeral, Palmer received a note in the mail from his father. Trenton Cray had gotten the results from his wife's postmortem and wished to share these with his son.

Palmer—Your mama died of a bad stroke, but you already knew that. What I wanted to tell you was that when they did her autopsy, they also found lung cancer in both of her lungs. She had it a while, because it had spread to her kidneys and her bladder. You have to wonder about things sometimes. I talked to the doctor and the long and short of it is that she would have been gone soon anyway, even if the stroke hadn't taken her. He said that she had six months, maybe, and that at the end it would have been a slow and painful road. She would have lingered, and it would have hurt her a lot, and she wouldn't have been able to get her breath. Instead, she went in her sleep without any pain. So if you are still thinking you caused your mama's stroke, which you didn't, you need to think about the fact that even if you did, you saved her from a horrible death. I don't know what some people would call this. Her sisters would probably say it had to do with her good connections with the Lord. But you know what I think. Take care of yourself.

—Daddy

"Sloppy luck," Palmer said when he read the note. He knew that was exactly what his father would call a quick, painless death rather than an agonizing, slow one. He showed the note to Cheddar.

"Sloppy luck," his cellmate agreed. There was no getting around it.

Mama has passed away. She died of a stroke. I know you liked her a lot and she felt the same way about you. She always called you her good son. You had her snowed but I didn't mind because it took the pressure off me. I miss her more than I can say. She wasn't perfect for sure, but she always tried to be the best mother she could be. I bet she walked ten thousand miles over the years stepping out to the porch to smoke her Marlboros so I wouldn't breathe her secondhand smoke.

If you run into her over there, explain to her that I wasn't at her funeral because they wouldn't let me out for it. That was hard, not being there. I mean, prison is prison and I understand that it is supposed to suck. That's kind of the point. If it was great, it wouldn't be much of a punishment and guys would be lining up to get their three squares a day. But then something like Mama dying comes up and you realize just how different your life is from normal people's lives. I've got a feeling that it will be like that even after I get out. Once you've been in here, nothing is ever the same as it was before. Even if you could somehow forget what happened, the world won't let you. You're marked.

Mama was only 61 years old when she went, and that's too young to be dying. I used to like to look at the old family pictures and there was one of her as a high school girl back in the 70s. She had long hair and big glasses and she was wearing bellbottoms. She went from that to dead awful quick. What? Yeah, I know, 18 is a lot younger than 61 and for sure it is way too young to die. My bad. I wasn't thinking. My old man had them do an autopsy on her. I would've passed on that, I think, but she was his wife longer than she was my mama, and you know how he is about having to get to the why of things. He's always been like that. He'll worry and pick at something until he understands it and he needed to know why this happened.

When they cut her open it turned out that Mama was really sick with cancer and she wouldn't have lasted much longer anyway. I think it was better that she went fast with the stroke but I guess that no one but her will ever really know the truth of that. I recall how much your grandma suffered when she died with her cancer. That was the summer we stayed outside as much as we could because it hurt so bad to even see her. It was a terrible way to go. I remember her crying and begging to die. If she had been a dog they would have put her down but she was someone's grandma so she had to suffer. I felt bad for your mama for having to tend to her, and I'm thankful that Mama was spared that.

When you're in prison you have a lot of time to think. I've been thinking about The Big Plan. Mama always thought that there was a plan for the world. God's plan, she called it. But I swear I can't see it. I mean, look at everything that's happened to our families. You're dead. Mama's dead. I'm in prison. What kind of plan is that? And think of your poor old grandma. There was a woman who never hurt a soul in her life, a lady who believed in God on the throne and sweet baby Jesus in the manger and all the saints in heaven. And she found herself at the end of her days begging her own daughter to please kill her and put her out of her pain. What kind of plan is that? If I was a big shot and some guy who worked for me came up with a plan like that, I'd fire him and dog walk him out the gate.

The same goes for Mama. A stroke took her out quick and clean and saved her from a long slow death. I've been told what a mercy it was *that God was watching out for her. The people who tell me that are usually the same ones who believe just like Mama did that the Bible is the word of God, but I don't think I buy it. Think about it. People believe that the Bible is the word of God because the Bible says that the Bible is the word of God. Remember when we were back in school and they wouldn't let us use a word in its own definition? This seems like the same kind of problem to me.*

I have to admit that the way she went was better than the way she could have gone and I am truly grateful that she didn't suffer. But the idea that God sent a stroke to save her from cancer just pisses me off. How stupid is that logic? How can people be so blind? Why not just prevent the cancer in the first place? Why not just prevent all cancer, everywhere? Mama spent about as much time on her knees as anyone I know and she deserved better than to die at 61 whatever the cause, just like you deserved better than to smash into a tree when you were 18.

A lot of guys in prison end up getting religion, and that's fine for them. I've got nothing against it. It doesn't cost me a dime and I hope it helps them as much as some of them claim it does. The nights are long in here and we all have our different ways to get through them. But the longer I am alive and the more that happens to me and to the people I love—and just to people in general—the less likely I am to see some caring and loving God driving the bus. If there is a God and if there is a plan in motion, then shame on him! And I'm not whining because I'm in prison. I did what I did and I got what I got and most days I can manage to take it like a man.

When you look at the Big Picture, what has happened to me doesn't amount to much. But what about all the poor folks who haven't done anything wrong? People like Mama or your grandma? They keep getting blindsided just like the guilty people. The way I see it, he either isn't there, or if he is, he's got a real mean streak. Or maybe he really just couldn't care less. Which is worse? Seems to me there's a problem either way. Okay. I'll settle down. Morris says that my grief is manifesting itself as a generalized anger toward the structure of the universe and the inevitable nature of death. He is a pretty good guy for a shrink, but sometimes I think he's just making this stuff up.

4

The Rodney Thing

Palmer was slow to recover from the news of his mother's death, partly because he had to make the measured voyage to full acceptance of the fact before he could even begin to grieve the loss. In the immediate aftermath of her journey to a finer reality, it was almost as if her departure were a fable to him, a grim fairy tale with an ending neither happy nor enlightening. As had been the case when Rodney died, Palmer arrived quickly at the cognitive realization that his mother had taken wing, but the emotional component of the equation lagged far behind. His brain knew because he had been told, but his heart didn't really believe. Eventually, however, he was able to layer enough distance between himself and her demise to allow him to begin to creep up on the loss from behind. After a sufficient amount of time went by, he managed to pull up even with the event, and then, finally, he worked his way past it.

He still blamed himself for her death, and he thought it likely that he always would, but the pain of the wound slowly subsided until finally it was a dull throb that was barely noticeable most days, provided he didn't poke at it. He and Cheddar went back to business as usual. They quietly slipped into the warm current of mindless endeavor, and from time to time one or the other would float to the surface to see what day it was, or what week. In this manner they saw two additional years pass, and thus it was that Palmer was nearing his third anniversary as an incarcerated felon when he encountered his second momentous milestone.

"Cray, you've got a visitor," the guard said through the open door. It was free time on the cellblock, and most of the inmates were out in the common area, playing checkers or cards. Palmer looked up from the book he was reading. It was Tolstoy's *War and Peace*, a perennial favorite from the Sweetwater State Correctional Facility library, both because it took a long time to read and because most of the characters residing within its covers regularly encountered worse circumstances than those experienced by the average Sweetwater inmate. During the time he had spent in the State's custody, Palmer had read many of the classics of literature—*Moby Dick, The Last of the Mohicans, Babbit, A Connecticut Yankee in King Arthur's Court*— first because they made the days disappear, and later because he had found a love for the written word.

"Who is it?" he asked as he marked his place and got to his feet.

"What am I, your social secretary?" the guard asked. His name was Chambers, and he was a new hire who didn't like Captain Cray, his boy Palmer, his nephew Cheddar, or much of anything or anyone else in North Georgia as far as Palmer could tell. He was a guard of the variety that liked to rest his right hand firmly on the handle of his baton when he talked to a prisoner, just in case trouble arose and he needed to whip it out and cut down on short notice. All of the old hands at Sweetwater—inmates and guards alike—gave him a wide berth when they could. He seemed about as stable as river stones on a steep bank.

"Sorry," Palmer murmured. Chambers reminded him of a lot of things, but none of these was social secretary. It had been a stupid question, and he normally avoided those, but the news of a visitor had caught him by surprise. Since his mother's death, visitors had been few and dwindling. His father didn't visit because his father didn't visit. His uncle had chatted with him every now and again, but only as an extension of his weekly visits with Cheddar, and only when such was allowed by the guards. The ladies from the church had been out to see him on one occasion, but that visit had been painful for all involved and was not repeated. The Nickel sisters were regular visitors for a little while, but their visits had tapered from weekly to occasionally. Finally, Tiffany stopped coming altogether, and after a few more months, Kaitlyn had followed suit. In a note written by Tiffany soon after they stopped visiting, she explained that the sight of Palmer in prison made both sisters sadder than they could bear.

Palmer had enjoyed their visits the most, but he was forced to admit that he had mixed feelings about seeing the pair. He was happy to enjoy the pleasure of their company, but the sight of them always brought back memories of finer days that did not involve guards and locked doors. They had through no fault of their own come to represent everything that he knew he was missing, and he, too, was left with a deep melancholy after nearly every visit. When he saw Tiffany, he felt bad because she couldn't have Rodney. And when he saw Kaitlyn, he felt worse because he couldn't have her. He was often depressed for days after they went back out among the free, and when they ceased their visits, he reluctantly realized it was probably for the best.

The Nickel sisters' effect on Palmer notwithstanding, visiting day was generally a treat for the large majority of prisoners, an event to look forward to and savor, like a trip to the fair. But more often than not, the act of visiting an inmate was an ordeal for the visitor. It was difficult to view a loved one, or even a liked one, in the prison setting: locked up, sometimes in shackles, dressed in Sweetwater Blues with a number stenciled over the pocket and on the leg of the pants, smiling and trying to be brave while assuring the visitor that all was well when, in fact, all was about as far from well as it could possibly get. Most people found that they couldn't sustain the sheer effort of forced cheerfulness. Spouses and mothers were the exception because it was their job to be, but for everyone else the tendency was to slack off on the visiting schedule after a short time. Well-meaning loved ones would begin to defer the unpleasant task as long as possible and regrettably have something more important to do on visiting day. Since Palmer's mother was dead and he had no wife, he had slowly but steadily become a card-carrying member of the legions of the forgotten.

Thus he was somewhat excited as Chambers walked him to the visitor's area. When he arrived there, he was directed to the last station. He was still considered an escape candidate even after three years of time served, so he was in the isolation room. Cheddar had explained to him that if he went five years without an escape attempt, his status as a flight risk would be reviewed, and perhaps he could begin to receive visitors face to face. Palmer walked past eleven occupied visiting cubicles before arriving at the twelfth, tucked in down by the far wall.

Sitting there on the stool over on the good side of the glass—the side that had access to the door, the hallway, and the world beyond—was Rodney's mother, Kathleen Earwood. She looked at him with her gray eyes, nodded, and smiled slightly. It was a distracted effort. He sat and picked up the receiver with an odd sense of trepidation. This uneasiness was due in equal parts to the fact that he actually had a visitor for a change combined with the fact that this caller was Rodney Earwood's mother. He wasn't normally apprehensive in her presence and had always liked her quite a bit, but he wasn't sure what to expect this time. She had smiled when he sat, it was true, but on the downside, he had killed her only son. Plus, he had been in Sweetwater State Correctional Facility for a good long while, but this was her first visit. Given the nature of his crime, he felt he had a sufficient understanding concerning the nature of her long absence. The part he was wondering about was why she had come to see him now.

"Hello, Mrs. Earwood," he said. He had been given permission years ago to use her Christian name, and he had done so on more occasions than he could recall. But now he was unsure of the appropriateness of using her first name. He was unacquainted with the generally accepted protocols surrounding conversations with the mother of someone he had augured into a tree, so he decided to begin in the formal realm and then to play it by ear from there on in. It all depended on how those critical first few exchanges went.

"Hello, Palmer," she replied. "It's good to see you." She smiled once again. "You're looking well. Are they treating you okay?"

Palmer nodded at this most ubiquitous of all greetings. His mother had asked it every time she came, as had most of the other visitors he had received. The truth was that they were treating him well enough, considering where he was and why he was there, although his answer would have been much the same even if they had been waterboarding him or routinely beating the soles of his feet with broom handles. What happened at Sweetwater State Correctional Facility tended to remain on the premises. This was an unofficial policy that effectively kept the guards happy, and everyone from the oldest lifers on down to the newest men in the three-bunk cells liked contented guards. It was almost an obsession among the inmates. They all knew that as bad as any given day had been, if they managed to anger one of their keepers, intentionally or otherwise, then tomorrow could always be worse.

"Yes, ma'am," he said. "They're treating me just fine."

He had not seen her since the day he had been sentenced. The time between then and now had not been kind to her, and she looked to have aged twenty years during those three. Her thick brown hair was streaked with white, and the puffy bags under her red eyes spoke of sleepless nights or perhaps strong drink. Her skin looked stretched and thin, like it had shrunk a half-size or so but she had decided to wear it anyway. Her mouth had acquired a pinched look, as if she were either in chronic pain or expressing constant disapproval, or some miserable combination of both. Palmer noticed that she exhibited a slight rocking motion even though she sat on a straight stool. She was only two years older than his mother had been when she had died, but she looked much older than Laurel Cray's sixty-one years. Losing her only son had been hard on Kathleen Earwood.

"I guess you're wondering why I'm here," she said tentatively. Her rocking seemed to pick up tempo. Palmer thought that perhaps it was a tic.

"Yes, ma'am," he said again. He hadn't intended to bring up the subject of her sudden visit, but since she had, he was indeed curious.

"The simple truth is, I wanted to see you." She paused then, as if waiting for his response. Her rocking slowed almost to a stop, like a rowboat on a quiet pond.

"That's fine. You can come whenever you want to. It'll be good to have the company." He felt a stirring of happiness and a twinge of interest in a larger version of the world than the shrunken existence he currently led, a small reality that included Cheddar, their cell, the prison kitchen, and the armload of woe caused by Napoleon Bonaparte when he had decided to invade Tsarist Russia in *War and Peace.*

"I've wanted to come several times since the judge sent you here, but Harris wouldn't hear of it. He was dead set against me coming. You remember how he is." Palmer nodded. He knew exactly how Rodney's old man was: loud, argumentative, opinionated, and most times just downright mean. He knew all this, and he knew from Rodney that Harris was a hard drinker and a wife beater as well. Harris Earwood was Kathleen's second husband and Rodney's stepfather. They had married when Rodney was three.

"I remember," Palmer said. Kathleen had sounded apologetic when she spoke, and Palmer wasn't sure if this sheepishness was due to the dearth of her visits or the errant ways of her husband. Maybe it was both.

"I have always given in to him to keep peace in the family," she continued. "Not just on the subject of visiting you, either." Palmer was aware of many of her marital accommodations in the name of civil harmony, and he thought that not wanting to be beaten for defying a violent husband was a perfectly acceptable reason for not coming down to Sweetwater State Correctional Facility on visiting day. It would certainly keep him at home. But he couldn't say that because he wasn't supposed to know about the physical abuse. Rodney had sworn him to silence when he told him, and the fact that he was now gone to the long home didn't relieve Palmer of his obligation to honor the agreement. A promise was a promise.

"Peace in the family is a good thing," he said.

"I apologize for not visiting you sooner. I should have been coming to see you all along." She wasn't crying, but her eyes sparkled where tears had formed, and her rocking had picked up speed.

"It's okay," Palmer said. "I understand about Harris. You don't have to apologize. He never was all that crazy about me, anyway, even before...what happened. Besides, it looks like he must have changed his mind about you coming to visit." He was feeling his way slowly through the conversation, like he was tiptoeing barefoot across a gravel road. There was something eccentric about this visit that he had yet to identify.

"No, the truth of the matter is, he never really did," she said. Her voice had a faraway, wistful tone for the briefest of moments. "Change his mind, I mean. Instead of changing his mind, he changed his state of residence. We split up about a month ago, and he's moved back to Asheville." Palmer hadn't expected this news. The information that his dead friend's mother was sharing with him was too personal. Palmer felt almost voyeuristic as he became privy to details he had not asked for and had no desire to know.

"I'm sorry to hear that," he said. He was indeed sorry to hear it for her sake, but he had to admit that he wasn't that upset to see Rodney's father gone. Harris Earwood had been a taste that Palmer had never been able to acquire. Rodney hadn't liked him, either, and he used to be fond of noting to anyone who seemed interested that his stepfather was a dick. Neither Rodney nor Palmer had ever understood why Kathleen continued to put up with him. Fear, Palmer supposed. Maybe habit on top of that. It had always been his opinion that Kathleen Earwood could have done much better than Harris, and Rodney had always agreed.

"Don't worry about it," Kathleen said. "I'm really not all that sorry. Mostly I'm just tired. I haven't loved him in a long time, and I haven't liked him in a longer time than that. It takes a lot of effort to pretend. It wore me out." Palmer could sympathize. Living with Harris Earwood would have worn him out years ago. But matters of the heart were difficult to predict, and there was just no accounting for some people's taste.

Once again, Palmer was struck by Kathleen Earwood's extreme candor. He hadn't seen her in a long time, and even back when he saw her regularly, the nature of their relationship was simply that she was his best friend's mother. They were separated by a wide chasm of age, gender, point of view, and experience, and that was without even adding in the sad fact that he had flown her only son into a tree.

"Kathleen, you don't have to tell me this." He had decided that since he knew the inner secrets of her recent breakup, the use of her first name was once again permissible. "It's private."

"Who else am I going to tell it to?" she asked simply. "The girl down at the dollar store is sweet, but I don't know her name. You're the closest thing to family I have left." He supposed she had a point, at that. Her son was dead, her husband had flown the coop to Asheville, and her closest friend—his own mother—had smoked herself into a premature and hopefully uneventful trip to heaven. "I'll stop if you want me to," she said.

"No, no, it's okay with me. We can talk about whatever you want to. I just thought you might feel odd later, after sharing this personal stuff with me."

"I feel odd all the time, anyway," she said. Her rocking had returned, as if to illustrate her assertion. What the hell, Palmer thought. It wasn't like he had anything else to do for the next seven years or so. They could talk all she wanted.

"Tell me what happened with Harris," he said. "Why did you decide to run him off?"

"You know how he was," she repeated. "He was sort of stubborn, kind of opinionated, awfully loud, and usually obnoxious. What you didn't know was that when he got drunk, sometimes he hit me." Palmer nodded. He was now officially privy to that information. "He never hit Rodney, though. He started to, once, when Rodney was just a little boy. I put a gun to his head and told him that if he ever hit my son, I would kill him where he stood. I guess he believed me, because he never made like he was going to hit him again."

"I like that," Palmer said. "You should've just shot him then."

"No bullets."

"I like that even more," Palmer said. "Why didn't you just pack Rodney up and leave?"

"I was foolish not to. I can see that, now. But I was afraid to leave. It's a funny thing about hindsight; it's always really clear. It's like I have a telescope, and I can see all of my mistakes, all of my should-haves. But back then, I didn't have any family left, and I didn't have a job or any money, and I had a little boy to take care of. It was important to me to have a husband, and I thought I could make Harris into the man I wanted him to be. But I found out that people are like they are. You can't change them. I worked hard for years trying to change him, and what happened instead was that I ended up changing myself."

"I wish he had been a better husband to you. You deserved better."

"We all deserve better, mostly," she said. "But what we deserve doesn't have much to do with what we get, or what we have to settle for. Harris turned even meaner when Rodney died. He was so bitter sometimes that I could barely stand to be around him. The thing is, on one level I understood everything he was going through, because there were days when I felt the same way." She looked at Palmer with haunted eyes as she shared this confidence. "Some days I was so mad at you that I wished Rodney had lived instead of you. I'm sorry for that. It wasn't Christian of me. It wasn't right."

"Don't worry about it. I feel that way myself, about half the time."

"You hush." She put her hand to the glass as if she were covering his mouth.

"No, it's okay," he said. His heart went out to her. "I expect it's natural to feel that way. Both for you and for me." She seemed to feel better to have the admission out in the open, like she had confessed a great and terrible sin and had received absolution.

"Right after you were sent here, I wanted to start coming to see you. Whenever I thought about you being in here, it broke my heart." She blinked a few tears. Her rocking ceased, only to be replaced by her right leg shaking in a sporadic manner. "I hope you know you've always been just like my own son."

"I know it. You told me plenty of times."

"Well, don't ever forget that I love you. You're my last connection to Rodney. It's almost like I can see him sitting beside you. I even talked to your mama before she died about visiting you, just to make sure she didn't mind."

"What'd she say?"

"I'm here."

"Well, yeah, but she's gone."

"That doesn't make any difference. If she had said no, I would have respected that, even now. But that didn't happen. She was happy for me to come visit you." Her face hardened. "But Harris wouldn't hear of it. He dug in his heels. At that time, I didn't think I could stand to lose my marriage on top of losing my son, so I didn't press him too hard. I was afraid of being alone." She paused as if waiting for a response.

"Alone is not good," Palmer agreed, but even as he said it he had the thought that sometimes, alone was clearly the better alternative. At least, that seemed to be the case with Kathleen Earwood and her absent husband.

"But I did keep the subject out in front of him, and I brought it up from time to time. Every time I mentioned it, he got mad. Finally it came down to Harris giving me an ultimatum. He told me that if I ever brought up the subject of visiting you again, he would leave. And that was the exact moment I realized I was no longer interested in being married to Harris Earwood. It was like a light bulb came on inside my head. I had put up with him for over fifteen years, but I had finally had enough." She stopped speaking and sighed. Then she shrugged, as if to indicate that what was done was done. "Suddenly I knew he just wasn't worth the trouble any longer. I knew being alone was better than being with him. It was time for a change. So I told him I was going to start coming to see you on Sundays and I didn't care if he liked it or not, and that maybe it *was* time for him to go."

"Good for you," Palmer said.

"We had a terrible fight that lasted all day, and he left that night." She looked sheepish as she continued. "He tried to change his mind and make up, and I had to put him under the gun again to get him on out. I haven't heard from him since. My lawyer has, but I haven't." She took a sip from the bottle of water she had purchased from the machine in the hall. Several moments passed as she rocked quietly, staring at the water bottle. Palmer wasn't sure if the visit was over, or if they were just on intermission.

"Was it loaded this time?" he asked. He really wanted to know.

"Yes."

"Do you think you would have shot him?"

"Yes."

"I don't know what to say," he said finally. He was in jail finishing up the third year of a ten-spot, but at that moment he had the impression that he was better off than she was. She looked up at the sound of his voice and began speaking again, as if she had just been primed.

"Once I started being honest with myself, I realized that we were like water and dirt. All we ever did was make mud. We were long past the stage where we could make it work. Maybe there was never a time when we could have. Well, let me take that back. I could have given in like always, but I wasn't interested in making the effort. It was time for a change. Thank God we never had a child together."

There was another long, uncomfortable silence. At least it was uncomfortable for Palmer. He had to admit, though, that the image of Kathleen putting a gun to Harris's head, twice, was pleasing. Finally he ended the hush.

"I'm sorry your marriage broke up." Palmer could see Kathleen's left hand through the glass as it rested on the table. He noted the indentation around her third finger where her wedding ring had recently clung.

"It was just time, that's all. We had worn out on each other. I guess even back when I did love him, I loved him in spite of him, if that makes sense. I suppose I was younger then, and I had more energy. Plus, when I married him, he seemed to love Rodney, and that was all I needed to see. A woman can love any man who is good to her children, and I needed a husband, so when he asked me to marry him, I did. But Rodney became less important to him as the years passed, and finally it seemed like Harris gave up on Rodney completely. Now he's given up on me, too."

"That's his mistake."

"Well, that's his choice. I'm tired of living the life I've been living. I want to try to salvage what I can from whatever's left of my time. I'm ready to move on. Losing Rodney made me realize just how precious life is. I don't want to waste any more of mine."

Palmer nodded slowly. He advocated moving on for anyone who had the means to do so and the mobility to make the trip. The silence grew long again. He could sense a pattern in the cadence of their conversation: short bursts of talk followed by lengthy pauses. After several moments, he once again leapt into the breach.

"I never got the chance to tell you this, but I'm sorry I killed Rodney."

"Well, of course you are," she said, once again putting her hand to the glass pane as if she were shushing him. "You don't have to say it. Not to me or to anyone else. It's over and done." There was a quaver in her voice as she reassured him.

"I didn't mean to do it," he continued. He had wanted to tell her this for quite some time; he needed to say it, needed to speak the words.

"I know you didn't," she said sadly. "You boys just ran out of luck. That's the thing about luck. It always runs out, and sometimes it runs out at the worst times."

Palmer nodded. He knew exactly what she meant.

"I appreciated you testifying for me at the trial," he said.

"I was glad to do it. I wish it had helped more. Your lawyer thought it would have a big impact on the jury, but I'm not so sure it had any effect at all."

"I'm sure it helped," he said. "The Hanging Judge might've given me life if it hadn't been for you." It wasn't much of a joke, but it was the best he could do.

"Your sentence did seem harsh," she said. "I talked to several people after the trial, and most of them thought so, too. One of the women who served on the jury told me she would have voted the other way if she had known the judge was going to give such a stiff sentence. She thought you were guilty, but not this guilty. I had my own lawyer research the case, and he told me that the conviction and sentence would both stand if they were appealed. Of course, he mostly does estates and divorces."

"Thanks for having him take a look. J. Randall Crane said the same thing. He said the sentence was on the heavy side of legal, but it was legal. So it looks like seven more years of the quiet life for me." He smiled at his small witticism, but she didn't. He was trying to make light of circumstances that had no bright side, and his efforts fell as flat as unleavened bread.

"I was sorry about your mother," she said. Palmer nodded. He noticed that she had begun to rock again. "She was a good mother to you, a good friend to me, just a good woman in general. I never worried about Rodney when Laurel Cray was taking care of him."

"Thank you." He wanted to say more, but there really wasn't much else to say, and her simple testimonial had moved him past the point of speech, anyway.

"I went to the funeral. The church was absolutely full, and there must have been fifty people standing outside. It had been raining hard all day, but when it came time for them to move her from the church to the gravesite, it stopped raining. The sun came out, and the sky was blue. There were birds singing. I thought you would want to know that. It was like God wanted her to have a nice service before he brought her home."

He was probably feeling bad about that cancer, Palmer thought.

"I appreciate you telling me about it," he said. "I didn't have any details about her funeral." He had not seen the casket, or stood by the grave, or heard the preacher's words of comfort, and he had an enhanced sense of loss for having missed these things.

"Trenton didn't tell you about the service?" She seemed surprised.

"No. We haven't talked about it. He's still too sad to bring it up." Palmer spared her the detail that he hadn't talked to his father at all since the morning after his mother had died, and that barring a prison break or any other untimely deaths in the immediate family, the conversational moratorium was likely to continue for at least seven more years.

"Bless your daddy's heart. He loved your mama so much." She reached one of her long impasses. Palmer waited her out, just to see if she would restart on her own. Finally, just as he was about to give up and throw out another possible topic of conversation, she spoke.

"Tell me a secret about Rodney."

"Ma'am?"

"Tell me something about Rodney I don't know. You were his best friend his whole life. I was just his mother. You knew a lot more about him than I did. Tell me something about my son that I don't know."

Palmer gave this request some consideration. There were a great many things he knew about Rodney that his mama did not, and some of those details needed to stay that way until the skies split and the seas gave up their dead. Finally, though, he chose a fact that he thought she might like to hear, a happy detail.

"Rodney loved Tiffany Nickel."

"My Lord, Palmer, I knew that." She smiled as she spoke.

"Well, how about this? He was going to ask her to marry him soon."

"He never said anything about it to me, but I knew that, too. I could tell by the way he talked about her."

"This is harder than I thought. Here's one. Rodney was planning on joining the Army. He was already scheduled to go take his physical."

"Now *that* I didn't know."

"He was pretty excited about it. He wanted to spend four years in the service. Then he wanted to go to college. The Army will put money into a college account for you, and he was going to get an enlistment bonus, too. When he got out, he was going to use the enlistment money and what was in the college account to go to school. He was going to go to law school." Palmer always had trouble envisioning Rodney in a three-piece suit, but he had to admit that he would have made a good attorney.

"I knew he wanted to be a lawyer someday. As smart as that boy was, and as much as he loved to argue, I always thought he'd make a good one. But I never knew he was thinking about joining the Army to pay for it. When did he decide on that?"

"He'd been talking about it ever since the tenth grade, when we went on a field trip to the quarry up near Jasper."

"I remember that trip."

"They were set to blast that day, and they let Rodney flip the switch to shoot off one of the dynamite charges. He thought that was the greatest thing he'd ever done, and he decided right then that he liked to blow stuff up. It wasn't long after that trip that he started talking about joining the Army."

"I wonder why he didn't tell me about it."

"Well, he figured you'd worry. But he was going to tell you soon." Actually, Rodney's plan had been to enlist, leave, and have Palmer tell Kathleen all about it the day after he'd gone. Palmer had resisted this scheme, and the jury had still been out at the time of Rodney's death with respect to the method of notification.

"He was right about that," she said. "I would have worried. That's the part they never tell you about being a parent. You never, ever stop worrying. If anything, it gets worse when your children get older and you can't protect them anymore. I was worrying the night that he died." She was quiet for a moment. Then she spoke again. "His father was in the Army, you know. His real father, I mean, not Harris. He was killed in an accident while I was pregnant with Rodney." Palmer nodded. Rodney used to talk about him all the time, even though he had never known him. Kathleen looked at the plywood partition separating her from the adjacent visitor, but Palmer knew she was seeing across the years, viewing a place and time better than the one she now occupied. She snapped back to the present and looked at her incarcerated host. "Thank you. I appreciate the confidence. Would you be willing to tell me something about yourself? Something I don't know?"

"I don't know, Kathleen." It had been different talking to her about her own son's expired dreams.

"Please?" she asked.

Palmer was on the horns of a medium-sized dilemma. During his imprisonment, he had become reticent about speaking of his own hopes and plans. He had become superstitious. He believed, along with Cheddar and most of the rest of the inhabitants of Sweetwater State Correctional Facility, that to talk too much about the future was to jinx it. Life after prison was a gossamer dream, fragile and

100

rare. To voice a hope or share a plan was to risk its annihilation. To share a secret desire was to hazard its destruction. But he hated to disappoint Rodney's mother, and she had shared much with him. So he decided to take the safe path and share a dream no longer in the queue, an obsolete desire once held by a young man before he became a felon.

"Rodney was going to join the Army. I was going to join the Navy."

"The Navy! Did you want to blow things up, too?"

"No. I just wanted to go somewhere. Going somewhere is all I have ever wanted to do." They were both silent then, as the realization descended upon Rodney's mother that, given the nature of Palmer's secret, the punishment he had received was appallingly cruel. Palmer was well aware of that cruelty and had been for some time. He had made his farewells to Hong Kong, Istanbul, the North Sea, the Horn, and all the rest. These places and many more were, like his mama's funeral, on the moon. It was impossible to get there, and foolish even to try.

But that was not why he joined her in silence. Rather, he had emptied himself of words and simply had nothing else to say. They continued to sit in peace until a guard came up beside Kathleen, caught her attention, and tapped his watch. She nodded at the man and turned to make her good-byes.

"It looks like it's time for me to go," she said gently. "Do you mind if I come back? I just realized that you might not want the company." She rocked slowly as she awaited the answer.

"You can come back whenever you want to," he answered. "I've enjoyed talking with you. You've been the high point of my year."

"I need to warn you that sometimes when I come to visit, I'll want to talk about Rodney. Not always, but sometimes."

"That's all right. He's a good topic of conversation."

"Do you need anything?"

101

"I've got everything I need."

"Okay, then. I'll see you next week?"

"Next week it is," Palmer said. "I'll have a good secret ready for you." She nodded and arose. The guard escorted her out. Palmer sat at his station and slowly tapped his fingers. He watched the door long after she had passed from view, watched until his own guard tapped the back of the chair with his baton to remind Palmer that he, too, needed to vacate the visiting area and head back home.

Cheddar was asleep when Palmer arrived back at the cell, but he awoke when his cellmate entered. He loosely held the copy of *War and Peace*, which he had apparently been trying to read before dozing.

"You know, this book sucks," he said without preliminaries.

"How would you know?"

Cheddar wasn't much of a fan of the written word, and of all the many, many authors he disdained, Tolstoy was way on up the list.

"I read the damn thing is how I know, all the way up through the sentence that says 'Mercy on us, what a violent attack.'"

"Cheddar, that's the first sentence."

"Well, I know what I like, and I know what I don't like. It doesn't take me all day to make up my mind like it does some people I could name. And I didn't like it. If I ever run up on Tolstoy, I'm going to kick his ass."

"He's dead."

"Good. Sounds like someone else thought his book sucked, too," Cheddar said, vindicated. "Who came to visit?" He hopped down from his bunk and handed the book to Palmer. Each took vicarious pleasure in the other's visitors, and it had been a while since Palmer had contributed to the visitor pool. Cheddar was all ears.

"It was Kathleen Earwood," Palmer said as he relocated his place in the text and slipped his bookmark back in.

"Oh, shit. How did that go?"

"It really didn't go too bad, considering all that has happened to her and to me. We had a pretty good talk."

"How was she about, you know, the Rodney thing?" The Rodney thing was Cheddar's term for Palmer's planned apology to Kathleen Earwood for killing her son. Cheddar and Palmer had discussed the issue at various times over the past three years, with Cheddar weighing in on the side of Palmer being out of his mind for planning even to bring up the subject if he ever saw his victim's mother again. In Cheddar's view, any action besides turning tail and running was foolhardy and bound to bring regret.

"We talked about him a good bit. I told her I was sorry about everything, and she told me that she didn't blame me for what happened. She said that we had just run out of luck." He looked at Cheddar. "That's what it was, you know. We just ran out of luck. If the Camaro had been six inches to the right or a foot to the left when we hit that dip, Rodney might still be here today." Palmer knew that being sober wouldn't have hurt, either, but he didn't wish to discuss that at present.

"That's what I've been telling you for three years. Sometimes, bad stuff just happens. There's no rhyme or reason to it. You can drive yourself nuts worrying about causality."

"Worrying about what?" With the exception of "son of a bitch," Cheddar had used very few four-syllable words during the past three years, and he had never uttered this particular one at all. Palmer was intrigued.

"Causality, man. You know. Aristotle? Cause and effect? What, you think I don't read? Give me something worth reading, and I'll zip right through it."

"Well, Kathleen Earwood agrees with you and Aristotle that sometimes things just happen."

"She's a smart woman."

"She just got smarter. She finally ran her old man off."

"Harris?"

"Harris."

"Harris Earwood is a waste of air. I'm surprised someone hasn't done him in."

"According to Kathleen, she almost did. Twice. Once when he tried to smack Rodney a long time ago and again about a month back when he wouldn't leave."

"I don't know if I ever told you this, but he used to buy a little product from time to time."

"Harris Earwood was on meth?"

"Yeah, and he owes me some money."

"It might be tough to collect that. He's gone to Asheville, and you're here."

"Well, it's not like he was going to pay me, anyway. She should have just shot him and been done with it."

"I think if he ever comes back, she probably will."

Your mama has started visiting me on Sundays. That's fine by me. I can use the company, and so can she. As far as visitors go, I'm pretty much down to none. Morris tells me that I'm depressed and that some visitors will help that. He says I've got the Sweetwater Blues. Great. I have a counselor with a sense of humor. It doesn't get much better than that. Whenever he tells me that I'm depressed, I say that I'm twenty-two years old and locked up in a cage with Cheddar Cray for the next seven years. What could I possibly have to be depressed about?

Your mama's not herself. I don't want to worry you, but she looks bad and she's not acting right. She seems forgetful, and sometimes she uses the wrong words or the wrong names. I suppose there's good reason for that, though, kind of like there is for me being depressed. A lot has happened to her over the last four years, and it has been the type of stuff that can grind you down. I don't want you to get yourself into a twist over it. I'm going to keep an eye on her. Well, as much of an eye as I can, anyway, considering where I am. No, that's all right. Don't even mention it. It's the least I can do for a guy I ran through a tree.

Speaking of things happening to her, I need to tell you about one of those right now. Are you sitting down? Can you even sit down? Well, grab hold of something, anyway, because I don't want you to float off in the middle of this. Harris and your mama have split up. Would I kid a dead guy about something like that? She has finally handed that boy his walking papers and put him on the highway. She ran him all the way back to Asheville. And that's not even the best part. The best part is, she told me that she had to stick the barrel of a gun to his head to persuade him to go. I think if Harris ever comes back, your mama ought to put a couple of slugs into him. She doesn't have to shoot anything important. Just wing him to let him know she's serious. Maybe a leg or a shoulder.

You know how we used to wonder why she even put up with him? She told me a little about that, and since she's your mama, I'll cut you in on the secret. After she lost your real father, she found herself on her own. She was in a tough spot. She had a kid, no money, no job, no family, and no prospects. And then along came smooth old Harris, probably wearing that light blue leisure suit we found in his closet that time. You just know he looked sharp in that thing. I bet he had a couple of gold chains hanging around his neck and lots of starch in his collar. Back when he first showed up, he wasn't a drunk, or at least he wasn't one in front of your mama. And she told me that he was good to you to start with. I believe every bit of that, because it would have been a deal breaker with her if he hadn't been. She would have sent him back to Asheville right then, leisure suit and all. Anyway, one thing led to another, and before your mama knew what hit her, she was married.

Once he had her reeled in, his persona started to slip around the edges. You like that word? Persona. I learned it from Morris. It means the person you are pretending to be. If I keep picking up the lingo I might be a psychologist someday. I could work with convicts. That would be great. Anyway, Harris was trying to be Husband and Father of the Year, but he couldn't hack it because deep down inside, he was a dick. I know that because his stepson told me and dead men tell no tales, or at least not any big ones. It could even be that he had good intentions, although I'm not wanting to give him the benefit of the doubt. As time passed, more and more of the real Harris started slipping out. By the time your mama figured out that her husband was someone else entirely from the guy she married, the train had already left the station. She was stuck like a car in a ditch.

Cheddar told me that Harris used to buy meth from him. We always knew he was a drunk, but I never thought he was a druggie. Cheddar says it wasn't every week, but it was pretty regular. That explains a lot. You remember those times he got crazy mean? I bet he was flying Air Cheddar. Cheddar also told me that Harris stiffed him. Cheddar is a redneck capitalist. He has a long memory and a strong sense of ownership. He wants his money and he's not going to forget about it. Your old man had better watch it. If he's still alive in 2030 or so, Cheddar might just ease up to Asheville to pay him a visit. I might even give him a lift just so I can watch their reunion. I never realized that my cousin was a badass until I started living with him. I guess I should have, though. He was in a rough business and he did all right until his wife turned him in. He's not a big guy, but like he told me once, you don't have to be big as long as your gun is.

5

Mexican Radio

The year 2002 evolved into 2003, and 2003 blended into 2004. Midway through that year, on June 11, Palmer Cray turned twenty-four and marked his fifth anniversary as an inmate. It was a momentous day, or at least what passed for one at Sweetwater State Correctional Facility. He had reached the halfway mark of his sentence, and regardless of Cheddar's well-meaning advice about the dangers inherent in keeping track of time, from this point forward, Palmer would be counting the days down to zero. The computation was a simple one. He had five more years to serve. Five years times 365 days per year equaled 1,825 days. There would be a leap year in there somewhere, maybe two depending upon the luck of the draw, so to be safe he'd call it 1,827 days until he shouldered his sack and walked out that gate. 1,827 days until he had a frosty bottle of beer. 1,827 days until he got close enough to a female to smell her perfume. 1,827 days until he was free to choose what he wished to have for supper, and to eat that meal from a china plate with silverware rather than from a plastic tray with a plastic spoon. 1,827 days until he was free.

To commemorate the occasion, Palmer went on a shopping spree at the prison store, which was located in the visitor's building across the yard. While being escorted to the facility, Palmer took deep breaths and walked with a spring in his step as they traversed the 100 yards between buildings. On both sides of the walk, basketball games were in progress on fenced and locked individual courts.

Palmer felt good on this day. He knew he had a long time left to serve, but he had crested the hill. He looked up at the buttermilk sky and sniffed the breeze. The air smelled heavy and damp. There would be a thunderstorm later, he decided. It was a hot June, and he hoped the coming rain would bring some cooler air with it. He looked past the inner and outer fences to the fields beyond and noted that they could use the rain. The prison had been built in farm country, and farming still went on around it at all four points of the compass. In that respect, Sweetwater State Correctional Facility served as a giant steel-and-block scarecrow in the agrarian countryside.

Palmer arrived at the prison store, which was in fact a ten-by-ten room adjacent to the visitor's area. It was actually more of a large closet than a proper room. It was open three hours each weekday and all day Sunday. The store was normally staffed by a trustee named Faro, who could be found during business hours propped up on the small counter in front of several racks of merchandise. Faro had once been a professional dealer in a casino, but it was his proclivity toward bigamy rather than that mildly disreputable career that had landed him in Sweetwater. Still, he was a good storekeeper. Inmates could buy toilet articles, candy and assorted snacks, cigarettes, postage, writing materials, and other odds and ends. Prisoners were not allowed to hold cash, but friends and relatives could deposit money into store accounts on the convicts' behalf, and as long as the inmates had a positive balance and weren't in the isolation block, they could come by to shop. And for those inmates who insisted on dealing in cash even though it was forbidden, Faro ran a thriving black-market enterprise on the side.

Beginning with Palmer's very first month in stir, $100 had been credited to his account each month. This was quite a large sum of money considering that all it could be spent on were snack cakes, smokes, shampoo, toothpaste, and other similar odds and ends. Thus Palmer could afford to be generous, and he was. He had arranged it with Faro so that Cheddar could come by whenever he wished to make a purchase. This accommodation had cost Palmer a carton of Pall Malls because it was against the rules for one inmate to sign against another's balance, but he had gotten Pittypat thrown in for the price, and while Pittypat was alive, he was allowed store privileges on Palmer's account as well. As for the source of the money, Palmer assumed that it was Trenton, but he had only seen his father once during the first five years of his sentence—on the forlorn occasion of his mother's death—and the subject of who was funding the store account hadn't come up during that cheerless conversation.

While he was at the store, Palmer purchased a spiral notebook, a pack of Camels, a Hershey's chocolate bar, and a Baby Ruth, which he believed to be the finest candy in the world. He also bought a small oscillating fan for their cell; it was already like a furnace in there, and most of the long summer was still in front of them. He intended to sit in front of the fan, smoke a Camel, eat the Baby Ruth, and begin his countdown to freedom in the notebook. The Hershey bar was for Cheddar, whose teeth had continued their decline over the past five years even in the absence of the dire influence of methamphetamine, thus making it impossible for him to share in the delights of a Baby Ruth candy bar. The peanuts were the problem. Cheddar had lost about half of his teeth by this point, and he had exhibited the unfortunate tendency to lose every other one. This predisposition caused him to bear an uncanny likeness to a jack-o'-lantern, at least from the shoulders up, and peanuts tended to hang in the gaps.

After returning from the store, Palmer sat in the cell and worked on his notebook. He had turned on their little radio and was listening to it while he worked. The radio had been a welcome addition to the cell. Palmer had purchased it at the store two years previously. Prison regulations dictated that radios and other audio devices could only be used with headphones or earpieces, but the guards did not strictly enforce this regulation as long as the volume was kept low and there were no complaints. It was a small clock radio, and Cheddar had taped over the LED clock face so that they would not constantly be reminded of the time. Because of its location inside the concrete and steel walls of the cellblock, the inexpensive receiver could only pick up five or six stations. But those came in clearly, and there was some variety, including a country station, an oldies station, a couple of talk stations, and two broadcast sources that fell under the broad canopy of Mexican Radio. Tuning in to any of these beat listening to nothing.

Presently, Cheddar arrived back from his work detail in the kitchen. "Happy Birthday," he said. He sat on their single folding chair, another addition to the décor of cell number B-134. It had been borrowed from the common area of the cellblock. This practice was technically against the rules as well, but it was allowed with prisoners who had shown the good sense to lay low and not make trouble for the guards. This was a code of behavior that both Cheddar and Palmer held absolutely sacred, and their commitment to institutional civility had paid off for them.

During the five years of their mutual confinement, Palmer and Cheddar had also acquired a deck of cards, a small hot pot, a pair of mugs, a diverse selection of wall art, a throw rug, a CD player, and a

110

combination chess-and-checker set. They were the proud owners of most of the comforts of home, and compared to some of the cells on the block, theirs was positively opulent. They lived in the Hilton of B-block. They were the rulers of the land of the swells. The wisdom of their policy of peaceful coexistence with the authorities was evidenced by the fact that many of these items were contraband, but all had been through more than one inspection—known as tossing the cell—and had survived unscathed.

"Have a Hershey bar," Palmer replied. His cousin smiled like the Cheshire cat at this unexpected treat. He took his gift and carefully removed the wrapping. These moves were slow and deliberate; Cheddar was determined to slip into the Hershey gestalt and enjoy the entire experience. He broke off a square of chocolate and tucked it carefully between his cheek and gum, like a discrete dip of snuff. Then he closed his eyes as the flavor overwhelmed his taste buds with pleasure. He loved chocolate, but he hated dentists, so he had to be careful about the substances that came in contact with his ruined teeth. Sweets and cold items were likely to initiate a throbbing jaw that could last for hours.

"Thanks," he said after the square had melted. He carefully eased another into its place. "What are you doing with the notebook? Starting another journal?"

Palmer had faithfully written in his journal every day since coming to Sweetwater. It had become an addiction with him, but unlike some of his cousin's compulsions, Palmer's habit would not take decades off his life or turn his teeth orange. He usually worked on his journal during the relative calm of the period between supper and lights out. Most residents of the cellblock hung out in the common area during that time. There was one television per cellblock mounted high on the wall in each common area, and on the days that no inmates had misbehaved, two hours of viewing was allowed. But Palmer was more of a cellbody. He had gotten in the habit of keeping to himself early in his sentence, and so far he had enjoyed success with the tactic. His journal was a living document that had expanded to several volumes of composition books. These were stacked on top of Palmer's locker, which was mounted to the wall opposite the bunks.

"I have been to the mountaintop, and I have seen the Promised Land," Palmer replied. "It's all downhill from here. I'm making a five-year countdown calendar. Every night before I hit the bunk, I'm x-ing off one of these boxes." He flipped to the back page of the notebook and pointed to the big box drawn there. It was the one he had drawn first. "When I get to this one, I'll be walking out the front gate."

"You know you shouldn't pay that much attention to time." Cheddar shook his head in disapproval. "It's a mistake. Time is your enemy. It starts slowing down when you think about it. We're cellmates. If it slows down for you, it might slow down for me."

"I'm still counting down."

"You're making a mistake."

"I've made them before," Palmer replied absentmindedly as he traced out squares in the spiral notebook. There was no arguing that point.

"It'll drive you nuts," Cheddar warned.

"Too late," Palmer said.

Cheddar broke off another square of chocolate and slipped it into his mouth. Apparently, he forgot himself in the heat of the moment and bit down. The inadvertent contact between sweet chocolate and a raw nerve caused him to grimace. "Shit," he said.

Palmer looked up from his project. "Cheddar, you ought to get all those teeth pulled. They're just going to keep giving you trouble. Look at it as one of the few benefits of being in here. We have a dental plan. It's like you work for a Fortune 500 company that has guards in the towers and bars on the windows. They'll put you to sleep, yank those bad boys out, and when you wake up, it'll all be over. It won't even hurt."

"But then I won't have any teeth."

"Nobody can pull one over on you."

"When I get out of here, I'm going to need a woman. I plan on being permanent point man on the pussy patrol. How am I supposed to get a female to pay attention to me if I don't have any teeth?"

Palmer could see where this could be a problem. "They'll give you false teeth," he said. "A set of straight, white, odor-free, useable false teeth, the kind of teeth a man with your plan needs. Plus, you'll be able to eat a candy bar."

"Women can spot false teeth a mile away," Cheddar said in a dismissive tone.

Palmer looked at Cheddar's Halloween smile, streaked as it was with Hershey's chocolate. He knew he should break the news to his cousin that his chances for immediate or even somewhat delayed post-incarceration intercourse ranged the reduced gamut from slim to not ever in this universe, but he could not bring himself to do it. The pussy patrol had come to symbolize all that was good in life, and, as Cheddar had once told him, it was unwise to deprive an inmate of hope. Palmer had no wish to be cruel to his cousin. If Cheddar thought that a willing assortment of amorous women was a mere seventeen years in his future, it was fine by Palmer. If Cheddar believed these ladies would be standing outside the gate, topless, perhaps, waving signs printed with CHEDDAR—OVER HERE or WILL SCREW FOR HERSHEY BARS, then who was Palmer to lay waste to the dream? Maybe Cheddar would meet a good-hearted blind woman with impossibly large breasts and a sinus condition, and then everything would work out fine. Stranger things had happened in the long history of the pussy patrol. He would hold this good thought for his dentally challenged relative, and the future would just have to take care of itself.

"You want a Camel?" Palmer asked, changing the subject. Camels were the cigarette of choice on B-block. Their lack of a filter tip eliminated waste and evidence, and they were strong cigarettes that packed a lot of nicotine into each puff, so even the worst tobacco addict could get by on only a few per day. Strictly speaking, smoking in the cells was prohibited for the sensible reason that some of the convicts were arsonists. Cigarettes were allowed out on the yards and in the common areas near the butt cans, and they were only supposed to be lit by a trustee, a reliable veteran of prison life who was accountable at all times for the location of the lighter. But many of the inmates had acquired lighters of their own, including Palmer and Cheddar, and they had become quite adept at sneaking an occasional cigarette in the cell when the guards' attentions were directed elsewhere.

"No, I'm good," Cheddar answered. He pointed at Palmer's new notebook like it was a plague rat. "Let's get back to that. Why have you decided to keep a calendar all of a sudden?"

"Five years is not all of a sudden. Today at 4:15 pm, it will be my fifth anniversary. Five years ago today, I walked into this cell for the first time. I've been here for exactly half of my sentence. Every day of that first five years was an uphill battle. I felt like I was crawling through a swamp on my hands and knees most of the time, and I don't even like to think about what I would have done without your help." Cheddar inclined his head as he accepted the compliment. Palmer continued. "Every day was miserable. But I'm at the top now. And down at the bottom I can see an open gate. Gravity's on my side. It's all about momentum from here on out. And I'm keeping track from now on, too. Faro told me about a guy he knew who was doing a stretch down at Coastal State, and they messed up somehow and kept him two weeks longer than they were supposed to. When they found out, they didn't say they were sorry or anything. I just want to be sure that they don't screw up at the end of my sentence and keep me too long." Even one day extra would be one day too many.

"You can't always put a lot of faith in what Faro says," Cheddar noted diplomatically. "That boy would climb a tree to tell a lie rather than stand on the ground and tell the truth. And I'm telling you, if you start checking off the days, it'll make the time go slow."

"It can't go any slower than it already has. I swear to God, Cheddar, it feels like I've been in here for a hundred years."

"I thought you were doing all right."

"I thought I was too. I wasn't thinking about anything but one day, just like you told me. Then it hit me like a bucket of cold mud this morning on my way back from the store. I'm having another birthday behind bars. I'm twenty-four years old. Out there in the world, I might celebrate by going out for a nice, juicy, thick steak. Then maybe I'd have a few ice-cold beers or even a couple of stiff drinks. I might even get drunk, if I could find someone to drive me." Palmer couldn't say for sure if he had been rehabilitated, because he really didn't know what that meant, but he had vowed early on that he would never again drive under the influence of alcohol.

"I heard that," Cheddar said, caught up in Palmer's birthday vision.

"And then, later on, I'd get laid." Palmer liked the way this last statement sounded so much that he said it again. "I'd get laid." He took a deep breath. His teeth—and other parts as well—ached at the thought of it. He took a look out the door, and once he saw that it was clear, he tapped a Camel from the pack and lit it. "That's what I'd do if I was outside," he said.

"Man, oh man," Cheddar said. "Steaks and cold beer and women." It was obvious that every bit of that plan sounded fine to him.

"But instead," Palmer continued, "it looks like I'm in for another night of Mexican Radio and checkers." At sundown the local

115

stations went off the air, and the only two frequencies their clock radio could retrieve from the night sky were a pair of clear-channel Spanish-language stations. The music was upbeat and catchy, but neither of them had any idea what the announcers were saying, and they always messed up the words when they tried to sing along with the music.

"I thought you liked Mexican Radio and checkers," Cheddar said. He sounded offended, as if he had invented both Mexican Radio and checkers with his cellmate specifically in mind.

"What's not to like?" Palmer replied absently. The activity wasn't cold beer, porterhouse steak, and hot, tangled love, but it was a five-star evening by Sweetwater State Correctional Facility standards. He looked out the window at the darkening sky. That storm wasn't far off now.

"You should cheer up," Cheddar said. "It's your birthday, and like you said, you're halfway home."

"I was as happy as a burglar in a pawn shop until you got here," Palmer noted. He carefully held his Camel between his fingertips as he got the last puff. Then he dropped the miniscule butt into the toilet and flushed the evidence.

"It was that notebook that did it."

"I won't write in it in front of you."

"Thanks."

"It's all right." There was no getting around the fact that a birthday was a milestone, and as such, it was a guaranteed bad day. Palmer should have just slammed his hand in the door upon arising that morning and gotten it out of the way.

"I got you this," Cheddar said as he dug in his pockets. He retrieved a bent pack of Camels from his left pants pocket and a crushed, partially melted Baby Ruth bar from his right. "It's not much, especially since you already got the same thing for yourself."

"It's hard to buy for the inmate who has everything."

116

"Tell me about it. I was going to surprise you later, but you need a pick-me-up right now. So here you are." He handed the modest gifts to his cousin. It was a gracious gesture. Palmer knew it was the thought that counted, and he accepted the presents in the same vein they were offered. The fact that he had paid for them himself made no difference whatsoever.

"You shouldn't have," he said. "I told you not to get me anything."

"I know, but hey, a birthday only comes once a year," Cheddar noted.

"Thank God for that. I think I'd have to kill myself if they came twice."

"Amen," Cheddar said. Then he had an idea. "Hey, I know what we can do. Tonight we can play *chess* while we listen to Mexican Radio. Or we can deal up a few hands of cards. We could even fire up the CD player and listen to some American music. That would be a change of pace." They seldom played the CD player because they only had three CDs, and these had been listened to many times.

"You decide," Palmer said. "It'll be like a surprise party, that way."

Palmer had only made four x's in his countdown-to-freedom book when another in a seemingly endless series of Wednesdays rolled around, bringing with it his weekly visit with Morris. Morris shook Palmer's hand as they sat at the small wooden table in the largish room. Several other tables occupied the area. Most of these were empty, although what appeared to be attorney-client conferences were going on at a couple of them.

"How was your birthday?" the counselor asked Palmer.

"I had a great day. I got a pack of broken Camels and a melted Baby Ruth bar. Then I listened to mariachi music from Jacksonville, Florida, while I played gin rummy with a reformed meth dealer who has a naked woman with big boobs tattooed on his chest. Actually, I'm not that sure he's reformed. It might just be lack of opportunity. He is a lousy gin player. He owes me somewhere in the neighborhood of twenty-five million dollars, and that's at a penny a point with him keeping score. I'm not counting on spending the money, though, because I feel like it may be hard to collect the debt. Later, after lights out, I listened to him play the hand flute up in the top bunk. It's not that he was indiscrete, but a cellmate knows these things, and our cell's pretty small." They were quiet for a moment. Then Palmer finished his narrative. "So I guess you could say that my birthday was about like last year's. Thanks for asking, though. How did your week go? Did you have any hot, juicy steaks? Did you sip any tall, frosty glasses of cold beer?"

"It sounds like my week went better than yours did. And no, I didn't do any of those things." Palmer thought he was lying through his teeth, because if he, Palmer, were on the outside, he would do them every single day. Morris jotted a couple of notes on the legal pad he had placed on the table before him. "You were in a much better frame of mind last week. You seemed almost chipper during our conversations. What happened?"

"I sort of got into a bad frame of mind on my birthday, which also happened to be my anniversary day." It seemed to Palmer that they had this same conversation every year. He wondered what was the point of writing everything down if Morris wasn't going to review the notes from time to time. "It was just that I hit a milestone, I guess. Two of them, actually. You know the deal. We've talked about it. Holidays are bad. Birthdays are bad. Anything out of the ordinary is bad. The anniversary of the day you go to prison is extra bad, especially if it's *on* your birthday. I've got the Hanging Judge to thank for that." They had indeed discussed the phenomenon, but he wasn't sure that Morris really understood the issues involved or the way Palmer actually felt when one of these milestones was encountered. He wasn't certain that anyone who hadn't done a little time could possibly understand. It was like trying to explain quantum physics to a stone.

"I think we need to talk about it some more."

"No point in talking about it," Palmer said. "It just is. It's a fact of life. In five more years, the problem will go away. Until then, there's nothing I can do about it but brush and floss regularly and avoid greasy foods. I'm screwed."

"What do brushing, flossing, and avoiding grease have to do with prison milestones?"

"Not a thing," Palmer replied. "Not a thing. You need to work on that sense of humor." The psychologist wrote a few words on his pad.

"Again, you sound particularly discouraged today."

"I always feel like this. I just don't talk about it much."

"Would you like for me to talk to the prison doctor about trying a different antidepressant? You've been on Prozac for quite some time. It's not unusual to have to change medications after you've been on one for a while."

"Good luck with that. I'm not on Blue Cross in here, you know. They buy the cheapest stuff they can find. They bring it in here in a dump truck. A guy who mops the infirmary said that they get medicine that's out of date, because they get a better deal on it that way." That inmate was known by his peers as Doc, and he was generally a reliable source of information despite the five years he was doing for car theft.

"I don't think that's what they do, and I don't mind checking into another antidepressant for you."

"Don't. The Prozac is fine. Plus, the side effects sort of work to my advantage."

"Side effects?" Morris asked.

Palmer shook his head. "I thought you were an expert on this stuff," he said. "Prozac takes the lead right out of a guy's pencil. Luckily, it's not the worst thing in the world for me right now to have the libido of a rock. It kind of takes the edge off the day when you're not dealing with being horny all the time. A functional sex drive is a liability in prison. It can get you into a whole lot of trouble. I'm surprised that they don't have everyone on the stuff. They ought to grind it up and dump it into the mashed potatoes and the coffee. I have a safe cellmate, and we live on a pretty quiet cellblock, but there are places in Sweetwater where you don't go alone—the showers, behind the laundry, out in the wrong part of the yard. They had a rape over in A-block just last week." As was the case with most of the inmates, Palmer was a bit of an expert on the subject of prison rape. He had avoided being a participant, thus far, and he approached each new day with the intention of keeping it that way. Turning twenty-one in prison doing ten years without parole had made him a careful man.

"I heard about that as I was checking in," Morris said. "One of the guards told me they're on lockdown over there until they get it sorted out."

"I heard that too." Palmer had heard that the victim was offered protective custody—solitary confinement in the isolation block—but had refused. He couldn't say that he blamed the guy. The isolation cells were the worst: twenty-three hours out of twenty-four with nothing but a Bible and your thoughts. He shuddered. If you weren't messed up when you went in, you were when you came out. He was surprised that the guy had even reported it. The reportage was what had earned him the offer of protection, not the rape. Most rapes went unreported because it was the generally held view among the inmates that it was better to be a bitch than a snitch. A rape victim might receive a little sympathy and perhaps even some peer protection after the fact, but once a man went to the guards, he was branded a snitch for his entire sentence. The name would follow him from prison to prison and from state to state. It was the mark of Cain.

"Let's get back to you," Morris suggested. "Sex seems to be on your mind this week."

"You think so? I'm twenty-four years old—supposedly in my prime—and I've been laid exactly three times in my life, all by the same girl, a girl I had to send away for her own good. The first time we made love, it took about fourteen seconds, and the last time we had sex was six years ago. If I'm lucky, my next window of opportunity will be opening in five years, assuming I don't get my nuts cut off in here and that I can find a woman who wouldn't mind consorting with an ex-convict. You know something? You might be right. Sex could be on my mind."

Morris looked over the tops of his glasses. Then he wrote on his pad. "Aside from the libidinal issues," he asked, "is the Prozac still working for you? How is your depression? How is your mood?" He was casually jotting one fact and then another onto his pad as they talked. In addition to the notes, there were circles, lines, stars, and arrows. He was a doodler.

"I suppose the stuff's helping. It's not doing any harm, anyway. Except to my dick, and maybe that's temporary. I have good days and bad days, but like I said, I doubt if they'll change it to something else, so why talk about it?"

"Let's do a quick little evaluation. We've done these before, so you know the drill. Answer truthfully. Do you feel sad?"

"I'm in a prison, and I have to stay here five more years. I live in a closet with a methamphetamine dealer named Cheddar. Be serious. What do I have to be sad about?"

"How's your anxiety?"

"I'm in a prison with seven hundred criminals. They all received the same blanket threat from my old man not to mess with me, which makes a large percentage of them want to mess with me. What would I have to be anxious about?"

"How's your appetite?"

"Functional, considering the food and the company." The food wasn't bad, but it was always the same. Breakfast every morning was scrambled eggs, oatmeal, and toast. Lunch was potato chips and one of several varieties of sandwich: tuna salad, peanut butter and apple jelly, egg salad, pimento cheese. For the main meal of the day, supper, an inmate could chart his course and mark his calendar according to what was being served on any given day. On Monday, it was always beans and cornbread with banana pudding for dessert. Tuesday brought Salisbury steak, mashed potatoes, green beans, and peach cobbler. Wednesday was the day for beef stew with slices of loaf bread, and there was always room for Jell-O. Thursday spawned meat loaf, creamed corn, lima beans, and the rest of the Jell-O. Friday was turkey-rice pie and cherry cobbler day. Saturday featured hamburger steak, mashed potatoes and gravy, English peas, and ice cream. Sunday's fare was chicken legs, baked potatoes, green beans, and sugar cookies for dessert. The menu never changed. As for the company, it spoke for itself.

"Do you still have feelings of guilt about Rodney?"

"According to the State of Georgia, I am officially guilty of getting drunk and running my best friend through an oak tree. Something like that will get on your mind and stay there. I also feel guilty about Mama. She worried herself into an early grave over me." Palmer couldn't explain it, but he felt worse about his mother's death than he did about his friend's, even though he had been an active participant in the latter. It was just that Rodney had placed himself in harm's way voluntarily. He had been along for the ride in more ways than one. Laurel Cray, on the other hand, had been blindsided by the entire affair. She had been an innocent bystander, but the fallout from Palmer's and Rodney's joy ride had killed her just the same.

"Are you feeling suicidal?" Morris always lowered his voice when he spoke the forbidden word, as if saying it loudly would give it power.

Palmer gave the question a long period of consideration before answering.

"You know, today that's kind of an interesting question. I really don't think about killing myself nearly as much as I used to, and even back at the beginning of all this, when I was giving the idea a lot of thought, I don't know that I would have done it. The idea of it appealed to me, but the reality of being dead scared me. But now, sometimes I think that being dead wouldn't be the worst thing that could happen. You know what I mean? It seems like it might be peaceful. At least it would be quieter. All I'd hear would be the gentle winds of eternity." A thought occurred to him. "Unless Mama was right. Then I'll be hearing my own screams of torment for the rest of time. That would really suck, so I kind of hope she's wrong. Either way, though, I don't think I'm suicidal, but I don't know that I'd fight all that hard to stay alive if something came up. Especially if the way out didn't seem like it would hurt too much. The pain has always been the kicker for me. I could never think of a way that I was sure wouldn't hurt except for pills, and I couldn't get enough of the right kind of pills in here."

"What do you mean by quieter?" Morris asked.

"There wouldn't be all this dialogue going on in my head all the time. All those voices that spend their days telling me how I've ruined my life would be gone. I'm getting tired of them. I know what I've done. I don't need to be reminded. As a matter of fact, it

123

used to be a one-sided conversation, but lately I've been taking up for myself and talking back."

"Are you saying you hear voices?"

"You'll have to speak up," Palmer said loudly. "I can't hear you over the crowd."

"Palmer, this is important."

"I talk to myself in my head all the time. I always have. And every so often, I swear I can hear Rodney talking to me. It's his voice and everything. That one is something new. I call him Dead Rodney."

"How long has that been going on?" Morris was scribbling and doodling furiously as they discussed Palmer's unexpected company. One especially long arrow left the page about halfway down the right margin and regained its footing on the following sheet.

"Dead Rodney has been around a few months now. He's no trouble, and he doesn't eat much. I thought I might keep him."

"That's the sort of thing you might mention a bit sooner next time," Morris said. He sounded perturbed, although whether it was with himself or with his patient, Palmer couldn't say.

"Next time," he said.

"How do you sleep?"

"Not so hot."

"Why do you think you sleep badly?"

"What, did you just get here? Did aliens abduct you and suck your psychology degree out through your ear? Take everything we've ever talked about, roll it all up in a nice, tight package, and lay it on a stained, six-inch thick, worn-out mattress. Then cover it up with a scratchy sheet and a thin wool blanket. That's why I don't sleep. I have bad things on my mind, and my bed sleeps like an Army cot."

"Do you feel irritable?"

"If you ask me any more questions, I may have to kill you."

"I'm going to call that a *yes*. Angry?"

"If you ask me any more *damn* questions, I may have to kill you again."

"Another *yes*. Do you have feelings of worthlessness?"

"Most days I feel like the sorriest person to ever draw breath. The rest of the time I think Cheddar is and I'm running a close second."

"Tell me why."

"Are you kidding? I killed my friend. I killed my mama. I broke my girlfriend's heart. I am a waste. Everyone who gets near me ends up dead or sorry."

Morris wrote for another moment or two after Palmer quit speaking. He looked at the words and squiggles on his legal pad for a short interval. He scratched his thin hair and chewed on the end of his pen. Then he tossed the legal pad onto the table and spoke.

"I think your depression is getting significantly worse. Considering that you're already on the highest allowable dosage of Prozac, I think I should talk to the prison doctor about a change of medication for you."

"Uh-uh. Don't do it," Palmer said.

"A different drug might be more effective in treating your symptoms. You might also get your erection back."

"I don't need it right now. Talk to me in five years."

"A change in meds might be beneficial," Morris repeated.

"It might not be. I might just be depressed because this place is depressing. I bet I'll be fine just as soon as I walk out the gate."

"Let's take that bridge when we come to it."

"We will, but in the meantime, don't bother the doctor."

"Why don't you want me talking to the doctor?"

"Right now I'm just a face in the crowd. I'm no different from a hundred other guys in here who are depressed because they've thrown it all away. But if you go telling the doctor that I need more treatment, or different meds, or that I'm suicidal or mentally unstable, I'll be out of here faster than this." He snapped his fingers.

"You hate it here."

"I do for a fact, but it could be worse. They'll ship me down to Central State or over to Augusta. Those are a couple of places I need to avoid. If you think I'm depressed now, wait till you see me in one of those joints. This place sucks, but at least I'm used to it, and I don't want to break in a new cellmate or learn the ropes at a different prison. Especially a prison where no one's got my back. So please don't do me any favors. Just leave well enough alone. I'm asking as a favor. I promise you I won't kill myself. I won't make you look bad."

"It's not about how I look, Palmer. It's about how you are doing."

"I'm doing all right, and I'm not planning on offing myself. It's not going to get much better than that until I get out of here."

This is going to sound like a seriously crazy question, but I need to ask it anyway, so humor me. Have you been talking to me? I mean really talking, as in making noises with your mouth or whatever it is you have instead of one. I've been hearing your voice for a while now. It's not all the time or anything. Just every so often. When I do, it sounds like you're standing behind me, talking in a real low voice into my right ear. Sometimes I turn around when I hear you, because I forget myself and think for a minute you're still alive. I expect to see you standing right there, but you never are. Or at least, if you're there I can't see you. Before you hear it from someone else, I call you Dead Rodney. Well, because it sounds like you, and you're dead. I don't know why I only hear you with my right ear. Maybe I have a better eardrum over there or something like that.

You haven't answered my question, but I think it's you. It's not like I have a lot of choices here. Either you're really talking to me or I've gone nuts. I don't think I've gone over the edge, but that's one of those things

126

*you can never be sure about. Someone who had actually gone off the deep
end probably wouldn't think he had, so I might be as crazy as a shithouse
rat right now and just not know it. I know when I told Morris about
hearing you, he got a little excited, and he's a professional psychologist. I
get the feeling he thinks I might've gone a little stir-crazy. He wanted to
talk to the prison doctor about me and see about changing my medication
but I told him no. I don't have anything against the doctor and I want it
to stay that way. In prison, you want to stay below everyone's radar,
including doctors. You want to blend in with the surroundings like a
chair. The fewer people who know your name, the better off you are.*

    *If I had it to do over again I wouldn't tell Morris I can hear you.
Telling him just shook him up and he's hard to deal with when he gets
upset. It's not like you're telling me to go out and kill someone or that I'm
really Jesus or anything. You're just being a smartass like you used to be.
You always liked to stir it up and then I'd have to help clean up the mess.
Do you remember that time were drinking beer in the Camaro outside of
the American Legion dance in Calhoun? And you made a wisecrack
about that girl we saw walking across the parking lot, something about
the way she was shaking her ass? And then before we knew it her brothers
and her cousins and her boyfriend were dragging us out of the car and
beating the tar out of us? I thought they were going to kill us right there
in that parking lot. Good times.*

    *Those boys might still be pounding on us if the girl with the nice
backside hadn't made them knock it off. I always meant to look her up
and thank her for that, but prison got here first. Anyway, they all went
on into the dance until it was just the biggest of her brothers at the door.
Right about the time he turned to give us one more hard stare, you
hollered*—Hey man, I'm sorry I was talking about your sister's sweet
ass! *Oh, man! It was a good thing that the Camaro didn't have a dead
battery or we'd have gotten our asses kicked twice that night. You used to
just love to run that mouth, and it looks like you haven't changed much
since you died.*

*Like the other day, I was in the kitchen rinsing trays when this guard named Murphy came in for a cup of coffee and started messing with me. I was running about an hour behind with my job, and Murphy was all, like—*Cray, what are you, a union man now? *The dishwasher was stopped up all morning and I had to wash most everything by hand, but Murphy didn't care about that. Some of the guards are just guys trying to make a living and there's nothing wrong with them or with that, but some of them are real assholes. Murphy is one of those.*

*Anyway, I didn't say anything, because he was just aching to thump me. I've been thumped before and can't say that I recommend it. And then I heard you say—*What's this little prick's problem? Are you going to let him talk to you like that? *You sounded so real that I turned my head before I thought. Then Murphy wanted to know what the hell I was looking at, but I didn't pay him any mind. I went back to scraping trays, but then you said—*If I had a foot I'd kick his ass. *That made me smile, and then Murphy wanted to know what was so funny. It was going downhill and I was heading for trouble when one of the cooks came over and bailed me out. He refilled Murphy's coffee cup and gave him some cookies. Then he got him talking about fishing, and Murphy forgot all about me. But I've been thinking about it ever since. It sounded like you were there, Rodney. It sounded like you were standing right there.*

6

The Head Bull's Boy

Inevitability is a force of nature on par with gravity, magnetism, and time. It is as certain as death and as unavoidable as taxes. It can occasionally be fooled, but not for long and never permanently. It can sometimes be outrun if enough energy is expended, but it cannot simply be ignored. Palmer Cray realized these truths after the fact, of course, because his hindsight was just as acute as anyone's, but prior to his encounter with Razor Smithfield, he had allowed himself to become lulled into a dangerous sense of complacency. Up to that point in his captivity, no one had called him to task for his parentage, and since no one had, Palmer had let himself believe that no one ever would. It was a natural, wishful mistake, the kind made by reasonable people who just want to be left alone, but it was a bad error in spite of that. Inevitability is inevitable, and it will have its due.

Razor Smithfield was a minor legend among the Georgia community of convicts. His given name was Peter, but he hated that name with a seething, unholy passion because it had been his father's before him, and he and his father had never been able to see eye to eye. He had been called Razor ever since the commission of his first felony, which had occurred during his fourteenth summer, when he brought his father low with an old straight razor he found at the landfill. The instrument had a broken and yellowed bone handle and had not been stropped in years, but it was plenty sharp enough to simultaneously give Razor a nickname and to make him an orphan and a ward of the state. Because he was so young and in light of the fact that his father was whaling away at him at the time of the slicing, Razor had not been tried as an adult for the crime. He was sent away to the boy's home and spent the following four years in youth detention before being released from custody soon after his eighteenth birthday. The authorities hoped that he would overcome his slow start and make a decent life for himself, as was their wish for all of their charges. But the bad habits he picked up from the other rowdy boys during his incarceration combined with the inescapable fact that he had liked the sensation of killing a man made him a poor candidate for rehabilitation, thus he continued on his path toward mayhem and ruin. Thirty years later, most of which he spent in one or another of several penal institutions for various crimes of violence, Razor Smithfield became Palmer Cray's problem.

Palmer first realized that he was dancing with the devil one morning at breakfast when he was manning the egg station in the serving line. As each inmate scooted his compartmentalized plastic tray into position along the steam table, Palmer plopped in one large spoonful of reconstituted eggs from a jumbo stainless steel pan. With over seven hundred trays requiring the exact same attention as each slowly slid by, it was not a challenging job, and since it was not, Palmer spent a fair amount of his time gathering wool. Sometimes he thought about his life before Sweetwater, and occasionally he dreamed about how it would be once he breathed free air again, and more often than not he considered on nothing much at all. It was during one of these inattentive moments that a generous dollop of watery powdered eggs inadvertently found itself on the back of Razor Smithfield's hand.

"Watch what you're doing, you stupid son of a bitch!" Razor said. He slung his left hand as if it had been burned by acid, and the offending eggs sailed over Palmer's shoulder into the kitchen behind him, where they landed with a splat.

"Easy, friend," Palmer said as he snapped back to the present, which was much less pleasant than the memory he had been examining. "It was an accident." At one time he would have objected to the epithet on general principle, especially from a stranger, but he had heard and seen quite a bit worse during his time in stir and had become mostly desensitized to insult. Plus, he really didn't care. The words and the man who spoke them meant less than nothing to him, and all he wanted was to finish his shift and get back to his cell, where he felt relatively safe. A good book and a honey bun awaited him, and discussions about eggs were not in his plans.

"I ain't your damn friend, and I don't care if it was an accident or not!" Razor Smithfield said. For the first time, Palmer took a long look at the man before him, and he had to admit that he didn't like what he saw. Smithfield was a new arrival at Sweetwater State Correctional Facility, and Palmer had seen him out in the yard. Cheddar had told him who the new inmate was, and what he was, and how he was, but Palmer did not yet know him, although that appeared to be about to change.

He looked as if he had ridden the hard trail and had seen his share of trouble. He had mean eyes—crazy eyes, Cheddar would say—that gleamed a bit, as if they were primed for mischief. His head had been shaved but now held a week's gray stubble scattered over a tattoo of a skull and crossbones. His ears didn't match, and he had a general shortage of teeth. A scar ran through his left eyebrow, causing it to droop. He had additional tattoos on both hands, both

131

arms, and his neck. The underlying theme for this body art seemed to lean toward death and destruction. To Palmer, he looked like trouble with a capital T.

"This doesn't have to be a thing," Palmer said. He offered a dish towel with his left hand. His right hand still held the long-handled, stainless steel serving spoon, and he thought he might hold on to that a while. The dish towel was not accepted, and Palmer placed it back on the steam table. Several hungry voices from the chow line chimed in their agreement that a thing was not necessary, or that if a thing was necessary, could the thing wait until after breakfast, because some people were hungry.

"It's a thing," the man said.

"Let's don't do this," Palmer replied. He was aware that he was very calm, and that surprised him. He realized that he was in for some trouble, although he still wasn't quite sure why, and he knew from his talks with Cheddar that Razor was a dangerous man. Palmer analyzed the scene objectively, as if it had nothing to do with him. He kept his opponent's hands in view, because the trouble would come from there. He had once heard it said that a potential adversary always telegraphed a move with the eyes, but in Palmer's experience, it was the hands that needed to be watched, always the hands. The man looked at him expectantly, almost eagerly, like he couldn't wait for it to be go time. It was apparently still Palmer's turn to speak, and since he didn't know what else to do but felt that some action was necessary lest they stand there all day, he decided that he had had enough of this. He dipped out another scoop of eggs and slapped them into the tray. "Have some more eggs," he said to Razor Smithfield. It seemed as good a catalyst as any.

"I don't want any more eggs!" the man said in a voice that was mostly a growl as he made his move. His right hand shot up from his side and Palmer saw the tool it contained, a stabbing instrument whose parents were a sixteen-penny nail and a broom handle. Palmer instinctively took a step backward while swinging hard with the serving spoon. The spoon and Razor's hand met in no-man's land, out over the egg pan. When metal met flesh, there was a surprisingly loud pop. Razor cussed and dropped the tool. Palmer swung again, hard, and smacked Razor in the nose. Drops of blood and spittle flew. Whistles blew as the guards became aware that malice was afoot and turmoil likely. Razor grabbed his nose with his left hand while Palmer plucked the tool from the eggs and spirited it away under the steam table. From start to finish, the incident had taken a long two seconds.

"I'll kill you for that!" Razor said through his hand. Blood dripped like ketchup onto his replacement eggs.

"What are you going to do? Pull a tool on me? Too late, asshole! You already did that." Now that it was over, Palmer was angry.

"You'll see what I'll do!" Razor warned with menace.

"What the hell is your problem, man?" Palmer continued. He shook his head. This trouble plus whatever the aftermath was—and there would without a doubt be an aftermath, and most likely an ugly one—was over one lousy, poorly aimed spoonful of eggs. Maybe he ought to smack the guy again. As Palmer gave the idea some serious consideration, two guards ran up, and Razor quickly slid his tray down the serving line.

"What's going on here?" one of the guards asked Palmer. His riot baton was in his hand and his eyes were alert; he reminded Palmer of a coiled spring. The other guard had moved to flank Razor, and he, too, had limbered up his persuader.

"Guy's nose started bleeding," Palmer said, gesturing with the spoon at Razor as he gave a half shrug. Regardless of what was going on with Razor Smithfield, Palmer had no intention of being the con who ratted him out to the guards. Right now he had a crazy person out to kill him over some eggs, and that was bad enough, but if he brought that situation to the attention of the authorities, Palmer knew it could get worse. He would become an instant persona non grata in the prison, and no one would have his back. Cheddar might even cut him loose over something as serious as ratting out another prisoner. Rats tended toward short life expectancies in a prison setting. He picked up the ruined pan of eggs, moved it aside, and replaced it with a fresh batch. And even though he had grown quite fond of the one he had, he fetched another steel spoon as well.

"What about it, Smithfield?" the guard asked. "What's your version? Why are you bleeding like a stuck hog? What happened?" He was tapping his stick against his thigh like he was counting down the seconds to zero.

"You got eyes," Razor said. "It's like the kid said. My nose started bleeding. I got a condition." He removed his hand from his nose to demonstrate, and as soon as he quit pinching his nostrils, the blood again began to flow, although it did seem to be slowing down.

"Yeah, we all know about your conditions. Your nose looks like someone tagged you pretty good. You running that mouth, Smithfield?" Razor shrugged his shoulders and attempted to look innocent, which was an ineffective strategy on his part. The guard just shook his head. "Move on down. People are hungry. If that don't stop bleeding soon, go see the doc. And be real careful. I've got my eye on you." The two guards remained in place as Palmer went back to serving eggs. As he dipped, plopped, and paid extra attention to his aim, he wondered what had just happened. Aside from their recent brief but intense exchange, all he knew about Razor Smithfield was his reputation, and from what he had seen firsthand, it was well deserved. The man was crazy, and apparently he had no issues with stabbing a total stranger over some errant eggs. Great.

"Crazy," said Palmer. The guard who had planted himself in the vicinity of the egg pan for the duration of breakfast looked at him quizzically, and Palmer realized he had spoken aloud. He shook his head to indicate that it was nothing and went back to dishing eggs.

He was ready for this meal to be over so he could go back to the cell and regroup, but time had slowed to a crawl, and the line of hungry inmates seemed to stretch all the way to the next county.

Unlike minutes, word travels fast in a prison, and by the time Palmer's shift was over and he had made the short journey back to the cell, his fame had preceded him. A couple of his comrades had given him the thumbs-up on the way back, and he had received a high five and a slap on the back from a bare acquaintance out in the common area. Razor was not a popular convict at Sweetwater, it seemed, even though he had only been there a short while, and anyone brave enough or foolish enough to whack him with an egg spoon was automatically elevated to celebrity status. As he entered the cell, Cheddar was there to greet him.

"Are you crazy? What the hell have I told you about Razor Smithfield! I told you to stay the hell away from him, is what I told you! He's killed more people than AIDS! He killed his own daddy, for Christ's sake, and they don't even know how many others he's done in." Cheddar just stood there shaking his head. The enormity of Palmer's actions seemed to have left him momentarily adrift.

"Thanks, I'm fine," Palmer responded. "Didn't get stabbed or anything."

"Of all the people in the entire place to screw with, you had to pick that guy? You must have a secret death wish!"

"I didn't pick anyone, I wasn't screwing with him, and I don't have a death wish! I got some eggs on his hand, and he went nuts. He came at me with a tool, so I hit him a couple of times with a serving spoon. It was self-defense. There wasn't anything else to do." Palmer didn't know why Cheddar seemed so upset. He wasn't the one who almost got stabbed.

"It doesn't matter what the reason was. That boy is full-blown crazy. He's one of the ones that shouldn't even be in this prison. They ought to open Alcatraz back up for him. They should put a

135

chain on his leg with a cannonball welded to it. And now that he has a hard-on for you, he's going to try to kill you when he gets the chance." Cheddar sat on the bunk and stared at the floor, as if the solution to this dilemma might be written there. He couldn't have looked more upset, even if Razor were after him instead of Palmer.

"You worry too much," Palmer said, although, truth be told, he was a bit worried as well. He'd had a few small scuffles since coming inside, some pushing and shoving and hollering, but now he had graduated to the big leagues. Now he had a homicidal maniac after him.

"You don't worry enough!" came the reply. "Now that you've gotten yourself on Razor Smithfield's bad side, we'll see how you like it. And he's the kind of guy who will kill everyone you know once he gets through with you! That puts my ass in the sling, too. I like my ass, and I don't want it to be in a sling!"

"I think I must have already been on his to-do list, which I don't get, because the only time I ever even saw him before today was when I was out in the yard with you," Palmer said. "All I did this morning was accidentally get some eggs on his hand, and I told him it was an accident, but he didn't want to hear that. It was like he was just looking for a reason. He just blew."

"What kind of knife did he have?" Cheddar asked.

"What does it matter what kind of knife he had?"

"I want to know. What kind of knife did he pull?"

"He pulled this kind of knife," Palmer said, producing the shiv. He hadn't known what to do with it after breakfast, but at the last minute he had tucked it into his drawers. He handed it to Cheddar, who took it carefully at first, as if it might be hot to the touch. He looked at it briefly before spiriting it away under a sweatshirt stacked on top of the locker.

"Wicked," Cheddar said.

"Yeah," Palmer agreed.

"You just whipped Razor Smithfield and took his knife away from him," Cheddar said in a monotone, like he was reading from a scroll. "You disarmed the most dangerous inmate since Big Al Capone. With a spoon." He shook his head. "I've been worried about you all this time for nothing. I think *you* should start watching out for *me*. Maybe we ought to hire you out to cons in trouble. We could make some spare cash that way. Some cigarette and honey bun money."

"What was I supposed to do?" Palmer asked. "Let him stab me?" Getting stabbed to avoid being stabbed later on didn't make a lot of sense, even in a place like Sweetwater, which existed outside the realm of sanity and the rules of logic.

"No, I guess not," Cheddar said in a petulant tone, all the while managing to sound a bit unsure about this answer. "You say it seemed like he came looking for trouble?"

"Well, he was either looking for it all along or else he got awful pissed off over some eggs. And he had the knife with him. Why would he carry a weapon to the dining hall unless he was looking to use it?"

"Some guys always carry," Cheddar said. "Maybe he's one of those."

"Maybe," Palmer said. "What I don't get, though, is why he would make a play in the dining hall. It's crowded in there. Lots of witnesses. Always three or four guards. I can think of better places to ice someone."

Cheddar nodded. "I can too," he said. "I don't know what's going on. I'm going to go see Faro and ask him what he's heard." Faro was like the Sweetwater prison newspaper. If anything worth knowing was going on within the walls, Faro would have the details, and if the price was right, he would share them. Cheddar looked at Palmer. "You stay in here and lay low. If anyone but me or a guard comes through the door, stick that shiv into their eye." Palmer nodded. Cheddar had made him paranoid. Subdued, he watched as his cellmate slipped on his jacket and headed out the door.

While Cheddar was on his reconnaissance mission, Palmer spent the time thinking about what had happened in the breakfast line. It seemed that he had an enemy within the walls despite his earnest ten-year mission to avoid trouble with anyone. It was too bad about the egg incident, but that had been an accident, and Razor's reaction to it was out of proportion. Palmer thought carefully about the events of that morning, and specifically he tried to remember if Smithfield had slipped his right hand into his pocket before the attack. If he had, then maybe he was just crazy, but if he hadn't, then the knife had been in his hand the whole time, or maybe in his sleeve, which meant he had come looking to stab Palmer. But try as he might, Palmer could not remember, and he was still mulling the issue when Cheddar returned from his hour-long trip to see Faro.

"What did Faro say?" Palmer asked as soon as Cheddar entered the cell.

"What didn't he say?" Cheddar replied as he sat on the bunk. "Man, we have got some big-time trouble."

"I figured we might have when a guy I didn't know tried to stab me in the breakfast line this morning," Palmer noted. He sat on the toilet opposite his cousin and leaned in close. There was no use sharing their business with the whole cellblock.

"Well, you were right about one thing," Cheddar continued. "It wasn't the eggs that pissed him off, although I'm guessing they didn't help much, either. Razor definitely came looking for you. He's on record saying that he plans to send you to see Jesus."

"Why? What does he have against me? I never met him, I don't know him, and I haven't done anything to him." Palmer thought about Razor's nose and amended his statement. "Well, at least not before today."

"You're the Head Bull's boy," Cheddar said conversationally. He looked from side to side after he spoke, just to be sure the coast was clear.

"That's no secret! Everybody knows it. And you're the Head Bull's nephew. No one's tried to kill either one of us yet!"

"Things change. The worm has turned."

"But why?" Palmer asked.

"Guess where Razor came from."

"I don't know where he came from. I don't care where he came from. I just want to be left alone."

"He came from Reidsville," Cheddar said, ignoring Palmer.

"Okay. He's from Reidsville. That's a big prison. Guys transfer in and out all the time. What's it have to do with me?"

"Razor is from the same Reidsville that your daddy sent Mondo to."

"Who is Mondo?"

"You never listen!" Cheddar said, exasperated. "I might as well be talking to the wall for all the good it does to tell you anything. You'll end up dead one of these days because you never hear a word I say, and then you'll be sorry!"

"I guarantee I'll be sorry, but I still don't know who Mondo is."

"You remember when you first got here and I told you that your old man had shipped off a guy who was laying for you? A guy named Mondo who was looking forward to meeting you in the showers?"

"Okay, yeah, I remember that now." Palmer nodded his head. "I had just forgotten his name."

"Well, Mondo and Razor were cellmates down at Reidsville. The word Faro heard was that those two boys had set up housekeeping and were swapping more than recipes, but that ain't the problem."

"Are we going to get to the problem soon," Palmer asked, "or will Razor kill me without me ever knowing why?"

"The problem is this," Cheddar said with a glare. "Mondo got his killing a few weeks ago, which proves that there is a God, in case you have ever had doubts. They found him with a sharp stake stuck in his heart, like he was a vampire or something. Would I like to get a look at the guy who could kill Mondo with a sharpened stick!" He shook his head in admiration. "That was one bad hombre!"

"Finish the story!" Palmer said in an urgent tone.

"Sorry. I got caught up in the telling, just like Grandma Cray used to do. After Mondo got himself planted out behind the prison, they shipped Razor up here so he wouldn't beat half of Reidsville prison to death while he was tracking down whoever iced his boyfriend. It was probably a pretty smart move. Razor ain't ever getting out, so he wouldn't have much to lose if he killed everyone in Reidsville."

"Or me," Palmer said. He was trying to connect the dots, but he still didn't see that any of this pertained to him. He hadn't known Mondo, and he didn't know Razor, and he had replaced the eggs. Everything ought to be square and everyone involved happy.

"Or you," Cheddar agreed. "According to Faro, Razor blames you for Mondo making his unscheduled trip to hell. He figures that someone killed Mondo to get to him, and he thinks that if he had never met Mondo, then Mondo would still be alive. And since he wouldn't have met Mondo if he had not been sent to Reidsville in the first place, that's why the crazy son of a bitch wants to kill you."

"How can he blame me for that?"

"Don't know, but he does."

"That's the craziest thing I've ever heard," Palmer said. "Do you believe that crap?"

"It doesn't matter what I believe. Razor thinks it. He's crazy. Just like I've said all along."

"I've got a mean, crazy guy trying to kill me over something that happened before I even got here," Palmer said quietly. "That's just stupid."

"Give the man a cigar," Cheddar said. "Razor Smithfield is a dumb ass, all right, but you'll be just as dead if he gets up next to you. He's crazy, but he's deadly. What we have to do is keep you away from him until word of this gets to your old man. Once that happens, he'll put a stop to it. He'll put him in isolation or ship him on off. Maybe he'll ship him down to Valdosta. I hear the roaches down there are big enough to name."

"Won't that cause me more problems?" Palmer asked. "This whole thing was caused in the first place by the old man shipping Mondo off."

"It might cause some problems down the road, but whatever they are, I guarantee you they will be smaller than having Razor trying to shank you. Anyway, look how long it took for this deal to come back around to haunt you. The next time paying the piper is due, you might be out of this place."

"Don't take this wrong, but I did shut him down with a spoon. Maybe he's not as big and bad as everyone says." Palmer hoped he wasn't, anyway.

"Uh-uh," Cheddar replied. "He's every bit as big and bad as they claim. Trust me when I tell you that nobody wants any of that. Don't you get cocky and start thinking you're bad. You just got lucky. That's all it was. He underestimated you, and now you've used up all the luck you had. What am I saying? You used up all the luck everyone in the whole state had. Next time he'll kill you, and then he'll make a run at me."

"What'd you do?"

"I know you," Cheddar replied. "That's all it takes. I'm a dead man by association. Razor's probably out warming up by killing the chicken that laid the eggs you slopped on his hands. Then he'll kill the cook. It's only a matter of time before he works his way up to me." He tapped his chest to emphasize the point.

"So what do we do?" Palmer asked.

"Your old man doesn't know that Razor wants to put you in a box. We've got to let him know somehow without it looking like you ran to Daddy for help. You and I have worked real hard at making you into just one of the guys. Most days you are, and we don't want to lose all the ground we've gained now." Cheddar thought for a moment. "Of course, we don't want you dead, either." It was a fine line to tread.

"So what do we do?" Palmer asked a little louder.

"My old man is due to visit tomorrow. He's bringing my boy by. I'll tell him what's going on. Then as soon as the visit is over, he can get the word to your old man. Once he does that, Razor will be on the next van out of here."

"That sounds like it might work." Palmer was heartened. "What should we do in the meantime?"

"I have to go pull the lunch shift. You lay low. Stay in the cell. Whatever you do, don't go to the yard or the showers. If he makes a run at you, it will be in one of those places."

Palmer nodded, glad for the advice.

"Sit here, face the door, and read," Cheddar continued. "Slip that tool up in your sleeve just to be safe. I'll be back in a few hours."

Cheddar left, and Palmer followed his instructions to the letter. He retrieved the homemade knife and slipped it up his sleeve. Then he sat on the toilet with the prison library copy of *The Old Curiosity Shop*, slid around on the john so he faced the door, and tried to take his mind off his troubles and pass the time. At first he looked up from his book every paragraph or two, but gradually he settled into the rhythm of the story so that his glances toward the corridor were fewer and farther between. Time passed, and the words of Charles Dickens transported him to another age of the world. Thus it was that it had been several minutes since his last peek when, as he was turning from Chapter the Fifty-second to Chapter the Fifty-third, he looked toward the door once again.

There stood Razor Smithfield, complete with crazy eyes, ugly smile, broken nose, and another knife. This one appeared to have started life as a piece of hard, brittle plastic, something with a handle like a putty knife or an ice scraper; it had subsequently been sharpened to a point on a rough surface, such as a concrete block wall. It was not an elegant weapon, but it looked sufficient to the task of killing a man.

"What the hell?" Palmer asked, although he did not really expect an answer.

"I told you I was gonna kill you," Razor growled. "It's time for that." He was just steps away from Palmer, and he crossed that distance quickly. Razor seemed to move in slow motion, yet Palmer barely had time to react. He straightened his arm, slipped the tool out of his sleeve and into his hand, and stabbed in an upwardly direction. This move was strictly instinct; there was no plan. His arm was fully extended before Razor arrived, so when he did, the old con impaled himself on his own shiv. His eyes bulged in surprise, and an "oof" escaped his lips. His replacement weapon, the sharpened plastic, clattered to the concrete floor. His hand wandered to his wound, and he looked down at Palmer's hand gripping the broom handle protruding from his chest. Then he dropped to his knees with a confused look on his face. Palmer let go of the handle, and when he did, Razor toppled like a field pine on a windy day.

"You stupid old man," Palmer said quietly. He looked at his assailant and shook his head. "You couldn't just let it go. You had to be a badass." He didn't know what to do now. The last thing he had set out to do this day was stab someone, yet here he was. He felt nauseous and strangely cold. "You stupid old man," he repeated to

Razor Smithfield. He sat there a moment until his breathing slowed, and then he stood. *The Old Curiosity Shop* dropped to the floor.

Palmer had a cell full of trouble and needed to think. He stepped across the cell and looked out into the corridor. Everything seemed normal. No guards were running toward the scene of the crime, no alarms were blaring, and the occupants of the cell across the way were absent. He crossed back to Razor and kneeled beside him. The old man was breathing, and his eyes were open and watery. He looked at Palmer with hatred. Palmer was inclined to help the man regardless, but he had no idea how.

"Kill you," Razor rasped. His arm flopped to the concrete floor as he appeared to lose consciousness.

"Yeah, well, you let me know how that works out for you," Palmer replied. He noticed that there wasn't much blood, and he wondered if the business end of the tool, the sixteen penny nail driven into the end of the broom handle and ground to a wicked point, had punctured anything vital in there. As he was trying to figure out the next step, he heard a noise behind him at the door. He turned in a panic, and there stood his cousin.

"What the–?" Cheddar asked. He looked confused, as if what he saw could not be reality.

"I'm glad it's you," Palmer said. "I had company while you were gone." He gestured at his handiwork.

"Did you kill him?" Cheddar's voice was a loud whisper.

"I think he's alive right now, but he doesn't look so hot." Razor stirred and moaned at the triage assessment.

"Oh, hell," Cheddar said. He leaned back out the door, looked both ways, and resumed his original position. "Oh, hell," he repeated.

"Uh-huh," Palmer replied. "I think that about covers it."

"Do you think he's dying?" Cheddar continued to stand in the door, perhaps to block the view in the cell from the prying eyes of the world.

"What am I, a doctor? He's got a homemade ice pick stuck in him all the way up to the handle. If he's not dying, he's missing a real good chance." Palmer thought that Razor probably was dying, given the location and depth of the stab wound, and he had not yet begun to form an opinion about how he felt about that. If the man died, he would be the second man Palmer had killed outright. It was getting to be a habit.

"What do you think we should do with him?" Cheddar asked.

"You're asking me? For a guy who always has an opinion about everything, you've picked a bad day to turn shy and come up stupid. I don't know what to do! You're the professional criminal in the family. I just kill people by accident. What did you do the last time something like this came up?"

"This is a first for me," Cheddar admitted. "Did you have to stab him?" He seemed obsessed with the issue of Palmer's culpability in the incident.

"I didn't stab him. He stabbed himself. All I did was hold up the knife." Palmer nodded at the plastic knife. "He was about to stick that into me." They were both quiet a moment, and then Razor broke the silence.

"Kill you," he said again. His eyes were closed, and a trickle of blood dribbled down his cheek.

"Shut up," Palmer and Cheddar said, more or less in unison, but halfheartedly, as if they were distracted. They had both heard quite enough from their guest. Razor complied, and Palmer and Cheddar further considered the overall situation. They could hear a rattle when Razor drew breath. It was a strangely forlorn sound.

"We've got to get him out of here," Cheddar finally said. "If the guards find him in here, we're sunk. You got any ideas?"

145

"Well, we could dress him up as a broom and push him down the corridor to his cell, but I have to tell you that I think we'll get caught."

"Quit being a smartass."

"Sorry. That always happens after I stab someone."

"Well, this is serious. We have got to lose Razor. How about over there?" Cheddar hiked his thumb at the empty cell across the corridor from theirs. "Humpy and Baxter are both at work. Let's drag him over there and leave him. When they get back, they can call the guards. They've both got good alibis because they're both working, so they probably won't get nailed for stabbing him. Everybody wins."

"Everybody but Razor," Palmer noted. It seemed only right to bring it up.

"Razor can bite me," Cheddar replied. "He was a lot of damn trouble standing up, and he's even more trouble laying down, and I don't like trouble. If he'd kept his ass where it belonged, we'd all be in better shape."

"Dragging him over there would be kind of a dirty thing to do to Humpy and Baxter," Palmer noted. He liked Humpy and didn't want to see him get stuck with a problem he had no part in creating. If it were just Baxter he was chunking up under the bus, things might be different. Baxter was a loudmouth from up north somewhere, and Palmer felt that the overall quality of life on the block would trend upward if Baxter spent a month or so in isolation for having a dead guy in his cell.

"They'll get over it," Cheddar said.

"There's another problem," Palmer said, "and this is sort of the deal buster. Razor's not dead. If they get him to the doc before he dies and he saves him, he might talk. If he does, that'll be my ass for sure." Razor rasped at this, as if he perhaps objected to listening to a conversation that dealt with his own immediate future and its probable briefness, but his noises were getting softer, as if he were slowly fading away. Palmer wished that the fading would go a tad quicker. Razor coughed blood, as if to indicate that he was passing on as quickly as he could manage.

"Well, then, we can't let the doc save him," Cheddar said quietly. His eyes met Palmer's, and they both knew what he was saying.

"Aw, man, I can't do something like that," Palmer said. "You want me to kill him?" He pointed at the prone Razor. "Holding up a knife for the old bastard to run into was more like a reflex. I wasn't trying to stab him so much as I was trying to keep from being stabbed." He held his hand in the same defensive position to demonstrate.

"He'd do it to you in a minute," Cheddar replied. He walked over, bent down, and picked up Razor's plastic knife. He held it up for Palmer to see, in case he had forgotten what it looked like. "Remember why we are having this conversation. Remember why he came here." He touched the point of the makeshift knife with his fingertip. "Sharp," he said.

"Believe me, I remember what he was trying to do. It's one of those things I'll never forget. But the difference between me and him is that he's a criminal and I'm just trying to serve my time the best way I can and then get the hell out of this place." He shrugged. Surely Cheddar could see that Razor Smithfield and Palmer Cray were two completely different kinds of men. At least, Palmer hoped they were.

"Serving your time the best way you can and then getting out of here means eliminating this little problem before it becomes a big problem," Cheddar said, pointing at Razor like he was a broken yard ornament. "You already mostly killed him, anyway, whether you meant to or not. You would really just be sort of finishing up what you started. Think of it as having a good work ethic. The kind that made this country great."

"I already told you no. I'm not going to do it. Putting the tool into him was different. I didn't have any choice. It was in the heat of the moment. It was self-defense. It was him or me." Palmer spoke quickly and ticked each point on a finger as he listed them.

"Calm down. I know it was. You know it was. Even he knows it was." Cheddar nudged Razor with his toe. "The question is, will the judge know it was? This could add time to your sentence. Even if it was self-defense. You know the ways of judges. There ain't a one of them that wouldn't have done the same thing if Razor had come at them, but they'll land all over you for it. You're a convict. They're not going to see this your way." That was a sad fact of prison life, and Palmer knew it. He was guilty until proven innocent, probably for the rest of his days.

"Yeah, I know," he said. "Judges suck. But I can't do it. I had to do the other thing. There was no choice. But this will be murder, and I just can't do it." He hoped it wouldn't add more time to his sentence, and he hoped his old man didn't catch too much grief over the matter, because he couldn't just kill a man in cold blood. It was quiet in the cell for a moment, and then Cheddar spoke.

"Well," he said. He looked at Palmer. "Can you at least make yourself scarce a while?"

"That I can do. Why?"

"If you can't do it, I've got to."

"There's got to be another way."

"There is no other way! If he lives, he rats you out. And even if he doesn't, sooner or later he will come at you again. If he lives, he'll get you. And if he gets you, he'll get me too." Palmer could see the logic, and he hated that he lived in a place where Cheddar's line of reasoning made perfect sense. The plan had a few flaws and might not work, but it was the only course of action that even had a chance. He nodded, giving his blessing.

"How are you going to do it?"

"My business. Take this and get rid of it." He handed Palmer the plastic shiv. "Make sure it goes away and doesn't come back. Then get back down here and help me drag Razor to a better place." Palmer accepted the weapon and turned to leave, but as he did, Razor made a choking noise. His eyes bulged, and he arched his back. He looked at Palmer, and there was panic in his gaze. He knew his time had come. He jerked once, and then he was still. Palmer had no illusions about Razor Smithfield. He had been a thoroughly bad man—trouble all of his days—and the world would be a much better place without him. But even so, it would be a long time before he forgot those desperate, fearful eyes.

"Looks like I'm off the hook," Cheddar said. "Check the corridor."

Palmer went to the door and casually looked both ways. "Clear," he said.

"Well, get over here and grab the other half."

Palmer did as he was instructed, and they were back in their own cell in less than a minute, the deed done.

"Thank God the camera got smashed, or we would have been screwed," Cheddar said as he unrolled some toilet paper from their modest supply and began to wipe up the blood. Palmer stayed on watch near the door. The remains of the camera in question hung prominently high on the wall at the end of the corridor, where until very recently it had assumedly provided a panoramic view of the comings and goings on the cellblock. It had been smashed the previous week by a new inmate named Rivers. Rivers had been prone to tears since the day of his arrival and had earned the nickname of Crimea as a result. After less than a month of imprisonment, he had gone over to the dark side and been dragged off in restraints after first destroying the surveillance device with a well-thrown copy of *Bartlett's Familiar Quotations.* He was running through the cellblock naked at the time—quoting Franklin Delano Roosevelt—and it was determined by the prison administration that perhaps Crimea Rivers was too high strung for general population.

"Sloppy luck," Palmer replied.

Once the cleaning up was completed to Cheddar's satisfaction, he and Palmer headed to the yard for some fresh air and healthful exercise after first making one small side trip to divest themselves of Razor's replacement shiv. They had left the original buried up to its wiped-down handle in Razor's chest. They figured there would be a bit of ruckus when Razor's body was discovered, but they knew that the guards would tear the prison apart looking for the murder weapon, so they left it where it was easy to find. Palmer and Cheddar lingered in the yard and discussed the details of their story right up until the alarm sounded, signaling a lockdown, at which point they knew it was time to conclude their deception.

"They'll probably question everyone on the corridor, so just be cool," Cheddar said *sotto voce* as they walked past a nervous-looking new guard posted at the entrance to their building. "Try not to act like you just killed a guy with his own knife."

"Thanks for the tip."

When they got back to their cellblock, they were greeted by the sight of most of the guards at Sweetwater State Correctional Facility, including the silent figure of the captain of the guard, Trenton Cray, who stood aloof from the crowd, taking in all the details. Razor's sheet-covered body was right where they had left it. With the knife handle sticking up under the sheet and the boots poking out the end, Razor looked as if he were asleep in a pup tent. Palmer and Cheddar were both searched before being escorted to their cell and locked in. All other residents of the cellblock received the same treatment as they returned from wherever they had been. Palmer noted that

Humpy and Baxter were not to be seen, and he hoped that Humpy, at least, didn't come to too much grief over the wayward body in his cell.

Over the next two days, Palmer and Cheddar were questioned separately and as a team. The interrogations were carried out by an investigator named Southern, who was on loan from the state police for the occasion. During the questioning, Palmer and Cheddar stuck strictly to the story they had agreed upon. They didn't know Razor. They didn't know what happened. What knife? They were in the yard when Razor met Jesus. Humpy and Baxter were good guys. Well, Humpy was, anyway. In the end, no one was called to task for the crime. The general consensus within the walls among both the inmates and the guards seemed to be that Razor was long past due, and that his luck had finally run out. No harm, no foul.

"That wasn't so bad," Palmer said to Cheddar after the cellblock had settled back to what passed for normal. "The investigation, I mean. Not the other part. We might could have just left him in here."

"Maybe," Cheddar said, looking up from the book he was reading. "But I promise you that Southern went after Humpy and Baxter harder than he came after us. It's always better to be safe than sorry."

"I guess so. I just hope it's over."

"He's dead, he's in the ground, and no one got blamed for it. How over do you need?"

"You know what I mean, I hope someone doesn't come looking to settle the score because he's dead."

"Don't worry. No one knows who did it, and no one cares that he's dead."

"Word always gets out about something like this."

"Well, if it does, you'll probably have guys chipping in to buy you a carton of Camels. Everyone I know is glad he's gone." He looked down at the book in his hands, *To Kill a Mockingbird*, and then he looked back at Palmer and held up the dog-eared copy as he quoted his favorite line, the one uttered by Heck Tate as he solved the murder of Bob Ewell.

"'I may not be much, Mr. Finch, but I'm still sheriff of Maycomb County and Bob Ewell fell on his knife.'"

"So did Razor Smithfield," Palmer replied. It seemed that it was for the best.

I know I'm in prison but sometimes it feels like I'm in a prison movie. It's like I'm watching myself be in here. Whenever something bad starts heading my way, I want to holler and tell myself to duck, but sometimes I don't see it coming in time, and when that happens I can't get out of the way quick enough. Sometimes you holler at me to look out and that helps. But sometimes you don't, so you're not as reliable as you could be. Anyway, I didn't see one coming again just the other day. I tell you, it just keeps on getting better and better in here all the time. Now I have two deaths on my hands. Yours and some old badass named Razor Smithfield. He was bad news and now he's dead news, and I promise you no one's going to cry because he's gone. I'll tell you about it but it was one of those deals where it felt like you were right there with me the whole time anyway, but I need to talk about this, and what else do you have to do but listen?

This guy Razor showed up at the prison a few weeks back, and the word on the tiers was that he was looking to fill a hole with me. He had this hard-on for me because his boyfriend had gotten himself killed down at Reidsville. Exactly! What did that have to do with me? Some people are stupid and some are mean and this guy was both. The first time he came at me was in the chow line. He tried to stab me and I busted his hand and his nose with a serving spoon. After that he was really pissed. I think the guards knew what had happened but no one was dead and they hate to fill out paperwork so they turned a blind eye. I went back to serving eggs and Razor headed off to bleed on his breakfast. I don't like to brag, but I popped that old man a good one. If he hadn't been crazy that might have ended it. But he was and it didn't.

Anyway, later on that same day he came at me again. This time it was right in my cell! Cheddar was working lunch and I was just sitting there minding my own business and reading a book when he tried it again. I had kept the knife he used at breakfast but he had another one from somewhere. He ran right at me so I stuck his old knife up, kind of protecting myself, and he ran right into it. Yeah! He ran into his own knife! He stabbed himself! That old man looked real surprised and kind of acted like his feelings were hurt, but what did he expect? I mean, Mama taught me to respect my elders and I'll do it when I can, but she didn't tell me I had to let them stab me.

When Cheddar came back from the kitchen he saw what had happened. At first he was acting sort of pissed, like he had to come back to stabbed guys laying around the cell all the time. I didn't take that to heart though. I mean, what choice did I have? After Cheddar got over his mood, we decided to drag Razor into the next cell, thinking that when the guards found him we wouldn't get blamed for sticking a tool into him if he was across the way. But the problem was that Razor was only mostly dead right then and if we left him that way he could rat me out for stabbing him or he could heal up and then come back another time for a visit, probably from behind and in the dark. Cheddar wanted me to finish him up but I couldn't do it. I really shouldn't have had any problem with the idea of sending him on home to Jesus, but I did. I guess I'm just not a killer at heart. Some of us have it and some of us don't.

So Cheddar told me to get scarce and he would do what had to be done. But Razor died just as I was leaving so it turned out that neither one of us had to put the pillow over his face. I have to tell you that I don't really know how to feel about all of this, but I do know that Razor Smithfield's not trying to kill me every time I turn around and I can live with that. We dragged him across the corridor to the empty cell. We left the shiv in him. Then we got out of there and waited for Razor to be found. About an hour later the horn for a lockdown blew and we figured that Razor had just become officially dead and would now receive his backdoor parole. We came back to our cell and there were guards everywhere. Even in a prison, finding a dead guy with a knife in him is a pretty big deal.

They locked us down and tossed all the cells. Razor's other knife was in the dumpster behind the kitchen by then and no one was going to stick their hand in there. While I was being strip searched I looked across the corridor at Humpy and Baxter locked in their cell. They were standing at the door and Humpy sort of had a grin on his face. I never did find out what he was smiling about, but I figured maybe he was glad to see Razor dead just like I was. The guards asked a lot of questions and the lockdown lasted two days, but I think pretty much everyone was happy to see Razor gone to the big barbecue, so no one ended up in bad trouble over him. My old man was there but he never said a word. He spent a lot of time looking, and I caught him looking at me a couple of times and one time he sort of raised his eyebrow. But he didn't ask and I'm not volunteering any information.

I'm glad I didn't have to finish Razor off. It's bad enough that I was holding the knife up when he ran into it. I feel different about killing him than I felt about killing you. I will be ashamed and sad the rest of my life for killing you. I didn't intend for it to happen and sure didn't want it to. But Razor had it coming and he got what he got. As bad as he was, though, I didn't expect to see him afraid as he died. I guess when it comes down to it, everyone wants to live forever and nobody wants to go. I know I don't, and I'm glad you never saw it coming. Maybe when my time comes, I'll be just as lucky. Now hurry up and read this before I tear up the pages and flush them. Sometimes the guards look through my journals when they're tossing us and I'd hate to get another twenty years for admitting in writing that I put Razor Smithfield out of everyone's misery. It needed to be done but I don't want any credit for it. I didn't do it for the bragging rights. We'll let it be our secret.

7

Happy Holidays

The first day of December was gray as a battleship and bitter as an unmarked grave. A chill had settled onto Sweetwater State Correctional Facility and clung there like a blanket of fallen snow. The cellblocks were heated, but the cells were built of cold steel, unyielding concrete, and hard time, and they held no warmth to speak of. The inmates adjusted to the chilly temperature by wearing jackets, extra socks, sweatshirts, and suits of long underwear sent from home. Some wore gloves and watch caps as well. The days were physically shorter but seemed longer, as if time itself were stretching in honor of the upcoming holidays. The fields around the prison stood forlorn and bare. They had been picked clean and deserted for the winter season, and it would be spring before they heard the rumble of the tractor and felt the bite of the harrow. Now they belonged to the deer and the crows. Clumps of mistletoe hung from the trees that gathered in the rocky island at the center of the field to the south of the prison, and hickory nuts clung to their boughs like despondent yuletide ornaments. To the north of Sweetwater, cattle stood ruminating in the pasture, silent and watchful as they considered the bleak landscape and chewed their cud. The surface of their small pond hissed with delicate ice.

Palmer sat in B-134 and worked a crossword puzzle. He was attempting to come up with a six-letter word for corrupt practices while deliberately trying to forget the fact that another Christmas would be upon them in a matter of weeks. Just as Cheddar had told him when he first arrived at Sweetwater prison, the December holidays were the worst. As Christmas neared, fights became more likely, depressions deepened, and thousand-yard stares in the common area increased dramatically. Every cell in the isolation block was occupied, either by inmates placed there for their own good or by those transferred there for the protection of others.

Palmer was not immune to these seasonal side effects, and he tried to stay as busy as possible. His mama had always believed that busy hands were happy hands, and she had raised her only son accordingly. Thus he worked the crossword puzzle even though it annoyed him. He normally avoided puzzles of all types because he wasn't proficient at solving them, but he had run out of reading material. *The Jungle* by Upton Sinclair was a surprisingly quick read, and he had finished it a full two days before his scheduled library visit. He had tried to read Cheddar's latest Regency romance in the interim but had given up after only a few pages. It simply wasn't his genre. Cheddar's taste in literature veered toward the historic, and he had taken a shine to Regency romances. He was currently reading *Sprig Muslin* by Georgette Heyer.

Palmer sighed and gnawed on the stub of his pencil. January would be along soon enough, and then they would all be safe from the perils of holidays for a while. Cheddar walked into the cell. He had been to the store to see Faro on a matter of great importance and was back to report on his progress.

"Man, it's cold outside," he said as he blew on his hands and rubbed them together. Winter weather had arrived promptly on November 1 and had made itself at home ever since. He removed his denim jacket and hung it on the hook mounted inside his locker door.

"It's cold in here, too," Palmer said. He wished they were permitted to buy space heaters for their cells, but the warden seemed to think that was a good way to get his prison burned down and did not allow it. Sweetwater wasn't very old, and when it was built, effective climate control had been around for decades, so Palmer assumed that it had been deliberately designed with cells that were hot in the summer and cold in the winter.

"What happened to this global warming I keep hearing about?" Cheddar asked.

"That's just for people on the outside," Palmer said. "They make us freeze our asses off in here because they can. It builds character, and that's a good thing for convicts. Plus, if you're worrying about how to stay warm, you don't have time to plan escapes. What's a six-letter word for corrupt practices?"

Over the long course of Cheddar's prison career, he had become a world-class practitioner of the arcane art of crossword puzzle resolution. He bent down and looked over Palmer's shoulder at the puzzle for a moment.

"Abuses," he said.

Palmer tried the word and it fit. He nodded his head.

"You never miss. When you get out of here, you ought to write crossword puzzles for a living."

"Who's your boy? I am the crossword king. I've got good news. Faro told me that he could get it. He said it would cost us twenty dollars and a pair of long johns. He said it would take him a week. He said we could wait until delivery on the twenty, but he wants the long johns as soon as he can have them. I told him to go ahead and get it coming." He dragged a sweatshirt over his head. "How are we going to pay for it? I only have three dollars, and if I give up my long handles, I'll freeze to death."

"Don't worry about it. This is my treat. It will be my Christmas present to both of us."

In addition to operating the prison store, Faro ran a small, unofficial specialty shop on the side for inmates with exotic tastes and hard cash. His partner in this enterprise was one of the cooks, a man named Cookie who worked as the courier from the outside in exchange for half the profit and virtually none of the risk. The item that Cheddar and Palmer were referring to was a pint of real, honest-to-God, made-at-a-distillery Kentucky bourbon. They had the hard cash, or at least Palmer did, and with delivery in a week, they had plenty of time to scratch up a pair of drawers. Neither man had enjoyed the taste of bonded liquor for several years. Over Mexican Radio and checkers one recent night, they had decided that it was high time to patch that hole in their lives. Their plan was simple. In fact, it had but two components. First, they would buy a pint of liquor from Faro. Then, on Christmas Eve night, they would sit in the cell, smoke Camels, eat Baby Ruths and Hershey bars, and drink their bourbon. While thus engaged, they would listen to the greatest hits of Lynard Skynard courtesy of Cheddar, who had won the CD in a poker game. It wasn't a grand plan when compared to other Christmas celebrations throughout the world, but by Sweetwater State Correctional Facility standards, it was big doings. Santa Claus was coming to town.

"Well, I did get us Lynard Skynard," Cheddar noted. He wasn't bragging, but facts were facts. While securing the musical portion of their upcoming holiday celebration, he had risked three unopened packs of cigarettes and a Hershey bar as he bluffed a busted straight.

"You did for a fact, and that's going to make it even more special. It wouldn't be the same if we had to listen to Mexican Radio

159

while we got drunk." Palmer was certain that people got drunk while listening to Mexican Radio all the time, and he wished each and every one of them well during this season of peace and brotherhood. But he was ready for some tunes he could sing along with.

"Do you think a pint will be enough to get us drunk?" Cheddar asked. There was some concern on this score. They had hoped to be able to afford a fifth or even a quart, but inflation had come to Sweetwater State Correctional Facility, and twenty dollars and a pair of long underwear didn't go as far as they used to.

"It'll have to be. All I've got is twenty dollars. It's been a long time since either of us has had a drink of hard liquor. I think a pint will put us right."

"I hope so. I need to get good and drunk and take a break from reality."

"Reality is way overrated," Palmer agreed. "What's a seven-letter word for pirate? The second letter is o."

"Corsair," Cheddar said without looking. "That's an easy one." He grabbed his blanket from his bunk and wrapped it around his shoulders. Then he picked up his romance novel and headed for the common area, where it was warmer.

"You'll get your ass kicked if you take that out there," Palmer said.

"Everyone's too cold to fight."

"Well, at least put your jacket on. The guards will give you trouble for taking a blanket out of the cell, and you look like you're wearing a shawl."

The week passed without incident, and Sunday blew in breezy and cold. Palmer began his day early with a shower and a shave. There was no set time assigned for showers on the weekend, and he had found that earlier was better when it came to accessing an adequate hot water supply. His shower was followed by a breakfast of rubbery eggs, oatmeal, and cold toast, but he ate his fill regardless because it was a long time until lunch. Then he worked a half-shift in the kitchen, first scraping and cleaning the breakfast trays, then doing the setup for the midday meal. This amounted to opening loaves of bread and hauling tubs of pimento cheese from the cooler. Cookie was working that day, and he met Palmer at the cooler and delivered the pint of Heaven Hill bourbon while Palmer was gathering up the final containers of pimento cheese. Cookie slipped the pint into the front pocket of Palmer's pants. They were quite baggy, and the bottle would not show if he put his hands in his pockets.

"Thanks," Palmer said.

"Not a problem. Glad to help. You and Cheddar have a merry Christmas." Cookie had once done some time in juvenile detention due to a misunderstanding involving a Mazda Miata owned by his former middle school principal and a gallon of black paint owned by Cookie. Thus he was sympathetic to the plights of many of the inmates. He was a kindred soul who knew just how quickly action could turn to regret.

"You want me to pay you or Faro?" Palmer asked. He had carried his little wad of twenty crumpled one-dollar bills for two days in anticipation of the handoff. The long underwear had already been delivered to the storekeeper, who had immediately slipped them on.

"Pay him. He handles the money. That's how we do it." Cookie picked up a gallon jug of mayonnaise from the wooden shelf in the cooler. Then they both stepped out to the marginally warmer kitchen.

"Can I ask you a question?" Palmer asked. Curiosity was not a desirable trait in prison, and normally Palmer did not succumb to its forbidden allure. But this particular question had been on his mind all week, and he figured he was relatively safe posing it to Cookie.

"Sure. I might not answer, but I don't mind you asking."

"You could make more money without Faro. Why do you cut him in?" By Palmer's reckoning, Cookie could make twice as much if he went solo. What he might lose in volume would be more than offset by this increased profitability.

"I've been asked that before, and I usually tell the guys who ask to mind their own business. But I'll tell you, because I think you'll understand. Faro is my uncle. He's my dead father's brother. He's family. You've got to take care of your family. You've got to help them if you can."

"That's a fact," Palmer said. He was living proof.

"He doesn't need the money so much as he needs to feel like he's still got his hand in the game. You know what I'm saying? Before he got into the jam that sent him here, he had been in business his whole life, buying and selling stuff. It didn't even matter much what it was. He was a born trader, a wheeler and a dealer. He can't live without it. It's in his blood. If I cut him out, it would kill him."

"You're a good guy, Cookie," Palmer said.

"I don't know about all that," Cookie said gruffly, warding off the compliment like a swarm of bees. He put Palmer to work hauling cases of potato chips from the back dock while he began the preparation of two thousand pimento cheese sandwiches. Once the chips were brought in, Palmer joined the assembly line with Cookie and two other men, and together they prepared the noon meal.

Palmer was released from duty at 11:00 am. He and the pint of Heaven Hill made a nervous journey back to B-block. He arrived at the cellblock to discover Cheddar lounging in the common area. Palmer gave his cousin the barest of nods, and Cheddar hopped up from his chair and joined his cellmate. They walked the final hundred feet to the cell in lockstep and entered one after the other. Palmer stepped to the back of the cell, as far from the door as he could manage.

"I've got it," he said quietly. He pulled the pint bottle form his pants pocket and slipped it into Cheddar's pillowcase as they had previously agreed. Then he arranged the pillow so that no telltale signs were visible. The owner of that bedding stood careful watch in the doorway. Because so much was at stake, Palmer would have preferred to shut the door while hiding the hooch, but it was a prison rule that only guards were allowed to open and close cell doors. All the cell doors stood open between 7:00 am and 8:00 pm unless there was a general lockdown. A closed door during that time stood out like a lighthouse on a dark, rocky seacoast. It was a smoking gun, an admission of guilt.

After the concealment was complete, Cheddar left his post at the door and fell back to Palmer's position. "What does it look like?" he asked as he sat next to Palmer on the bottom bunk. There was barely contained excitement in his voice. This was a big moment, perhaps the high point of his sentence thus far.

"It looks a lot like a pint of bourbon," Palmer said.

Cheddar nodded, as if he had known that fact all along.

"What brand did they get us? George Dickel? Ancient Age?"

"Heaven Hill."

"Heaven Hill? We gave them twenty dollars and a union suit, and they got us the cheap stuff?" Apparently it was a seller's market.

"What did you expect? That's capitalism. The less they spend on what we buy from them, the more money they make. It's the same thing they do at Walmart, except they deal in tractor-trailer loads there. The way I see it, bourbon is bourbon. The first drink will kill our taste buds. After that, it'll be smooth sailing." Palmer didn't mind Heaven Hill. It was what Houston Bibb sold at the bootlegger's, and Palmer had cut his bourbon teeth on it. "Of course, if you're too good for Heaven Hill, I'll just drink the whole pint."

"No, no, that's all right," Cheddar said. "I can't wait. Can I have first drink?" Before Palmer could answer, they heard a

163

commotion out in the common area. There were loud voices and shouts, and someone blew a police whistle. A bell clanged, which was the signal for all inmates to leave the common area, return to their cells, and wait. A con named Reeves stuck his head into their cell and explained the ruckus.

"They're tossing the cells," he whispered loudly. "Four teams, working fast. Hide it if you got it!" Then he looked back over his shoulder before continuing his journey to the cell next door, where he intended to follow his own advice and conceal his unapproved belongings.

B-block had been tossed just the previous week, so Cheddar and Palmer had thought their bourbon would be safe. Now they had a problem. The four two-man teams of guards currently tossing the cellblock had revealed the flaws in that theory, and they were in danger of being caught. Almost as if by design, there weren't that many good hiding places for a pint of bourbon inside a prison cell.

"Oh, shit," said Cheddar. "Dammit. Hide it! Hide it!"

"Settle down," Palmer replied. "I did hide it. If they come in here and see you like this, they'll know something's up."

"We need to hide it in a better place," Cheddar hissed. "They'll find it there. They always toss the pillows."

"Well, why did we hide it in the pillow?" The idea had originally been Cheddar's.

"Because we thought no one would look! Do something! They're coming!" Cheddar stood and leaned casually in the doorway to give Palmer more time. Palmer reached up into the pillowcase and removed the bourbon. Where to put it? Under the mattress? No, both mattresses would be in the floor momentarily. Maybe behind his journals? Uh-uh. The journals would hit the floor right after the mattresses did. He was considering just slipping it back into his pants pocket and hoping for the best when he had an epiphany.

Palmer laid the bottle gently in the bottom of the toilet bowl. He pulled a handful of toilet paper from the roll, wadded it, and dropped it on top of the pint. Then he stepped up to the bowl and peed on top of the basin's contents. Once finished, he zipped up and was just beginning to turn toward the door when he heard his cellmate speak.

"Good morning," Cheddar said pleasantly, just like he had nothing to hide.

"Step out," the guard said to Cheddar. "You know the drill." Palmer noted that it was Murphy. He was accompanied by a new guard, one Palmer had not seen before. The attrition rate for new guards at Sweetwater State Correctional Facility was close to forty percent, and about as many new guards arrived each month as did prisoners. "You too," he said to Palmer. "Don't take all day about it. Chop, chop."

They both stepped out and watched impassively as the pair of guards entered the cell. The new man observed as Murphy expertly patted down the blankets on both bunks before snatching them to the floor. Then he grabbed up each pillow and felt for contraband. Cheddar nudged Palmer gently. He had been correct. Murphy tossed the pillows onto the floor before flipping both mattresses. "Nothing," he said, sounding disappointed. He moved on to the lockers. He opened Cheddar's first and inspected its contents thoroughly. Then he moved on to Palmer's locker and rambled around in it. Finally he raked the tops of both lockers with his hand and inspected with interest the items he had knocked to the floor.

"It's clean," he said to the new man. Murphy turned toward the door as if to leave, but then his eye came to rest on the toilet bowl. "What the hell?" he asked of no one in particular. Palmer stiffened. "Which one of you boys needs to be toilet trained?"

"That's me," Palmer said. "I was just finishing up when you had us step out of the cell." The new guard reached for the handle.

"Leave it," Murphy said with disgust in his voice. "They don't pay us to clean up after criminals." He was shaking his head as he left. The two guards stepped to the next cell and began again. "You toss this one," Murphy said to his partner.

Palmer and Cheddar reentered their own cell and began to straighten up the mess left by the inspection. According to prison policy, they had fifteen minutes to get the cell squared away. As they worked, Cheddar looked over his shoulder at the door. Once he had satisfied himself that the coast was clear, he eased up close to Palmer and whispered to him.

"Where'd you put it?" he asked. Palmer nodded toward the toilet. Cheddar stepped over and looked in the bowl. Then he glanced at Palmer in confusion. Palmer nodded again at the commode. Cheddar picked up an empty plastic clothes hanger from the floor and probed in the bowl. Then he smiled. "You're a genius."

"I'm not a genius, but I'm smart enough to know that since I'm the one who put it in there, you're the one who has to get it out." It was a fair division of labor.

"No problem. I'd pull it out of there with my teeth if I had to."

Palmer eased over to the doorway and stood lookout while Cheddar hooked the hanger under the bottle and scooted it up the side of the toilet bowl. Then he flushed twice to rinse away the bulk of the makeshift camouflage. Finally, he picked up the Heaven Hill with his fingertips, placed it in the sink, and washed it thoroughly. After the bottle was cleaned and dried, he hid it back in his pillowcase. He sat on the chair and watched as Palmer returned from sentry duty and retrieved the last of their personal effects from the floor.

"The guards are getting cagey," he said. "Back-to-back cell inspections just a week apart? That's pretty slick. I bet they found a truckload." He found himself wondering if they should try to hide the pint back in the kitchen for a few days in case the guards decided to come back for an unprecedented third toss. It was probably a good idea, but the thought of the pint of Heaven Hill being on its own, cold and lonely in the kitchen, filled him with anxiety. He wanted it where he could see it, regardless of risk. He picked up his journals and placed them on top of his locker. The cover was completely torn from one of the notebooks, and the binding of another was ripped. "I wish Murphy would take it easy with my journals."

"They're looking for shanks," Cheddar said. There had been a stabbing in A-block the day before. It wasn't fatal, but it was apparently sufficient motivation for the guards to make an unexpected check.

"Well, they're not going to find one in a composition book."

"Those guys on A-block really piss me off," Cheddar said. "Everybody over there thinks he's the baddest ass in the prison. All they do is lift weights and fuck with each other. You know me. I believe in live-and-let-live, and if that's how they want to spend their days, that's okay by me. But this time they almost cost me my Christmas whiskey, and that brings it down to a personal level. What they need to do over there is knock it off. At least until Christmas."

Palmer agreed. Whenever an inmate misbehaved, it was hard on them all.

"We came that close to getting caught, and that's a fact," Palmer said. Although he had only had it a short while, the pint of Heaven Hill had become precious to him, like an uncut blue diamond. It represented all that was right and good in the world, and he was loath to lose it to the likes of Murphy. Apparently, though, getting drunk and listening to Lynard Skynard on Christmas Eve was meant to be. It was almost as if Baby Jesus himself was watching over the cell.

Again they heard loud voices. They sounded like they were drifting over from the next cell, the one occupied by Reeves and his cellmate, Spunk Foster. Cheddar hopped up and poked his head out to see what was going on. From where he sat, Palmer heard Murphy's voice.

"What are you looking at, Cray? Get back in your cell."

"Sorry, boss," Cheddar said. He snatched his head back in like a turtle facing off with a cat. He came back to the bunks. "They found a shank and some raisin jack next door," he said. "The shit's going to hit the fan now." Sweetwater State Correctional Facility was an equal-opportunity prison. Thus whenever contraband was found, the cell's occupants were punished equally. Normally the price paid for having illicit items in the cell was forfeiture of all privileges for a specified period. But the discovery of a weapon always guaranteed a trip to the isolation block. Knives were a big deal, and the one discovered in Reeves's and Spunk's cell would likely buy them each some time in solitary confinement.

"If I had to bet, I'd say that the raisin jack belonged to Reeves and the knife belonged to Spunk." Palmer didn't care much for Spunk Foster, but Reeves was a pretty good guy who made a nice batch of raisin jack.

"That damn Spunk," Cheddar said. "All the time wanting to be bad. All the time going to stick somebody. You know the deal. The shank belongs to both of them now. Reeves is going to have to pay the price, too. What they ought to do is put Spunk over on A-block and see how he likes that." This plan would make Spunk—an avowed and outspoken Aryan Brother—one of the few Caucasian residents of A-block, although he would not be likely to retain that address long.

"He wouldn't make it to supper," Palmer said. "They'd cut him into small pieces and mail him home."

"Too bad for Spunk. At least we'd be rid of him."

"The isolation block is full," Palmer said. "I wonder what they'll do with our neighbors." He figured they'd probably graduate a couple of the current residents early so that they could accommodate

168

Spunk and Reeves, although Palmer had seen guys transferred to different facilities over something as lethal as a knife. He hoped not, because he'd miss Reeves, although they could transfer Spunk to hell, or A-block, for all he cared. The man was trouble, and Palmer liked to avoid trouble.

"I wonder what they'll do with that raisin jack." Cheddar said. He had a taste for the illegal prison brew, and it was a long time until Christmas Eve. From next door, they heard the toilet flush. The sound was accompanied by the usual clamor of pipes in the wall.

"I guess that answers your question," Palmer said, aware of the subtle irony of the situation. If Reeves had put the raisin jack in the toilet to begin with, it might have escaped Murphy's attention.

"What a waste," Cheddar said. He sounded sad.

Out in the common area, another two-man team of guards had come over to assist with the aftermath of the contraband discovery. They could hear that Reeves was taking his medicine with quiet, resigned dignity, but Spunk was cursing the guards, their wives, their sisters, and their mamas.

"I'm not so sure I'd be pissing off the guards like that," Cheddar said. "A lot can happen to a guy while he's in isolation."

"Spunk's not too bright," Palmer replied.

"Mean, though," Cheddar said. Palmer nodded. It was a fact.

Reeves and Spunk were searched, after which they were handcuffed for the walk to isolation. They could look forward to a cavity search when they arrived at their destination, and to a sufficiency of quiet time after that. After the pair was marched off, Murphy came back into the cell with Cheddar and Palmer. He sidled over to the toilet and looked down at the clear water in the bowl.

"Now, that's better," he said. "You boys keep it that way, and we'll be just fine." Palmer nodded and Cheddar smiled. They were happy to have been of service. Murphy left, and both inmates breathed a sigh of relief. They had dodged the bullet coming and going.

"I thought I was going to die when they tossed the cell," Cheddar said. "I just knew they were going to run up on our bourbon any minute, and I didn't even know where it was."

"I thought I did a pretty good job disguising it," Palmer replied. "But I did get nutted up when the new guard made like he was going to flush the toilet. If he had hit that handle, we would have been done for." Cheddar nodded in agreement. They might not have drawn solitary time over the liquor, but they would have received other punishments, such as removal of store privileges, suspension of visitation rights, and confiscation of other personal belongings. And the worst punishment of all would have been the loss of the booze.

"We got lucky," Cheddar said. "Maybe we even had some sloppy luck."

"Maybe," Palmer said, but he was dubious. "I think sloppy luck would be more like if Murphy found the bourbon, confiscated it, put us on the chain gang, took the bottle home, had a sip, and then dropped dead because it was poisoned."

"I guess you're right. But poisoned or not, I'm drinking it."

After the excitement of the morning had come and gone, Palmer was hoping that the remainder of the day would be somewhat calmer. He and Cheddar began the afternoon with pimento cheese sandwiches and potato chips in the dining hall.

"These are great," Cheddar said as he bit into his second.

"Old family recipe," Palmer replied.

After lunch, Cheddar reported to the kitchen for two hours of cleanup duty. Palmer adjourned to the cell and his crossword puzzle. It was visiting day, and he thought perhaps Kathleen Earwood might stop by, although a visit from her was no longer the sure bet it had once been. When they had started their weekly visits, she had not missed a single Sunday for over a year. She had stepped into the weekly rotation where his mother had left off and seemed to be trying to do her best to fill Laurel Cray's role, at least as far as visitation was concerned. Since that time, however, her performance had deteriorated. At first she had begun to skip the occasional week. Then she worked up to missing two consecutive visits. He supposed she was running out of steam as most visitors did, and he guessed that eventually he would see her no more. But for now, at least, she came more times than she didn't, and Palmer enjoyed the company whenever she did. Beggars could not be too choosy, and he would take what he was offered.

Palmer had also begun to be more and more concerned over her mental state. She often seemed forgetful during their meetings, occasionally misplacing times, places, and names. Sometimes common words eluded her, and when this happened, her speech would grind to a complete halt until she could retrieve the proper noun or verb. Additionally, she had forgotten his name a couple of times recently. Once she had called him Rodney during a conversation, and as they talked he had realized that she was speaking with him as if he were her long-gone son. And sometimes she just talked nonsense, her conversation rambling this way and that like a runaway hound. Her appearance had become unpredictable as well. Some Sundays she was dressed to the nines with clothes pressed, hair done, and nails polished, while on others she was unkempt to the point of slovenliness. Palmer knew from his own experiences with the dark side that many of her symptoms could be explained by depression, and he wondered if that was indeed her malady.

At 2:00, the new guard stuck his head in the cell to tell Palmer that he had a visitor. As Palmer walked past him, he noted that the man's nametag said Llewellen. He wondered if the man was related to that pile of Llewellens who lived over by the quarry next to the Alabama state line. He certainly had the traditional Llewellen look—close-set eyes, oversized ears, flat chin—and if he was a member of that clan, Palmer had concerns about his fitness for this particular position. The Llewellens were known for their meanness, and they had a reputation for having a crazy streak on top of that. Palmer felt that the combination of these two factors made his choice of career an unfortunate one. Several Llewellens had been to Sweetwater in past years, although the guard standing beside Palmer was the only one to have ever come through the front gate in a paid capacity. It must be getting harder and harder to find prison guards, Palmer thought. Hiring a Llewellen was only a short step away from handing the keys to the prisoners and having them keep an eye on themselves.

Palmer arrived at the visiting area. It was as crowded as a Baptist church at Easter time and nearly as loud. He scanned the crowd until he spotted Kathleen Earwood. She was sitting across the room at a small table next to the door. He waved at her and caught her eye. Then he threaded his way through the space between them and sat opposite her at the table.

"Hello, Kathleen," he said.

She frowned at him for a moment. Then she smiled and took his hands in hers.

"Hello, Palmer."

"I'm glad you came today. I guess I must be getting in the Christmas spirit. It makes me want to see people." Different people, anyway. He had been seeing the same old people all day, and they hadn't done that much for him.

"I never miss a Sunday," she replied as she patted one of his hands. Her fingers felt bony, and she looked like she had lost some weight since her last visit.

"You don't miss very many, for sure," he replied. She looked confused at this, but he paid scant heed as he continued. "You look nice today."

"It's cold out," she said.

Palmer didn't see a coat. He hoped she'd hung it up in the outer room or at least left it in the car. "Maybe we'll get some snow." A little snow might even make Sweetwater prison look festive for the holidays.

"What were you saying about Christmas?" she asked. She looked at him intently.

"I was just saying that I like this time of year and that it's good to see people at Christmas. It's my favorite holiday."

"Me, too," she said. "I'll be glad when Christmas comes."

"It won't be long now," Palmer said.

Kathleen looked confused again, as if he had spoken in French or Latin. There seemed to be a slight disconnect between the conversation he was having and the one she was trying to have. She began to speak.

"Christmas," she said. "Snow. You were talking about snow. I miss the snow. I used to love when it snowed when I was small."

Palmer looked at her. She appeared to be calmly inspecting the backs of her hands as they rested on the tabletop. He thought he ought to say something, but he wasn't quite sure what that might be. "Kathleen, are you okay?" he asked.

"I am," she said. "Just fine. What were we talking about?"

"Christmas and snow."

"That's right. Christmas. I have some gifts to send you." All gifts and parcels had to be mailed rather than delivered in person so that they could be inspected, and regardless of whether they were mailed from the back side of the world or down the street, the process always seemed to take about three weeks. "I'll mail them to you this week so you'll have them in time for Christmas." She took a deep breath and smiled at him sadly. "What time is it?"

Palmer looked at the clock on the wall and told her the time.

"I haven't been here our whole two hours," Kathleen said, "but I have to go early today. My car is making a funny noise, and I have

173

an appointment with Ottis Lee Lamb over at the junkyard to look at it."

"Ottis Lee? I know him. I used to buy car parts from him all the time for my Camaro. I worked for him one summer until Mama made me quit."

"Why did she make you quit?"

"I came home smelling like cigars, and she didn't want me to smoke."

"Well, she was right about that. He still smokes those foul cigars, but he is a good mechanic. Anyway, I need to get the car seen about."

"Are you okay to drive?"

"What an odd question. I'm fine." She did seem closer to normal than she'd been at the start of the visit.

"We've had a good visit," Palmer said. "You go on. Tell Ottis Lee I said hello."

She nodded and they both stood. She gave him a long hug. "You're a good boy," she said. "Mama loves you." She released him and walked to the door. The guard opened it and let her out.

I've been here nearly seven years, and I've only got three more to go. That's if I don't screw up and get any time added on, and that's starting to look like a pretty big if. The problem is that with the way I've been acting lately, I just might screw up. Everything is irritating the piss out of me. Stuff I used to be able to let go gets on my mind now and stays there and eats away at me slow and quiet like Mama's cancer.

The other day a guard got up into my face about my shirttail and I came this close to popping him, which would have been a bad, bad mistake. I never told you that we have a dress code here? It's true. They actually have a dress code in a prison. So if I get stabbed tomorrow but I'm not dressed properly for the occasion, I could be in big trouble. They could drag me to isolation and leave me there. When we're outside of our

174

cells, we have to be wearing an undershirt and our denim outer shirt has to be buttoned up and tucked in. We're some of the best dressed convicts in the country. If they weren't worried about guys hanging themselves they'd probably have us in neckties too.

It's all about who is in charge. They make us do it because they can. Cheddar says he has been at other prisons where they don't care what you wear as long as you're dressed in something. The thing is, I've never had a problem with the dress code before and I don't really have a problem with it now. It's a shirt. Who cares about a shirt? If they want it tucked in, they can have it tucked in. If they want me to wear it like a turban I can do that too. I actually have more of a problem with wearing the T-shirt all the time. In the winter it's okay because it's cold on the cellblock, but it gets hot in here between April and September. Sometimes by the end of the day I have to wring out both my shirts and hang them up to dry.

Anyway, I was on my way to the kitchen to work my breakfast shift. I was in a hurry because that bunk had felt pretty good and I'd gotten an extra five minutes so I was still tucking my shirt into my pants as I left the cell. Llewellen had opened the cell door and was standing out in the common area twirling his stick. When I came out, he was all, like— Cray, get that shirt tucked in. I just stopped walking and stood in place. I swear it was almost like he had backhanded me. I was obviously tucking it in, but he was screwing with me anyway. I mean, my hand was stuck down in my pants. What did he think I was doing? Playing with my dick? I wanted to take that stick from him and tune him up with it. He was every guard who had ever given me trouble and I wanted to take him down.

Llewellen just loves being a prison guard. He's never going to quit. He'll still be here when Cheddar goes home, I guess. They'll probably let him move in when he retires and bury him out back when he dies. They had him over in A-block for a while, until three of the inmates jumped him one Saturday night. They took away his radio and beat him *unconscious with it. The whole prison got locked down for five days, because it looks really bad when a guard gets beat up, and especially when one gets it as bad as Llewellen did.*

Those three guys over in A-block all drew extra years and got split up. One's at Reidsville now, and the other two are at Augusta and Savannah. Still, I bet they think it was worth it. Whacking a guard with his own radio is big news in here. Those guys are famous now, like Elvis or someone. They're heroes. But they're not in so great with the guards, and you can bet they're still catching hell about it, even though they're at different prisons now. That all happened a while back, and Llewellen was out on medical leave for a couple of months. The odds were five-to-two against him coming back at all. I had a pack of Camels riding on him just hanging it up and staying home with Mrs. Llewellen and the kids, drawing a nice check every month. But he cost me that pack of smokes when he decided to come back in just enough time to tell me that my shirttail wasn't tucked in quick enough to suit him.

When he told me to get myself tucked in, it was like I felt something tear in my brain. I could actually hear a ripping sound. I started to turn around. I was in motion, and I was going to let him have it. It was time for a Llewellen sandwich. It was thump day and I had him in my sights. Then the strangest thing happened. For once in his life, he had the sense to see what was coming. He saw that I was pushed one step too far. And then he threw me a bone. He actually saved me. He said—Think about it, Cray. *He could see what was about to go down. Maybe those boys in A-block beat some sense into that thick Llewellen head. And now I owe him one. It's a hard thing to owe a Llewellen.*

Cheddar says I've got a bad case of the seven-year itch. That's what they call it when you've been here for a while and the place starts getting to you. It doesn't always have to be seven years but for some reason it usually is. Everything gets on your nerves. I've only got three years to go, but I am fed up with this place right now. The sameness is starting to get to me. I am running out of steam. I hate the cell. I hate the food. I hate my job. I am tired of Cheddar. Mexican Radio sucks. I have read every single book in the library, and now I am starting to read them all over again.

I'm packed in with seven hundred guys, but I feel alone. Three years left is better than ten years left, but I still have a long way to go before I get out of here. I officially do not care about anything anymore, and that's dangerous. Look at Llewellen. There was no way to win if I'd confronted him, but I was about to anyway because I didn't care. And I didn't really even make a decision to do it. It was just sort of happening. I'll have to keep an eye out for that, or I'll find myself doing the full fifteen plus maybe a little extra for bad behavior, and some of that will be in isolation. The seven-year itch is bad, for sure, but a case of the fifteen-to-twenty-year itch would kill me dead.

8

Cheddar's Liver

Time passed as slowly as a glacier receding over a scarred landscape, but it did pass, and eventually Palmer found himself well into his seventh year of captivity. He had survived his bout with the seven-year itch without serious harm, although his successful navigation of that impediment had been due in large part to luck rather than skill, which is often the way of the world. He was prone to the occasional attitudinal relapse when the planets aligned just so, but he somehow managed not to be in the wrong place at the wrong time most days and thus avoided many situations that might have brought his demeanor to the attention of the authorities. And during the few instances when he might have fallen afoul of a guard regardless of his intentions or luck, the gods of human incarceration had placed Cheddar there as a buffer to help him during his time of travail.

Cheddar had undergone similar itchy periods on two separate occasions during his own prison career, and he understood what Palmer was going through. More important, he had learned the coping skills necessary to hold at bay and eventually defeat the seven-year itch when it reared its prickly head, and these he was more than willing to share. So Cheddar mentored his cellmate on the exceptionally fine arts of turning the other cheek and letting the sleeping dog lie. He instructed him on the skill of disregarding what he could not change and swallowing down what he could not vent. These were lessons well taught and learned, and they were put to good use on the morning when Palmer's seven-year fever broke and he was finally able to lay the demons to rest.

"This is harassment," Palmer had said on that occasion. They were standing in the common area while Murphy and a new guard tossed their cell. It was 9:00 on a Saturday morning. The two guards were nosing around for whatever they could find, looking for serendipitous swag. Traditionally, the guards and the inmates both liked to slack off a bit on the weekends and take a break from the general insanity of the prison experience. This meant that weekend tosses were almost unheard of unless there had been an escape attempt or an assault with a weapon. Since there had been neither during the past week, Palmer felt that the current Saturday fishing expedition was nothing more than a blatant intrusion into his private space. There were people in his home throwing his possessions onto the floor, and it was rubbing him raw on principle. It was simply uncalled for. How would the pair in the cell feel if he went to their homes and did the same? If it weren't for the multiple strands of razor wire, the towers staffed with armed corrections officers, and the attack dogs between him and the guards' houses, Palmer was tempted to try, just to see how they liked it.

"I can't argue with you there," Cheddar said. "It is bullshit for sure." He hadn't been awake long and looked scruffily unperturbed. He spoke in a prison whisper that only Palmer could hear. Over the years the pair had come to be able to communicate so quietly with one another that it was almost as if they were psychic. Even his shrug was perceptible only to Palmer. "But what can you do? Maybe he's teaching the new bull how to shake down a cell while it's quiet."

"There you go putting a positive spin on things again," Palmer said with lips that barely moved. "They're doing it because they've just got to be screwing with someone all the time. That's the only reason." The inspection should have been no big deal because they had no serious contraband in the cell, but Palmer was coming to a slow boil over what should have been a routine occurrence.

"It's not worth it," Cheddar said. "Let it go. They'll be gone in a few minutes, and no harm done. Just settle down."

"What's not worth what?" Palmer asked. He watched as Murphy turned Cheddar's pillow out of its pillowcase before throwing both items onto the floor. He stepped on the pillow as he moved to the lockers.

"Running your mouth at the guards is what. Don't play dumb with me. You know exactly what I'm talking about. Take a deep breath and calm down. Try counting to ten."

In the cell, Murphy swiped his hand across the top of a locker and raked Palmer's journals into the floor. He looked Palmer's way with a mischievous grin. Palmer gritted his teeth. His hands made fists at his sides. There was no need to treat his belongings that way. Cheddar had seen the swipe and the grin. He nudged Palmer in the ribs and elaborated on his advice.

"He's playing with you now, boy. He knows you're on a short fuse. Don't let him win. Count to ten like I told you. My mama always used to tell me that I should count to ten when I felt myself getting mad at somebody. She said it would keep me from saying things I didn't mean and doing things I'd regret."

"Thanks for sharing that," Palmer said. "Your mama was a smart woman. Maybe you should've listened to her and counted to ten before you got that tattoo." It was a cheap shot and Palmer knew it, but he needed to lash out, and unlike Murphy, Cheddar was not likely to thump him with a baton and throw him into isolation.

"I wasn't able to count at all when I got the tattoo," Cheddar replied, oblivious to the jibe. "And I'm serious as the AIDS about this. You need to pay attention to what I'm saying. You're standing here getting pissed because they're tossing the cell. Don't try to tell me you're not. I know you better than anyone, and I've been in your shoes besides. The unfairness of it all is just killing you. But if you run your mouth, Murphy will tie you up nine ways from Sunday. He's just looking for an excuse, anyway. Look at him. Stepping on my pillow? Throwing your books in the floor? You know what that's about. He knows he's getting under your skin. If you give him the chance, he'll be thumping on that head for you. Then he'll thump me because I share a cell with you. I don't feel like getting thumped. It hurts. So just choke it on down, count to ten, and keep your lips pressed together before you get us both into trouble. I don't need to be on Murphy's hit list and neither do you. Now count."

"This is stupid," Palmer said.

"Count."

Palmer hesitated. Then he began a slow count in his head. When he got to ten, he took a deep breath.

"There," he said. "I counted." Strangely enough, he didn't feel quite so outraged. Perhaps Cheddar and his long-lost mama were on to something with the counting. Had she counted to ten before she climbed into that Kenworth? Palmer suspected she had, and then had gone anyway. There were some things that counting couldn't fix. But Palmer felt a bit better. He would still like to meet Murphy on the outside some fine Saturday morning for a nice long chat about the importance of respecting others' belongings. After their talk he'd like to throw all of his stuff into the floor and then thump him if he acted like he had a problem with it. But it could wait. Life was long, and

Palmer was patient. He had all the time in the world. Murphy's time would come, and Palmer planned to be there when it did.

"Good," Cheddar said. "Did it help? Are you calmer now? Sometimes you have to do it twice. I knew a guy once who counted to a hundred. Everyone thought he was retarded or deaf when he didn't answer them, but he was just counting."

"It helped a little. I don't think I'll count to one hundred. But they still don't have the right to treat our stuff that way." He nodded at the pair in the cell.

"Sure they do. They have the right to do whatever they want. This is a prison, and we're prisoners. They're guards. They got hired in the first place because they like to screw around with people. There's a question on the application that asks: Do you like to fuck with people?"

"No there's not."

"I swear to God it's true. I've seen it. And if you answer *no*, you're out. They might let you work in maintenance or in the office, but you're not getting a job as a guard." Cheddar made a slight gesture in the direction of the cell. "This particular set of guards gets paid to screw with us, and look what a fine job they're doing. Their yearly bonus is probably based on how well they do it. These two are up for raises, I bet. Just remember that part of messing with us is messing with our stuff. It's not like you've never had your cell tossed before, and there's nothing in there to worry about, anyway. All of our good stuff is hidden in the kitchen. So this inspection is no big deal. It doesn't matter. Don't make something out of nothing. Guys like us can't afford to get pissed on general principle. We'll come out on the losing side if we do. If we get pissed off, we'll get pissed on. Now, here they come. Keep your mouth shut and your eyes down."

Meeting a guard's gaze was considered to be an aggressive stance, and as such, there was a rule against it. An inmate could draw punishment for the act up to and including isolation. Murphy and the new guard stepped out into the common area. Palmer took a quick glance as the new one walked past him. She looked to be in her late twenties or early thirties. She was a big, muscular woman with short brown hair and an abundance of freckles on her arms and nose. Her name tag bore the name Curtin.

"You boys are clean," Murphy said, as if they hadn't already known that fact. He grabbed his belt on each side of his buckle. "Now hop in there and get that cell put back together. I want it squared away in fifteen minutes. Chop, chop." He clapped his hands twice as he spoke.

"Right, boss," Cheddar said. He began to chop.

The two guards stepped to the next cell, the one occupied by Reeves and a new boy who went by the name of T-bone. T-bone was a young and promising car thief, and Cheddar and Palmer believed with all their hearts that he was a vast improvement over his predecessor, Spunk. Spunk had been transferred to Hays State Prison up in Chattooga County after assaulting a fellow inmate with a basketball as they were both on the way back from the exercise yard. The pair had been chatting about the contested outcome of a recently completed basketball game, and they apparently were unable to arrive at unity of opinion concerning the results of that contest. The guard was standing a mere five feet away when the assault occurred, but Spunk had jumped on the guy anyway. He was one of those inmates who had no truck with consequences, which was the main reason why Cheddar and Palmer both liked T-bone much better than they had liked Spunk. He seemed much less prone to maim one of them, or to frail away with a basketball on the basis of a lost bet or even a mere whim.

Palmer followed Cheddar in and helped him reassemble their home. Cheddar reinstalled the mattresses on the bunks and made the beds while Palmer retrieved their scattered belongings and repacked the lockers. They had performed this ritual many times before, and their moves were economical and sure, like robotic devices on an assembly line. In less than ten minutes, everything except Palmer's frame of mind was shipshape and as good as new.

"How about a cup of coffee?" Cheddar asked in an accommodating tone. He had already taken the hot pot to the sink and was filling it. "A good hot cup of Joe will help us take our minds off our troubles."

"I don't know."

"I've got canned milk." Cream in their coffee was a luxury usually saved for birthdays and holidays. Cheddar was hauling up the big guns in an attempt to make his cellmate feel better about the ragged start to their day.

"I guess some coffee would be good, at that," Palmer said. His cellmate had persuaded him with the canned milk, as he had known he would.

"That's the spirit. I've got a package of Vienna Fingers, too." Vienna Fingers were their second-favorite treat, lagging only slightly behind Oreos. Honey buns brought up the rear of the prison trifecta of sweets.

"You know what?" Palmer asked in a conversational tone.

"What's that?"

"I just hate it when he says chop, chop." Murphy was still stuck in Palmer's craw like a fish bone, and it would apparently take more than canned milk and Vienna Fingers to hack him up.

"Damn it!" Cheddar said. He sounded frustrated. "For Christ sakes, let it go, will you? I thought we were going to have some coffee and chill out. Murphy's an idiot. He's been saying that since the day he hired in to this place. I wish I had a dollar for every chop I've heard. He probably says it at home to his wife before he screws her. He probably says it to his kids before he sends them to school. Hell, he probably says it to his dog when he throws him a bone. I've heard

184

him say it to some of the other guards, too. Why would you let it bother you now?" He shook his head in exasperation.

"It just does." Palmer shrugged.

"That's because you're letting it. You're letting Murphy and the rest of them get away with you. You're out of control."

"So you're telling me that you like it when the guards screw with us?" Palmer asked. His tone was belligerent.

"What I like doesn't even begin to come into it. We're so far away from what I like that you can't even get there from here. What I like is in a whole other universe. Over there they have women with big boobs, and they have beer, and TV, and air conditioning. Over there I don't have to use the john in front of my cousin or take showers with guys who like what they see. But in this world, I'm a state prisoner, and here I've got jack. They can pretty much do whatever they want to me—including killing me—and get away with it. I don't get to have a say, and it doesn't matter what I like. The only way it could be any worse is if I was a state prisoner in Texas, or maybe Mississippi. Or if I was doing time in some federal pen. That's just how it is. And you're sitting right here beside me and know the deal just as well as I do. Now, you need to knock this off. I mean today. As in right now. Get your ass off your shoulders. I'm serious. Murphy always says chop, chop. It's just something he says. He probably doesn't even know what it means. It's nothing to get bent out of shape over. Neither is any of the other stuff that's been getting under your skin. There isn't anything you can do about any of it except get yourself in trouble." He plugged in the pot and fetched their mugs plus two packets of instant coffee from his locker.

"Well, I wish he'd stop."

"You know, maybe if you wish just a little bit harder, he'll stop. Be sure to close your eyes tight and cross your fingers. Hey, I've got a quarter hidden in my shoe. If you want, you can throw it in the john and make your wish."

"Smartass," Palmer said.

"Dumbass," Cheddar replied. "I guarantee you one thing."

"What?"

"Letting Murphy know that something he does is pissing you off is not the way to get him to lay off. If you think he says it too much now, just let him know how much it bothers you. It'll be chop, chop city then, for sure. Chop, chop this and chop, chop that. That's the kind of guy he is. He was trying to piss you off this morning, and you almost took the bait. What you have to do is ignore it when he pulls that crap, just like you always have. It doesn't mean anything." Cheddar poured the contents of the coffee packets into the cups. Then he continued with Palmer's attitude adjustment.

"No matter what you do, he's not going to stop saying it. And the guards are not going to stop tossing the cells. And Llewellen or someone else just as stupid is always going to rag you about your shirt. And some new guy is always going to try to get over on you. Those are just the facts of life! Listen to me. You've let yourself get into the habit of being pissed off at every little thing. It happens to everyone in here after a while, so you're not even special. But it's a luxury you can't afford. So far you haven't gotten into any scrapes, but that's because you're lucky and because I've still got your back. But you are cruising for a bruising. You're asking for it, and you're going to forget yourself one of these times, and then there'll be the devil to pay. You'll have your privileges taken away. They'll stick you in isolation. They'll add more time to your sentence. If I hadn't been standing beside you this morning, you probably would have done it right then. I'm telling you, you can't win. There's no end to all the crap they can do to you, and there's a world of hurt waiting for you when they do."

"I can't help how I feel."

"You can go tell that to Morris, because I don't want to hear it. You can help it, and you'd better start. You're not some scared kid

186

anymore. You have made your bones. You're a grown man who has survived seven years in a Georgia state penitentiary. If you can do that, you can do anything you put your mind to. So don't tell me you can't help it. You can help it if you want to. Plus, you're not nearly bad enough to be acting all big and tough all the time."

"I can take care of myself," Palmer said defensively.

"You're not going to like this, but I'm going to say it anyway, because you need to hear the truth. There are some bad people in here, and you're not one of them. That's just the truth. You stick up for yourself all right, but when it comes to B-A-D bad, you're not. I'm badder than you are, and there are still about two hundred good old boys in here who scare the shit out of me. So you need to back down and ease up. Because if you don't chill out, then one of two things is going to happen. Either a guard is going to take a notion to tune you up, or else some inmate who thinks you got smart with him will."

"But—"

"But nothing. I'm telling you to knock it off. Notice I didn't say I'm asking. I said I'm telling. If you won't think about yourself, think about me. When you bring down that whole mountain of trouble, it won't just bury you, you know. It'll get all over me, and probably all over Reeves and T-bone. Some of it's bound to get on your old man, too. Everything you do in here involves him."

Palmer considered Cheddar's words. It was true that he had been in a funk. It was a fact that he had been popping off at fellow inmates and staring at guards, and that both actions were different recipes for the same sort of disaster. He supposed a case could be made that he had been looking for trouble, at least on a subconscious level, and that if he wasn't careful, he was going to get what he was looking for. Perhaps Cheddar was giving sound advice. Stranger things had happened in the history of the world. Palmer decided to give easing up an earnest try. Maybe Cheddar's count-to-ten method would be effective. If not, he could try twenty. After that, he'd just have to see what he saw.

"You might be right," he said. "I'll try get back to where it all just rolls off me." Today was the first day of the rest of his sentence.

"I know I'm right. And don't just try to get there. Get there. Trying is for losers. Doing is for winners." Cheddar passed a steaming mug of coffee to his cellmate. He had split a third packet of grounds between the two cups so that the brew was good and strong.

"I thought we were having cream," Palmer said. He took an appreciative sip.

"We might have cream tonight, if you chill out in the meantime. We'll just have to wait and see how that goes. But the Vienna Fingers are off the table." Cheddar did not reward foolishness in others, although he was often blind to the trait in himself.

"What did you think about the new guard?" Palmer asked, changing the subject in an attempt to comply with Cheddar's wish that he let his ire go. He declined to comment on Cheddar's withholding of the canned milk and the Vienna Fingers, which was an attempt at behavior modification, Sweetwater style. "Her name is Curtin."

"Are you kidding me?" Cheddar asked. He took a loud slurp of his coffee. "What did I think of her? I think I'm in love! Did you see the titties on that girl? If Murphy hadn't been standing there, I would have thought I had died and gone to heaven." Curtin's bosom had indeed been ample, and her uniform was cut in such a manner as to prominently feature her badge on her left breast, like an official State of Georgia pasty. "If she was my woman, I'd never leave the house again."

Curtin's bosoms were not the topics that Palmer wished to discuss. He had a larger issue on his mind.

"Didn't you think it was kind of odd that they let a female corrections officer walk a beat down here in the cells?" It had struck

Palmer as a strange and unwise choice. There had always been female guards at Sweetwater State Correctional Facility. At any given time, fifteen to twenty percent of the officers at the prison were women. It was an equal-opportunity bad job that chewed up and spat out men and women at about the same rate. But today was the first time in seven years that Palmer had seen a female patrolling in the cellblock. He thought it was a questionable idea, and dangerous for Curtin's sake.

"I don't know why they decided to put her in here," Cheddar said. "But all I can say is, it's about time they did. They ought to get us a redhead and a blond, too. We live in a fine country, and I'll cut any man who says different. I'd give a hundred dollars just to go out on a date with her."

"You don't have a hundred dollars," Palmer said. "All you have is a quarter in your shoe."

"She doesn't know I don't have a hundred dollars," Cheddar said. "And she won't know unless you tell her. Man, did that backside look fine, or what?"

"Any backside would look good to you," Palmer said. "If my mama was still alive, you'd probably be checking out hers on visiting day."

"Aunt Laurel did have a nice butt for a mature woman," Cheddar said. "Bless her heart." This was not quite the reaction Palmer was expecting.

"Watch it," he said. "That's my mama's butt you're talking about."

"Sorry," Cheddar said. He shrugged as if to indicate that the pleasing roundness of Laurel Cray's now-defunct fanny had not been his fault in the least, even though it was apparently his problem. "I swear I meant no disrespect." He clasped his hands and bowed his head in an attempt to demonstrate his regard for his departed aunt.

"I'm sure she appreciates the compliment if she's listening in," Palmer said. "But getting back to Curtin, I think it's crazy that she has been given cellblock duty. Yeah, yeah, you're in love with her. I get it." Palmer held up his hands to ward off further commentary about Curtin's various assets. "My point is that I guarantee you're not the only person drooling all over the floor when she walks by. She's locked in here with 700 guys who haven't been laid recently. Some of them haven't gotten lucky since Nixon was president. And I'm talking about the first time he was president. Putting her in here is like locking a glass of sweet tea in a room with 700 thirsty, violent diabetics. Someone's going to be tempted to try to sneak a drink before it's over. You wait and see. If I was the warden, I'd be worried about her safety. If I was Curtin, I'd be worried about my own safety. Even with Murphy in here with her, something bad could happen to her. Things could get out of control. Hell, *especially* with Murphy in here with her, something could happen." Murphy rubbed people wrong. It was his way, and there was no getting around the fact.

The guards always patrolled the cellblocks in pairs, and there was video backup on top of that, because what had happened to Llewellen was not an isolated incident. Corrections officers and inmates squared off fairly often, and every year more and more guards in the prison system were assaulted and injured. Guard duty was no walk in the park. It was tedious and dangerous work for not a great deal more than minimum wage. Palmer wasn't sure why anyone would even want the job, and even though Curtin looked like she could take care of herself, he wondered why she had made the decision to walk out into harm's way.

"I have to admit you don't see women in the blocks too often," Cheddar said. "But I have seen it before. We had one down at Arrendale. Now, that was a mean woman." There was a mixture of deference and admiration in his tone, as if he were a gladiator referring to a highly respected foe. An image of Bay-Annette came to

Palmer's mind. She was one mean woman, as well, and she didn't even get paid to be. Maybe Cheddar liked them that way. Perhaps it was the element of risk that excited him, the chance of injury or death.

Cheddar continued. "Her real name was Masters, but we all called her Thumper. I'll let you figure out why. The word on the tiers was that she was a lesbian who hated men, but I think that was a bunch of crap. She actually was a lesbian, which was such a damn waste if you ask me, but she hated everybody. If she even thought you were checking her out, you'd find yourself sitting in an isolation cell for a week or two with a knot the size of a softball on the side of your head." His right hand meandered of its own accord to his temple and rubbed a spot there in fond remembrance. She had apparently made a believer of Cheddar. "She was one you didn't have to worry about, though. No one in their right mind was ever going to mess with her. She could have walked through the cellblock naked, and guys would have looked the other way." Then Cheddar had a thought. "I didn't see a wedding ring on Curtin's finger. Do you think she dates ex-cons?"

"I'm betting not. There's probably a rule against it. There is against everything else." Or there might not be, Palmer thought. It could be one of those situations that no one thought would ever come up.

"You're probably right. I can just see the warden coming down against it. It's easy for him to be particular, though. He's got a woman. He's probably got two."

"Well, someone has to take up the slack while we're out of circulation," Palmer said. Cheddar nodded and sighed at the unfairness of a system that would allow wardens to have abundant female companionship but would deny that same boon to a few deserving inmates. It just wasn't right.

"Screw the warden," Cheddar said after a moment. He had reached a decision. "I think she's hot, and I'm going to ask her for a date when I get out of here. Do you think she'll wait for me? I've only got sixteen more years to go." The time would pass before he knew it.

"You've got Bay-Annette waiting for you. She's enough of a woman for any man. She might even be enough of a woman for two men."

"Bay-Annette's probably waiting for me with a gun," Cheddar clarified. His errant hand gravitated from his temple down to his chest, to the unfortunate body art that had brought so much woe into his young, promising life. "Besides, I'm through with her."

"Twenty-five years is a long time," Palmer said. "Surely she'll have gotten over that tattoo by the time you get out. And don't you think it would break her heart if you showed up with Curtin? The last thing you want to do is break Bay-Annette's heart. Not if you ever want to sleep again, anyway." Palmer was pretty sure that he wouldn't want to get anywhere near a woman who had sent him up for a quarter of a century, but to each his own, he supposed. Seven years in jail had taught him not to judge, lest he be judged.

"She does take disappointment hard," Cheddar said. "And she doesn't like women whose chests are larger than hers. If Amber had little ones, I probably wouldn't be here now." He stopped speaking as if he were giving his last statements some consideration. Then he continued. "But again, I'm done with her."

"Nonsense. She's your wife. She's the mother of your boy."

"No, really. And even if I was interested, she wouldn't wait."

"She'd never do that to you."

"Twenty-five years is a long time. Women have needs, too, you know. It's like with Vienna Fingers. If you get used to having a Vienna Finger every day, you develop a taste for them."

Palmer nodded. He knew just what Cheddar meant.

"We ought to have one right now," he said.

"This is serious," Cheddar said. "Once you've got the taste, if someone takes the Vienna Fingers away, you get to missing them. After a while, Vienna Fingers are all you can think about. They're all you want."

"So you think Bay-Annette is pining away for a Vienna Finger?"

"I know it for a fact. She's bound to be." He looked conspiratorial for a moment. Then he leaned close and shared a confidence. "She loves Vienna Fingers, and I don't want to sound like I'm bragging, but I have really good Vienna Fingers."

"I'll take your word for it," Palmer said. Seven years of close proximity and too much information made for a bad combination. "Forget the Vienna Fingers for a minute. I guarantee you that she'll be waiting for you. You two are a match made in heaven. No one would ever dream of taking her away from you." At least, not anyone who knew her, Palmer thought. "Plus, even if she just had to sneak in a cookie or two in the meantime, they wouldn't be as good as the real thing. You said so yourself. It'd be like she was eating the store brand." Cheddar appeared to think about this analogy a moment.

"Look," Palmer said, "when it gets to be time for you to get out of here, don't even let her know you're coming. Just head on over and walk in unexpectedly, like you own the place. Which you do. That way she won't have time to plan anything, like loading her pistol or moving away. Surprise is your ally. It can only be good news for you. I think you should plan on taking along a coffee can as a peace offering. They always seem to put her at her ease. That's the way you want her. Nice and relaxed." Bay-Annette loved coffee cans better than raccoons loved garbage.

"She does like to get her hands on a coffee can," Cheddar admitted. Bay-Annette had been back to see him three times since the fateful day when he had capitulated and sent her to dig up a Sanka can in the interest of peace in the family and their son's

193

continued good health. Now she was into him for a Hills Brothers, a Maxwell House, and a Folgers as well. Each time she sought financial succor from her husband, she had a good reason to do so, and each time she left, she had a twinkle in her eye, a spring in her step, and the directions to another burial site tucked into her bra. At the current rate of consumption, Cheddar might have one last coffee can left to bear before him as a peace offering when the time came to reunite with Bay-Annette. "I just can't say no to the bitch," he admitted. "She's running through my money like General Sherman ran through Georgia on the way to the sea, and I'm letting her do it."

"She is your wife, though, and the mother of your child," Palmer pointed out. "It's sort of like you're taking care of your family." He believed that if he had a wife and son on the outside, he would try to support them if he possibly could. He was certain that at the very minimum, he would keep the coffee cans coming for as long as they lasted. Of course, if he did have a wife on the outside, it wouldn't be Bay-Annette, so he could afford to be noble of intent and magnanimous of thought. It was easy to call them from the cheap seats.

"That argument would carry a lot more weight with me if she hadn't turned me in to the law in the first place," Cheddar noted.

"You could be right," Palmer admitted. As far as potentially unfixable marital difficulties went, sending a spouse to prison for a quarter of a century had to be well to the right-hand side of the bell curve. Getting over it could be a problem.

"I may change my mind, but right now I feel like these twenty-five years will always be between us."

"Something like that would be hard to get over," Palmer agreed.

"Of course, I'd still like to screw her again."

"Well, naturally." It went without saying.

"I had intended to live out my life with what was in those cans," Cheddar said. "At this rate, though, it looks like I'm going to have to get a job when I get out."

Regardless of whatever else Cheddar's prison sentence might have accomplished, it had instilled in him a sense of abject fear and penitent shame with respect to his previous career as a dealer of methamphetamine. As his years in Sweetwater had dragged by, he had grown ashamed of what he had once done for a living. He carried a burden of guilt for the lives he had helped ruin and the pain he had caused, both to his customers and to his family. At the same time, he had come to be extremely fearful of ever again making or dealing meth, lest he once more fall afoul of the law—or, worse, Bay-Annette—and have to come back to prison for the remainder of his natural time. This fear extended to all manner of other illegal activities as well. So if his coffee can fund ran out as it seemed destined to do, he was going to have find some honest work. Cheddar had never before labored in the traditional sense of the word, and the prospect of having to do so when he got out was unsettling.

"A job's not so bad," Palmer said.

"Easy for you to say."

"Well," Palmer said, trying to improve Cheddar's mood, "you're getting to be a pretty good cook. I've seen you scramble eggs for seven hundred inmates. Maybe the Waffle House will give you a shot. Even late on Saturday nights when all the drunks are hungry, you won't have to cook for seven hundred." Palmer tried to imagine Cheddar feeding seven hundred hungry drunks in a Waffle House on a rowdy Saturday night and found that he could not. The scene was too incomprehensible, the concept too surreal.

"I don't want to work at the Waffle House," Cheddar replied.

"Well, then, how about at Denny's?" he asked. Maybe Cheddar would be happier in a classier setting, one in which the seats in the booths were upholstered.

"Denny's? You want me to go work at a Denny's? That'll be lots better. Thanks." He shook his head. He had arrived at a low point. "Just kill me now," he said.

"First you have to tell me where the rest of the cans are buried," Palmer replied. There was no use in both of them having to hire on at Denny's.

The rest of that year passed and became another, and in the spring of 2007, Palmer became aware of Cheddar's illness. He probably would have noticed it earlier if they had been separated from each other for any length of time at all, but they were constantly in one another's company. They lived together, they worked together, and they ate and slept together. Under those circumstances, gradual changes in appearance and demeanor were hard to spot. So when Cheddar first began to be tired all the time, Palmer just thought he needed to get more rest and perhaps to take some vitamins. When Cheddar complained of feeling achy all over, Palmer assumed that he—like about twenty other inmates on B-block at the time—had a lingering case of the flu and advised him to take a couple of aspirins and call him in the morning. When Cheddar began to pick and nibble at his food, Palmer chalked it up to the lack of variety if not carbohydrates in the prison fare. And when Cheddar developed a tremor in his hands, Palmer believed it to be a nervous tic, one of an infinite variety exhibited by many of their prison mates, an occupational hazard associated with being a professional felon in a violent and unpredictable setting. Thus it was only in retrospect that the gravity of these symptoms was brought home to him. Palmer's hindsight turned out to be twenty-twenty, although in point of fact it wouldn't have done either man a great deal of good even if Palmer had managed to stitch together a diagnosis much earlier. What Cheddar had was hard to treat and impossible to cure.

"You're yellow," Palmer said to Cheddar as he walked into the cell. He had been working the early shift in the kitchen and was now returned from that duty to retrieve his cellmate for breakfast. They were planning to eat in the kitchen with the cooks, where the extra bacon roamed free, and where fresh coffee flowed like spring water from a hillside.

"I'm as brave as anyone in here," Cheddar replied. "Braver than T-bone." T-bone was having adjustment issues and had developed the habit in recent days of softly crying late into the night. They heard him fairly frequently after lights out, along with Reeves's occasional *T-bone, for Christ's sake, will you go to sleep?*

"No, I mean you are actually yellow in color. There's a word for that. What is it?" Palmer tapped his forehead while he thought for a moment. Then he snapped his fingers as his Sweetwater High School education kicked in and the word came to him. "You're jaundiced."

Their window faced the east, and the morning light as it streamed in had caught Cheddar in profile and frozen him there. He looked just like an actor who was standing in a yellow spotlight. Actually he was more beige than yellow, the color of a manila envelope, a sickly shade that was oddly complementary to his teeth. His eyes, however, were as yellow and feral as those of a hungry winter wolf at the rise of the full moon. It wasn't a good look for him. The skin color reminded Palmer of the time years ago when his mother had bought a first-generation tube of sunless tanning lotion and had conscientiously rubbed the substance on in the name of beauty until she bore a fair likeness to a summer squash. As for the eyes, well, they were just plain creepy, even allowing for the fact that they were Cheddar's.

"Bull," Cheddar said. He was standing at the ready, poised at the toilet just about to make his morning water.

"It's not bull, Cheddar. You are yellow. Look at yourself!"

Cheddar viewed his forearm. Then he looked at the back of his hand. He leaned over and inspected his face in the small steel mirror mounted on the wall.

"Well I'll be damned," he said. "I'm turning yellow." He assumed his former position and looked down. "My dick's even yellow," he noted. Then he looked up at the ceiling and began to urinate. As soon as he did so, however, Palmer took double before offering yet another comment.

"Cheddar, you're pissing blood."

Cheddar looked down. It was true, although his pee wasn't blood-colored so much as it was a dark muddy brown, the color of coffee grounds or dark molasses. But either way, blood red or coffee brown, there was apparently a problem with Cheddar's plumbing.

"Do you think I could get a little privacy here?" he asked.

Palmer averted his eyes. The pair had an unspoken understanding concerning the public nature of their sanitary facilities and the private nature of the need to use them. Thus they each looked elsewhere as much as was possible given the dimensions of their small cell. For Palmer, at least, the lack of privacy while performing his daily functions was among the worst parts of being in prison. It made him feel like a lower form of life, an unevolved specimen, and it contributed to his feelings of inferiority with respect to the free people of the world, those lucky souls who had a bathroom door and were able and even expected to close it when the moment of truth arrived.

"Sorry," Palmer said. "I wasn't thinking." He inspected the tops of his shoes. "But in my defense, your dick is yellow and you are pissing blood. I felt like I ought to mention it."

"Yeah, I know. I've been peeing brown for about a week. I haven't had any trouble with it in a long while, and it caught me by surprise."

"A week? That's not good. And what do you mean you haven't done it in a while?" In his view, peeing brown was a big issue even if you only ever did it once. The mere fact of russet urine must surely always imply serious physical malady. What else could it signify? It seemed like a peck of trouble to Palmer, but Cheddar was very blasé about the whole affair, like it was no big deal at all. Visions crossed Palmer's mind of intrepid eighteenth-century British explorers hacking their way through equatorial jungles while beset by exotic diseases such as blackwater fever, dengue, and beri-beri. He wondered what was wrong with Cheddar. It couldn't be good, whatever it was, and it might even be contagious.

"Hold on a minute and let me finish what I'm doing here," Cheddar said. He sounded exasperated. "You know I don't like to talk while I'm taking a leak."

Palmer waited while Cheddar completed his business, flushed the toilet, and then stepped to the sink and washed his hands before drying them on his pants. While at the sink, he admired his yellow features once again in the mirror. "Nice," he said grimly. "I look like a banana."

"What's going on, Cheddar?" Palmer asked. "Why are you turning yellow, and why are you peeing brown? And why did you say that it hasn't been brown in a while?" Palmer realized that he had posed a plethora of whys before breakfast, but brown pee and yellow skin brought many intriguing questions with them, questions that literally begged for some answers. Cheddar sat in their chair and sighed.

"Brown pee is not so unusual," he said. He sounded defensive, like he had been caught stealing a piece of penny candy from a kindly corner grocer or copying the answers from a fellow student's test paper.

"Maybe on your side of the family it isn't such a big deal, but over here where the normal people like to hang out, pee is sometimes yellow, sometimes clear, and never, ever the color of a Yoo-Hoo. I've been around for twenty-seven years, and in all that time I haven't ever had to take a single brown pee. As a matter of fact, I've never even seen any until today."

"Okay. Brown pee is maybe a little unusual."

"Maybe just a little bit. So what's going on?"

"I've got a condition," Cheddar said.

"I thought you did." It appeared that Palmer was going to have to drag it out of him. "You want to know what my tip-off was? Your yellow skin and your brown pee. That plus the fact that you look like you've been hit by a log truck and left by the road three days in the sun. So what condition does all that to you? Is it something to do with your kidneys?"

"No, it's more of a liver thing," Cheddar said quietly.

"A liver thing?"

"I've got chronic Hepatitis C. That's what's got me turning colors."

"What?" Palmer was surprised. They had lived together for over seven years, yet this was the first he had heard of Cheddar's problem.

"Hepatitis C. I've had it for a while now." He cast his eyes downward, as if he were ashamed of his illness. "I haven't had a bout of brown pee since before we started bunking together. I was kind of hoping I was through with it, that maybe it had cleared up on its own."

"Do you know how you got it?" Palmer had of course heard of Hepatitis C. Everyone in prison knew what it was and how it was generally transmitted. A fair percentage of the inmates had acquired this knowledge the hard way.

"It's hard to say. If I had to bet, then I'd say that most likely I either caught it from Amber, or else I got it while I was getting this tattoo of her. Either way, she was probably involved." There was regret in Cheddar's voice, as if all things having to do with Amber had somehow not been worth the price he was having to pay.

"When you said you caught it from Amber, does that mean you got it from having sex with her? I always heard you couldn't get it that way." The word around the tiers was that heterosexual love was safe.

"It's a funny thing about that. We can put a man on the moon, but we can't figure out what the deal is with Hepatitis C. One doctor told me that I could get it from sex with Amber. Another doctor told me there was no way I could get it from sex with her. Of course, neither of those doctors looked like they were old enough to shave, so maybe they just hadn't covered that part with them yet. Who knows? I like to think that having sex with Amber was probably when I got it, because if that was it, then at least I got laid. It was either that or from her needle. She used to boil it, but I don't know if that helps or not. She was a smack addict, and I was pretty heavy into all types of drugs back then. We shot up a few times. I didn't care that much for it, but she just loved it. She needed that good sick every day."

"So you got Hepatitis C from having sex with Amber, or from her needle, or from the tattoo artist." They had narrowed the list, and Cheddar was correct; Amber was in some way involved with all of the potential causes.

"Yeah. Unless I caught it when I got raped while I was doing that nickel at Hays State. That was before I met Amber. If that was the case, then she caught it from me." The list was expanding again, and the theory of Amber as causation had taken a blow as well. "I hope I didn't give it to her," Cheddar lamented. "I thought a lot of that girl."

"You got raped at Hays?" Palmer was suddenly flooded with questions that he'd never be able to ask. It was morbid curiosity, he knew, but it was also human nature, and he couldn't help it. He had come close to having a similar experience himself a couple of years back, and only the serendipitous arrival of an unexpected guard had saved him from a fate worse than Cheddar's.

"A lot of guys do. There's more fucking going on in that place than there is in a Reno whorehouse."

"You've never said anything about it."

"I was never going to, either. It's one of those things a guy doesn't talk about much. But it just sort of popped out today."

"What happened?"

"I told you. I got raped. The son of a bitch who did me was a piece of work named Gibson. He was serving forty years for a little bit of everything, including raping an old lady who lived in his trailer park. That old woman was eighty-three years old, and they ought to have fried him for that, but instead they put him in prison. He nailed me in the back of the laundry while two of his buddies stood lookout. I'd been at Hays State about three weeks when it happened. I was just a punk kid, not much older than you were when you first got here, but I didn't have anyone watching out for me. The shame of it nearly killed me."

"What'd you do?"

"What do you think I did? I hurt him just as fast and as hard as I could. I slipped up behind Gibson a couple of weeks later and put a tool into his kidney. I jiggered it around in there real good, too, so there'd be plenty of damage. It was my intention to kill him, but the last I heard, he was still alive. That's my bad luck and his good, I guess, but if he ever transfers here, I'll finish the job." There was a look in Cheddar's eyes that Palmer had never seen before, a flinty stare that foretold mayhem and violent death.

"I never knew that you'd stuck someone."

"What, did you think you were the last hard man? Did you think you had the patent on stabbing?"

"I just never knew. That's all. Don't get wound up."

"You know the deal. It's something else you don't talk about. Word has a way of getting around in a prison. I've seen it too many times. A con will brag about stealing some stuff or beating up a new fish, and the next thing he knows, he's sitting in isolation for a month or so, reading his Bible and wondering who talked." He put his finger to his lips. "The walls have ears," he said mysteriously.

"I'm sorry Gibson got to you."

"Don't be. It's not like I was running around in panty hose trying to get laid. He busted me with a chair leg from behind. You can still feel the crease in my skull. When I came to, it was over. I didn't even know who had done it until I heard it in the yard." There was a hard look in Cheddar's eyes.

"Did you go to the guards?"

"You know better than that. Or you ought to by now. You never go to the guards about anything. A snitch is a dead man, pure and simple. They put me in isolation for my own protection. While I was in there, I made my plan. When I got out I sold all my stuff, and I bought a shank. I didn't have the full price, but the guy I bought it from didn't like Gibson from a long way back, so he gave me what he called a deep discount. He said he'd give me the knife for what I had to trade if I promised to stick it in deep when the time came. I told him we had a deal and I bought the knife. Then I did my best to kill Gibson." He shook his head. "I never have been any good with a knife, though. I got him in the kidney, but I was trying for his liver. There's only one of those, and if I'd gotten him there, he'd be worm food right now, provided the worms weren't too particular." He looked at Palmer and shrugged at the irony of the situation. "And that's the problem with me. Hepatitis C goes for the liver, and it has camped out in mine. I haven't had any trouble with it in a long time, though, and I was hoping it had faded away. Sometimes it does, they say. They call it spontaneous remission. The bug's still in there, but it's asleep and not bothering anything. I've read about cases that only flared up once or twice before they just went away for good. I guess not this time, though. I'm not that lucky." He smiled ruefully. "Leave it to me to catch a good dose." He shrugged. "At least the son of a bitch didn't give me HIV. They tested me for that about six months after I got tapped. That was to give it time to show up if it was going to."

"You've had Hepatitis C the whole time we've been cellmates and you never told me?" It seemed to Palmer like a fairly large omission. "What if you gave it to me?" He had a sudden strong desire to wash his hands and scoot a bit farther away. He fought this urge out of courtesy and respect for his cousin and friend.

"Like I said, I was hoping it was in permanent remission. Anyway, you can't catch it just by living with someone. Or at least, that's what they say. You can only get it by sharing infected needles or by having sex with someone who has it. Sometimes you can get it from blood transfusions, but that doesn't happen much anymore. And you can catch it from tattoo artists if they're dickheads who don't sterilize their needles." He shrugged. "And sometimes you can pick up a case of it by getting raped at Hays."

"Still, you should have told me."

"Should have, would have, could have, blah, blah, blah," Cheddar said. He stepped to the door, looked both ways, and lit a Camel.

Palmer took the pack and lit one as well. "What's that supposed to mean?" he asked.

"There wasn't any point in telling you. All that would have done would have been to get you all nutted up, kind of like you are right now."

"I'm not nutted up."

"You stay nutted up. You may be the most nutted up person I've ever met, at least in prison, but I know you can't help it, so I don't blame you. Look, I can't do anything about the fact that I have it, and neither can you. I thought it had gone away but it hasn't. You can't catch it from me unless we shoot up together or we dance the horizontal love tango. I don't have any drugs, so that one's out. And don't take this wrong, but you're not my type, so that's out, too. It looks like you're safe."

"What are you going to do now?"

"I guess I'll go to the infirmary. See what the doc has to say. But it probably won't be much. He'll tell me to lay off the smokes for a while and try to get plenty of rest until it goes back into remission. He might put me on some vitamin D. Sometimes they do and sometimes they don't. It kind of depends on the doctor. I guess I'll need to go light on Reeves's raisin jack. That's too bad, because this last batch only makes you gag a little bit." Palmer nodded. Reeves had indeed hit his stride.

"What about medicine? Won't he give you something to take?"

"This is one of those $5,000 per month diseases," Cheddar said. "Guys with good health insurance plans who aren't serving twenty-five years for manufacturing and dealing meth get interferon, mega vitamin D, and all those other high-priced drugs. I'll get a pat on the ass and an aspirin from a guy we all call the doc because nobody can pronounce his name. Unless he's out of aspirin. Then I'll just get the pat on the ass."

"They have to treat you."

"They absolutely have to treat me. But they don't have to spend any money on me, and they damn sure don't have to cure me."

Cheddar is real sick. He has the bad kind of hepatitis and after all he has survived in this world it may be the thing that kills him. His liver hasn't had a happy life anyway, and this stuff is making it worse. His

205

skin is yellow and he's pissing brown. He's lost weight and he was already too skinny to start with. He has had it the whole time I've been in here with him, but it was in remission and wasn't bothering him too much. But now it has flared back up and I've got a bad feeling about it.

I talked him into going to see the doc but it didn't do him much good. They gave him a shot and some pills, and then they ticked him off when they started talking about sending him to a medical isolation block because sometimes hepatitis is catching and they thought they ought to isolate him. I guess he finally hollered so loud about it that my old man heard the noise, and when he did that put the stop to the talk about Cheddar moving to the hospital, or at least it did for a while. If he gets to where he can't get up they'll move him on over, but for now they sent him back to our cell and then they tested me because we live together.

They did take him off work details for a while because he needs rest plus they don't want him hanging around the kitchen. They took me out of the kitchen too just to be on the safe side. I'll miss kitchen duty but guess what I'm doing now? I finally got my wish. I'm on the road crew and it's pretty sweet. We go out and work most days on the state right of way. We have this school bus but it is painted white instead of yellow and it's labeled State Prisoners. They've got grating welded over the windows, which seems kind of stupid because as soon as we get to where we're going, they open the door and let us walk right down the steps. The driver is strapped and another guard with a scatter gun rides along with him, but they're both pretty good guys who don't mess with us as long as we do our work. The work is easy. We ride to one road or another in the county and pick up bottles and cans and garbage. We weed eat along fences and around signs. Sometimes while I'm working, I forget I'm a prisoner for a minute or two.

I suppose they think that I won't run now that I've served seven and only have three to go. I guess they're right about that. Sometimes while I'm out there on the road I'll look at the woods and think about just running up in them and disappearing from the face of the world. I can almost see myself slipping into the trees. I think I could make it but I'm afraid of what would happen if I didn't. It's not the guns that worry me. I'm more afraid of drawing penalty time than I am of getting shot at. Plus even if I did get away I'd have to keep going for the rest of my life. That's a long time to have to look over your shoulder. Seven years into a sentence is the wrong time to run. If I ran now, the seven years I've served would have been for nothing. The time to boogie is at the beginning when the years are all out in front of you. That's when it's worth the risk. That's when you have the least to lose.

When I'm out on the road I can see people's houses and sometimes I just look at them and imagine the lives of the people inside. I saw one the other day that was a little gray pre-fab job with maybe two or three bedrooms and a carport on the side. There was a blue minivan that I figured was the wife's car and an old Chevy truck that must have been the guy's. They had a swing set and a couple of little bikes in the yard, and there was a clothesline in the back with some wash hung on it. I thought maybe this couple had been married for six or eight years and had two or three kids. I imagined he was a millwright over at the paper mill and maybe she was a stay-at-home mom at least until all the kids were in school. I had the husband pegged as kind of a jerk who didn't really deserve her, but I figured that she was a good woman who had married for life and that she would get the boy straightened out and turned into a keeper eventually. Anyway, it was like these imaginary people were real and I knew them. I have made up several families up and down the roadways. I'm not sure why I do this but I think it's because these families have lives and I'm horning in on theirs because I don't have one of my own. I'd ask Morris what it means but I know he'd make a big deal about it, and once he got to picking at it all the fun would be gone.

Cheddar is laying up most days when I get back from the road. He looks like hammered death and says he feels worse than he looks. Mostly he just sleeps and reads and smokes. Sometimes I can get him to eat a candy bar and listen to Mexican Radio but not often. That worries me because it doesn't take much energy to suck on a Hershey bar and listen to a mariachi band. Some days he doesn't feel like going to the dining hall so I keep enough honey buns and coffee in the cell to make him happy. Besides being my cousin, he's been my best friend for over seven years now. I wouldn't have survived in here without him. My old man picked right. Cheddar made all the difference. This place would have chewed me up and spit out my shoes. I wouldn't have made it until the weekend. I hope he gets to feeling better soon. If he dies, I don't know what I'll do, but I know I don't like the thought of three more years in here without him.

Shame on me. Here I am talking about Cheddar like it's a done deal, and he's not dead yet. I need to have some faith in him. He's been shot, stabbed, blown up, beaten, and run over, but he's still here. He survived being married to Bay-Annette and he's walked out of every jail he ever walked into. He's tough and he may pull through yet. He told me once that you're not dead until you're dead and I guess he's right about that. If you're alive, there's hope. If you wake up in the morning then you're still in the game, or at least you are for one more day.

9

The Meanest Son of a Bitch in the Valley

Fall is a time for change, even at Sweetwater State Correctional Facility, where not much ever changes. The hot days of summer had crawled past in slow motion, each seeming longer and more miserable than the last, but the days were now dry and cool, with deep blue skies and wispy, high clouds. The *Farmer's Almanac* called for an extended, raw winter, and in anticipation of this, the nights grew lengthy and biting, and each dawn brought a sparkle of frost. In the fields around the prison, the hay had been harvested and the cornstalks cut and chopped for silage. Cattle slowly wandered the dormant land. Overhead, the occasional flock of geese sailed the sky. The countryside rested and waited for spring.

Inside the walls, the cells were slowly acquiring the chill they would keep for the next few months. Cotton gloves and long underwear once again became the big sellers at the prison store. It was a hard season in one way or another for most of those marooned at the prison. Some of the inmates were beset with a sweet melancholy as they thought of family they missed and time they had forfeited, a gentle sadness that always seemed more prevalent during autumn as Thanksgiving and Christmas approached. Other cons, those with longer sentences or with no families other than their brothers in crime and their fading memories of better lives, felt the deep angers they normally held intensify and their desires to punish magnify.

The best of the prison guards sensed this undercurrent of emotion and made allowances. These jailers were usually those with the most experience, but not always. Sometimes just plain common sense allowed a new hire to see what a thoughtless veteran could not; men in bondage could be pushed quite far, but there was always a breaking point. In light of this realization, the occasional defiant stare was ignored and the odd disrespectful comment disregarded.

It was a time of transition in cell B-134 as well. Cheddar Cray was in the process of making his peace with the world, and Palmer Cray was in the process of making his peace with that. Cheddar was convinced that his time was near and had spent the prior several weeks putting his affairs in order as best he could, given his location and the nature of his worldly goods. He had made Palmer aware of the locations of the remaining coffee cans and had made his desires known about the disbursement of the money they contained. Palmer had not wished to be burdened with this information or with the responsibilities that came with it, but Cheddar had insisted, and Palmer owed him, and that was that.

"Can't Uncle Cullen do it?" Palmer had asked. "He's been doing a pretty good job so far."

"Daddy's getting old and his leg hurts him all the time. He doesn't need to be walking through the woods or digging holes."

Palmer still hoped for a recovery, but he had to admit that such a miraculous outcome seemed less and less likely as the weeks went by. Cheddar continued to look bad and feel worse, and Palmer was forced to admit that the end seemed near.

"How do you feel?" Palmer asked on the Friday that Cheddar set sail upon the eternal sea. He hung his denim jacket on the hook inside his locker and rubbed his hands together briskly. It had been a chilly day out on the road, and the crew had come back early for that reason. Now that he was inside and out of the wind, he was beginning to warm up.

"I feel like I'm dying," Cheddar replied absently. He did not open his eyes when he spoke, and there was a deep weariness in his voice. "How do I look?"

"You look like you need a honey bun and some hot coffee," Palmer said. Cheddar did sort of look like was dying and had for some time, but Palmer thought it would be unkind to mention that fact. Plus, Cheddar didn't look all that great when he was well, so it was a loaded question. "How about it? I've got some sugar for the coffee."

"A honey bun and some coffee would hit the spot. You got any smokes?" Cheddar opened his eyes and coughed. On top of his other health issues, he had recently caught a cold, and it had dug in deep and now sounded like pneumonia.

"The doc says you shouldn't smoke," Palmer said as he got out his pack and tapped out a Camel. He felt it was his duty to remind Cheddar of the doctor's warning even though he didn't think it made any difference at this stage. He certainly wasn't going to deny him a cigarette. Cheddar was a grown man and could make his own choices, at least for a little while longer.

"Well, he smokes two packs a day, so what does he know?" Cheddar accepted the smoke and a light from his cousin. "And since my liver is killing me anyway, I don't know how much good quitting is going to do me." He drew deep and coughed for several seconds. "See," he croaked. "Better already. Just what I needed to set me right."

Palmer tossed him a honey bun and ran water into the hot pot. "You're not dying," he said. "You're just having a relapse. This'll pass in a week or two and you'll be back to your old self."

"Right."

"Coffee will be ready in a minute. Did you go to lunch today?" Cheddar had been skipping lunch for the past couple of weeks.

"Nah. I wasn't hungry, and I wasn't in the mood to walk down there."

"You've got to eat, Cheddar."

"What are you? My wife?"

"If I was your wife, I would have left you by now."

"Smartass," Cheddar said. "I'll eat this honey bun, but I won't like it." He ripped the wrapper with his teeth and took a small bite. "Stale. Faro's selling old stock again." He chewed for a moment. "How was it out in the world today?"

"It was great. We cleaned up about three miles of highway, and I killed a snake." It had been a rattler. Palmer had scared up the reptile accidentally when he chased a piece of newspaper up into a culvert. Luckily the snake was sluggish, or the ensuing duel might have had a different outcome.

"Lucky bastard," Cheddar said as he sat up. He coughed, grimaced, and put a hand to his chest.

"I don't know about that," Palmer replied. He was afraid of all manner of snakes and didn't care who knew it, and he had not felt particularly lucky when he encountered this one. "He was a big one, and I did the snake dance when I first ran up on him."

"How did you get him?"

"To be honest, I really don't remember. I think we were both trying to get away from each other as hard as we could, and then he was dead. Maybe he was an old snake and had a heart attack. I know I almost did."

Cheddar snorted.

"You and your snakes," he said wistfully. "If I ever get over this hepatitis, I'm going to try to get on the road, too. I could use a change of scenery. Wave at a few women. Kill a few snakes. You talk about the sweet life."

"That's a good idea."

"Did you get the rattles? I'd like to give them to my boy." Since he had become sick, about the only thing that could get Cheddar out of the cell anymore was a visit from his son, and even those seemed to tax his strength.

"Sorry, man. I didn't even think about that. A guy on the crew named Zombie from over on C-block got them. He collects them." The water in the pot had started to bubble and steam, so Palmer prepared a cup of coffee for each of them. He put extra coffee and sugar in Cheddar's cup, thinking that the strong, sweet brew would perk him up.

"Not a big deal," Cheddar said. "I just thought he might like a set of real rattlesnake rattles. That's the kind of thing that would have been a big deal to me back when I was a kid."

Palmer nodded. "Tell you what," he said. "I'll try to trade Zombie out of them come Monday. He's already got three or four sets of the things, and he's got about five more years to work on the collection, so he can spare one. I bet he'll swap them for a pack of Camels." Cheddar nodded and closed his eyes. He raised his hand as if to say thanks.

At some point during the conversation, Palmer realized that loud voices were coming from the corridor. They had begun as little more than the usual background noise that drifted in from the common area, but now they had grown louder and more urgent. Several different voices blended together into a commotion. Due to the poor acoustics of the corridor, Palmer was unable to hear what was said. The words bounced back and forth like tennis balls as they echoed off the walls. He patted Cheddar on the foot before stepping to the door to isolate the cause of the disturbance. He slipped into the corridor and looked to his left. At the far end of the cellblock stood Murphy and Curtin, the two guards assigned to B-block that afternoon. They had their hands on their riot sticks, and they were facing a small group of inmates. Most of the noise was coming from the prisoners. Maybe Murphy had been trying to toss a cell and the inhabitants objected. Or maybe he had run that mouth to the wrong inmate at the wrong time, and his *chop, chop* was now coming home to roost. With Murphy, you never knew. At that moment, one of the prisoners—a large man called Tiny Poteet who was doing a hard quarter for murder—stepped up and swung what looked like a short piece of pipe at Murphy. The makeshift club connected with Murphy above his left ear, and he managed to look surprised even as he dropped like a stone. When he hit the floor, it sounded like a sack of feed dropping. Everyone was still for a moment, and even Tiny looked surprised. Then Curtin snapped to action and tried to bring her nightstick into play, but Tiny was a bit quicker as he caught her on the backswing with his pipe, and she joined Murphy on the floor.

This was a bad situation. Palmer was frozen in place and didn't know what to do. Two guards were down, and the leader of the group currently in charge of their welfare had not only put them there but was also serving twenty-five years with no possibility of parole for dispatching the mother of his children by blindsiding her with a George Foreman Grill. Palmer looked up at the camera entrusted with keeping an eye on that portion of the cellblock and noted with disgust that it was still broken.

"What's going on?" Cheddar hollered from his bunk.

"Something bad," Palmer replied. "Stay in there!"

As he watched, Tiny Poteet and two of his crew grabbed Murphy and began to drag him into Tiny's cell. Murphy stirred and looked as if he might be attempting to resist, and Tiny whaled him again with the pipe. Without giving much thought to his actions or their consequences, Palmer began moving toward the gathering at the end of the corridor. Tiny and his cronies continued to pull Murphy into the cell. Palmer wondered if he was still alive; that last tap had been savage, and Murphy was no longer stirring. Palmer didn't care much for Murphy, but he hoped he wasn't dead. He also wondered what Tiny and his buddies planned to do next.

Palmer arrived at the prone form of Curtin just as Murphy and his captors entered their cell. He took a deep breath, grabbed each of Curtin's wrists, and began to pull. He couldn't do anything for Murphy at present and doubted if anyone could, but he didn't like Curtin's chances if he left her unconscious on the floor. His plan was to drag her into the nearest cell and close the door behind them. The door would lock, and that would activate a signal on the big control panel at the guard station outside of B-block. Once that light came on when it should not be on, Palmer hoped the cavalry would quickly arrive. It was not a great plan, or even a good one, but he couldn't think of a good one right then, and it beat a lifetime of regret if he did nothing. He already had more than plenty of that. Curtin was heavy, and Palmer had only dragged her two steps when Tiny and his crew emerged from the cell.

"Looks like you have your hands full there, Cray," Tiny said. His soft, girlish voice sounded odd coming from such a large man. "Maybe you can get your old man to help you with that." Palmer declined to answer and leaned in to his task. He had about ten feet to go, and the odds of making the safety of the nearby cell were not good, but he was not a quitter. He saw a motion out of the corner of his eye, but before he could react, Cheddar kneeled down and removed Curtin's riot stick from her belt.

"Keep dragging," he said to Palmer. The trip down the corridor had left him panting. He coughed and spat. Then he stood and pointed the weapon at Tiny and began to move toward him. His hand shook, and he looked as if he might pass out.

"I've got one of those, too," Tiny said as he tapped Murphy's stick against his leg. He smiled unpleasantly. Palmer was entering the door of the cell, so Cheddar had bought sufficient time to complete Curtin's rescue. Palmer dragged her on in, then dropped Curtin's arms and stepped back to the door. He planned to grab Cheddar and drag him in as well, but as he reentered the corridor, he saw that Cheddar had covered the distance to Tiny and was now standing before him. Palmer started toward the group gathered in front of Tiny's cell.

"Why don't we see whose is bigger?" Tiny asked conversationally. Without preamble, Cheddar slammed Curtin's riot stick into Tiny's crotch one, two, three times. He had always told Palmer that if a fight could not be avoided, then hit first, hit hard, hit dirty, and then run like hell just in case your opponent had allies.

"You talk too damn much," Cheddar said to Tiny. He managed to sound both infinitely weary and threatening at the same time, and he had sent Tiny into a world of pain that was probably unlike any he had previously known. Tiny dropped his weapon, fell to his knees, and began to retch. One of his cronies leaned down to snatch up the weapon, and Palmer, who had just arrived on the scene, took advantage of his fortuitous position by kicking hard and breaking out most of his front teeth. He fell forward with a shout just as another of Tiny's crew, a pimp called Cadillac serving three to nine for being a pimp called Cadillac, swung a roundhouse right with a homemade blackjack—a can of SPAM in the toe of an athletic sock—that caught Cheddar square in the sternum.

Cheddar sat down hard as Palmer scooped up the freed nightstick. He and Cadillac faced off, one with a State-issue riot stick and the other with SPAM in a sock. Tiny was still making retching noises on the floor, Cheddar was in the middle of a hard bout of coughing, and the con that Palmer had kicked wasn't saying much at all. The other two members of Tiny's crew had faded back into the cell and appeared to be reconsidering their recent rash behaviors.

"I'm good with calling this a draw," Palmer said. He bent and grabbed the back of Cheddar's collar with his free hand, but his eyes never left Cadillac.

"I'm good with fucking you up," Cadillac said in an ominous tone, but he had already given himself away. The fight had gone out of him, and now he was just trying to look tough for the conscious members of his crew. If he had planned to make a move, Palmer thought, he would have made it in place of the threat.

"You need to see about your people," Palmer said as he began to drag Cheddar toward the safety of the cell where he had already stashed Curtin. "Tiny's nuts must be all the way up in his throat. Why don't you check him out?"

"You're mine," Cadillac said. He swung his sock once to emphasize the threat.

"Next time," Palmer responded. He dragged his cousin as he made his strategic withdrawal. Cheddar was much lighter than Curtin had been, and in no time at all they were in the cell with the door slammed behind them. Palmer grabbed Curtin's radio from her belt and keyed the transmit button.

"Hello! This is Palmer Cray in B-block. Hello! Come in! There are two guards down in here. Murphy's hurt bad! I've got Curtin in 140 with me! Send in the troops! Watch out for the boys hanging around 137! They're the ones causing the trouble." He heard the panic in his own voice and realized that he was not as calm as he thought he was. He dropped the radio to the floor and turned to check on Curtin and Cheddar. Curtin was looking at him, but her right eye was bloodshot and not focusing well. Tiny had clipped her a good one with that pipe, and Palmer thought she probably had a concussion.

"Thanks," she said. Her voice was a whisper. Then she rolled over on her side and threw up. While she was thus occupied, Palmer kneeled by Cheddar to inspect the damage. Cheddar's complexion was pale, and his skin was cool to the touch. He hadn't spoken since taking the hit.

"Are you okay?" Palmer asked.

"Do I look okay? What did he hit me with?"

"SPAM in a sock," Palmer said. Cheddar nodded, as if that confirmed his suspicions.

"It felt like SPAM. I guess it could have been worse. It could have been jack mackerel in a sock."

"Why is that worse?"

"Bigger can," Cheddar explained. "Jack mackerel in a sock can mess you up." He placed both hands over the point of impact. "My chest really hurts."

"Just lay back and take some deep breaths. It'll ease up in a minute, and then you'll be all right."

"No, I won't. Tiny got me in a real bad mood, and then one of his boys hit me with a can of SPAM. My head hurts, my heart hurts, and as soon as I'm back on my feet, I'm going to kill that hog-headed bastard."

"Tiny or the other one?"

"I don't even care. Pick one and surprise me. I can't believe he hit me with a can of SPAM."

"Well, you kind of started it when you tuned Tiny up with the stick."

"That's no excuse. And I didn't start it. I was trying to finish it." He looked over at Curtin. "How is she doing?"

Curtin tried to sit up, grabbed her head with both hands, and fell onto her side, facing them. She was breathing hard, but she was breathing, and Palmer took that as a good sign.

"I bet she has a concussion," Palmer said.

Cheddar pointed at the key card still hanging around her neck. "You think there is just one of those, or do you think Murphy has one too?" he asked. It was a good question, and Palmer was a bit taken aback by the fact that neither he nor Cheddar could answer it after seven years behind bars. He had thought that between them they knew just about everything there was to know about Sweetwater State Correctional Facility, but apparently there was always one more detail to assimilate.

"I don't know," Palmer replied, "but I hope the guards get here before we find out." Cadillac swung a mean can of SPAM, and if he came through that door, Palmer would have to deal with him. As if on cue, there were two loud pops from out in the corridor followed by shouts and frantic footsteps.

"They're on the way," Cheddar noted. He delicately sniffed the air and frowned. "Tear gas. God, I hate tear gas. That's another reason I'm going to kick Tiny's ass when this is all over. He went and got me gassed for no good reason." He began to cough as the odor got stronger. Palmer went to one of the lockers and got two T-shirts and a washcloth. He wet these at the sink and then placed one of the shirts in Curtin's hand while giving the other to Cheddar. Then he sat down between them and held the washcloth over his own mouth. From the corridor they heard four shots followed by an anguished scream followed by silence.

"Rubber bullets," Cheddar said. "I hope they shot him in the nuts."

"Who?"

"I don't even care. Pick one and surprise me." The silence continued. They heard shuffling outside the cell door.

"Sounds like it's about over," Palmer noted.

"Well, it might be about over, and it might not," Cheddar said in a matter-of-fact tone. "You know we've got a problem, right? We are the wrong people in the wrong place at the wrong time. We're convicts locked in someone else's cell with an injured female guard during a prison riot. This is your boy Cadillac's cell, by the way. If we had a little more time, I'd pee all over his stuff. Anyway, when they come in here, they'll probably kill us both just to be on the safe side." He raised his hands and nodded to Palmer to do the same. "Maybe this'll keep us from getting our asses shot off."

"Good idea," Palmer said as he raised his hands.

"You boys know I've got your back," Curtin said, "but it's not a bad idea to keep those hands up for a few more minutes just the same. They'll be kind of excited when they come in." Palmer was surprised that she was conscious, but her kind words would come in handy when it came time to explain. "I owe you both," she continued. "If there's anything you ever want me to do, then all you have to do is just let me know."

It was quiet a moment. Then Cheddar spoke. "If you really mean that, do you think I could have a look at your boobs before they come in here and kill me?"

Her good eye popped open, and she looked at him hard. Then she smiled and tried to shake her head.

"You are a strange man, Cray. No, you can't see my boobs. I'll tell you what, though; look me up when you get out, and I'll see what I can do." At that exact instant, the door was jerked open and a flash-bang grenade was tossed in. Curtin, Palmer, and Cheddar all tried to holler, but no one was listening. The bright flash was accompanied by a noise so intense that Palmer felt it rather than heard it. The last thing he remembered seeing was a phalanx of armed guards in vests rushing through the door. And then there was nothing at all.

Cheddar is dead. It just doesn't seem right and I feel almost as sad as I did when you and Mama died. Cheddar's been the biggest part of my world for as long as I've been in this place, and now he's gone. He watched out for me and taught me the ropes and that made all the difference. So if you don't care, put in a good word for him if you can, and keep an eye out for him. He takes things personally sometimes, and he'll take being dead hard at first.

It wasn't the hepatitis that got him, or at least not directly. What killed him was a heart attack, and when he had it he died on the spot. What brought it on was a ruckus we had in here. A convict named Tiny and some of his boys took down two guards, Murphy and Curtin. No one in here—guard or inmate—can figure out what they hoped to accomplish with that move, but I guess you don't have to be a rocket scientist to be a convict. I don't think they thought about it much at all. I guess there's sorry and then there's Sweetwater sorry, and these boys were Sweetwater sorry. Maybe Tiny just got pushed too far and before he realized it, he had stepped off the edge. I'm not speaking up for him. I hate him. But I know what it is to get pushed too far, and Murphy was always one to shove when he ought to just let a man alone. He was long on balls and short on good sense. He liked to pick at things.

Anyway, Tiny and his boys hurt Murphy really bad, and Murphy died about a week after they brained him. But before they could do the same to his partner, me and Cheddar stashed her in a cell and waited with her in there for help to arrive. Yeah, I said her. Her name is Curtin, and Tiny laid an iron pipe up against her ear and gave her a concussion. So check this out. Tiny and his boys were in one cell with Murphy, who was hurt bad and dying. Cheddar and I were in a different cell with Curtin and we were trying to protect her. I had called all of this in on Curtin's radio, but then I dropped it on the floor and it broke. My old man told me later that the guards were trying to call me back but I wasn't answering. They weren't sure what exactly was going on, so they decided to just come in and take everyone down.

It was a circus but I don't see that they could have done anything else. We were in the cell waiting for the good guys to get there. We were talking to Curtin and she said she owed us one, and Cheddar asked her if he could have a little look for saving her. Yeah, that boy wasn't right all the way up to the end of his time. He came right out with it, and Curtin told him to come see her when he got out and she would see what she could do. Right then the door snatched open and someone tossed in one of those flash grenades. It knocked me out, but it took Cheddar right on out of the world. There was a big stink about it because the guards had killed an inmate with non-lethal force. Then there was a bigger stink when Curtin told everyone we had saved her from getting it like Murphy did.

Since it was an accidental killing, they did an autopsy because that grenade wasn't supposed to kill anyone. That's when they found out that it was Cheddar's heart that had done him in. My old man said that the meth and the cigarettes and the hepatitis and the case of pneumonia he had plus being scared by that grenade was all just too much. His ticker gave it up and he came on over to your side of the world.

If you see him, you better be careful because I know he'll be pissed. I can just hear him now cussing away because he got his killing while he was trying to do the right thing. I don't know how many times he told me that being a hero would get me killed, and that he never wanted to see me doing the right thing unless there was a payoff in it for me. Then he went and caught the slow train because he was a bona fide hero himself. Tell him that if I get the chance I'll take a look at Curtin's boobs for him. On second thought, maybe you better not. He'll be pissed off for sure if you do. He was a bad enemy to have when he was alive and I'd hate to think what kind he'll be now that he's dead.

10

Free at Last

When Palmer awoke, he had the worst headache he could ever remember having. It was much worse than the one he suffered after the wreck, although he had had a week's worth of coma to get used to that one before he ever became aware of it. Or at least, that was the way he remembered it now. The thought crossed his mind that headaches were like childbirth; you forgot how bad they were between episodes. Then he realized that he had no idea what childbirth was like, and he wondered where that comparison had originated. He was disoriented for a moment, but then he saw that he was in his bunk at Sweetwater prison. That was good, because if he was here, then the guards hadn't killed him after all, so maybe whatever else was going on could be fixed. There was a soft buzzing in his ears, and he was very thirsty. He was also quite tired, his eyes burned, and he thought he might just take a nap. He turned to his left to get comfortable, and there on the toilet sat Trenton Cray. He looked old and used up.

"What day is it?" Palmer asked. He hadn't seen his father face to face since his mother had died, yet this was the only thing he could think of to say to him. It seemed inadequate to the moment, but it was all he had.

"It's still Friday," Trenton said. "You were out for about three hours." He shifted in his seat and crossed his leg. Palmer noticed tiny balls of white lint on his father's blue sock and that his shoes needed a shine.

"How's Curtin?" Palmer asked. "She got smacked pretty hard."

Trenton nodded. "She took a bad hit, but the doc says she's going to be fine. She told us how you and Cheddar saved her. You boys are heroes. I'm proud of you both." He spoke quietly, as if those words were for Palmer's ears only.

"What about Murphy?"

"He's not so good. He's in the hospital now. He may die." Palmer shook his head slowly. He wasn't surprised. He had seen the blows delivered, and that second one, at the very least, had looked like a killing blow.

Palmer sighed. Murphy was a troublemaker, but that was more like a misdemeanor than a capital crime in Sweetwater. In that spirit of compassion, he wished Murphy a long and mildly painful recovery followed by an early retirement. It was the least he could do.

"What about Cheddar?" he asked as he pointed to the upper bunk. "Is he up top?"

Trenton shook his head and then cleared his throat.

"Cheddar is dead," he said. "He shouldn't be, but he is." That truth settled slowly on the chilly cell like a November frost.

"How did that happen?" Palmer was confused and more than a little stunned. It was a long journey from Curtin's boobs to the afterlife, and he was curious about the path Cheddar had traveled from one to the other and about the speed with which he had made the trip.

"I don't know, and neither does the doctor. He just died. When the guards came into the cell, you were out cold, Curtin was hollering at them not to shoot, and Cheddar was dead. They tried to revive him, but it was a no go."

"He was afraid we were going to get shot."

"He wasn't shot. He just dropped dead. We'll do an autopsy. Then we'll know what killed him."

Palmer nodded absentmindedly. He wasn't even that curious about the how of the incident. Knowing wouldn't change a thing; his cousin would still be dead. He felt sad, but more than that, he felt empty. Cheddar hadn't been much, but he had been just about all that Palmer had, and now he was gone.

"Does Uncle Cullen know?"

Trenton nodded. "I called him a little while ago. He's going to tell Cheddar's wife and that boy. There's really no one else to notify. No one knows where his mama got to, and you and me are the rest of his family." It was true. Living Crays had become relatively scarce of late, an endangered species seemingly headed for extinction.

"What about Tiny and Cadillac and the rest?" Palmer asked. In light of the news about Cheddar, he sort of hoped that a rubber bullet or two had strayed into lethal territory.

"They all lived," Trenton said. He sounded a little disappointed at this, and Palmer shared in his disappointment. "They're all shackled to bunks in the hospital block. Once they heal, it'll be isolation until they stand before the judge. After that, they are all headed for deep, nasty holes for a long, long time. They'll be in for worse than that if Murphy dies, and the way it looks, he probably will. It'll be a needle then."

"So what happens now?" Palmer asked. It was a broad and complex question that covered many topics.

"The prison is on full lockdown for at least a week, so you should be safe in here until we can get you moved to another prison. If I can't get you into a transitional facility, I'll try for a county jail."

"Moved? I don't want to move." Palmer hadn't thought about his own safety, or about having to move to safeguard it, or that at the very least he would need a new cellmate. He had not been in this newest reality long enough to begin making any plans. Ironically, he hated Sweetwater with all of his heart, but he was inclined to stay where he was, nonetheless. Better the devil you know, he supposed.

"It won't be safe for you in here," Trenton said. He sounded ashamed of the fact that he would unable to protect his own son, but it was the truth. Plan A, Cheddar, was in the morgue, and there was no Plan B aside from keeping Palmer isolated until he could be moved.

"So you think I'm going to get stabbed because I saved a guard's life?" Things had happened so fast that it had not occurred to Palmer that he might be in a jam for saving Curtin. He supposed it made sense in a Sweetwater State Correctional Facility sort of way, although he felt oddly disconnected from the conversation, as if he and Trenton were discussing some other inmate's fate.

"I think it's just a matter of time before someone makes a run at you," Trenton said. "You know how it is. About half the men in here are like you. They made some mistakes, but they're trying to get past that and maybe move on. All they want to do is survive, serve out their time, and someday go home and live out the rest of their lives. The other half of the population is bad news, pure and simple. They hate everything and everybody good and decent in the world. They're not going home, mostly, or if they are, they'll be old men when they do. Those are the ones who won't let you alone for doing the right thing. You know the deal. Once you go to the guards, you're cooked. They'll get you, either for saving Curtin or for helping me nail Tiny and his boys to the wall. If Cheddar was still here you might be okay, because then you would have someone watching your back. Your cousin was my hole card, but he's gone now. I don't have anyone else I trust enough to put in his place."

"Maybe they'll leave me alone because I'm the Head Bull's boy," Palmer said. It was a poor attempt at levity, humor of the graveyard variety at best, but the attempt fell on deaf ears because Trenton took it as a serious statement.

"That just makes it worse," he said. "I thought things might get better for you in here after you took Razor Smithfield's knife away from him and killed him with it, and it seemed like they did for a while. But there are just too many people who want to take you down because of who I am. I hate it, but it's true." He shifted on the toilet. "It's been a problem since the very first day you got here."

"I didn't know you knew about Razor," Palmer said. This day was just packed full of surprises.

"I'm getting a little long in the tooth, but I try not to miss the important things. My son killing the meanest snake in the snake pit is an important thing."

"How did you find out?" Palmer asked. It didn't really matter now that he was caught, but he wanted to know. He and Cheddar had worked hard at being clever, but it looked as if it had all been for nothing.

"You know the broken camera up on the wall?" Trenton asked as he pointed in the general direction of the common area outside the cell.

"Yeah, I know it. That thing has been broken forever."

"It just looks broken. It works fine."

"Oh."

"All the recordings from the cameras come to me. On the day that Razor died, the video showed him coming to your cell. Then it showed Cheddar arriving a little while later. Then you and Cheddar were dragging Razor across the corridor into the other cell. I put all that together with the trouble you had with him in the breakfast line, and it was clear what had happened." He stood and put his hands in his pockets. "I had already started trying to find someplace to put him as soon as I heard about him making that move on you at breakfast. As a matter of fact, I had already given the order to stick him into an isolation cell until I could ship him out. But he was too quick for me, so you had to take care of him yourself."

"He came at me with a tool."

"I figured that. We never found it, so you did a good job getting rid of it."

"It was him or me. I didn't have a choice."

"I figured that, too, so don't ever feel bad about doing what you had to do. Look, no matter what happens to me, Razor Smithfield won't come back to haunt you. That DVD burned up in our fireplace at home. You and I are the only two people alive who know what happened to him, and I'm not talking. No one's asking questions, anyway. He was a blight on the world, and not a single soul misses him."

Palmer nodded in agreement. He certainly didn't miss Razor, and no one he knew seemed to be struggling with the loss, either.

"What did you mean when you said *no matter what happens to me?*" Palmer asked. "Are you in trouble again because of me?"

"I may be in some trouble. We'll just have to see. But it's not because of you. If anything, you made it better."

"What do you mean?"

"We had a hostage situation, and now we have a dead inmate and two hurt guards. One of them will most likely die. None of that is supposed to happen in a prison, and someone is going to have to take the blame for it. That's just the way it works. Usually in a case like this the warden takes the fall. Wardens are kind of like ship captains. They don't really have anything to do. The only reason to have one is so that there will be someone to blame if the ship sinks.

Our ship took on a little water today. If you and Cheddar hadn't stepped in, it might have sunk."

"So let the warden take the hit. That's why he gets paid the big money. You said so yourself."

Trenton sighed and shook his head. "I owe the warden some favors. When the search for the guilty begins, I guess I need to be standing at the front of the line."

"I suppose the favors have to do with me?"

"It doesn't matter," Trenton said. He stepped slowly to the door. "Are you hungry? Thirsty? Need something to read?"

"No."

"Okay. I'm shutting the door. Someone will bring you breakfast in the morning. We'll get this sorted out. Get some rest." Trenton stepped into the corridor, and the door closed with a click.

Palmer sat alone in his cell. It was a small space, but it seemed empty without Cheddar there. Palmer stood and began to pace. When the lights went out at 9:00, he paced in the dark. He was as nervous as a cat, and the back and forth movement of the pacing seemed to help. Tears began to flow silently down his cheeks, and as they did, he remembered Cheddar's advice on his very first day at Sweetwater about not letting anyone see him cry.

"It's okay," he said to Cheddar. "No one can see me in the dark, and all my best friends are dead." As he shuffled the night away, sometimes he spoke to Cheddar, and sometimes he spoke to Rodney, and sometimes he talked to no one at all.

The week that followed passed slowly even by Sweetwater standards. Palmer remained isolated in his cell for the most part, although he was visited several times each day by guards who brought him food, news, and occasionally diversion. It seemed that his actions of the previous Friday had elevated his status among the guards from lowlife convict to celebrity bordering on sainthood, albeit one that must remain under lock and key lest he disappear into the night. Thus in addition to three squares each day he was provided a variety of snack cakes, cigarettes, magazines, and tantalizing tidbits of information from the world beyond his locked door: Murphy had died, so Tiny, Cadillac, and the boys were all sweating it out in isolation and facing murder charges; Curtin was healing nicely and planned to return to Sweetwater in a couple of weeks; the prison remained on lockdown with about half the inmates cursing the concrete floors that Palmer walked on while the other half thought he had done a good thing; Cheddar had died of a heart attack and his remains had been released to Bay-Annette; the Head Bull was to be relieved of his command and forced into early retirement.

A week after the day that Palmer would always remember as Black Friday, the door snatched open and in walked Trenton Cray accompanied by his boss, a man Palmer had never seen on the cellblock before who was known to one and all simply as The Warden. Palmer had never heard his actual name spoken and wondered if even his old man knew it. The Warden and Trenton walked to the bunk occupied by Palmer and stood side by side before him. Palmer marked his place in the book he was reading and stood up. He didn't know what was happening, and he feared the worst.

"Even though we have never met, I feel like I know you," The Warden said as he extended his hand. Palmer took it and shook. He had no idea what was going on, but he knew that it would take literally no time at all to count the number of inmates who had shaken The Warden's hand, so something unusual was up.

"Good to meet you," Palmer said quietly.

"The pleasure is all mine," said The Warden. "I don't get to shake the hand of a hero every day. Especially one who is in a cell!"

Palmer cut his eyes to his father, looking for advice about whether or not to chuckle at The Warden's little joke, but Trenton's face was a stone. Palmer was alone at the tiller in uncharted waters.

"Happy to help," he said. He found himself being careful not to give even a hint of offense to The Warden. Regardless of what was going on, here was a man who had total power over Palmer, and Palmer was certain that they both understood this. Cheddar had once observed that it was always a mistake to piss off a guy who could have you killed, and Palmer believed this to be good advice.

"You did a good thing last Friday, and I would like to do a good thing for you in return." The Warden smiled as he spoke.

"Thanks," Palmer said. "I appreciate it." If he were offered a choice of rewards, he was going to ask for a hot shower while an armed guard stood at the door. A week of cold sponge baths in the sink had left him with a healthy desire for hot water and soap. The Warden reached into the inside pocket of his suit jacket and pulled out a folded document. He unfolded it, produced a pair of reading glasses from his shirt pocket, and slipped them on. Palmer listened as The Warden read two short sentences. He then folded the paper, handed it to Palmer, and again shook his hand.

"Congratulations," The Warden said. Palmer wanted to speak, but he found he lacked the ability at present. The words that The Warden had read were jangling around in his head. He finally managed a nod and a smile. The Warden patted him on the shoulder, then turned and left the cell. It was quiet. Palmer sat on his bunk and looked up at his father.

"I don't recall him ever coming to an inmate's cell like this before," Trenton said. "Not in all the time I've known him."

"What the—?" Palmer asked as he held up the folded page. He knew it wasn't a trick because his old man would have had nothing to do with that, but he really could not believe what was happening. Of all the many things he had wished for during the long nights of captivity, never once had he dared hope for this.

"It's a pardon. A full pardon. Effective now. You're going home." Trenton Cray favored his son with one of his rare smiles.

"Why?"

"The governor likes it when someone saves one of his guards."

Well I've got some good news. They let me out early. I still can't really believe it. For seven years I went to sleep every night thinking about how it was going to be when I got out. I got so good at it that I could just think of the word free a few times and I would fall asleep and dream the good dreams. Now I don't have to dream it anymore. I can go where I want and do what I please. No one gets up in my face. I can shut the door when I need to take a leak. I can have a beer. I can sleep with a woman if I can find one who will sleep with an ex-convict. Like Faro used to say, it's all gravy and good times.

No, the prison didn't burn down and I didn't escape. The governor gave me a pardon. I feel like I'm in an old movie! When the governor got word that Cheddar and I had saved a guard, he took an interest in what was happening at Sweetwater. I'm not sure how he went from there to issuing me a pardon, but I'm not bitching or asking anyone any questions. Right now I'm staying with my old man, but I've been thinking about moving on and leaving no forwarding address, just in case there has been a mistake and they decide to put me back in jail. You never know about these things. The government makes mistakes all the time and then they just go about their business while poor suckers like me get the shaft.

There was a story told by an inmate about a guy down at Macon State who was released early by mistake. All the time they were out-processing him he was telling them that it wasn't his time to go and that he had more years to serve, but they wouldn't listen and in the end they almost had to drag him out the gate. A few days later they figured out that they had screwed up and turned the wrong guy loose and so they sent the sheriff to pick the poor guy up. But that's not even the bad part. Once they had him back inside the walls they charged him with attempted escape, put him in isolation for a month, and added time to his original sentence. *I know! How messed up was that? That's why I almost don't trust my pardon. What if it's a mistake? What if they change their minds? What if the governor was drunk and now he has sobered up? I'm telling you right now that if they send the sheriff after me, he'd better bring two or three deputies with him, because it'll be a big job getting me into the backseat of that car.*

The weird thing about leaving jail was how fast it all happened. From the minute that the Hanging Judge handed me my sentence until the minute that The Warden read me my pardon, time seemed to pass at half speed. Every hour took two hours to live through. Every week took two weeks to drag itself by. I won't even tell you how long the years took. But once I got my pardon it took less than a fast hour to become a free man. Time had speeded up again. It was almost like we were running. My old man wanted to help me pack, but all I took was a sack full of my journals, the Sweetwater Blues on my back, and a pack of Camels. I left everything else to Reeves and T-bone next door. They'll be in good shape on trade goods for months.

When I walked out that gate I was born again. They wanted the Sweetwater Blues back, but I dug in my heels and my old man backed me up. I had earned the right to burn those things, and that was what I intended to do. The old man dropped me at home and left me to settle in while he went back to the prison. It was kind of weird and a little scary being in that house by myself after all that time. I felt like I was in a museum. Nothing had changed. The same magazines were in the rack. The same water stain was on the bathroom ceiling. The house still had just a hint of Marlboro Menthols and the smell of Mama's hand lotion. Everything was just the way it had been the day I left.

I went into my bedroom and changed into some of my old clothes, and then I took my prison denims and a can of charcoal lighter and a bottle of the old man's bourbon and headed to the trash barrel in the backyard. As I burned my Sweetwater Blues I toasted all the dead people standing there in the yard with me. I tossed back two shots for you, and I sipped one for my mama, and I even put one away for Murphy, who was a dickhead but not one who deserved to be beaten to death. When it came time to honor Cheddar, I just tipped back the bottle and finished what there was. Then I sat on the concrete picnic bench where I had eaten so many egg-olive sandwiches as a boy, and I cried until I couldn't cry anymore.

11

Promises Made and Promises Kept

Palmer's first week of freedom was not much different from his final week of incarceration. He was mostly alone during both, and much of his time was divided between staring at the walls, pacing the floors, sleeping, and wondering what was going to happen next. But there were a few more amenities available to him as a free man, and the fact loomed large that he could go outside anytime he wanted to, even though initially he did not want to. He was on freedom overload, and too many daily factors were under his total control. It was unsettling, and as an antidote he kept four walls around him at all times. Still, he was certain that eventually he would have the desire to venture out into Sweetwater the town, and in the meantime he was quite content to eat take-out pizza whenever he was hungry and to watch the real estate auction channel whenever he didn't feel like staring, pacing, or wondering. He was oddly drawn to the auction channel and its sad mission to cash in peoples' dreams and dispose of abandoned properties in once vibrant cities, but mostly he watched because it was the only channel he could squeeze from the satellite using his father's double-handful of remote controls. Technology had overtaken him while he was in stir, and as soon as he began to care a bit more about what he watched he intended to learn the ins and outs of Trenton Cray's entertainment system.

As for the senior Cray living on the property, he was gone each morning when Palmer awoke, and he returned each evening after dark. He didn't discuss the goings-on at the prison much, but from the way he looked and from their previous conversation on the subject, Palmer had the impression that his father was dealing with more than just a bit of bother and that his career with the State would soon be over. Thus he was not greatly surprised the Thursday that his father arrived home in the middle of the afternoon looking adrift and bemused, like he was a country boy lost in a fog in the big city. He came into the den and sat in the recliner. Palmer was watching the real estate auction channel while he munched on a slice of sausage and mushroom pizza. He had missed pizza a great deal while he was inside the walls, and he was methodically working his way through his list of favorites. Once he finished the current selection, pepperoni and green pepper was up on deck.

"What are you watching?" Trenton asked. He reached over and grabbed the final slice of pizza from the greasy cardboard box on the coffee table.

"This is the real estate auction channel." Currently on the block was a four-bedroom, three-bath fixer-upper two blocks from the beach in Panama City, Florida. It was advertised as ocean-view property, and perhaps from the peak of the roof it was.

"I didn't even know we got that station," Trenton said absently as he chewed a bite of pizza. "Are you looking to buy a house?"

"No. Just passing the time. You're home early."

Trenton frowned as if remembering something unpleasant. Then he shrugged and looked at his son.

236

"The hammer dropped today. The Warden cut me loose. I've been trying to remember the last time I didn't have a job, and I'm not sure I can. I think maybe it was when I was fourteen. That was the year I went to work gathering eggs in Branton MacAllister's chicken house. Now there was a tough fifty cents an hour." He smiled in remembrance.

"The Warden should have kept you. After all the times you made him look good over the years, he owes you better than this." Despite his father's opinion to the contrary, Palmer had thought that Trenton would somehow weather the current storm at the prison. Apparently he had been incorrect.

"No, it was fair. I told you that someone was going to have to go. After Murphy died, it was a sure thing. I was the captain of the guard, and one of my men got killed in the line of duty. I should have had procedures in place to prevent it. I should have trained my guards better. I should have had Tiny in isolation. I should have fired Murphy before he got himself into trouble. I should have been holding my mouth differently. Pick one, or pick them all. And even if I had done all of those things, it would still be on me." He sounded tired, and he sounded sad on top of that. "You know the old saying. You're only as good as your last thirty days. My last thirty days weren't so great."

"I don't know who did what to who," Palmer replied, "and I have nothing for Tiny and the boys, but you know Murphy was no angel, right? I didn't see who started the trouble, but if I was going to bet, I'd put my money on Murphy stirring up something he should have just left alone. He really liked to mess with people. That was his thing, and you know it. I don't think he could even help himself. He's been up in my face more than once, even though he knew I was your son."

Trenton sighed and appeared to gather his thoughts.

"He was kind of a mixed blessing," he said, "and I probably should have cut him loose years ago. But it's awful hard to find someone who actually likes being a prison guard, and he loved coming to work every day. I've always thought that people who were happy in their work did a better job. Well, whatever shortcomings he had are between him and the Lord now."

It was true, Palmer supposed, although he couldn't quite suppress the errant thought that if Murphy was assigned gate duty when he arrived at the city of angels, then the entire concept of heaven as payment for living a good life had just lost a touch of its shine, and it was no longer the reward it had once been. It also occurred to him that if Murphy got up into the wrong angel's face, then the issue of what to do with Murphy in heaven would only be a short-term problem. They'd chunk him out the side door, and he'd be on his way south in no time.

Father and son watched real estate television in silence for a few minutes. The fixer-upper in Panama City had garnered a few bids but would probably not make its reserve. As the auction drew to a close, Trenton offered an observation.

"It was time for me to move on. I lost my interest in that job when your mama died. Even before that, if you want to know the truth of it. In the early years at the prison I thought I was making a difference in the world, that I was fighting the good fight. But the harder I worked and the longer I stayed, the less it seemed that what I did mattered. The crimes just got worse and worse, with the worst of them being so bad that you couldn't even get your mind around them. There were always more inmates to stack into the cells, and every year it seemed like the mean ones got meaner, the young ones got younger, and the stupid ones got stupider. I decided right after I buried your mama that I was going to hang it up once I finally got you out of there and back home. So The Warden did me a favor. He

238

saved me the trouble of quitting. This way I got to keep my pension."

"I know what you're saying about it all just going to hell. Some of the guys I knew inside thought we were in the end times. They believed that was why people and what they did seemed to be getting worse all the time. They thought we were at the end of days." Palmer didn't believe in the concept of the arbitrary end of humanity via the hand of the Almighty, but he knew plenty who did and who seemed almost eager for that time to arrive.

"There are always people who think that. You know your mama did. People have been thinking that way for two thousand years, looking for the Rapture or the end times or Armageddon, whatever you want to call it. I think it's just an excuse, but I never told your mama that, for sure. She was a sincere true believer and wanted the best for everyone, but for some folks it's an excuse to be judgmental and for others it's an excuse to do what they want."

"What do you think about the actual idea of end times?" Palmer had never heard his father speak on the subject before. "You know, God calling us all to account."

"I think that God has better things to do with his time than to create humans with all of their weaknesses and then set them up for failure by making them have to try to be something that most of them just can't be. Somebody that mean and crazy would belong in Sweetwater prison, even if he was the Lord." Trenton stood and looked at Palmer. "Why go to all that trouble to create humanity just so you could send people to hell? Why not just put them all in hell to begin with and save that middle step? And for that matter, why create people in the first place if all you want to do is burn them up? It just doesn't make any sense to me. None of it. I guess that's why I'm not a preacher." He shrugged. His wife had always handled the theological issues in the family. She had been good at it, and he had always been happy with the arrangement. Now he was obviously out

239

of his depth, adrift and uncertain. "Of course, I also think it doesn't matter what I think, or what anyone else does, either. We'll all find out the truth of it one way or another on the day we die. Until then, it's all just speculation, just a bunch of talk by people who have no more idea what's going to happen than I do. No one knows, and the ones who holler about it the loudest are the ones who know the least. Enough of that! Let's talk about something else. You want to go see Mama? Maybe we'll stop by Rodney's plot, too."

"I do," Palmer replied. "I'd like that a lot. And after we do that, if it's okay with you, I'd like to stop by and see Cheddar. It's hard for me to believe he's gone. We spent a lot of time together in that little cell, and I miss him. The last time I saw him, he was talking about Curtin's boobs." He smiled as he remembered what turned out to be his cousin's final request.

"That sounds about right," Trenton replied as he headed out the door.

The trip to the cemetery marked a turning point in Palmer's post-Sweetwater experience. It was something that he knew he had to do before he could move on, but he had been putting it off. As he stood silently at his mother's grave, a calm descended upon him, and he experienced a sense of completion. He had said good-bye to her many times since her passing, but the parting had never seemed real to him until he stood before her stone and bade her farewell. Laurel Cray lay in a well-tended grave under a gentle green slope in the shade of a gnarled magnolia tree. She resided among her kin under a marker that bore a simple cross, her name, the two dates that set the endpoints of her time upon this world, and a quotation from Galatians: *And let us not grow weary of doing good, for in due season we will reap.* A small bouquet of fresh-cut flowers had been placed at the base of the stone. It was a calm, serene spot for the long rest, and Palmer felt better than he had in some time for having seen it.

"I like the verse," Palmer said to his father. "It suits Mama to a tee." Laurel Cray had always believed that a combination of works and faith led to the gates of heaven, and that works were the more important of the two components.

"It was one of her favorites," Trenton replied. "She picked it out a long time ago. I think she always believed that she might go before me, so she had it all planned out."

"The flowers are nice."

"I bring her different ones every week. She always loved fresh flowers."

"I miss her."

"I do too. I always will."

"The worst day I spent in prison was the day of Mama's funeral," Palmer said. He hadn't realized that he had spoken until he heard the words. "Do you think you'll see her again?"

"I do," Trenton Cray said in a quiet, gravelly voice. "I do."

The next stop they made was at Rodney's grave. Trenton stood to the side while Palmer stepped forward to pay his respects. As he stood before the stone, Palmer read the inscription. *Rodney Earwood: Only The Good Die Young.* He liked the epitaph, and even though he could think of one or two exceptions to the rule, in general he had no serious issues with it.

The visit to Cheddar's grave involved a trip to a different cemetery on the other side of town, a boneyard that Palmer had always dubbed The Creepy Graveyard. It was a treeless place, a barren hillside in plain view of the four-lane highway. It occupied the land immediately adjacent to the super Walmart that had come to Sweetwater the town just prior to Palmer's incarceration in Sweetwater the prison. It was one of those cemeteries that featured flat horizontal stones, assumably so the lawnmower could drive right over the top of the departed without having to stop and trim around them. There was a sales office in a trailer at the back of the lot, and a dumpster beside that, and a large sign painted on a 4-x-8-foot sheet of plywood offering plots beginning at just $895 apiece or two for $1700. An angel was painted on the sign, but Palmer thought she looked a bit sheepish about being there, as if she were underemployed and knew it, but had had to take what work she could find when she got to town until the hard times passed and something better presented itself. Several of the gravesites had small LED lights to commemorate the fallen, and at night The Creepy Graveyard looked as if it were overrun by vagabond spirits bereft of all hope of peace, dignity, and eternal rest, each wandering the land on its separate way to the afterlife, or to the Walmart, or perhaps to nowhere at all.

Cheddar's grave was on the steepest part of the hillside right up near the top of the hill, where he had a view for all eternity of the sales trailer, the dumpster, and the four-lane highway in the distance. The raw clay from his recent burial was heaped in a red mound over him. There was no stone, and there were no flowers. Even the grass was sparse this high up.

"Poor Cheddar," Palmer said quietly. He was still breathing hard from the hike up the hill. "This must be one of the $895 plots. I bet they had to winch him up here." He looked at Trenton. "Why did Bay-Annette do this to him?" It looked personal to Palmer, like she had surveyed all available resting places in the county before selecting the absolute worst one she could find.

"She said she was broke," Trenton said. "After she told me that, I gave her the money to put him down decent, and I gave her one of the family gravesites over in the other cemetery to boot, but she stuck him up here anyway. I don't know what she did with the money I gave her." He shrugged. "I guess it doesn't matter. What's done is done, and I don't think Cheddar cares."

"What does Uncle Cullen have to say about this?"

"He was pretty mad about it when he saw it, once I got him up here with his bad leg, but she was Cheddar's wife, and she had the right to put him wherever she wanted to, I guess. I told him that once the mound settled and we got some grass planted on it and a stone set in place, then it wouldn't be so bad."

"It'll still be pretty bad," Palmer noted. He hated to disagree, but facts were facts.

"I know. I was trying to put a good face on it for my brother."

"He would have gotten a better view out behind the prison," Palmer said. The little potter's field behind Sweetwater State Correctional Facility was at least flat, and it overlooked some of the prettiest farmland in the state. It was well kept by an old inmate named Armet, a man who had much more respect for the dead than he had ever had for the living. There was even a graceful, tall windmill out in one field, and its three white blades seemed to tick off the moments of eternity as they completed each revolution. Palmer had spent many hours over the last seven years just watching that windmill as it slowly turned in the Georgia breeze.

"That's a fact," Trenton said. "Cheddar was a pretty good boy—except for being a meth dealer, you understand." Palmer nodded. He knew just what his father meant. "I didn't think he was a bad man so much as he was a weak man with bad habits, but I have to say that he did all right by you." Trenton sighed. "I never really believed he'd get out of jail, you know, and I guess I was right. Sometimes I have a sense about these things. I thought Sweetwater would be the death of him one way or another. Well, he's in a better place now."

"It'd have to be a better place than this," Palmer said, looking around. He was irritated at the treatment his cousin had received, and he knew he needed to get over that before he visited Cheddar's bereaved widow. "This reminds me. I've got to go see Bay-Annette before long. I've got some coffee cans for her. I was going to dig them up for her, but after this, I think maybe she deserves to spend some time on the shovel."

Trenton nodded his agreement. Some things in life could be forgiven, but sticking someone into the Creepy Graveyard when it could be avoided was not one of them.

The cemetery visits were cathartic for Palmer, and after them he found that he was no longer afraid to present himself out in the wide world. He had several items of housekeeping to attend to, and he enlisted Trenton's aid as chauffer and financier since he had no money of his own to speak of, no car, and no driver's license. The first stop he made was to Morris Cato's office, which was in a restored loft over the drug store in Sweetwater's historic downtown business district. The counselor had scaled back their visits to once per month about a year prior and had made his most recent trip out to the prison about a week before the unpleasantness with Tiny. Palmer wanted to touch base with him before the next counseling session came due and he drove out to the prison for nothing. It was bad enough going there when there was a reason.

"Nice," Palmer said as he strolled into the small reception area and inspected the paneled walls, overstuffed chairs, and subtle lighting. Morris had been standing at the front desk conferring with his receptionist when Palmer dropped in. "This is a really great place. Maybe I'll look into the counseling business. You boys seem to do okay for yourselves."

"You didn't escape," Morris said as if he were hoping his statement was the truth but wasn't quite sure it was. He took a step back as if to distance himself from his client in case guards from Sweetwater burst in and began indiscriminately spraying the office with bullets. "Tell me you didn't escape."

"Thanks for the vote of confidence," Palmer replied. "I thought you were supposed to know me even better than I know myself. So you should know I didn't escape. I'm not the escaping kind. They let me go." He sat in a comfortable chair and crossed his legs.

"Why did they do that?"

"Maybe we could sit down in your office and talk about it," Palmer suggested. He was fairly impressed with the lobby, and he really wanted to take a good look at the inner sanctum as well.

"Yes. Of course. Come on in." Palmer hopped up and followed him into the next room. It was a large office with refinished hardwood floors, exposed brick walls, and an open ceiling with modern light fixtures hanging from rough-hewn rafters. A desk, computer table, and side chairs occupied one end of the room. In the center of the open space that comprised the rest of the office was an oriental rug ringed with comfortable leather chairs and practical coffee tables. Morris motioned Palmer to a chair and sat in the adjacent one.

"Sweet," Palmer said as he rubbed the leather on the arm of his chair. "It must have really bummed you out to leave all this and come out to the prison to talk to a bunch of bad-ass criminals. I don't know if I could have done it. No wonder you were always asking me about being depressed. You were projecting!" Palmer enjoyed referring psychological lingo back to its source because doing so always seemed to make the source frown. The source frowned and looked at his watch.

"Okay. We're sitting. Talk to me. We only have about twenty minutes before my next appointment."

Palmer relaxed in the wingback chair and related the tale of implausible events that had led to his release. As he spoke, Morris nodded and jotted and offered the occasional encouraging noise. The account took ten minutes in the telling, and when Palmer finished, Morris sat quietly for a moment, tapping his pen on his legal pad while slowly shaking his head. Finally he spoke.

"That is an amazing story."

"I know!" Palmer said. "I would have dragged a guard up into a cell years ago if I had known it was going to get me out of there. But I keep thinking the governor has made a mistake, or that he's going to change his mind and send the state police to pick me back up. If he does, I want you to hide me, because I'm not going back. I'm serious."

"That's a natural reaction to unexpected good news. The anxiety, I mean. It has to do with you feeling that you don't deserve your good fortune. We all tend to feel that way when something good comes about unexpectedly. It'll pass. I'm sorry about your cousin, by the way. He seemed like he was a good friend to you."

"He was, and I am sorry he's gone, too. He deserved better than to keel over dead, especially when he had just done something that might have gotten him pardoned." Palmer reached for a piece of toffee candy from a cut-glass compote on the table. He unwrapped it, popped it into his mouth, and savored the richness of the treat and the fact that good things were just there for the taking out here in the free world. "Maybe this was some of that good old Cray sloppy luck. I don't know. Maybe dying of hepatitis is a really bad way to go, and a quick heart attack was a better way. The thing is, I was kind of getting used to the idea of the hepatitis doing him in sometime later on down the road, but he was as tough as a piece of jerky and I still thought he might beat it. Even if he didn't, I thought there would be more time before he was gone." He paused for a moment. "And I know for a fact that he would have liked to have been on this side of the bars just one more time, even if it was only for a day or two."

"We always think there will be more time, right up until the moment it is all gone. It's one of mankind's primary defense mechanisms against the fear of dying and the unknown. If you would like to talk about it some, we can have a session next week."

"Maybe we better hold off on that," Palmer said. "I don't know how much you cost now that I don't get you for free, but I don't have a job yet and Trenton just lost his. We may have to scale back on luxuries like heat, food, and mental health for a while."

"Your father lost his job at the prison? He *was* the prison. What happened?"

"Someone had to take the rap for Murphy dying and for all the rest of the trouble, and he was standing at the front of the line. When the axe swung, it took his head off right at the shoulders."

"I'm sorry to hear that. I like your father. He is a genuine person and an honest and good man. Those are rare commodities these days. Tell him if he needs to come by for a talk, it's on the house. Don't you worry about the money part right now, either. On your way out, go ahead and make an appointment for next week. We'll work out who owes what later on. I like to finish what I begin, and I'm not quite done with you yet." He held out his hand, and he and Palmer shook.

"Thanks," Palmer said. "You're a good guy." It was the first time in their extended acquaintance that he had said it, but it was true and he knew he should have spoken the words long ago.

The following day, Palmer undertook the chore he was dreading the most. It was time to go see Bay-Annette and begin the administration of Cheddar's estate. He would have preferred that this task had fallen to others, but such is the way of the world. He caught a ride with Trenton, who was on the way out of town for a few days to do a bit of rough camping, fly fishing, and mind clearing over on the Echota River.

"You need be careful of that gal," Trenton said to his son as he let him out in front of the house. Trenton Cray often referred to female persons as *girls* and to female persons who should not be trusted as *gals*. "She ain't even nearly right." From some of the stories that Cheddar had shared concerning her exploits over the years,

Palmer suspected that his father's assessment was accurate. "Now that Cheddar's gone, she'll be on the prowl."

"I'll be careful," he said. "But I need to see her and the boy. I promised Cheddar I would take care of this, and I owe it to him."

"I know you do. You want me to come in with you?"

"Nah. It'll be fine. I only have one thing she might be a little interested in, and she'll be as tame as a kitten once I start talking about coffee cans." Palmer exited the truck and stood in the dirt road next to the mailbox.

"You got a way home?"

"I'll walk. It's only four miles, and it's been a long time since I could walk that far in a straight line."

As Trenton drove off, Palmer looked at the house. It was an old structure, and Cheddar had told him that Bay-Annette had inherited it from her parents, who had inherited it from theirs. It was an L-shaped, single-story dwelling with a small front porch in need of screening and a larger back porch in need of replacement. The house may have been painted at one time, but now all that could be seen was raw, weathered wood. The tin roof showed streaks of rust, and there was a sway in it that bespoke a longtime leak. The mailbox beside him was open and empty, and it bore several bullet holes plus the stick-on letters C, R, and Y. The A had fallen off at some point through the years and was now wherever the winds had carried it, or perhaps it had been shot. Palmer walked to the house and stepped up on the porch. The floorboard squeaked and gave significantly with his weight, but it held.

He knocked on the door and waited half a minute for an answer. Then he knocked again, louder this time. After another thirty seconds with no answer, he turned to go, but then he heard a sound from behind the door that sounded like a soft drink can being opened. A moment later, he heard a long, loud belch. He tried the doorknob and found that the door was unlocked. He opened it and peeked into the house. He saw a gloomy room with yellowed linoleum on the floor and faded blue paint on the walls. Dust motes floated, gently nudged by the air entering through the open door. There in the middle of the living room floor, sitting cross-legged with his back to Palmer, was Cheddar's teenaged boy, Dakota Blue. He was wearing ear buds and playing some sort of video game on the television. Palmer walked slowly into the boy's peripheral vision. He killed two or three more bad guys on the screen, then pushed the pause button on his controller and looked up at Palmer. He removed his ear buds and nodded his head as if he had been expecting a visitor. When he reached for his drink, Palmer noted that it wasn't a soft drink after all.

"Hello," Palmer said. "Do you remember me?" He had seen the boy a few times from afar on visiting days and had viewed a recent photo that Cheddar had kept taped to the wall of the cell, but it had been quite a while since they had been face to face. He looked like a younger, pre-methamphetamine version of his father, a Cheddar with good teeth, no tattoos, and perhaps the hope of a future.

"You're Palmer, my old man's cellmate. And his cousin." Dakota Blue Cray took a sip from his can of beer. It was Pabst Blue Ribbon. Palmer did some mental arithmetic and came up with the boy's maximum possible age, which was just shy of sixteen.

"You're a little young for that, aren't you?" Palmer asked. This wasn't what he had intended to say, but it was what had come out. He could have kicked himself. He had been noticing of late that occasionally his words just did whatever they wanted to, regardless of his own wishes, and that tendency was beginning to trouble him.

"Said the drunk driver who killed a guy when he was eighteen by smashing him into a tree," Dakota Blue replied. He looked Palmer in the eyes as he spoke, challenging him.

"Ouch," said Palmer, and that was all he had as a reply. The kid had guts, a mouth, and a bit of a mean streak, but he was right.

Palmer wasn't his father, and it wasn't his place to correct him. He barely knew him, and with his track record, he certainly had no business informing anyone about the evils of alcohol. Palmer supposed it wasn't the kid's fault that he was a chip off the old block. Sometimes these things just happened. "Is your mother here?"

"Dude. Who do you think gave me the beer? She's in there." He gestured toward the closed door in the opposite wall of the small living room. Palmer assumed it was her bedroom.

"Is she decent?" he asked.

"Never has been before and she probably didn't decide to start today. But she usually has her clothes on by now." He replaced his ear buds, took another sip of beer, and went back to his video game.

"Cute kid," said Palmer. He stepped to the door and knocked.

"Yeah?" came a voice from the other side. Palmer opened the door but remained at the threshold. Bay-Annette was on the bed, sitting on top of the quilt. There was a newspaper spread out before her, opened to the page with the crossword puzzle and the horoscope. A cigarette burned in an ashtray beside her. She wore jeans and a T-shirt, and her blond hair was gathered into a loose ponytail that served to highlight her dark roots. She wore no makeup, and the creases, lines, and smudges that were the inevitable signs of a hard life were clearly visible, but there was no denying that she had once been quite pretty and still wasn't too hard on the eyes. In fact, she was the finest thing Palmer had seen up close in years. She looked up from her paper, and when she saw who was standing there, she smiled, but the smile did not extend to her hard, calculating eyes.

"Hello B—um—Annette," Palmer said. "How have you been?"

"Well I'll be damned!" she said. "Palmer Cray. You're out!" She stood up from the bed, stepped to him, and enveloped him in a courtesy hug. He had noticed that she was not wearing a brassiere when she had risen, and he confirmed this fact during the hug. It had been a while since he had hugged any woman, brassiered or otherwise, and an unbidden stirring of desire came to him. He fought his impure thoughts to a standstill.

"You're right," Palmer said. He held Bay-Annette out at arm's length as if to give her a good look.

"What am I right about?" she asked, confused. Her voice was husky from too many years of smoking cigarettes, pot, meth, and crack.

"That I'm out," he said. "It's good to see you. I wanted to come by to tell you I'm sorry about what happened to Cheddar."

She frowned when she heard her deceased husband's name, as if the mere syllables brought back memories best left unrecalled.

"It was his time," she said vaguely.

"You have my condolences."

"Look, I know you were probably close to him, but I'll be honest and tell you that I'm not that sorry about losing him. I didn't hate him enough to kill him myself, but now that someone else has done it for me, it's time for me to move on."

Palmer had not really known what to expect from Cheddar's widow, but he supposed he was not greatly surprised by her lack of abject grief over the loss of her husband. She had, after all, been the one to send him to the slammer in the first place, and even though he had been gone a long time, they had navigated more than a few rough spots during their time together on the highway of love.

"Well, I'm sorry anyway. I know he had some ragged edges, but he died trying to do the right thing, and I think that's important. I don't know if they told you any of the details, but he died helping me save a guard. He was a hero. Maybe it made up for some of the bad things he did along the way." He felt as if he were eulogizing his cousin, and perhaps even apologizing for him a bit, but it was important to him that Cheddar be remembered in a favorable light.

"Hey, I didn't leave his dead ass out at Sweetwater," Bay-Annette pointed out a bit defensively. "Although by rights I should have. I picked him up from the prison, and I buried him up high, just like he always wanted."

"Yeah, I went by the gravesite," Palmer said. "It was high, all right. Nice and quiet up there." Maybe he had been too hard on Bay-Annette. Maybe Cheddar had actually wanted to spend eternity looking down on the roof of the Walmart where, according to urban legend, everything that was needed to manufacture methamphetamine could be purchased at one convenient location.

She closed her eyes and nodded.

"Better than he deserved, that's for sure," she said. Then she opened them wide as a thought occurred to her. "Wait a minute. You're out way too early. Did you make a run for it? If you did, I can let you stay and rest up for a bit, but then you have to get out of here. This is one of the first places they'll look." She sounded a bit excited as she spoke, and she looked over each shoulder as if she might spy a pack of bloodhounds sneaking up slowly, hoping to get the drop on her visitor and perhaps tree him before he broke and ran. "I don't need any trouble with the law. I've had enough of that to do me."

"No, I didn't cut out. They let me out for helping the guard. They gave me a pardon. No parole officer, no supervision, no nothing." Even after more than a week of breathing the free air of North Georgia, every time he said this, a smile came to his face.

"I'm really glad to hear it," she said. "I never thought you deserved all that time, anyway. They hit you way too hard for no more than you did. It wasn't like you meant to kill him." These were the right words to say in the present situation, but they were spoken without affect, and Bay-Annette was gazing over Palmer's shoulder as if she didn't have any idea what to say next. Now that he wasn't a fugitive, she had apparently lost interest in his company and his conversation. Palmer decided that the time for pleasantries had passed.

"Anyway, I came to see you because Cheddar asked me to," he said. "He left you something." Her eyes snapped to his and held there. It seemed he had regained her attention.

"I hope it has to do with coffee," she said slowly and distinctly. She swallowed loudly, as if she could use a cup right now.

"It actually has more to do with coffee cans."

"Thank God!" she said. "I thought maybe he had died before he told anyone where they were. The idea of all that money buried where no one could find it was just too much to take. It was keeping me awake at night! Tell me where the rest of the cans are. Wait a minute. Let me get a pen and a pad so I can write it all down. There are still a lot of them, right? He never would tell me for sure, that bastard, but I always knew they were buried all over." She bustled around the small room gathering the items she would need for the information transfer. She picked up her cigarette from the ashtray on the bed, and from the top drawer of her nightstand she removed a note pad and a pencil. "You know what? A map would be better. I think there is one stuck in the back of the phone book." She brushed past with another jiggle, and Palmer cast a glance in spite of himself. He had developed a fairly insistent headache, and the visit was nowhere near over. Bay-Annette came back with a small map of Sweetwater and the surrounding area. She sat down on the edge of the bed and handed the map and pencil to Palmer.

"Just put x's where the cans are buried, and then we'll come up with a plan for digging them up," she said. "Don't worry. I'll pay you for your time and trouble." Palmer looked at the map—thoughtfully supplied by Cherokee Bail Bonds: We Post, You Coast—before sighing and handing it and the pencil back to Bay-Annette.

"I can't do that," he said. He dreaded what he knew was coming next.

"Why not?" she asked. Her voice rose about half an octave as she spoke, and she leaned forward aggressively.

"That's not the way Cheddar wanted it done. He wanted me to give you one coffee can now, maybe two if you were in a tight, and then one every six months or so until Dakota Blue turns eighteen. After that, each of you gets one can every year until they run out." Cheddar had been very specific in his instructions, down to which coffee can went to which beneficiary and when the transfers were to be made. It was all written down in one of Palmer's journals next to Reeves's recipe for raisin jack.

"But I want them all now!" Bay-Annette explained, as if perhaps Palmer had misunderstood the situation and this would clear the matter up for all concerned.

"I get that, and if it was up to me that's what we would do, but he wanted to spread it out and make it last. He was afraid you would spend it too quickly if you got it all at once." Cheddar's exact words had been, "The bitch will run through that money like shit runs through a goose," but Palmer saw no need for direct quotations. At a time like this, paraphrasing was the better part of valor, and it would suffice for the task at hand.

"Screw him! He's dead! He doesn't get to have a say anymore! I earned every penny in those cans and more besides, and I want it! He's just doing this because I put him in jail!"

Palmer had to concede that she might have a good point, but he was bound by his pledge to his cellmate regardless of the fairness of the disbursement schedule.

"I think he just wanted to be sure you were taken care of," he said.

Bay-Annette was quiet for a moment. Then she looked at Palmer. "I helped him make that money, you know. He did most of the selling, and a whole lot of the taking, by the way, but not many people can cook a batch the way I can. So I'm just as entitled to the money as he is. We're still married, and everything is supposed to be split fifty-fifty. I'll get a lawyer if I have to." Given the origins of the windfall, Palmer wasn't so sure that retaining counsel would be in Bay-Annette's best interest, so he tried to steer her away from that course.

"I believe you, Annette. I think you worked every bit as hard as Cheddar making that money, and you're going to get every penny. I swear. But I have to do it the way he asked me to. It was kind of a deathbed thing. I promised." In truth, Palmer was tempted to just give it all to her and be done with it, but he had a nagging suspicion that Cheddar was correct in his assertion that it would be a bad mistake to do so.

"Damn him! Damn him straight to hell!" Bay-Annette yelled. "He got me pregnant! He got me hooked! He blew me up! He blew me up again! He gave me the clap three times, plus God only knows what else I probably caught from him. And now I can't get hold of our nest egg? Now I can't get some start over money?"

"Really, I think he just wanted to take care of you." Palmer repeated. He was trying to find a way out of the minefield, but he was trapped in the middle with tripwires all around. It wasn't fair. He had come to do the right thing. He was probably the only former resident of Sweetwater State Correctional Facility who wouldn't have just kept the money for himself, which was no doubt why he had drawn the duty, but he wasn't getting any credit for that. All he had come to do was to give away some money, and now he was the bad guy.

"You don't have to do anything he said, you know," Bay-Annette said. "You are holding all the cards. You can just hand it over and forget about what he wanted."

"I can't do that, Annette. I promised him."

"You can do whatever you want to do. He's dead."

"I owe him. I need to do it his way."

"He owes me!" she replied. "He owes me every dime and then some. Do you have any idea what it was like to screw Cheddar Cray?"

"Uh, no," Palmer replied. "We weren't that kind of cellmates." They seemed to have reached an impasse, and Palmer was about to suggest that perhaps it was shovel time when Bay-Annette suddenly upped her game.

"If I sleep with you, will you give me all the cans?" she asked.

"Pardon?" Palmer asked.

"You heard me! You were talking about taking care of things, so speaking of taking care of things, is there anything I can take care of for you? Is there anything I can do to make you change your mind?" She stood with an extra jiggle. "Anything at all? You've been out of circulation for a while now."

Palmer thought he was prepared for this question. Indeed, he had been warned by Cheddar that it would be forthcoming and that it would be best to not be caught by surprise lest he be swept away by the deluge.

"She'll offer to make your toes curl up if you'll give all the coffee cans to her at once," Cheddar had said. "I won't tell you she's not good, because she is. And I won't hold it against you from wherever I am when I'm dead if you decide to go ahead and ride the love train. Life is short, and the love train doesn't always make a stop in your neighborhood." He had gestured at their surroundings to make his point, and it was true that the love train did not seem to run to cell B-134 in Sweetwater prison. "But watch out for Bay-Annette. She's the mother of my boy and the best lay I ever had, but she'll screw your brains out one minute and then cut your throat while you're sleeping the next. You can't trust her. Remember how I got here!"

Palmer did remember how his cousin had gotten to Sweetwater State Correctional Facility, but as he stood before Bay-Annette with bliss just a few coffee cans away, his cousin's sad journey to a small

256

concrete cell was the last thing on his mind. What was in his thoughts at that moment was the wide chasm between right and wrong. He looked at Bay-Annette, and he knew that there wasn't much that he wanted more right then than some of her magical delight. He might have desired an end to world hunger more, or perhaps a cure for cancer, but not much else ranked higher at that moment than riding the love train. But as deprived as he was in matters of the flesh, he still was not willing to take advantage of the situation. He had spent nearly a quarter of his life among men who had chosen paths leading to regret, and he knew he was facing such a choice now. He also knew that a single regret often led to two, and that small regrets tended to herald larger ones, and that the path back from the dark side was arduous and full of peril, and that he already had a pretty impressive track record when it came to screwing up. So even though he wanted her about as much as anything he could recall, he decided to take a pass.

"Let's go dig up some coffee cans," Palmer said, offering an alternative activity while chiding himself for a fool as he listened to the love train chug slowly out of the station, its whistle sounding distant and forlorn.

"What?" she asked. She stepped back and looked at him with a touch of suspicion. "I just offered to screw you!"

"I know you did." He suspected she had seldom if ever had this offer declined. He couldn't quite believe he was declining it now.

"Oh, my God! You're gay!"

"That's not it. If your offer had been because you like me, or because you were curious, or even because you were horny and I just happened to be handy, then we would go at it right now. But not for coffee cans. I've already got plenty to be ashamed of. Now come on. There's a pair of Folgers cans right out there in the backyard, and I think we're going to dig them up for starters. Let's go."

257

"In the yard? In the damn yard? I'll kill him! I swear to God I'll dig him up and kill him! There were two in the yard the whole time he was away?" Actually there were four out there, but Palmer felt that no good could come from sharing that information.

An hour later, Bay-Annette and her son were contentedly counting bills at their kitchen table while Palmer slowly ambled home. His hands were in his pockets, and he kicked a stone as he shuffled along. It had been an odd day, and he liked that he was able to walk at the end of it without encountering any barbed wire while he contemplated all that had occurred, including Bay-Annette's parting words to him.

"Are you sure you wouldn't like to have a little fun?"

"The last time I tried to have a little fun," Palmer had said, "I ended up in prison for ten years."

I've been out of Sweetwater for a while now and I feel safe in saying that freedom may just catch on. I think I've done more interesting things during the last three weeks than I did the whole time I was in the slam. I've watched TV and been to a movie. I've been offered sex for coffee cans. I've had beer and pizza, steak, hot dogs, hamburgers, more beer, and more pizza. I've been to both cemeteries in town. I stopped by to see you while I was in the good boneyard. I pulled a few weeds off of you and neatened up the area. I also left some flowers for you, just because.

I have been having a hard time sleeping since I walked out of the gate. I have this dream almost every night where I'm out in the middle of the prairie. I guess it's the prairie, anyway. It looks like what I think a prairie looks like. There's not a tree or a hill in sight, and all I can see in any direction is tall grass, like the old amber waves of grain thing. The wind is blowing steady and cold, and it howls all the time, but it sounds like a sad steam whistle from an old locomotive more than it does the wind, and that kind of freaks me out. There are these huge herds of animals I don't quite recognize grazing all around me. These suckers are big! At first I think they are buffaloes, but once I get up close to them, they change into something else, and I can never quite make out what they are.

The animals can talk, but they only talk to each other and won't speak to me. I pick out a friendly-looking specimen and offer it a cigarette. Yeah, that does seem strange, but the reason I offer it a smoke is because several of them have cigarettes dangling from their lower lips, so I think offering it a coffin nail might be a good ice breaker. But the one I choose must be a non-smoking buffalo because instead of taking the Camel and lighting it up, he snorts and bellows and then starts chasing me. Or maybe he's a Marlboro buffalo.

The rest of the herd joins in the chase, but it's like we're running in slow motion. I run for a while and the ground I'm hoofing it over is covered with human bones wearing Sweetwater Blues. I look up, and there is a wall in the distance that kind of looks like the Great Wall of China with razor wire along the top, and I know if I can get to it I will be safe. No matter how hard I run, though, the wall doesn't get any closer but the things chasing me do. They nip at my heels and I can hear them breathing and yelling at each other to catch me and I always wake up right before they run me down, scared enough to wet myself but too afraid to go to the john. Sometimes I'll drift back off after the dream, but most times this is the end of my sleep for the night, and when the sun comes up I'm sitting on the porch waiting for it.

I told my dream to Morris and he got so excited that you would have thought that the buffaloes were after him. If he said classic once I bet he said it a dozen times while I was telling him about the dream. According to him, the big prairie in my dream is the world outside of Sweetwater prison, the wide open spaces, the land of the free and the home of the brave. The buffaloes are all the straights, the people who have not been locked up, and the reason they won't talk to me is because I am an outcast in society. Morris calls me the proverbial stranger in a strange land. It always makes me a bit nervous when he gets biblical

259

with me but he's got that little streak in him so what can I do? Anyway, the wall off in the distance stands for the safety of the prison walls, and all of the dead guys I'm running over are other inmates who tried to make it on the outside but failed, and according to my counselor I am longing for the safety of prison. I don't remember it being all that safe in there but I am an uneducated man, so what do I know?

I asked Morris why the buffaloes smoked and he said he didn't know. When I suggested that maybe it was because it made them look cool, he got a little bit ill with me and told me I needed to be serious. Then he asked me to tell him what I thought the dream meant. I told him that I didn't have a clue what it meant but I guaranteed him I was not itching to run and visit the Great Wall of China or to run back into the loving arms of Sweetwater State Correctional Facility, either. Before I'd go back over that wall, I'd let every buffalo there ever was run over me, back up, and then run over me again. Morris is a good guy and he's pretty sharp most days, but there's a lot about ex-cons he doesn't know. Me and the old man drove past the prison the other day on our way to the Creepy Graveyard, and I couldn't even look over at it. I'll never go back there. I'll die first.

12

What Comes Around Goes Around

As Palmer acclimated himself to the free world, he spent his days walking the town and reacquainting himself with many of the people he had known for most of his life. He found that Sweetwater the town had changed very little in his absence and its inhabitants had evolved even less, but that he had, in fact, become someone quite different during his seven years under lock and key. Everyone was friendly enough, to be sure, and greeted him as if they were genuinely glad to see him with his unfortunate trouble behind him and out among the free people once more. But as he reestablished contact with this small piece of the world and the people in it, he found that he viewed the town and its occupants with prison eyes. As he entered each building or room, he did a casual but thorough reconnaissance looking for choke points, dark corners, potential offensive and defensive weapons, and possible routes of escape, and as he shook each hand, he evaluated its owner with the risk versus return mentality that had been a survival skill in the jug but for which he had found no real purpose on the good side of the walls.

The fact that he had changed was apparent to him, although he took pains to hide this new harder self from others. It wasn't a case of not liking his new persona. He neither liked nor disliked how he now was, but he did realize that he was a very different animal from the young man who had once flown a Camaro into a tree. He had become a pragmatist while in bondage and knew that he was what he was because it was what he had had to become in order to survive. But he had also learned how to blend into the background and fit it, and he was trying hard to once again find his place in the little town of Sweetwater.

He had been free for a little more than a month before he finally worked up the courage to go visit Kathleen Earwood. He had heard that she was not doing well, that she had become reclusive and odd, and his natural first reflex was to feel responsibility and remorse, but that did not greatly surprise him because it was his first reaction to a great many things both past and present. He had also heard that she had remarried, this time to a local businessman by the name of Ottis Lee Lamb. He owned the junkyard out on the four-lane not far from the Creepy Graveyard. Back when he was a driving man, Palmer had purchased many parts for the Camaro from Ottis Lee Lamb and had received several more as gifts, and they had become friends. That car had eaten spare parts like they were candy.

"I need to go see Kathleen Earwood today," he told his father that morning. "I've been putting it off since I got out." He had intended that she be one of his first stops after walking out of the gates, but one thing had led to another, and the longer he waited, the less he wanted to go. If he didn't go soon, he might not go at all.

"I figured you were working up to that," Trenton replied, "and that you'd go for a visit when you got ready. She got married again, you know. She's been married about three years."

"I heard that in town."

"She hitched up with Ottis Lee Lamb."

262

"I heard that, too. I never would have thought it." Ottis was a robust, joyful man. He had always been known as a bit of a rounder, but he was a devout one. He liked to play cards, smoke cigars, and drink corn whiskey, but he believed in a just and loving God who wouldn't begrudge a man a little fun while he was on this earth. Kathleen, on the other hand, was quiet and demure and had most likely never rounded even once in her entire life, devoutly or otherwise.

"Love is strange," Trenton confirmed.

Palmer thought about what he knew of Ottis Lee Lamb. The man was in his late sixties, and he had owned the junkyard since inheriting it from his father one frosty morning in 1971 when the elder Lamb had made a serious miscalculation concerning the load-bearing capabilities of concrete cinderblocks and been crushed by a Chrysler Imperial while attempting to remove a transmission. By the time Ottis Lee located his father and removed the Imperial from on top of him, there was nothing left to do but provide a decent burial. Ottis Lee planted his father at the back of the junkyard, down by the creek and next to a pretty grove of poplar trees. He buried him deep and carefully positioned the Imperial over him as a marker. For years after, Ottis Lee was sometimes seen late in the evening, sitting in the Chrysler—now referred to as The Death Car—down by the creek as the sun set in the west, talking over the hard realities of the junkyard business with his departed father as he smoked Swisher Sweet cigars and sipped corn whiskey from a mason jar.

"Did he move in with Kathleen?" Palmer asked his father. He assumed he had, because Ottis Lee had always lived in a shed at the junkyard, and he couldn't imagine Kathleen moving out there. The shed was drafty, and snakes and rats occasionally dropped by uninvited.

"He did," Trenton said. "You know she's got something going on upstairs, right?" He tapped his temple to indicate which upstairs he meant.

"I heard that in town, too, but I sort of knew it already. She had some of that going on back when she used to visit me in the slam. I guess it got worse."

Trenton nodded. "Way worse," he said. "Ottis Lee is in bad shape too. He has something wrong with his breathing, something he got from asbestos. I guess it's from working around the junkyard his whole life. Brake liners used to be made out of asbestos, you know. He says he must have breathed in at least fifty pounds of brake dust over the years. I suppose it finally got to him."

"Well if he's sick and she's...you know, the way she is, then who is taking care of who?"

"That's a good question. Maybe they're sort of pitching in and helping with each other. I'll give you a ride over there after breakfast, and maybe you can find out."

Palmer still wasn't driving, and he wasn't in any particular hurry to get back to it. The State wanted him to jump through many hoops to get his license back, and so far the process had seemed to be more trouble than it was worth. Plus, he had found that he liked walking. Ever since his release, he seemed prone toward building up stress during the day, and when it got to an uncomfortable level— usually signaled by his desire to slap someone—walking helped to relieve it. He would have never believed that being a liberated convict could, in its own way, be as stressful as being an inmate, but it was. Each kept him off balance, and each had a steep learning curve. Palmer hoped his new tendency for anxiety was a short-lived phenomenon.

"I think I'll walk," he said. "I'll be back by supper." It wasn't far to Kathleen Earwood's house, and Palmer supposed he could probably walk it blindfolded; he had made the trip countless times as

264

a boy. The route was six blocks over to Main, right on Main and three blocks down to Mill, then left on Mill and down four blocks to the Earwood home at the corner of Mill and Water. He whistled as he walked at a brisk pace, his hands in his pockets, and soon arrived at his destination.

He stopped in front of the Earwood house, Rodney's boyhood home, and allowed himself a good, long look. The house was a two-story wood frame duplex pretty much identical to every other house on Mill Street. All the houses had once been mill houses owned by the Sweetwater Company, the now-defunct cotton mill that had been the town's main source of employment for decades. Generations of mill workers and their families had lived in the homes, sent their children to the mill school, received medical care at the mill clinic, and, when the time came, been buried in the mill cemetery. During the 1950s, the textile industry in the South began to reexamine its business models, and the houses were sold to individuals, most of whom still worked for the Sweetwater Company. Now the mill was gone, but the clapboard houses remained. The Earwood home had long ago been converted to a single-family dwelling, but from the outside it pretty much looked the same as it always had. Palmer stepped onto the porch and knocked on the front door. He waited a moment before knocking again. Close to a minute passed, and just as he was about to knock a third time, the door slowly opened. There before him stood Ottis Lee Lamb.

It had been a while since Palmer had seen the man, over eight years in fact, and although those eight years had not been kind to either of them, Ottis Lee had clearly had the worst time of it. He had always been a large man, standing six feet tall in his stocking feet, and in his prime tipping the scales at well over two hundred muscular pounds. Now he appeared to have shrunk. He was stooped over, and his faded blue denim overalls hung from his emaciated frame and puddled around his house slippers. He wore no shirt, and his grizzled, white chest hair contrasted starkly with his black skin. His weathered face was lined and cracked like old leather. He was completely bald, and his full white beard gave him a wizened appearance.

"Palmer? Palmer Cray! How are you doing, boy?" His large hand engulfed Palmer's and gave it a shaky squeeze. Palmer noted that although Ottis Lee had always had a booming voice, today he was speaking softly, almost in a loud whisper.

"I'm good, Ottis Lee. I'm real good." Palmer, too, spoke quietly, even though he had no idea why.

"I heard you were out of the jug and walking the roads," Ottis Lee said. "I knew you'd be by to see Kathleen directly. Lord, that was some bad business out there at the prison, killing guards and inmates and such, but at least it got you sprung. Come in! Come in!" He held open the screen and Palmer entered the front room. It smelled of Vicks VapoRub, Swisher Sweet cigars, and old age.

"It looks like congratulations are in order now that you're a married man," Palmer said. He stopped and looked at the picture of pretty Jesus hanging on the living room wall, that ubiquitous Southern deity with his long, thick hair and his compassionate brown eyes. The twin to the rendering was hanging on his father's living room wall, put there by his mother sometime long ago. Like most of his generation, Palmer had been raised on pretty Jesus, and looking at him brought his mother to mind, which made him sad. He hoped that she was up in heaven sitting with pretty Jesus right now, maybe sharing a Marlboro Menthol with him as they discussed the state of the world and the fate of mankind.

"Thanks," said Ottis Lee. "You know, it was a funny thing. I always said I'd die a bachelor, but here I am married and settled down." He motioned to a chair, and they both sat. Palmer noted that his host was constantly short of air, and that he would occasionally pause while speaking to catch his breath.

"I remember you saying it all the time," Palmer said. "You said that if the Lord had wanted you to get married, then he wouldn't have made you such a fast runner. You told me back when I was just a kid that if I got fast enough to outrun Rodney, then the girls would catch him and leave me be."

"I remember that," Ottis Lee said with a rueful smile. "I used to be a fast runner, but the good Lord has slowed me down some. These days, I'm just about stopped."

"I'm having a hard time imagining Kathleen chasing you around the junkyard until you got tired. She never struck me as the running kind. Are you sure you weren't chasing her?"

"Well, there wasn't much chasing going on by either one of us, if the truth be told. Once Kathleen ran Harris off, curse his North Carolina hide, she started bringing her car by the junkyard from time to time when it needed work. We'd known each other since Rodney was a boy, but it wasn't until after her sorry man left for Asheville that we became friends." Ottis Lee looked at Palmer over the tops of his glasses as he made his next point. "Harris Earwood didn't care much for people like me."

"Fast junkyard owners?" Palmer asked with a grin. "Cigar smokers?"

"Yeah, that's it. He hated every fast, cigar-smoking junkyard owner he ever knew. He thought we should all run back to Africa. I'm from Waycross. I'm not even really sure where Africa is." Ottis Lee was not much of a traveler, Palmer knew. He once admitted that during the one and only time he had ever left the country, he had spent the bulk of the following year on his belly in a stinking jungle hoping to avoid being shot, stabbed, snake bit, or blown up. Once he returned from that outing, he hung up his roaming shoes for good.

"That was Harris for you," Palmer said. "He never was one to let the facts or a map get in his way."

"That's the truth. Anyway, about the time that me and Kathleen became good friends, we also figured out something else. It came to us that neither one of us had a living soul in the world to help us through the burden of being old, and believe me, boy, it is a burden. It seems like the load gets heaviest when you are least able to bear it. As you get older, you start to think about what's coming next, and what that's going to be like. As bad as getting old is, getting old alone is the worst thing there is. We were both as alone as folks could be, and we were both afraid of that. Do you want to know what I was afraid of the most?"

"What's that?"

"I was afraid I'd die, and no one would find me for a while. You know I keep dogs out at the yard." Palmer nodded. Ottis Lee had always kept a noisy pack of big dogs as a deterrent to the theft of auto parts. "If no one was there to feed the dogs and I was laying there dead, well, you know what would happen next. I wouldn't blame them, you understand. They're just animals, and when they get hungry, they eat. But sometimes that would get on my mind and I couldn't think of anything else." He gasped a breath, coughed, and gasped again.

"That would be bad," Palmer agreed. He'd almost been eaten by Ottis Lee's dogs on two separate occasions, and he hadn't even been dead.

"I don't even recall what got us on the subject of getting old and frail and dying alone, but we were talking about those things out at the junkyard one afternoon after I replaced a bad alternator for her, and it turned out that Kathleen was afraid of the same thing I was. Of dying alone and being found days or weeks later. Then I said I wished we both had someone to be with, someone to make the empty time seem fuller. I was just thinking out loud like I'm prone to do, just talking, and then she snapped her fingers and said she had a good idea. I asked her what it was, and right there and then she asked me to marry her. I thought she was just messing around, but she convinced me that she was being serious."

"She snuck up on you! Reeled you in like an old river cat."

"Well, I don't know about that, but she did have enough sense to see a good solution for both of us. I was getting too old to live rough out at the junkyard anymore, especially in the winter, and she had this nice house with plenty of room. She was getting kind of low on cash since that devil went back where he came from, but I had enough money for two. She was a good cook, and I could keep the furnace running and fix her car when it laid down. And we'd both have someone to talk to and to get old with. Someone to help when sickness came." He nodded as if reassuring himself of the validity of the plan.

"Not to mention the fringe benefits of married life," Palmer pointed out.

"Lord, no, Palmer," Ottis Lee said. "I'm too sick for that, and I was too old for it even before I was too sick. No, I guess you would call what we have a business arrangement. It was plain that we would do better together than we were doing apart. Still, as good an idea as it was for us, I never would have come up with it on my own, and I almost didn't go through with it after Kathleen thought of it."

"Why not?"

"I've been a black man living in Georgia my entire life, and there's not much that folks can say or do to surprise me anymore. The world has changed a lot since I was a boy, and it needed to and that's a fact, but I wasn't sure it had changed enough to allow me to marry a nice white lady from town. When I was a young boy that was the kind of thing that could still get a black man hung, and not just in Georgia. People like to judge, and people like to get all up in

269

other people's business, and I'm too old and set in my ways to put up with any foolishness."

"You could have just lived together."

"Yeah, that would have worked out a whole lot better," Ottis Lee said with a wry grin. "No one around here would have had any trouble with that. As it was, most of my black friends quit coming around because I married a white woman, and most of Kathleen's white friends quit coming around because she married a black man." He shrugged. "At least the racism cuts both ways. But that's their problem. We have each other, and as it turned out, it was none too soon. She started to head downhill pretty fast not long after we got married, and I got sick last year. I'm still able most days to watch out for her, and she's still pretty good company for me even if she doesn't always know who I am. So we plug along. It's the best we can do."

"How are *you* doing?" Palmer asked. "Trenton told me you were having trouble with your lungs."

"You got eyes. I'm dying just about as fast as I can manage unless I just go over and lay down on the railroad tracks. The doc has given me six months to live twice now. The first six months he spent trying to figure out what in the Sam Hill was killing me and then trying to teach me the name of it. He's spent most of the second six months wondering why I wasn't already dead. I don't think he'll have to give me six more, though. The way I feel most days, it won't be long now."

"There's nothing they can do?"

"Not much that will make any difference. This mesothelioma is some bad business. It's a kind of cancer that you catch from asbestos. Once you get it, about the best thing you can do is tell everyone good-bye and get right with the Lord. Sometimes they can buy you a little time, but the kind of time they buy you is not the kind of time you want to have." He shrugged again, then wheezed. "So I'm not buying any. I don't want talcum powder shot into my chest, and I don't want to be cut open and scraped out, and I don't want any of that chemo, and for sure I don't want to be cooked nice and crispy with that radiation. I saw what that stuff did to my sister, and then she died anyway. Shoot, I think all it did was speed it up for her. She died the day after her final treatment. Well, not for me. Dying's bad enough without going through all of that."

"I'm sorry, Ottis Lee. I don't know what else to say." He found himself unable to look his old friend in the eyes.

"Don't fret, Palmer. We all die. It's just my time. Sure, I wish I had a few more years here, because *here* is a real nice place to be, but these are the cards I drew, so this is the hand I have to play. I've had a fine life, and now it's time for me to move on. I worry about Kathleen, though. Our business arrangement is breaking down. Her mind is in terrible shape, but she's pretty healthy from the neck down. I think she'll live a long time, and I don't know what's going to happen to her after I go. That's the only problem with our plan. Both of us don't have to die alone, but one of us still has to." He sighed. "I've prayed and prayed on it. I know the Lord is working on something. He won't let us down."

Palmer nodded. He was reminded of his mother's faith, and just as he had with her, he kept his doubts to himself.

"Where is she?" Palmer asked.

"She was up most of the night. Sometimes she is on a reverse schedule. She gets real lively about the time the sun goes down, and she usually falls out around daybreak and sleeps a few hours. That's why we're talking quiet." He smiled a sad smile. "Waking a woman with Alzheimer's is kind of like waking a sleeping baby. You don't want to do it unless the house is on fire."

"What does she do all night?"

"She walks. I bet she walks twenty miles a night, all of it right here in the house. She walks around the living room, down the hall, in and out of her room, back up the hall, around the kitchen, and

271

then back here again. She can't get upstairs because I've got it closed off. I had to do it when she started falling down the stairs. Now she just walks down here. She never gets tired, she never sits down, and she never gets to where she thinks she wants to be."

"Why does she walk?"

"Lord, that's a good question. Mostly she thinks she has to get to her Aunt Arabel's house, because her daddy is waiting for her there."

"Who is Aunt Arabel?"

"Arabel was Kathleen's great-aunt. She's been dead about forty years, but she's fresh as a daisy in Kathleen's mind. Her daddy's been dead nearly as long, but Kathleen is sure that they're both waiting for her over at Arabel's place. As near as I can figure, in her head she's walking through the neighborhood she grew up in. Bless her heart. Her doctor told me that he sees this kind of thing a lot in people like her. He said it seems like they're trying to get back to a place and maybe a time that was safe for them. I don't know about all that, but it is a fact that she is determined to go to Aunt Arabel's." He rested from speaking, then continued. "Back when this first started, I thought I could use facts and logic to show her that she was just confused. So we went for a ride one day, and we ended up at the cemetery. I showed her Aunt Arabel's grave, and her daddy's, and I tried to explain to her what was happening to her and why she was confused. She said she understood, so I thought we were going to be okay. On the way home, she pointed out three different houses that she thought were Aunt Arabel's, and she wanted to stop at all of them." He shrugged.

"If she's up all night, how do you sleep?"

"I don't, much. But when I do fall asleep, she generally leaves me be unless she gets hungry. She can't get out of the house since I nailed the windows shut and installed deadbolts on the front and back doors. So sometimes I catch forty winks while she walks her circle."

"She tries to leave?"

"Oh, yeah. She was bad to walk on out the door on her way to Aunt Arabel's. The last time she got away, she almost ended up in the river. That's when I got out the hammer. Now at least I know that whatever happens, it'll happen in here where I can try to keep her safe. About the only real problem we've had lately is when she wants to work in the kitchen. Sometimes she decides she wants to cook and turns on the stove, and a couple of times she started fires by accident. So I've started leaving the breaker shut off when I'm not cooking. It upsets her that the stove won't work, but she forgets about it quick enough, and at least we don't burn up in the night."

From down the hall Palmer heard a sustained, loud tweeting noise. Ottis Lee looked at him and nodded toward the sound. "It's her door alarm," he said. "It's like a door stop. When she tries to open the door, the alarm warns me and the door stop slows her up until I can get there. It's time to get her dressed. Wait here while I get her changed and decent. If you want to help out, you could put on the coffee. She likes a cup of coffee when she first gets up. It's one of the few things she hasn't forgotten about. Lots of sugar."

The old man shambled down the hall. The alarm stopped tweeting, and as Palmer made a pot of coffee in the kitchen, he could hear Ottis Lee's calm voice as he assisted his wife through her morning ablutions and into her clothes.

Several thoughts went through Palmer's mind as the coffee brewed. Apparently Kathleen was even worse off than he had imagined, and he was a bit concerned about how their reunion would go. Would she still know him, or would he be a stranger to her? Should he go along with her delusions, or would it be better to try to bring her back to reality whenever possible? He didn't know the correct answers to these conundrums, and Ottis Lee hadn't really said other than to share the story of the visit to Aunt Arabel's grave, including the disappointing outcome of that visit. And what about Ottis Lee? He looked terrible and assumedly felt worse than that. How long did he have? How bad would it be when he died? The house held too many problems for Palmer to absorb, not the least of which was that the house itself had become Kathleen Earwood's prison. Palmer understood Ottis Lee's need to put the place on lockdown and probably would have done the same if he had been in his shoes, but he had recently spent seven years in one jail and was now visiting another in his spare time.

When the coffee pot was full, Palmer poured a cup for each of them, adding several spoonfuls of sugar to Kathleen's. He had just set them around the small kitchen table when he heard quick footsteps approach. Kathleen Earwood entered the kitchen followed a moment later by Ottis Lee. Palmer was shocked by her appearance. She had never been a large woman, but now she was tiny and frail. Her hair had once been thick and brown, but now it was fully white and wispy thin. Her skin looked like translucent parchment. She walked bent forward with her arms hugged to her chest, as if she were trying to hold whatever was left of herself in. Ottis Lee had dressed her in a pair of sweatpants, a pullover cotton shirt, and slippers. Her eyes met Palmer's, and he saw a flash of recognition in them. For an instant, he thought that maybe everything was going to be fine after all.

"Rodney!" she cried as she threw her arms around him tightly. "My sweet baby boy! Lord bless us all! Where have you been?" He patted her back gently as he looked to Ottis Lee for assistance. The old man slowly sat at the table and took a sip from the coffee cup before him. He shook his head as he quietly chuckled. Then he looked at the kitchen ceiling and spoke.

"Thank you Lord, for revealing your plan," he said to the cracked and faded plaster, and to all that lay beyond that. He looked at Palmer and nodded his head once. "And thank you for putting my worries to rest. I know now that she will be cared for when I'm gone."

"But I—" Palmer began to say, but then he stopped. He had always said that he would pay Rodney back if he could, and here was his chance. Talk was cheap, and actions were all that counted. He was at the climax of an eight-year journey of guilt and regret, and what he did right now would make all the difference. He had an opportunity to make at least partial amends. He had killed Rodney, and he owed him more than he could ever repay. He couldn't bring him back, but he could help look after Kathleen. Now was when the rubber met the road, or when the Camaro hit the tree, as the case may be. Now was when he could step up and do the right thing or go home and soothe his conscience with more cheap talk and empty regrets. He sighed. It looked to him as if there were only one real choice.

"I've been away, Mama," Palmer said to Kathleen Earwood as he patted her again. "I've been away, but now I'm back."

I've been putting off telling you some bad news. One of the first people I met on the outside was your mama. She's in bad shape. I hate to tell you, but she's not right in the head. You remember when she used to visit me at the prison and it seemed like she was not quite herself? Well, that has gotten a lot worse. Your mama is all gone and there's someone else traveling around in her body. That person thinks I'm you. I mean she thinks you're still alive and that I am you and that she is my mother. It's a messed-up situation and I'm not sure how it's going to end. Not good, I expect, but we're sort of getting used to that, right?

The good news is that she is married again. Your new daddy is Ottis Lee Lamb so I guess that makes you a black kid now. He always wanted a son, and since Harris went to Asheville you need a father figure, so it looks like a match made in heaven to me. The bad news is that Ottis Lee is very sick and not likely to last much longer, but I don't

275

want you to worry about that. I'll take care of Kathleen when the time comes. Since she thinks I'm her boy, it's the least I can do. I'll do whatever it takes to see that she's okay. If it wasn't for me she really would have a son around to look after her. I'll make it right somehow.

Poor Ottis Lee has something called mesothelioma. It seems like a really bad way to go, but I have come to believe that there aren't many good ways. Maybe a quick and painless heart attack at age 100 right after the best meal you ever had followed by the best sex you ever had followed by a neat glass of high dollar Scotch and a Marlboro. But other than that, most people deserve better than they get, present company included, but what they deserve counts for exactly jack. Anyway, Ottis Lee spends his days taking care of your mama and trying to breathe. He really should be on oxygen and the hospice left a bottle, but he likes those Swisher Sweet cigars more than he likes to breathe and he doesn't want to blow Kathleen up, so he keeps it turned off and tucked into the corner.

Your mama's doctor thinks she has dementia and Alzheimer's. They're kind of alike, but not. Or maybe they are. I don't know. He says little pieces of her brain are dying, and they take her memories with them when they go. He told me that the wiring in her brain is starting to short out and that's why she is confused and forgetful and why she can mistake me for you and why it is perfectly logical for her to try to walk to a place 40 years in the past. There's no cure for it, but she has tablets for anxiety and tablets for sleep and tablets for when she gets agitated and tablets for this and for that. What she really needs is a tablet to make her take the others because she doesn't much like to take her medicine.

It's really strange what she remembers and what she forgets, and how that comes and goes. The older the memory is, the more likely she is to remember it. She doesn't remember Harris at all, but she does think that Trenton is your father. No, I mean that she thinks that Trenton is actually the guy she was married to before he died and she married Harris. But she thinks they're both young again. It kind of creeps Trenton out when she holds his hand and talks sweet to him, but he

276

knows she can't help it so he puts up with it because she is sick. She knows who Ottis Lee is and that she's married to him now, but she doesn't really know what that means and it's not a problem for her when husbands 1 and 3 are both in the same room at the same time. It seems normal to her and I swear it's starting to seem that way to me too.

So that's kind of where we are. I'm helping Ottis Lee watch out for her, and after he dies I guess I'll be on my own. That'll work out fine as long as your mama thinks I'm you because she is all about her little Boo Boo. Yep, she told me your little boy name, so don't be giving me too much lip if you don't want it spread all over town. Do me a favor. If you run up on Aunt Arabel over there, see if she'll give you her recipe for sugar cake. Your mama is driving me crazy for some of Aunt Arabel's sugar cake, but no matter what I try to pass off as the stuff, it's never quite right. The closest I've managed was a Twinkie. Be on the lookout for Ottis Lee. It won't be long before he makes the trip and it would be nice if some people he knew met him at the station.

13

Boo Boo and That Other Man

As time passed, Palmer came to realize that Ottis Lee Lamb was sicker than he looked, and that was the real shame of it, because he looked about as sick as a living human being could. Beginning with his lungs, his mesothelioma had slowly enveloped most of the internal organs worth mentioning and now held them tightly in its malicious embrace, and it was a short race against time before one or another of these gave out completely and left him stranded on the distant shore. His breathing became more labored as each day passed, so much so that he eventually had to trade in his beloved Swisher Sweets for the more conventional but far less satisfying oxygen tank. Most days he sat in Harris's recliner and watched old movies on television—Jimmy Stewart and Gary Cooper were his favorites—and most nights he attempted to sleep in that same overstuffed chair while Kathleen made pass after pass on her way to Aunt Arabel's house. His appetite had almost completely left him along the way, so Palmer made sure that each cup of coffee he served was loaded with as much cream and sugar as it would hold. He laid in a quantity of frozen chicken pot pies because that was all that Ottis Lee would eat, and at the same time he purchased an ample supply of bacon and eggs, because Kathleen would allow nothing else to pass her lips.

Eventually Palmer gave up trying to commute to his new job as caregiver for everyone living in the Earwood home and just moved in himself. He made the decision on the morning he let himself in and found Ottis Lee sprawled in the floor at about the midpoint between the recliner and the bathroom. Kathleen was making her circuit as usual, but she was attempting to help in her own way. She had brought Ottis Lee several coffee cups to cheer him up as he waited for rescue, and the fact that each contained a different liquid and that none of them contained coffee detracted not one whit from the noble gesture. She had also pitched in and dressed herself during the emergency, and as she shuffled by, Palmer noted that she had on pajamas under her housecoat, which was on backwards, and that one of Ottis Lee's denim shirts, inside out, covered that. As a final touch she had donned a brassiere, and Palmer was somewhat impressed that she had gotten both arms through the straps because straps often defeated her, and it bothered neither him nor Kathleen that the cups faced the rear.

"Lord, Ottis Lee," Palmer said as he kneeled down beside him. "Let me get you up from there." The old man was getting smaller and lighter all the time, and Palmer had little trouble scooping him up and relocating him from the floor to the recliner. Sometimes it seemed as if Ottis Lee might just disappear altogether before the end, and that all that would remain to remember him by would be his robe, his slippers, and a chewed up, cold cigar stub in the ashtray. "Were you on the way to the john or coming back? Do you still need to go?"

"I was…coming back," Ottis Lee gasped. He talked in snatches now, three- and four-word pieces wheezed out between breaths.

"Otherwise I guess...you'd be mopping up... behind me. I'm good...for a while." Palmer settled him into the recliner, replaced his oxygen cannula under his nose, and covered him with a quilt. He tucked it in tightly so the old man would warm up quickly. He had felt cold to the touch, and Palmer was worried that he would literally catch his death of cold from the episode.

"How long were you down there?"

"It was...around four o'clock. I guess...about five hours."

"Boo Boo, can we go see Aunt Arabel?" Kathleen asked as she paced by. She was on automatic pilot this morning, as she tended to be early in the day, and she did not even pause to hear the answer. As the day passed, her queries would usually become more insistent, and by sundown, she would be worked into a state of panic and rage at being denied the freedom to make her journey to see her long-departed kin. It was the same every day and had been for about a month now. Palmer needed to get her cleaned up, changed, and fed, but first he had Ottis Lee to deal with.

"Hey, Mama," he said to Kathleen. "Maybe we'll go later." To Ottis Lee he said, "Let's get your medicine into you. Then I'll make some coffee."

"I can't believe it," Ottis Lee said. His breathing was still labored, but no more than was now customary for him. "It's twenty steps...to the bathroom...and twenty steps back...and the trip...was too long for me. Plus, I hit everything...but the pot...while I was in there. I swear, Palmer...if you decide...to get old someday...you had best leave...your pride at the door. If you want my advice...die young."

"Thanks for the tip," Palmer said. "Do you hurt anywhere?" He was trying to determine how much pain medication was in order, and whether or not he needed to call the nurse. He looked at the schedule on the side table and saw that she was due for a visit that morning, anyway, so he decided to let her check him for breakage.

"Just the...usual places. I don't think...I broke anything...I'm still using. I tripped on my own feet...and once I got down in the floor...I wasn't strong enough...to get up. I knew...you would be along... and Kathleen...had my back...the whole time." He smiled weakly at his little joke.

"I saw that. I thought you hid all of her bras." Kathleen, too, was shrinking as the weeks and months went by, and she no longer had any real need for a brassiere, and they were trouble for all concerned, so they had been sequestered, and both men had been hoping that she would forget about the existence of this particular type of undergarment. But she had worn one every day and most nights for nearly all of her life and did not seem willing to give them up now.

"I did...but she tore up her room...until she found one. She kept saying...it wasn't decent...for a woman to go out...on a Sunday...without her brassiere. Said the preacher...and her daddy... would both say something...if she went out like that."

"It's Tuesday, and her daddy's been dead longer than I've been alive." Ottis Lee shrugged as Palmer pointed out the obvious.

"I guess...if you wear one...of those things long enough...you feel undressed...without it. Shirley calls it...one of her deep habits. She said...those are always...the last things to go." Shirley was Ottis Lee's hospice nurse. She was officially in charge of his health and welfare, and unofficially she took a peek at Kathleen every time she came out as well. Ottis Lee took some breaths and rested for a moment. Then he spoke again. "Once you get her...out of it... throw it...and the rest of them...away."

Palmer nodded. They had both come to realize that out of sight, out of mind was the best tool in their toolbox.

"I will. I'll burn them in the trash barrel out back. It'll look like the '60s around here. Maybe I'll grow my hair long for the occasion. Here. Take these." He handed Ottis Lee his morning medications.

Then he held out a cup of water with a straw. Ottis Lee took his pills with a frown and a gulp. He had not been sick much throughout his life, and it seemed he was having a hard time warming up to it now.

"I remember...the '60s. All those...sweet young things...and me a young buck...just free...and glad to be...alive." The memory seemed to sadden him, but he smiled in spite of it. "I never got...any of that free love...we kept hearing about...back then. But if it...was any better than...the little bit of...love...I was rousting out...it would have...killed me anyway. Good days. They were...good days."

"Good days," Kathleen said as she walked past them. "I feel good today, Boo Boo. You can give my candy to that man." She pointed at Ottis Lee. "That other man took my pills." Candy and pills were interchangeable terms to Kathleen, and that was mostly Palmer's fault. It was difficult to get the latter down her throat without employing subterfuge, and Palmer often resorted to hiding her medication in food and drink while hoping for a good outcome. Snickers Bars were the best for this purpose, but she was beginning to have a bit of trouble swallowing them because her tongue sometimes got in the way. According to her doctor this difficulty in swallowing was normal for Alzheimer's patients, and it would likely become more pronounced as her condition worsened.

"Okay, Mama," Palmer said to Kathleen. "Who is 'that other man'?" he asked Ottis Lee as he passed him the inhaler. Ottis Lee took two good hits, coughed, recovered, took one more shot for luck, and replied.

"I think...it's me. She started talking...about 'that other man'...after I fell."

"Boo Boo and That Other Man," Palmer said. "Sounds like a bad hip-hop act, or maybe a TV show."

"Don't make...me laugh. I'm too sick...to be laughing. I'll break...a rib."

"Are you hungry?"

"I was...but all those pills...filled me up." There were quite a few, and Ottis Lee made a point of fussing about the quantity every time he took the medicine.

"If I make you a pot pie, will you eat it?"

"I don't know."

"I got the kind with crust on top and bottom."

"I do...like that crust. Maybe I'll have...a little bite...or two."

"Okay, here's the flipper for the TV. I think there's a Western on this morning. You watch while I get Kathleen straightened out. Then I'll make her some bacon and you a pot pie. We'll all have a cup of coffee." Ottis Lee nodded, pointed the remote, closed his eyes, and fell asleep. It had been a long night.

Palmer removed the remote from his hand and left him to nap. He stepped into the kitchen, crossed to the electrical box in the utility room, and flipped up the breaker for the stove. Then he set the oven temperature and placed a chicken pot pie on a cookie sheet on the rack. As he began to prepare the coffee, Kathleen came into the room. She was carrying the doll that he had brought her at Shirley's suggestion after Kathleen had spent two very bad days looking for her baby, which she believed had been kidnapped by a hobo or perhaps inadvertently left at Aunt Arabel's house during a fire drill. He had placed the soft doll where she could discover it on her own, and at least for the time being it seemed to mollify her.

"I'll have us some coffee made in a minute, Mama," he said to Kathleen. "Are you about ready to get dressed?"

"You know I don't drink coffee, Boo Boo. I never have cared for it." Palmer nodded, and she wandered back out of the kitchen. Once the coffee had brewed, he poured himself a cup and took a couple of appreciative sips. He always hated to hit the ground running at the beginning of the day, but he had definitely had to do just that this morning. He preferred to enter the day at a more leisurely pace, to get his mind right, his plan made, and his coffee sipped.

As soon as he got Kathleen dressed and both of his charges fed, he needed to sit down and talk over the morning's events with Ottis Lee. He believed that they had arrived at yet another crossroads, one more in a long series of new normals, and at this place, Ottis Lee was no longer even able to take care of himself, never mind Kathleen. But he respected the old man, so he wanted to ask him what he thought they needed to do at this juncture. Palmer had thought for a while now that he would eventually need to move in, and he realized that perhaps he had waited a few too many days before doing so, but he wanted to ask Ottis Lee what he thought about the idea rather than tell him that the time for it had arrived. It was a little thing, a small courtesy, but Ottis Lee was at the stage of life where the big things were all tumbling out of his control, and that made the little things all the more important. Palmer unlocked the padlock on the cabinet that held all of the dangerous objects in the kitchen, including knives, matches, and Kathleen's medications. He selected her morning tablets and dropped them into the bottom of her tall sip cup. Then he crushed them with a wooden pestle and added hot coffee, cream, and four spoons of sugar. He stirred, added an ice cube, and popped the lid on the cup. Kathleen walked back in just as he finished relocking the cabinet.

"Your coffee's ready," he said.

"I have to have my morning coffee," she replied. She opened the refrigerator, placed her doll inside, and shut the door.

"Are you ready to get dressed?" he asked again as he handed her the sip cup. He didn't really expect an answer, but he wanted to plant the seed of the idea in her head so it would not take her by surprise later. "Be careful, now. It's still hot."

She took a sip and smiled.

"You make good coffee, Boo Boo." She hugged him.

"Well, you taught me how. Come on, let's go get dressed."

"I already got dressed," she replied.

"I know, and you look really nice. But today's a special day, so we have to dress up a little bit special for it. Shirley's coming to visit us. You remember her, don't you?"

"Well I guess I do! She's my daughter."

Palmer gently herded her out of the kitchen and toward the bathroom. He had found by trial and error that the best way to clean and change Kathleen was to first engage her in conversation. She didn't resist his efforts nearly as much, and if there was a part of her somewhere in there still concerned with modesty, then perhaps it would be distracted while he did what he had to do.

"If she's your daughter, then she must be my sister," Palmer said as he stripped her out of her clothing and removed her pull ups. The strong odor of urine reminded him that he still needed to clean up after Ottis Lee's pre-dawn bathroom run.

"You don't have a sister. You're my only baby." As she stood before him, he gave her a quick once over with a wet washcloth, dried her with a clean towel, and slipped on another diaper. Normally he would sit her on the shower chair and just let the warm water do most of the work, but that operation involved a level of commitment he could not spare this morning. After her sponge bath, he combed out her short hair and squeezed some toothpaste onto her toothbrush. He placed the business end in her mouth and began a brushing motion. She reached up and took over. It was a wonder to Palmer what she kept and what she lost. For some reason her brushing skills were still quite strong, and she went at it with gusto.

"Stop brushing and spit," he said after a few moments. Kathleen did, then swished and rinsed with the water he provided. He wiped her mouth and took the toothbrush. "Good! Bring your coffee, and let's go get dressed." She led the way, and he followed her to her bedroom. It was a shambles from the earlier bra hunt, but he managed to locate a sweatshirt, a pair of sweatpants, and her slippers.

She stood patiently while he dressed her, although she did offer a comment as he guided one of her arms into a sweatshirt sleeve.

"You forgot my bra," she whispered, assumedly so neither the preacher nor her father would hear and be scandalized by the omission. "I'll need my bra before we go to Aunt Arabel's."

"Okay," he said. "They're all in the washing machine right now. We'll get you one in a minute. Have some more coffee." She took another long sip, and Palmer could almost see the caffeine and the other, less traditional chemicals as they worked their way into her system. "Are you ready for some breakfast?"

"I just had a big breakfast, and I couldn't eat another bite." Palmer nodded, and Kathleen once again began her endless walk. Palmer let her get started, then went back to the kitchen. He checked the pot pie, which was not far from ready. He put a skillet on the stovetop, removed the doll and a pack of bacon from the refrigerator, and went on with his morning routine. He placed four strips of bacon into the heated pan and watched as they began to sizzle. Kathleen stepped into the kitchen without comment and retrieved her doll. She was carrying her coffee cup, but she seemed to have forgotten that fact.

"Have some more coffee," he suggested. She looked at the cup in her hand. Then she took a long drink, and then another. She placed the cup on the cabinet and cuddled her doll closer.

"This poor thing is freezing!" she said.

"You should find her a blanket," Palmer suggested. She left the room, and Palmer could hear her gently cooing to her baby as she went to find something warm for her. He browned the bacon, blotted it, put it on a sturdy paper plate, and placed it on a tray. Next he cracked and peeled one of the hard-boiled eggs he always kept ready in the refrigerator and put it beside the bacon. Kathleen still liked the taste of eggs, but she was no longer very adept at using utensils, so it was boiled or nothing. Then he removed the steaming

286

miniature pot pie from the oven, chopped it up with a spoon, and put it on the tray. Finally, he poured a half mug of coffee for Ottis Lee before topping it off with cream and sugar. Breakfast was ready. He took the entire spread to the living room and set it on the coffee table. It was around ten in the morning, and he had been working steadily since he walked in the door. Kathleen shuffled into the room.

"I'm hungry, Boo Boo," she said.

"Here's bacon." He handed her a crispy strip. "There's an egg for you too, if you want it." Then he turned his attention to Ottis Lee, who had begun to stir from his nap. "Cup of coffee?" he asked as he passed him the mug.

"Thanks," Ottis Lee replied as he accepted it with two shaking hands. Palmer helped him steady it as he took a sip. "You know...I like it black."

"I know. You like it black with a Swisher Sweet, but today you have to drink it with cream and sugar. You need the calories."

"You're not...my mama." Ottis Lee smiled, then took another sip.

"No. Your mama would have told you to hush, behave yourself, and eat what was put in front of you."

Ottis Lee nodded. "It's true. My mama...wouldn't put up... with much sass from us...young'uns. Lord...that woman...would cut a switch...in a ...minute."

"She was a smart woman. Are you ready for some pie?"

"Maybe...just a taste."

Palmer took the cup and replaced it with the cooled pie. Ottis Lee slowly worked at his pie with a fork until eventually he had worried every bit of crust from the little tin and had consumed it. Once he finished, he handed the remains of his breakfast to Palmer.

"That was...mighty fine. You're a good...cook."

"Eat a bite or two of chicken?" Palmer asked. "You need some protein. Maybe a carrot or a pea?"

"No. Just the crust. I surely...like that crust."

Palmer nodded. He was fairly pragmatic when it came to feeding sick people. Beginning with Cheddar back in Sweetwater prison and continuing now with Ottis Lee and Kathleen, he gave people what they would eat. By doing this, he cut down dramatically on both waste and resistance. It was a question of perspective. He had figured out early on that it wasn't the difference between a strip of bacon or some piecrust and a fully balanced and healthy seven-course meal. It was the difference between bacon or piecrust and nothing at all if the patient refused to eat, and some food was better than no food.

"How about a trip to the bathroom?" Palmer asked.

"I'm good." As Ottis Lee answered, the doorbell rang. Palmer stepped to the door quickly. He wanted it opened, shut, and locked back tight before Kathleen made another round through the living room. Open front doors agitated her. They exacerbated the desire to travel the mystical road to Aunt Arabel's house, and to all the magical lands beyond, and it was too early in the day for her to get wound up about hitting the road. He unlocked the deadbolt and opened the door. Before him stood Shirley Connely, Ottis Lee's nurse.

"Morning, Palmer," she said with a smile.

"Come in," he replied. She opened the screen and entered the living room, dragging her wheeled carrier behind her. Palmer quickly shut the door and locked it. He dropped the door key back into his jeans pocket.

"How is everyone?" Shirley asked. She was well aware of the quick entry protocol and moved away from the door.

"It's been one of those wild mornings," Palmer confessed. "But it seems to be quieting down a little now."

Shirley Connely was a traveling nurse for Tri-County Hospice, the agency entrusted with Ottis Lee's medical care as he navigated the rocky road from this life to the next. She was a compact woman with chestnut hair and compassionate eyes. As was the case with most of the healthcare professionals Palmer had met, she wore scrubs when she was at work. Today's were blue. He liked her, and he respected her medical expertise, her kind heart, and her commonsense judgment. She was a hospice nurse because it was her calling, not merely her job. She was in the business because she wanted to help people in trouble.

Palmer was on file with the agency as Ottis Lee's caregiver. He was actually listed as Kathleen's biological son and Ottis Lee's stepson, which was admittedly a bit of a tall tale, but it helped Palmer get the job done. This deception had been Trenton Cray's idea, and it was a good one. In the world of caregiving, relatives of any sort trumped well-meaning acquaintances, and a son was more likely to be heard than an ex-convict on a mission to repay the ultimate debt.

"What happened?" Shirley asked.

"Ottis Lee fell going to the bathroom and spent half the night in the floor. That got Kathleen all stirred up, and she's been walking to Aunt Arabel's house ever since."

Shirley nodded as she opened her bag and removed her stethoscope and her laptop computer.

"How do you feel?" she asked Ottis Lee as she carefully uncovered him.

"I feel...like you're the prettiest thing...I've seen all day," Ottis Lee replied. He was long past the ability to do most of the many things he had once loved to do, but he could still flirt, and Shirley was about his only opportunity.

"You're a sweet man, Ottis Lee," she replied. She listened to his heart and lungs and shined a light into each eye. Then she felt his head for bumps. "But I'm mad at you right now, so you can save your sugar talk for another time. I told you it was a bad idea to walk at night when you were here without Palmer. Maybe now you'll listen to good advice when you hear it. Do you think you broke anything?" She began to check all four of his limbs for movement and bruises.

"I think...all I broke...was my pride."

"Pride goes before a fall, and you're lucky that's all you broke. You know, you could use that." She pointed at the bedside commode chair strategically staged by the wall near the recliner. "It's here for a reason."

"I don't...want to," Ottis Lee said. "A man likes...a little privacy."

"I know it," Shirley replied. "I wouldn't want to use it in front of everyone, either. But I would if I had to. And you know something? Kathleen won't even notice what you're doing, and Palmer here can leave the room anytime you need to be alone for a few minutes. So you'll still have your privacy, and you won't end up with a concussion or a broken hip. You know what a broken hip means to a man in your condition?"

"It means...bigger trouble...than I've already...got."

"That's right. A lot of the time it's the beginning of the end. So use some good sense."

"It's hard...dying," Ottis Lee observed. "Folks say...life is hard. For some it is...I guess...but for me...life was easy...and fine. Dying is hard."

"You are mighty right about that, Ottis Lee," Shirley said kindly. "It's just about the hardest thing there is. I wish it wasn't so, but there's nothing much left but the hard part now." At that moment, Kathleen entered the room, her forgotten bacon clasped in one hand and her doll dangling by one leg from the other. She saw Shirley and stopped short, dropping them both to the floor.

290

"Who are you?" she asked.

"I'm Shirley, Miss Kathleen. I've come to see about Ottis Lee."

"We don't have him, do we, Boo Boo?"

"We could let Shirley take a look at That Other Man while she's here," Palmer suggested, pointing at the recliner.

"I'll have to see what Daddy says," Kathleen replied. "You know how he is about black folks." She squatted down and picked up her bacon. She took a bite, dropped it back, and left once again on her rounds.

"She knew who you were last time you were here," Palmer said. "And this morning she believed you were her daughter. I thought for sure she would remember you today. I don't suppose it matters, but whenever she remembers something, I take it as a good sign, like maybe she is fighting it off."

"It comes and goes," Shirley said. "Bless her heart. There is no telling what's going on in her mind." She slid the blood pressure cuff over Ottis Lee's bony arm. "Are you eating anything?" she asked her patient. He nodded as she pumped the bulb.

"Lord, yes. I had a big…breakfast this morning."

Shirley looked to Palmer for confirmation.

"He had the crust off a pot pie and most of a cup of coffee with cream and sugar. It was a big breakfast for him." He felt like he was ratting out a friend, but she needed to know.

"You're wasting away," she said to Ottis Lee. "We've got to get more nourishment into you. If this keeps up, I'll have to start bringing a child's cuff along with me so I can check your blood pressure. Do you like ice cream?"

Ottis Lee nodded. "I like chocolate."

"Good. Tell Palmer to make you a chocolate milkshake every day. Or a chocolate sundae with lots of syrup. You're going to blow away if we don't get some meat on your bones."

"I promise...I'll eat more," Ottis Lee said. "The next time...you come...I'll be as round...as a fattening hog."

"I hope so. How's your pain?"

"It's tolerable. It's mostly...a three or a...four. Sometimes it jumps... to a six."

"We can increase your medication some."

"Maybe just...for when it gets...up over five."

"The doctor wrote an order for a stronger medication if you needed it. There's no sense in you putting up with even a three all the time if there's something you can do about it. I'll call the pharmacy and have them fill the new prescription, and I'll let Palmer know what to do and when to do it." She made a few notes on her laptop.

"I thank you."

"How's your air?"

"About like...it was. I can't seem...to catch enough of it."

"The less you do, like trying to walk to the bathroom, the easier you'll breathe." He nodded. "All right," she said. "I have to head on to see my next patient now. Is there anything you need before I go?" She packed her bag as she spoke.

"If you get the chance...do you think you...could ask that... preacher...to come out again? I liked him...and I need to talk... about a couple of things...while I can still...sort of talk." He was referring to the agency's chaplain, but to Ottis Lee, all members of the clergy were preachers.

"I can call the office right now if you would like to see him today," Shirley said. Ottis Lee shook his head. "Well then, I'll see him in the morning, and I'll let him know." She leaned over the recliner and gave him a hug. "I'll be back the day after tomorrow unless you need me sooner." Kathleen popped into the living room, saw Shirley bidding farewell to Ottis Lee, made an about-face, and headed back down the hall.

"No hugs for baby," she said as she retreated. "No hugs."

"I'll walk you out," Palmer said. He walked ahead of Shirley to the door, unlocked the deadbolt, and gestured her out. He locked the door behind him before escorting her to her car. This was a ritual they had developed so that Palmer could hear information he needed without asking for it in front of either of his patients.

"I really like your car," he said as he walked around her red Mustang convertible. "If I ever start driving again, I may have to have one of these."

"The gas mileage is terrible, but I do love driving with the top down," she said as she loaded her equipment and supplies into the trunk. She slammed the trunk lid and came around to where Palmer stood.

"What do you think?" he asked.

"Usually when they start falling, that marks the beginning of a big change for the worse. Somehow you've got to convince him to quit walking around. A broken hip is a bad thing to have on top of everything that's already wrong with him. That would make his final days a pure misery."

"He's a lot worse today than he was yesterday," Palmer replied. "If he had been like this last night, I wouldn't have gone home. It seems like he went down overnight."

"It happens that way sometimes. They'll be doing so well that you think they're on the mend. Then all of a sudden, they're gone. I call it the last good day. I'm always happy for the patient when they have one, a last good day, but I want to warn the family to prepare themselves for what is coming next. Still, I've been doing this my whole life, and sometimes a patient will still surprise me. He's got some time left, I think, but it may move quicker now. Do you have someone who can stay here at night? I think it's time. He might be okay a while longer if he would just stay put in his chair, but if she gets into distress, he won't be able to help her. You could come some morning and find them both in the floor, gone."

"I'm staying from now on. I decided that when I saw him this morning."

"That's good."

"I waited too long, I guess, but I thought it was all right."

"It was, until this morning. It's a big step, and once you're in, you're in until it's over." She smiled ruefully. "Don't beat yourself up. Those two in there can handle that just fine without any help from you."

"His breathing is getting worse, his pain is creeping up, he's started falling, and he won't eat. He's talking about the good old days more and more, and now he's asked to see the preacher. I've got a bad feeling about this."

"He's making his peace and getting himself ready for the journey. People do that. On some level he knows his time is getting near. Can you get by the pharmacy today and pick up his new pain medicine?"

"I'll send my father."

"He should keep taking what he's taking now, but also give him one of these new ones twice a day. Make sure he takes them even if he thinks he doesn't need them. The time to take pain medicine is before you need it, not when you're already in trouble."

Palmer nodded. "I do have problems getting him to take his pain medicine sometimes. It's like he's testing himself to see how much pain he can take. I think his panting has as much to do with pain as it does with his mesothelioma. He says he doesn't want to get hooked. Sometimes I want to point out that he's sitting in a recliner chair watching old movies and waiting to die, so what does it matter if he's hooked or not?"

"Pain can make a person pant," she said. "But there's no need for it. We can keep him almost completely out of pain and alert at the same time if he'll let us. There is no need for him to hurt, but you're right. People of his generation are often afraid of strong pain medication and suffer when they don't have to. He trusts you, Palmer. Make him take his medicine. I never said this, but put it in his coffee if you have to."

"I'll see that his takes it," Palmer assured her.

"I'll see you Thursday," she said as she opened the door and stepped into the Mustang. "Call me if you need me sooner. Make him a chocolate milkshake!" She slammed the door, started the car, and left for her next visit.

Palmer lit a cigarette and stood in place taking puff after quick puff. One thing was certain. If he ever had terminal anything, and it was painful, and there was medication available to ease the pain, no one would have to tell him twice to take it. People were all different, he supposed, but it seemed to him that the best way to cope with dying was to be so high when it happened that he did not even realize that it had happened. His reverie was interrupted by a holler and a crash from inside, and he knew that his smoke break was over. He took one last puff, ground out the butt, and headed back to his duties.

Palmer unlocked the door and opened it slowly. Kathleen's back was to him. She was standing in front of the coffee table, which was upended. Plates, cups, bacon, medicines, and one lonely boiled egg were scattered across the floor. Palmer quietly locked the door and pocketed the key. Then he stepped up beside Kathleen Earwood.

"Kind of a mess," he noted.

"That Other Man did it," she said matter-of-factly.

"Why did he do that?"

"He was mad because he can't go to Aunt Arabel's house. It's his birthday, and Aunt Arabel made a sugar cake."

"He must have been pretty upset," Palmer said. He righted the table and began to pick up the scatterings. It had been two or three days since she had experienced an episode like this, and Palmer had been expecting another. Sometimes she became physically violent, but once the rage passed, she often had a good day. Palmer figured she was just handling her negative emotions the best way she could.

"Boo Boo," she said. "Oh, Boo Boo bear." She turned and walked toward the hall. He realized as she left the room that she was no longer wearing the sweatshirt he had dressed her in that morning. He sighed. It was early yet in what was obviously going to be a long day.

"I wish you wouldn't do things like this," Palmer said to Ottis Lee, who sat reclined and blanketed in his chair, panting as he watched the cleanup.

"You know…what a rascal…I am," Ottis Lee replied.

"What got her set off?"

"She saw you go out with Shirley."

"Whoops." Palmer had been careful, so perhaps Kathleen had been peeking.

"Whoops for sure."

"Can we have a talk?" Palmer asked as he finished neatening the coffee table and its contents. He dragged a chair close and sat.

"Yes."

"How do you feel?"

"I feel like…a Chrysler fell on me."

"What would you think about me moving in for a while?"

The silence grew long as Ottis Lee considered this proposal.

"I would…appreciate the help. And I would…surely hate that a…fine young man like you…gave up a big part…of his life…for a pair of pitiful…old folks like us." Palmer saw tears glistening in Ottis Lee's eyes.

"I'm not giving up anything. I have to sleep somewhere."

"You know…it's an all day…and all night job…around…here. I'm not really…the problem, though. My time…is coming soon. For

a little while...I thought...it was here last night...and it didn't...
bother me...that much. I'm about ready...for this to be over. When I
get to heaven...the first thing I...want...is a deep breath." He looked
at Palmer. "But Kathleen...could live for years."

"I know."

"Why are...you doing this? Helping with Kathleen? I never
really...asked you."

"I promised her son."

"But he's dead."

"That doesn't make any difference."

"Mercy me," Ottis Lee said. "We both made...the same promise. I...can't keep mine. But I can help you...keep yours." He was
quiet for a time. Kathleen walked into the room. She was still sans
sweatshirt, but she had found her bra and put it on, in a manner of
speaking. One strap was looped around her neck while the rest of the
undergarment hung like a cape behind her. She stepped to the table
and picked up the boiled egg.

"That one's dirty," Palmer said. "Let me get another one for
you." She looked at him with wariness, then took a bite. She walked
to the front door and stood before it for a moment, trying the
doorknob several times. Then she turned and addressed Ottis Lee.

"I can't open the door," she said.

"I know...darlin.' It's broken. We'll have to...get a man...to
come see about it."

"Daddy can fix it!"

"Well, then."

"Or maybe That Other Man can fix it."

"Maybe so. As soon...as...I get to feeling...a little better...we'll
call him."

"Daddy's going to be mad," she warned as headed toward the
hall.

"I'll speak to...him," Ottis Lee assured her. "It'll be all right."

To Palmer he said, "Bless her heart."

"You want me to bring you the phone?"

"Not just yet. But I have...a question. Do you know...a good lawyer? I need one...and mine's dead." Ottis Lee had always used Charnell Jackson over in Sequoyah for his occasional legal business, but that venerable attorney had recently died of a broken heart.

"The only lawyer I know got me sent to Sweetwater prison for ten years," Palmer said. "But he really didn't have much to work with, so it wasn't totally his fault. Will he do?"

"He'll have to. Does he make...house calls?"

"I'm sure I can talk him into it. What do I need to tell him you want?"

"I need for you...to be able...to take care of...business for Kathleen. Financial business. Medical business. Whatever. I have some money...in the bank...and I have the junkyard...which is worth a lot...but as they say...it's not very liquid. We also...need... to make it legal somehow...for you...to make decisions for her. We're...getting away with...telling everyone...you're her boy...but you're not...and someone may call...you out...on that when I'm gone."

"Okay, I'll give him a call."

"What's his name?"

"J. Randall Crane."

"What does the...J stand for?"

"I really don't know."

"Well," Ottis Lee said, and the tone of voice suggested that he wasn't completely sure he trusted lawyers with letters for names, but that he supposed he couldn't be too choosy, given his present situation.

"Okay, I'll set it up. I guess I better get Kathleen dressed again. Do you need to go to the john before I get busy?"

"No. Do we have...any corn liquor?"

"We do." Palmer always kept a bit around because Ottis Lee liked it.

"When you get back...can you bring...me a taste in a mason...jar? And a Swisher Sweet?"

"Sure, Ottis Lee. We'll have to turn off the oxygen if you're going to smoke."

"That's okay. It's not doing...me much good anyhow."

It's crunch time. Ottis Lee is all but gone. He can't eat, he can't breathe, he's starting to hurt pretty bad, and he's told me he's ready to go. Every so often he'll rouse up and ask for a mason jar of corn whiskey and a Swisher Sweet, but when I give them to him all he does is hold them and smile a sad smile. I think it makes him feel better just holding them, like maybe he's still able to do something normal, something that he likes to do. He told me once to die young if I could and he also said that you were one of the smart ones who had the good sense to get it over with quick, although as I recall, that wasn't exactly your choice.

Your mama is slipping too. She eats pretty well when I keep on her about it, but she's in constant motion sixteen or eighteen hours a day so she's as skinny as a rail no matter how much I try to feed her. We had some good months when I was her Boo Boo and she would usually do what I said, but now sometimes she forgets who I am and I can't do much with her besides just try to stay out of her way. Other times she thinks I'm a young Harris just hanging around waiting to screw her over, so I'm getting a combination of anger and all of the other negative feelings she has stored up in there somewhere. Either that, or something about me just pisses her off lately. It could be because I burned all her bras.

I took her to the doctor the other day and I don't think I'll be up for that again soon. I don't know how she was about doctors back in the day but I can tell you that she doesn't care for them much now. She cussed him like a yard dog. The doc told me he'd been called worse, but not lately. Anyway, he showed me some pictures of her brain over time and it is actually getting smaller. I talked to him about some of the things she has been doing and he just sat there nodding his head, telling me that these were normal behaviors for a person with her condition. I guess normal is one of those relative words because it feels anything but normal to me. I came away with some different medicine to try her on plus the definite impression that this is one of those diseases they don't know a lot about and I'm more or less on my own.

She got away from me the other day and it scared the bejeezus out of me. I was hiding the door key on the frame above the door and I guess she must have watched me put it up there. I wouldn't have thought she was capable of remembering where she saw it, what it was for, how to use it, and to only use it while I wasn't watching, but she surprised me and put all of those pieces together and escaped. I stepped out of the kitchen with breakfast for her and Ottis Lee, and he was asleep and she was gone. The front door was open and she had caught the midnight train to Aunt Arabel's. Luckily I had warned all the neighbors to be on the lookout and one of them had seen her and was escorting her back to me. She saw me coming toward them and she dropped like a stone and started crying right there on the sidewalk.

The thing is, I know she can't run free, and I know she'll never get to Aunt Arabel's or see her daddy again. I know she would already be dead if I wasn't feeding her and washing her and keeping her locked away from harm. I know the Kathleen we both knew is long gone and that the person living in that body now is like a scared little child. I know every bit of that, but that crying got to me. She doesn't look that much like your mama anymore, but she looks like her enough to remind me that I am basically keeping someone I know and care about imprisoned against her will. I've been there and know what that feels like, but now I'm on the other side of the bars. I'm the jailer now. I guess I take after my old man. I don't know what's going to happen next, but I know that whatever it is won't be good. Tomorrow is the enemy, and I don't think it is taking any prisoners.

14

Ashes to Ashes

Ottis Lee Lamb died on a sunny, raw, and gusty February morning, Groundhog Day, in fact, and his passing was just as unremarkable as the many thousands of other deaths that occurred that very day throughout the wide, hard world. He left this world in the same condition he had once arrived—alone—and it was the final, unavoidable episode of his life, the one death that he owed, and the one event he could not avoid. Ottis Lee met his end with the same grace and good humor that had characterized his entire life, yet to the pair who shared housekeeping with him, it was a day heavy with sadness. Palmer had grown close to him during the months of his illness and knew that he would miss his company once he crossed the wide river. The old man had not talked a great deal during his final weeks because breath was hard to come by in his part of the world, but his presence in the recliner had brought much comfort to Palmer. In retrospect, given the date and the bright sunshine, Palmer wished he had taken Ottis Lee outside for a brief taste of fresh air.

Perhaps if he had seen his shadow he would have been granted six more weeks of life.

As Shirley had predicted, Ottis Lee enjoyed one final good day prior to his reunion with his kin over on the heavenly shore. He slept well during the night and suffered none of the nightmares he had recently experienced featuring cold graves, hot fires, and dead friends and family from long ago and far away. He walked to the bathroom with assistance from Palmer, and he ate most of a chicken pot pie, including the peas and carrots. He sipped a small swallow of corn liquor from a vintage mason jar and savored a token puff from a fresh Swisher Sweet, the very last one in the box. He watched and snoozed through *The Cowboys*—starring John Wayne—followed by *Butch Cassidy and the Sundance Kid*—featuring Paul Newman and Robert Redford—and he even managed to share a few words with Palmer at the conclusion of the Western double feature.

"That was…a…good flick," he said after Butch and Sundance met their ends at the hands of the Bolivian Army and the credits rolled. Palmer nodded, and Kathleen began to sing from her position on the floor between the two men and the television. She had taken to sitting in the floor regularly as her condition progressed and her memory continued to wither.

"Flick a flicka crick a hick dick tricka flicka flicka my friend flicka hicka radicka dock." She sang in a monotone as she rose from the floor and headed for the hall.

"She's happy today," Palmer noted. The singing had been going on for about a month and usually involved single-syllable rhymes.

"Naw…she's singing…the…Sweetwater Blues," Ottis Lee gasped. Kathleen Earwood had once been a good singer, but her ability to carry a tune was now gone along with most of the rest of her, just another piece that had fallen by the way.

"Maybe we should hold off on saying flick," Palmer suggested. "Too many words rhyme with it."

"Okay...Slick." Ottis Lee started to laugh at his small jest, but as soon as it began, his laugh turned into a cough, and then it graduated into a wracking, shuddering full-body experience that seemed destined to burst Ottis Lee asunder and splatter him on the walls. It sounded to Palmer like the more phlegm he cleared from his lungs, the more he needed to clear. He couldn't get his breath, and Palmer could see panic begin to appear in his eyes. Palmer turned up the oxygen, sat him upright in the recliner, and pounded his back. He wasn't sure if this course of treatment was doing any good at all, but he didn't know what else to try, so he kept at it rather than stand by and do nothing. Finally, after what seemed like a short eternity, the coughing fit began to subside, and when it came to an end, Ottis Lee managed to snatch one loud ragged breath. Then he spasmed, and exhaled once, slowly. He caught Palmer's eyes with his own, now bloodshot, and as he stared, Palmer saw the fear in them turn to calm acceptance, and then he saw the calm fade into something else. Ottis Lee closed one eye, as if to share a wink, and he quietly slipped away. Palmer gently closed his other eye. He felt terribly alone at that moment. Ottis Lee had been his friend, a mentor of sorts, and his partner in caregiving, and even during the recent times when he had not spoken much, at least Palmer knew that a sentient, adult human being was sharing the many trials and few tribulations of caring for someone beset by Alzheimer's and dementia, the double whammy of oblivion. "Okay, then," he said to no one in particular, his voice devoid of affect. "It's all on me, now."

"Now now cow bow how how row," sang Kathleen as she reentered the living room. "Sow how bow now—" She stopped, silent, at the recliner containing the remains of Ottis Lee Lamb, her old friend, mechanic, husband, and departed caregiver. "Is That Other Man dead?" she asked. She reached timidly, like a child, and touched his cheek. Then she snatched back her hand as if burned. Tears began to run down her cheeks.

"He is," Palmer replied. He never knew when to lie to her and when the truth would better serve the situation, but in this case there wasn't much of a choice to make. She seemed to sense that Ottis Lee was absent, and his mortal coil did indeed have the look of vacancy about it. Palmer felt like he ought to be up and busy handling the situation, but he thought he would just sit a while first. The wind was out of his sails. He was suddenly very tired, and he stood knee deep in melancholy.

"What will we do?" she asked. It was a good question, Palmer realized. An answer would come to him, he was certain.

"We'll call the funeral home in just a few minutes. They'll come and get him. They'll take good care of him."

"Is that where he'll live now? At the funeral home?"

Palmer nodded. He took her hand and patted it. "He'll live there now."

"With Daddy?"

"With Daddy."

Kathleen pulled her hand from his and walked to the front door. She tried the knob, twisting it first one way and then the other. Then she reached up and felt above the door frame for the key, but it was no longer kept there. Finally she turned and left the room, hugging herself tightly as she walked. From down the hall, Palmer heard the door to her bedroom slam. Maybe she would nap for a while and give him time to get his thoughts arranged and his business done.

He stood and fished in his pocket for his cell phone. At his request, the landline to the house had been disconnected a few months back after Kathleen's fourth call to 911 in as many days to report her kidnapping at the hands of Boo Boo and That Other Man. The Sweetwater Police had been understanding all four times. They all had mamas, after all, or at least Palmer supposed that was the case, but once it became apparent that she was not going to desist

305

in her attempts to involve the law in her plight, the easiest remedy seemed to be to disconnect the phone. She still called 911 from time to time to report all manner of dire treatment, everything from being bathed and dressed to receiving medication, and it didn't seem to bother her much that no one now spoke back to her from the receiver. Palmer flipped open his phone, dialed the on-call number for Tri-County Hospice, and left a message for Shirley to return his call. She was on the phone with him in a matter of minutes.

"He's gone," Palmer said when he answered his cell. "He died about thirty minutes ago."

"Bless his heart. Did he slip out easy?"

Palmer considered the question. In deference to Shirley's compassionate nature, he was tempted to put the best face on Ottis Lee's passing, but in the end he stuck with the facts.

"Well, he went fast, at least, but it didn't seem like it was all that easy." He described Ottis Lee's final moments.

"I'm so sorry. I was hoping he would pass away in his sleep."

"Yeah, me too." Palmer was young enough to still be working on the many details of his philosophy of life, but he was certain that regardless of what else might or might not be true, it was a no-brainer that it was always best to sleep right through one's own death. Just go to sleep here, wake up there, and skip all of that unpleasantness in the middle. "What do I need to do now?" Palmer was pretty sure that all of the correct protocols had been covered with him at one time or another during Ottis Lee's final journey, but he had forgotten everything beyond calling Shirley and was at a loss as to what came next.

"I'll be there in about an hour to pronounce him. Have you called the funeral home yet?"

"No, I thought I'd do that when you got here. Getting him out of here is going to really freak Kathleen out, and I might need some help. Maybe I'll carry him to the porch and they can pick him up outside."

"Or maybe I can get her to show me something in her room when they are there," Shirley said. "Does she know he's gone?"

"Who knows what she knows?" Palmer asked. "She looked at him and touched him, and she cried a little and asked a couple of questions, but now she's off doing something else." Sometimes he thought that maybe she understood a little of what was going on around her, and sometimes he was sure that she had absolutely no clue. But at other moments, at times like right now, he wasn't sure either way, and those were the toughest and most delicate situations for him to handle.

"We'll see what we see when I get there," Shirley said. "Go ahead and call the funeral home, but tell them not to be in any hurry. I'm leaving another patient's house right now, but I'm over in Cherokee County, so I'm an hour away. If they get there before I do, just tell them to wait outside. They're used to it."

Shirley hung up, and Palmer made a quick call to Owen and MacGregor, Sweetwater's only funeral parlor. His call was handled by none other than Genuine Owen, founder and patriarch of Owen and MacGregor. He had been making final arrangements for loved ones for better than seventy years, and although he had sold half interest in the funeral home to the MacGregor Corporation several years back, it was only with the codicil that he be allowed to stay on in whatever capacity he deemed appropriate for as long as he wished. Genuine believed that busy hands gave a man a reason to get up in the morning, and his strategy for avoiding being finally arranged himself was to continue to make others' final arrangements for as long as possible. As the saying around Sweetwater went, Genuine Owen had put more people into the ground than the Spanish flu.

"Owen and MacGregor Funeral Home," he said into the phone. "Genuine Owen speaking. How may we assist you?"

"Hey, Genuine. This is Palmer Cray. Ottis Lee just passed away."

"My condolences to you and Miss Kathleen during this time of loss. I'll gather up the boys and get them on the way out there."

"Hold off about thirty minutes before you send them. The nurse from the hospice still has to pronounce him dead."

"I understand. And are the arrangements going to be any different than Ottis Lee and I discussed?" Ottis Lee had gone to visit Genuine Owen not long after receiving his diagnosis and prognosis, and over a quart jar of corn liquor and a pair of Swisher Sweets they had hammered out the pertinent details of his eternal sleep. He had wanted to be buried at the junkyard, under The Death Car with his father, but Genuine had informed him that, lamentably, due to town ordinances that had been passed almost immediately after that original automotive interment, this would not be possible. Ottis Lee had no real objection to breaking the law once he was dead, but since Genuine did, he had settled for cremation as a distant second best solution. Unfortunately, even though it was one of the tools in his box, Genuine Owen did not hold with cremation, and he never missed the opportunity to try to talk a potential customer or a bereaved loved one out of engaging in the practice. The issue wasn't money, or at least not completely, although it was true that the profit margins on cremations were much slimmer than they were on the more lucrative traditional arrangements.

Genuine had more money than twenty of him could ever spend, and he had acquired that large pile of cash by being fair, honest, and tenacious, but in this case, the issue had more to do with the mechanics of resurrection than it did with the price of burials in Sweetwater. Genuine Owen firmly believed that when Jesus came again and the dead rose from their graves for bodily ascension to the heavenly plane, the dead folks who had been cremated and who had no bodies to rise with or graves to rise from might be at a serious disadvantage and thus in for a disappointing eternity. At the very least they would be in for some fancy explaining at the pearly gates provided they even got that far. Genuine would not refuse a cremation request outright—he was a businessman, after all—but he felt it was his Christian duty to explain the possible downside of the practice in much the same manner as, say, a physician reading the warning label from a pack of Pall Malls before handing it over to a patient.

"Ottis Lee said to tell you that unless you've changed your mind about tucking him in under the Chrysler with his daddy, then he hasn't changed his mind about heading to the furnace. He wants to be cremated and scattered over the junkyard. He wants it to happen on a pretty evening in spring, right as the sun is setting. He wants Jackie Wilson to be singing 'Higher and Higher' on the stereo, and he wants me to be about half lit on corn liquor and smoking a Swisher Sweet as I toss him into the breeze." It was all written down in Ottis Lee's bold hand.

"Sometimes when people become gravely ill, they don't think straight," Genuine pointed out.

Palmer had been informed by Ottis Lee of the lingering issue of remains versus cremains, so he knew to be on his guard. "Sometimes when they've had a half quart of corn liquor before they make their funeral arrangements, they don't think straight either," Palmer replied. "But it's settled and done, and I'm going to honor his wishes."

"I would just hate for Ottis Lee to be denied the Kingdom of Heaven because the Lord didn't have anything to work with." Genuine Owen sounded truly worried on his client's behalf.

"For dust thou art, and unto dust shalt thou return," Palmer said. "The Lord's pretty smart, and He's handy besides. I'm sure Jesus can gather up enough of Ottis Lee to make it work. Anyway, Genuine, I don't want to fuss with you. You've taken care of just about every member of my family who ever died, including Cheddar, although I swear I don't know how you got him up on that hill."

"It wasn't easy, but the widow insisted. We had to use a come-along. He broke loose once and ended up down by the sales trailer."

"So I know you're a good man whose heart is in the right place," Palmer continued. "Ottis Lee Lamb believed in the Lord his whole life, and when the time comes, he'll find his way home. I know it in my heart." Palmer could sense that Genuine wasn't convinced, but before the debate could continue, he heard a crash. "Got to go, Genuine. Kathleen's into something!" Palmer snapped the phone shut as he headed down the hall. He arrived at Kathleen's door and turned the knob, but he was unable to open the door. Something was blocking it from the other side.

"Mama, are you okay?" he asked loudly. In recent days she hadn't often thought he was her little Boo Boo, but sometimes she still did, and addressing her as Mama remained his most productive tactic. He heard a rustle and a scrape from the opposite side, but she did not answer him. "Are you sitting in front of the door? Can I come in? Are you okay?" Sometimes Kathleen sat in the floor of her bedroom right in front of her closed door, effectively blocking the entrance to her room. Palmer had yet to figure out if she did it on purpose or if she just liked sitting in that spot, but when she sat there, somehow her weight seemed to double. "What was that noise? Are you hurt?"

"I want to go home," she said from her bedroom. He could tell she was crying.

"But you are home!"

"I mean my real home. I want to go to my real home."

"This is your real home. You've lived here I don't know how long. Twenty-five years, maybe. Maybe more than that."

"No. I guess I'd remember that. My real home has snow. I remember it from when I was a little girl. We all lived up north. Me and you and Daddy and Mama. We moved up there so Daddy could get a job at a car factory. Did you ever meet him?"

"No, ma'am," Palmer said quietly. Kathleen's father had died long before Palmer and Rodney were born, the hapless victim of unforgiving narrow arteries and insoluble fats.

"My mama was a cook in a diner in Michigan and my daddy worked at the Chrysler plant. He put motors into cars. I don't remember what my job was. And one time it started snowing. You have never seen so much snow in your life! It was at Christmas, but this was way back then, and it snowed for a week straight. It was up to my shoulders and over my sister's head. Everything was closed down. The Chrysler plant and the diner sent everyone home. My daddy couldn't get home, though. He was on his way when a calico cat ran out in front of him. It was Aunt Arabel's cat, and he never liked that cat. His car slid and hit a bump in the road and he flew into a tree. That killed him and another young boy besides. I don't know who that boy was, but it was because of the snow. My job closed down, too." She had been speaking quickly but stopped abruptly. He heard her begin to hum through the door.

"What was your job?" Palmer asked in spite of himself. Though she was clearly confusing her facts, Kathleen was talking more in one sitting than she had said during the entire previous week, and he felt that it was good for her, although he couldn't say why. Her humming subsided, and she began to speak again.

"I don't recall. I think I was a schoolteacher. No, wait a minute. That was my mama. She was a schoolteacher at the diner. She worked the graveyard shift and taught the men to read the menus. I worked at the funeral home with my sister. That Other Man is going to live there now. She made toast and I fixed the dead people's hair so they'd look nice when their families came to see them. That's how I found out about Daddy and that other boy so soon after they hit that tree. They brought them in for me to get them ready, but then

311

they wouldn't even let me look at the boy, even after I begged them. They had to put him right into his coffin and close the lid tight. His head was gone and the rest of him was somewhere else, so I couldn't make his hair nice. His mama cried and cried. They said her hair turned gray in a single day."

"Do you remember that boy's name?" he asked Kathleen.

"I don't. Dead people don't have to have names anyway. I think I was about six at that time. I was married to Rodney's daddy but I didn't have Rodney yet. I had a dog named John, though. I think he would have liked all that snow. Rodney, I mean, not John. John hated the snow and he wouldn't use the bathroom in it. It snowed for an entire week. We didn't have any electricity because all the trees fell on the power lines until they snapped. But the gas was still on, so we had heat in the kitchen and a stove to cook with. We had hot water, too, so we could take a bath. I have always despised cold bathwater. Mama sent me outside to play in the snow with my sister. I had on my blue wool coat and my plaid snow pants. Did I ever show that blue coat to you?"

"No, ma'am."

"Mama bought it for me. She said it matched my eyes. Laurel and I were digging a tunnel in the snow in our front yard. Laurel was my sister. She died, but not in the tunnel. It was later when her boy got sent away. We were in the front yard digging when this big snow blower truck came up our street. We lived on Ash Street, but I never saw any ashes except in the big barrel out back where we burned the trash. That snow plow had a big thing on the front of it that would go around and around. It sucked the snow right off of the roads and blew it up and out of the way through a big pipe on top of the truck. By the end of winter the snow was piled so high beside the roads that even Daddy couldn't see over the tops of it.

"Well, that plow came on up our street, and we were out digging a tunnel and playing with John. He didn't like the snow, but

312

he liked us. Daddy always said John was a barking dog, and barking dogs come to bad ends. John ran out to bark at the plow truck. I guess the man driving it couldn't see John because it was cloudy that day and getting near to sundown and John was a white dog and he got sucked up in that screw. The truck kept coming down the street, but now all the snow it was blowing was red, because John was dead and that was his blood. Some of John even blew onto me and Laurel as the snow plow went by, because the driver couldn't see us either, I guess. When we went inside the house to tell Mama about John, she screamed because she saw blood on us and thought something was wrong with us. Then she saw that we were all right, and she sat in the kitchen floor and hugged us and rocked us and cried and cried. She kept saying my poor babies over and over again. Poor John. Laurel never did get over him being sucked up in that screw, and finally it gave her a stroke and killed her."

"I'm sorry about John," Palmer said. No other words came to him at that moment.

"That's all right," Kathleen said. "He's in heaven now with That Other Man and Daddy. I told them at the funeral home that we needed to go shovel up John so we could bury him, but they were busy painting the floor. By the time they got around to him, it was too late. He had melted. The electricity came back on Tuesday, and Mama went back to work at the diner. Daddy was dead, but a man who looked just like him had moved in with us and started sleeping in the spare room. He went back to work at the Chrysler factory in place of Daddy. He must have known a little something about cars, because they never did catch on at the plant that it wasn't him."

"What was the other man's name?" Palmer asked. The story fascinated him. It was the story of her life, told in code.

"He said his name was Daddy, but I think he was just saying that so Mama would let him stay. It was hard times back then, and a lot of men lived on the roads. She knew that Daddy was dead along with John and that boy. She had stood right beside me at the funeral when they were both lowered into the ground. But sometimes she would forget herself, and then she would let that other man kiss her or call her Honey, and one time she made a little girl with him, and that was where your mama came from. He wasn't a bad man at all. He just needed a place to live, and I don't blame her for it, either. But he wasn't Daddy. Rodney was dead, too, by that time, but Laurel hadn't fallen into her stroke yet, so we were still sisters. We wrapped Rodney in the curtains to keep him warm until the snow melted away and the ground unfroze and we could bury him next to Daddy and that other boy. Mama was mad about the curtains, but that other man who looked like Daddy told her it was all right and then he bought her some new ones. They were white with lace edges and let a lot of light into the room. They were pretty. I liked them a lot." Her soliloquy abruptly ceased, as if a switch had been pulled. She sat quietly on her side of the door and he sat on his.

"Would you like to come help me get Ottis Lee ready to go to the funeral home?" he asked. "I thought we would put him in some clean overalls and a nice shirt." He heard her stir.

"He needs his hat," she said. "It might rain."

"We'll get his Mopar hat. It was his favorite." The door opened, and Kathleen stood before him. She was naked except for one sock. She had been crying.

"Boo Boo, I'm afraid," she said.

"Don't worry," Palmer replied. "We'll get through this just fine."

I haven't felt this low since Mama died. Ottis Lee went hard, and he deserved better than that but what's new? I guess that whole business has worn me down. Plus, I swear that Kathleen is going to put me into an early grave, but if you believe in karma I suppose that's fair because that's just what I did to you. The problem is that she never sleeps. It's like she has forgotten how to do it. She has medicine that's supposed to help her sleep but it doesn't do any good at all. I'm tempted to try her on a nice glass of wine at bedtime, but with all the medication she has in her I'm afraid she won't wake up. Killing one Earwood was bad enough. I don't want to have two of you on my conscience.

One of my problems is that I haven't been out of the house since Ottis Lee's funeral. Morris was by here to visit the other day and his big suggestion was that I needed to get out and have a Me Day from time to time. I swear I like old Morris but one of these days he's going to say something stupid like that and I'm going to have him slapped before I know what has happened. A Me Day would be great, but the only person willing to stay with her anymore is Trenton and sometimes Kathleen tries to woo him, so he's become skittish. And after she cut up so bad at Ottis Lee's memorial service, I'm not in any hurry to take her out for an Us Day, either. As bad as staying put is, it beats finding Kathleen in the other visitation room at Genuine Owen's place up in the casket with Pearl Peddycoarte, hollering about Aunt Arabel going to live with the angels. It took me and Trenton both to get her out of there.

I finally got a little nap the other night and I had a dream that scared me pretty bad. In this dream I was just the same as I always was in my mind but there was something wrong with me so that when I spoke or tried to do something, I got it all wrong. You can see where this is going, I guess. They diagnosed me with Alzheimer's and dementia but all that was really the matter with me was that I couldn't communicate with anyone. Whenever I tried to do something like put food into my mouth it would end up in my ear or in the DVD player. Whenever I tried to say something, nonsense would come out instead. Whenever I needed to turn left I would go right.

It was a terrible dream but it reminded me that no matter how bad it is to take care of Kathleen, that's nothing compared to being Kathleen. I used to think that having Alzheimer's and dementia was kind of a gentle way to go, that people just sort of gradually faded away, but now I know it is the worst of all the bad ways to die. I have watched piece after piece of your mama fall away, and now all that is left is a scared and simple creature who doesn't know what is happening to her, or why. It is a terrible and cruel way to go. Give me a can of beer, a Camaro, and a tree anytime.

15

Aunt Arabel's House

Palmer Cray awoke with a start from his stolen nap on the living room sofa. As a result of his chronic sleep deprivation, he had acquired the habit of falling asleep unexpectedly whenever he sat still for any length of time. He was both grateful for the rest and slightly guilty at having fallen asleep, and as he sat up, he sensed that something was missing. It was a moment before he realized that the backdrop of noise constantly provided by Kathleen was absent this morning. Normally she would be talking, or singing, or banging and slamming, but all of these sounds were conspicuous by their absence. Palmer was not one to look a gift horse in the mouth, so he grabbed some clean clothes, quickly headed to the bathroom, and jumped into the shower. He did not often get the opportunity to bathe unattended these days, and he enjoyed every moment of his solitary scrub.

Once finished, he dried and dressed. As he stepped back into the living room, he again encountered the silence. He figured that Kathleen must be sleeping late, but this did not surprise him. He had taken her to the quarterly visit with the neurologist the previous week and had come away from that appointment with a new selection of medicine to try, and new medications often made her sleepy for a few days. At that same appointment he had gained a hearty respect for the doctor's ability to absorb verbal abuse and a renewed suspicion that no one really understood the disease that was slowly but surely killing Kathleen. He looked at the clock and attempted to calculate the benefits of letting her sleep in versus the risks involved with her falling out of her routines. In the end his uneasiness at her silence won out, and he walked to her room and opened the door. Kathleen sat in the floor beside her bed with her legs folded up under her. She looked up at Palmer, and she smiled.

"Daddy's going to be mad," she said as she held up her pull-up for Palmer to inspect. He was taken aback by her position in the floor. He took the undergarment from her and tossed it into the trash can.

"What happened?" he asked.

"I don't know," Kathleen replied pleasantly. She didn't seem to be even the least bit upset concerning her predicament. Palmer felt a small tug of fear. She should be hollering for help and trying to stand, but she wasn't.

"Let me help you up." He stepped behind her, kneeled down, and reached under her arms and around her chest. He slowly stood, dragging her along as he went, but as he achieved the upright position, he realized that she was just hanging limp in his arms like a large rag doll. Her legs jerked around as if they were trying their best to remember what it was they were supposed to be doing.

"Can you get your legs under yourself?" he asked. She did not answer and continued to hang. "Kathleen. Help me. Use your legs. Can you stand up?"

"I can stand as good as you can, mister," she replied in an argumentative tone, but her actions belied her words. As if to

318

punctuate the sentiment, she began to wet herself. Palmer held her until she finished, then eased her onto her bed. She provided no help whatsoever. It was like he was dragging a sack of meal onto the mattress.

"I want you to stay right there a minute while I go get a washcloth. Can you do that for me?"

"Yes, Daddy," she replied. Palmer hightailed it to the living room and grabbed up his phone. He dialed 911 and waited. His call was answered on the second ring.

"911 Emergency."

"I need an ambulance sent to the corner of Mill and Water in Sweetwater. Over in the Mill Village. To the home of Kathleen Earwood. She is an Alzheimer's patient, and I think she has had a stroke. She can talk, but she can't walk." As he spoke into his flip phone, he stepped to the bathroom, where he wet a washcloth and grabbed a dry towel and a new pull-up.

"I'll get one rolling right away," the operator replied. "Please stay on the line."

"Can't. Got business to attend to. Hurry." He snapped the phone shut, unlocked and opened the front door, and hurried back down the hallway to Kathleen. She was exactly where he had left her, and she smiled once again when he came into the room.

"I want eggs," she said.

"We'll get a bite to eat in a minute." He gave her a quick wipe-off with the washcloth and a fast dry with the towel. Then he dropped the towel onto the floor to absorb the mess there. He slipped on her pull-up and scrounged through the dresser for a clean pair of sweatpants and a sweatshirt. He thought warm and comfortable would be the right choice in apparel for a trip to the emergency room. "How do you feel?" he asked as he worked.

"How do you feel?" she answered. She shook her finger at Palmer as if she were scolding him. He sighed. Now was not a good time for one of her new favorites: the mimic game. He sat her up and maneuvered her into her sweatshirt. Then he tackled her sweatpants one leg at a time. She neither helped nor resisted throughout the dressing process. She could move her legs, but she couldn't move them for effect.

"Do you have a headache?" he asked, trying to elicit something specific from her to share with the medical personnel when they arrived. He was fairly certain they would ask why he had summoned them.

"No, Daddy-oh."

"Do your legs hurt?"

"Legs. Eggs. Pegs." In the distance, Palmer heard a siren. The hospital was twenty miles away, but the ambulance service kept a unit staged at the Sweetwater fire station, so they should arrive in a moment. He slid the slippers onto Kathleen's feet, and she was ready for her journey to town.

"Kathleen, look at me. Some people are going to come visit us in just a minute."

"Aunt Arabel?"

"No, it's not Aunt Arabel this time. Some friends are coming to take us for a ride."

"I like to ride."

"I know you do. So when they come, I want you to be nice to them. I want you to behave." Sometimes she did fine with strangers, but sometimes she became physically aggressive around people she had not seen before, and for a little woman she still packed quite a wallop. Palmer hoped that he could avoid bloodshed by preparing her in advance.

"Behave," she said as she began to work her arm out of the sweatshirt sleeve.

He stopped her. "Let's stay dressed so we can go for our ride," he suggested.

"Will they take us to Aunt Arabel's house?" Kathleen asked.

"I think they might," he replied. "It's on the way."

The trip to the hospital was about as uneventful as such a trip could be. Palmer rode along with Kathleen so she would not become frightened, but she seemed to take the excursion in an ambulance in stride. He spent most of the trip providing Kathleen's medical history to the technician, and he hadn't realized quite how much of it there was until he began relating it to someone else. He had gathered up her medications in a plastic bag prior to leaving the house, and the technician was going through the bottles one by one and listing them on Kathleen's chart. The EMTs had started her on fluids as a precaution against dehydration, and she spent most of the ride staring with interest at the IV needle protruding from her arm. Palmer had not thought it necessary to stick her with the needle, but the EMTs had seemed not to hear him as he pointed out that she drank several cups of water each day and that it was filtering through her just fine if the pee they were standing in while they found a vein was any indication.

"We have to start an IV on everyone," the EMT had said apologetically as she worked. "You never know how a trip to the emergency room is going to turn out, and there might not be time later if they get in a hurry." The practice made sense to Palmer when explained in those terms, and he wished he had not fussed.

There was a whirlwind of activity once they arrived at the hospital. Kathleen was poked, tapped, prodded, recorded, evaluated, and stuck again. After it became clear that asking her for information was not the best way to get it, all questions concerning her history and her current state of health were directed toward Palmer. After her vitals were taken, several tests were scheduled, and Palmer and Kathleen found themselves parked in a curtained cubicle in the emergency room waiting for the diagnosis process to begin in earnest. Kathleen was connected to a monitor that measured blood pressure, pulse, and the oxygen content in her blood. She had become agitated during the initial examination and triage and had been given a dose of medication to calm her, so she slipped in and out of a light doze. Palmer had no idea how long the wait ahead of them would be, and he was considering joining Kathleen in a nap when the curtain whisked open and a large man in camouflage scrubs stepped inside. His black glasses rode at the tip of his nose, and his gray hair was combed straight back.

"Good morning," he said as he offered his hand. "I'm Dr. Compton."

"Good morning," Palmer said as he shook. "I'm Palmer Cray. Her name is Kathleen Earwood. I'm her guardian and caregiver. I'm the one who found her in the floor this morning and called 911."

"What can you tell me about Mrs. Earwood?" the doctor asked. He removed her chart from its place at the foot of the bed and began to read as Palmer spoke.

"She has had diagnosed Alzheimer's for about three years and dementia for about two. There is nothing else physically wrong with her that I know about except for high cholesterol and high blood pressure, and she's on medicine for both of those. Last night, she could walk. As a matter of fact, she could run. I had a heck of a time chasing her down and putting her to bed. This morning, she can't even stand. I found her in the floor beside her bed. She wasn't able to help at all when I got her up. When I dressed her, she was able to move her legs, but she didn't know how to use them. I hope that makes sense. She says nothing is hurting. Not her legs or her head or anything else. I thought maybe she had a stroke, so that's why I called the ambulance."

Dr. Compton nodded as he read and listened. "A stroke is a possibility," he said. "A lesion in her brain is another. Do you remember what time it was when you last saw her use her legs?"

"I got her to bed around three o'clock, and she was fine then. I found her in the floor about seven, and she couldn't walk. So sometime between three and seven, something bad happened."

The doctor made a note. "They told me that she got pretty upset a while ago," he said. "Is it normal for her to get that agitated?"

"*That* agitated is a little unusual, but it does happen from time to time. Most days she does okay during the daylight hours, but she starts getting sort of cranky around dark. Her neurologist calls it sundowning. She walks and talks all night long, and it's not a good idea to get in her way. But I think what got her so bent out of shape a while ago was the fact that we're at the hospital. She hates doctors. I usually give her one of these before we go to see any of her doctors, but I was afraid to give her anything this morning before we came down here, so you all were on your own." Palmer reached into the zip-lock bag containing Kathleen's medications and removed the bottle of anti-anxiety pills. He passed it to the doctor. Dr. Compton looked at the bottle, nodded, made a note, and handed it back. "Today they gave her a shot," Palmer continued, "which worked a whole lot better than the pills do, anyway." The doctor nodded again.

"That was a good decision to hold off on her medicines until we got a chance to take a look at her. We'll get her morning medications into her in a little while. When did she last see her regular doctor?" While he talked, he scratched the bottoms of each of her feet with a pin and nodded in satisfaction as first one foot and then the other jerked in the appropriate manner. He made another note on her chart.

"She saw her regular physician about three weeks ago. That's Dr. Pine from Sweetwater. She saw her neurologist just last week. He's Dr. Wilson from over in Sequoyah."

"How does she do with food?"

"She eats when I remind her, but she doesn't really like food anymore. She walks so much that she keeps losing weight. I feed her whatever I can get her to eat to try to keep her weight up. She likes milkshakes, so she gets a lot of those. I'm losing the battle, though. She just gets skinnier and skinnier."

"Did Dr. Wilson mention that anything unusual was going on with her?"

"Not really. He's not much of a talker, but he told me he thought she was doing okay for the shape she's in. Those were his words, not mine. He did an MRI because it was time for one, and he changed two of her medicines." Palmer couldn't remember anything else he thought worth mentioning.

"Do you have the new medications with you? And do you remember the names of the ones she stopped taking?"

"I do and I do," Palmer replied as he dug in his bag. He extracted two bottles, one small and one large. "Here are the two new ones." He dug around a bit more. "And here are the ones she has quit taking." He handed those over as well.

"Did he say why he changed them?"

"He has been trying for about a year now to find something to help her stay calm at night. Those are the latest in a long line of pills for that. So far they haven't been working, but they do help her sleep better once she finally goes down. She sleeps longer and deeper. Do you think changing her pills had something to do with her legs?" Palmer hadn't thought of it, but now that he did, it seemed sort of a good place to start looking. Back at Sweetwater prison, whenever something bad happened, the first thing the inmates usually did was look for what had changed in the general routine. Maybe it worked the same way in medicine.

"That's certainly one of the things we'll look at, but I don't think it's likely. These two medications are a bit unusual for treating her condition, but I've never heard of them having an effect such as we are seeing here. One good piece of luck is that she had that MRI last week. For one thing, it pretty much rules out a brain tumor. We'll do another one today, and if there has been an episode of some type involving her brain, it should show up, and then we'll have a pretty good chance of figuring out what happened." The doctor handed all of the medications back to Palmer, and he replaced them in the bag. At that moment, Kathleen stirred and opened her eyes. She yawned.

"Who are you?" she asked as she looked at the doctor. She reached out and grabbed Palmer's hand.

"I'm Dr. Compton. You're at the hospital. We're going to keep you here a little while and see if we can get you walking again. Will that be okay?"

"I know who you are," Kathleen snapped. "I saw you at Aunt Arabel's house, and we went to school together in Daddy's 1953 Ford. There was a hole in the floor and you could see the ground go by. One of my babies fell out and we never saw her again. And I guess I walk as good as anyone!" She made as if to demonstrate, but when her legs wouldn't cooperate, she switched her attention to another topic. "Who are you?" she asked again, but this time she was looking at Palmer. She snatched her hand back from his as if he had been taking a liberty to which he was not entitled.

"You know who I am. I'm Palmer. I live with you." Palmer was a bit taken aback. During his time as Kathleen's caregiver, she had thought that he was any number of people, sometimes simultaneously, but this was the first time she had not recognized him as someone significant from her life.

"Are we married?" She looked at him with wariness, as if perhaps he had wed her against her wishes while she was sleeping.

"No."

"Well, that's a relief. If we're not married, then we shouldn't be living together. It's just not right. If Daddy finds out, there'll be trouble. Big trouble." She began to wring her hands, perhaps in anticipation of the bad times to come once Daddy became aware of the living arrangements.

"It's okay, Kathleen. I was best friends with your son, and I knew Ottis Lee all my life. He was your husband. Do you remember him?"

"I never had a son." A single tear rolled down her cheekbone and dripped onto her pillow. "I always wanted one, but I never had one. I had three girls, but they all ran off."

"Well," said Dr. Compton as he replaced the chart in its holder. "I'll see about admitting her to the hospital, and I'll send in a nurse with the medications she needs this morning. I expect they have some paperwork for you as well. We'll get started on her tests just as soon as we get her into her room." He offered his hand once again, and Palmer shook it.

"Do us all a favor and send along a little pudding with the pills," Palmer said quietly with his back turned to Kathleen. "Otherwise you're going to have to give her another shot." The doctor nodded. Apparently he was well acquainted with the medicinal properties of vanilla pudding as it pertained to Alzheimer's patients.

"Do you have any questions, Mrs. Earwood?" Dr. Compton asked as he prepared to leave.

"Are you a hunter?" she asked, pointing at his scrubs.

He smiled. "No, ma'am. I just like to wear the outfit."

"My boy liked to hunt. He hunted all the time. A bear killed him."

"I'm sorry for your loss," he said. She looked as if she were about to speak again, but then her eyes fluttered and drooped closed, and she fell back asleep.

"She does seem a bit confused this morning," Dr. Compton noted.

"Yeah, she's all over the place today. This is a little worse than usual. I guess it's the excitement. Did you hear her ask who I was?" The doctor nodded. "That's never happened before," Palmer said. "This is the first time she has ever forgotten my face."

"That could be significant. We'll know more after we run the tests." Palmer nodded, and the doctor left the cubicle. Palmer sat back in what could have perhaps been the most uncomfortable chair in the southeastern United States and mused about the morning. He had been to doctors' offices and clinics numerous times with Kathleen over the past three years, but this was their first trip to the hospital. Dr. Wilson had told him that Alzheimer's patients tended to hold a certain level of physical and cognitive behavior for a while before nose-diving suddenly and without warning to a lower state, and he had seen this pattern several times with Kathleen. Given what he had witnessed this morning, he was certain that this had happened once again. But unlike the other times she had lost ground, this time she had forgotten how to walk and who he was, and all of that had happened during a four-hour nap.

During the remainder of the day, Kathleen was given an MRI, an EEG, an EKG, a PET, a complete blood workup, and a sonogram. Many of the tests were not as useful as they might have been if Kathleen's state of agitation had not interfered with the administration of the procedures, but some diagnostic information was obtained, and as a general rule of thumb, some was better than none. As the results from these examinations were posted to her chart, a picture began to emerge of what was wrong with Kathleen Earwood. Palmer had always assumed that the world of modern medicine was a high-tech place, but in spite of all of the machines and the scientific words and the complex procedures, the diagnosis was very nineteenth century. Kathleen was slowly forgetting how to be alive.

"We don't know for sure why she can't walk," Dr. Wilson said the next morning as he spoke with Palmer in the hall outside

Kathleen's room. Since he was her neurologist, he had been called in to confer. "Her legs seem fine. We can see no reason why she shouldn't be walking to Aunt Arabel's house right now. The MRI they did here yesterday shows an area that might be stroke damage, and that area doesn't appear on the one I did last week. So she might have had a stroke, but it doesn't look like a stroke to me, and her symptoms don't match what we normally see when a patient has suffered a stroke. What shows up on yesterday's MRI looks like old stroke damage, but she has not had a previous stroke." He sounded truly puzzled.

"What else might have caused this?" Palmer asked.

"I don't know."

"Have you ever seen someone just forget how to walk overnight?"

"No. But for want of a better explanation, that seems to be what has happened."

"So what now?"

"That's the big question. Her long-term prognosis should determine our course of action. If you, for instance, suddenly lost the use of your legs for no reason that we could see, we would be very aggressive with our attempts to get you back on your feet. But with Mrs. Earwood, we have to keep in mind that her underlying condition is going to almost guarantee poor rehab results. We can try some rehab, and maybe she can relearn how to walk, but I have to remind you that walking is an amazingly complex process, and she is in the stage of life where she is more likely to forget than to learn and remember."

"Help me, Doc. What I need is a little bit of hope. She doesn't watch TV, and she won't listen to the radio. She forgot how to read a long time ago, and she doesn't like being read to. She doesn't know who she is or who I am. She doesn't really like food anymore. About all she had going for her was walking around and around the house, talking about whatever popped into her head. Her entire life had kind of distilled down to that, and now that's gone, too. I think if there's even a small chance that she might walk again, we should try it. She's running out of reasons to be alive. We have to give her something. She doesn't remember the past, and she has no concept of the future. All she knows is right now, and if that is reduced to laying in the bed being afraid, it's too cruel. We've got to try to do better for her."

Dr. Wilson nodded. "I don't disagree. I just wanted to be sure you knew what we are getting into. I'll set up a rehab consultation, and we'll see what we can do." He made a note on her chart and departed for the nursing station.

Palmer let himself back into Kathleen's room and took a seat. She was asleep and snoring gently. Palmer looked at her, and he was startled by what he saw. Her face was puffy and pale, and the lack of color to her complexion made the dark circles under her eyes stand out even more. Her wispy white hair was matted with sweat. She was bone thin, and her skin had a papery look to it. Palmer realized that she looked as if she were dying. He didn't suppose that her appearance had changed this much since yesterday, so it must be the setting that allowed him to see her as she had become, in the harsh light of reality.

He sighed. He didn't know how this all was going to turn out, but he was in for the duration, and he swore to her silently that he would do the best for her that he could. When all of this had begun, she had thought of him as her son. Now, oddly and perhaps inevitably, he had come to consider her as one of the two separate mothers he had been blessed with. Due to the unfortunate circumstance of his imprisonment, he had been unable to do much for his biological mother at the end, and that inability to help had left an unfilled need that Kathleen now met.

"You get some more sleep," he said to her quietly. "I'm going down to the cafeteria for a bite to eat." He touched her on her head. She murmured, turned onto her side, curled into the fetal position, and opened her eyes.

"Where are we?" she asked.

"We're at Aunt Arabel's house."

"Is she here with Daddy?"

"They're both here. I'll round them up in a little while and bring them in."

"I'm afraid."

"Don't be afraid. I won't let anything bad happen to you."

"You're a good boy," she said as she drifted back off.

"And you've been a good mama," he replied, but she was already asleep.

The cafeteria was down three floors, and Palmer took the stairs because he needed to stretch his legs. Once he reached the dining hall, he began to feel a strange sense of déjà vu. The main entrée was Salisbury steak, and although he was certain that it was better than the Sweetwater prison version, the similarities between the hospital dining experience and the prison equivalent were too many to ignore. The food looked the same. There were guards posted at each of the doors. The trays and the utensils were plastic. There was a long, slow-moving line for the food and an indifferent soul dishing it out. Palmer wouldn't have been much surprised if Razor Smithfield walked up and tried to put a tool in him.

Once he had his lunch and a place to sit, Palmer picked at his food and drifted into a reverie of sorts. He noted that he had automatically sat facing the door with his back to the wall, but he always did that now so it was not remarkable. He looked at the faces of his fellow diners and found himself attempting to gauge the depths of their troubles by the looks on their faces. The young woman with the salad, the tea, and the look of unfettered despair had a gravely ill child here, perhaps, and he sent a prayer in her direction because it couldn't hurt. The old man with the misbuttoned shirt and the Salisbury steak had a look of such utter sorrow that he must be sitting the long vigil for his wife of many years, a woman he had brought to the halls of healing but whom he would not be taking back home. The youngish man in the dungarees and work shirt wolfing down the cheeseburger was here to get a baby. He could barely contain his excitement or hide his smile as he ate his lunch, and Palmer thought the man would likely smuggle the wrapped piece of pie back upstairs to his wife. Palmer felt voyeuristic in a way he could not explain. He had seen intimate details from the lives of total strangers, and the likely fact that none of the stories he had attributed to the people were true did not alter the intimacy of the moment. Palmer silently wished them all well as he scraped his tray and placed it on the conveyor. He hadn't been hungry, after all, and he needed to get back to his duties. He didn't want Kathleen to awaken alone in a strange place.

When Palmer arrived back at the room, the door was open, and both Kathleen and her bed were missing. The IV pole lay on its side, and used medical supplies and wrappers were scattered about the floor. In the bedside chair he normally occupied sat Kathleen's day nurse. She had been crying.

"What happened?" he asked. "Where is Kathleen?"

"She coded."

"I don't know what that means." He didn't know the term, but the condition of the room did not bode well.

"Her heart rate shot up to a dangerously high level. The doctor gave her a shot to bring it down, but it came down too far. Her heart stopped. The doctor did CPR until the crash cart got here, and they got her back going again. She's in CCU. She's on the vent. The doctor thinks she has a broken rib now because of the CPR. Her heart has speeded back up again. It's up and down and all over the place. They don't know what's going on, but she's stable for now and a cardiologist is looking at her case."

Palmer didn't know what to say. He was trying to get his mind around the new information, but he couldn't.

"I was only gone to lunch," he said, as if he were offering an excuse for his absence. He knew that if had been sitting right there in that chair when the episode began, not one thing would have gone differently. If anything, he would have been in the way. But he felt as if he had let her down, that when she had truly needed him, he had been gone.

"It happened quickly," the nurse said. Her name was Wendy, Palmer remembered. She was about his age, but she seemed very young to him.

"Can I see her?" he asked.

"I'll take you to CCU," she said. She led him down the hall to the elevators, then up one floor to the CCU. She spoke to a nurse at the nursing station before taking him back to one of the beds on the unit. Kathleen was unconscious, but her movements were constant nonetheless. She had been intubated, and a machine was doing her breathing for her. Her hands were restrained to the bed rails with padded Velcro straps, and the sheets were tucked in tightly around her. Several IV lines were plugged into the port originally installed by the EMT. Palmer supposed the woman had been correct after all. You just never knew what was going to happen in a hospital, and it was always best to prepare for the worst.

"Why is she restrained?" he asked Wendy. "I don't like that."

"So she can't pull the tube out."

"I hate seeing her like this."

"I know you do."

"What happens now?"

"We'll have to see what the doctors say. Let me take you to the waiting room. They'll talk to you there."

Palmer nodded. It seemed as good a plan as any. She led him to the CCU waiting room, which was a bit nicer and somewhat more intimate than the larger one downstairs. She left him there with her well wishes, and he sat staring at the television on the wall. He had waited only a short while when he was joined by Dr. Compton, the hospitalist; Dr. Wilson, the neurologist; and a tall, slim woman with what looked like a permanent worried expression. She introduced herself as Dr. Francis, the cardiologist. Dr. Compton led off the discussion.

"Did you speak with the nurse?" he asked.

"I did. She told me what happened. It sounds bad."

"It was a close thing," Dr. Compton said. "So what we have to deal with is a woman with severe dementia and Alzheimer's who still can't walk and whose heart rate is out of control. She is on the vent and has at least one broken rib and maybe a cracked sternum from the CPR, so we have to keep her sedated because of the pain." He looked at Palmer. "Normally, I would advise a heart intervention, just to get her stabilized."

Dr. Francis nodded at this. "There are procedures that can help control her heart rate, both on the high and low sides, but I'd like to see her a little more stable before we talk about surgery of any type. I am trying her on a different drug to lower her heart rate. It's not as quick or as effective as the one Dr. Compton administered, but it is starting to work, and it should slow her down."

"Why did the first medicine stop her heart?"

"The dosage is tricky, and she seems to be very sensitive to it."

"Why did her heart rate shoot up in the first place? Is it related to her Alzheimer's?"

"It might be," Dr. Wilson said.

"Or it might be completely unrelated," Dr. Francis added. "It seems like a condition called supraventricular tachycardia, but that is generally congenital with an early onset. A normal heart rate for Mrs.

333

Earwood would be between 70 and 80 beats per minute. Hers was more than 150. Oddly, when her heart stopped and was restarted, her rhythm should have reset itself, but it didn't."

"Tell me what I should do," Palmer said to the group. He had too much information and no idea what to do with it all.

"We should get her stable before we do anything else," Dr. Compton advised. "Going through a code is a very traumatic experience. We need to let her recover."

"I agree with Dr. Compton," said Dr. Francis. "After we have her heart rate down and she has recovered from her trauma, then we'll see about an intervention."

"And once we have her out of CCU and her heart rate stabilized," Dr. Wilson said, "we'll get back to her leg issues."

Palmer nodded. There was a good solid plan, and it sounded reasonable to him. But often the best-made plans are undermined by the capricious whims of cold reality. As they stood there in the waiting room, first one, then two, and then three beepers went off. The doctors looked at their handheld devices, and each of them spoke just a word or two before bolting toward the CCU.

"It's her," Dr. Wilson said as he headed out.

"No," said Dr. Francis as she caught the door and followed.

"Wait here," said Doctor Compton as he brought up the rear.

Palmer stood alone in the CCU waiting room. He considered calling Trenton, but he had nothing to report that would do anyone any good, and there was no use worrying him. He would just come and sit with Palmer, and he hated hospitals. Besides, Palmer didn't feel much like talking, anyway. So he waited, leaning against the wall with his hands in his jeans pockets and his eyes on the floor. He didn't have long to wait. When Dr. Compton came back in followed by the other two, the looks on their faces told him all he really needed to hear.

"We lost her," Dr. Francis said.

Palmer looked back at the floor. He hoped she was at Aunt Arabel's house at long last, and that she was now wrapped in the loving arms of all those who had waited for her there: Rodney, Aunt Arabel, Ottis Lee, Daddy, and all the rest. He wished her peace, and comfort, and good thoughts, and plenty of them.

"We lost her a long time ago," he replied. "Maybe now she has found her way home."

Your mama has passed away. She went from doing just fine physically to gone in two days from start to finish. I swear I never saw it coming. It was like once she started that final slide she couldn't get it all over with quick enough to suit her. I thought we had years to go. She was getting smaller and smaller and forgetting more and more, but physically she was strong. Everything was working more or less like it was supposed to. Then one night her legs quit working. I think she just forgot how to use them. Then her heart rate went crazy, and I think it was the same deal there. After that it was all downhill.

I am sad that she's gone but I'm grateful too. She didn't know much of anything at the end and she was always afraid. The fear was hard to see.

I was going to put her down with your real daddy because I thought she might like that, but I couldn't find him. I looked over at Mission Hill cemetery because she mentioned that church a lot when she talked about Aunt Arabel. And I looked over at Mount Olive Baptist because that's where she used to always take you to church. I even looked at the Sweetwater Cemetery, but he wasn't to be found. I didn't even bother with looking at the Creepy Graveyard because your mama wouldn't do that to anyone and besides, I think it was still a chert pit back when he died. So I don't know what she did with him.

I ended up having her cremated, and then I scattered her over the junkyard with Ottis Lee. Me and Cheddar's boy and Trenton and Uncle Cullen gathered out there at sunset and reunited her with her last and maybe best husband. Those two once made a pledge to look out for each other and I like the thought of them roaming the junkyard at night hand in hand, trying to make some kind of sense of the afterlife just like they did during this life. You ought to drop by and visit her if you get the chance. I know she'd be tickled to see you. She loved you even after she forgot who you were.

Speaking of the junkyard, I inherited it so I am now in the junk business. I hired Cheddar's boy to work there for me, and it turns out that he is a pretty good mechanic. When I say I hired him that's not quite the way it went. Actually I bought him from Bay-Annette. Yeah I know that buying people is wrong but I had my reasons. She came to Kathleen's memorial service, which was a nice one even if Genuine Owen did not approve of yet another cremation on his watch, and she was blasted totally out of her mind. I didn't know anyone could be that messed up and live to tell about it. After the service she came to me and tried to barter some personal attention for another coffee can. I told her I'd give her one the next day if she wasn't blitzed when I got there. She said we had a deal and staggered out to her car, and Dakota Blue drove her home.

The next day I went out to her house with one can like I promised. It was a good can, a Chase and Sanborn with about ten grand in it. She was alone and as sober as The Hanging Judge. She was dressed in not much and when I tell you that she looked mighty fine I'm engaging in what is known as understatement. No, I didn't take her up on her second offer of romance and shame on you. That's my cousin's wife you're talking about and I owe him a little respect even if he is dead and even if he did tell me it would be all right to try a little taste and to hold on tight if I did. So instead, I went to get a beer from the fridge, but when I went into the kitchen to get it I found a meth lab set up in there. You can't teach an old Bay-Annette new tricks.

The next part's kind of weird, but no weirder than me writing letters to a dead guy for ten years, so stay with me. I swear I saw Cheddar in there. He was standing in a dark corner—maybe floating is a better word—and looked at the meth lab and then he looked at me and shook his head. I heard him sigh, and I didn't even know that ghosts could do that. Right then I knew what I had to do so I went back to the living room and brightened Bay-Annette's day. I told her I'd give her the location of every single coffee can there was if she would clear out of town and leave Dakota Blue with me. She asked me what I was getting out of the arrangement and I told her I was getting the opportunity to save a boy from going down the same wrong road that his daddy and I had gone down.

She took my offer. To get the cans all she had to do was talk him into living with me until he was 18, and then she had to leave and never come back. She dropped him off on the way out of town and I guarantee you she didn't look in the rearview mirror once. I didn't tell her where they all were. I'm an ex-con and you know how we lie. I held four cans back as his college fund in case he wants to go someday. If he decides not to go, he can have the money for whatever he wants it for. I told him that to give him an incentive to stay. For now, we work at the junkyard. I run the part out front and he works out in the yard. Trenton has taken to dropping by to help. We don't really need any help but I think he just likes the company and to have a little something to do. Dakota Blue and I live in your mama's house, which I also inherited, and most days we seem to be doing fine.

Epilogue

It's been awhile since I have written you and I apologize for that. I don't seem to need to write as much anymore. Maybe I've finally gotten my head screwed on straight or maybe I'm having a light touch of Alzheimer's myself. They say what goes around comes around and that may be true. Or it could be that karma has a mean streak and a long memory. Or it could be that everything is random and no one is driving the bus at all. Who can tell? I don't claim to know the big picture or any such nonsense, but I do know what I know.

I felt like I owed you for the life I took from you and I intended to pay that back by taking care of your mama. I did the best I could for her every single day, and if she had lived longer I would be right there still. But along the way it became more about her and me than it was about me and you. Maybe that's how it had to be. I don't know. But I do know that I pay my debts, so if there is anything else you need just let me know. Your mama was on the house.

I felt like I owed Cheddar, too. He was a good friend to me on the inside and I wouldn't have made it without him. So I took care of his financial business and I got Dakota Blue away from Bay-Annette while there was still time to save him. And I did one other thing not too long ago. It was closing time one Saturday at the junkyard, and when I went out to shut the gate I saw a late model Camaro parked near it. Yeah, they're making them again, but they don't run the way mine used to. Two boys were sitting in it and they were talking to the kid. I didn't recognize them, but when I got up close I saw that they were drinking beer and that they were trying to get him to go with them.

I told Dakota Blue he couldn't go and I wanted to put a stop to the whole party, but when I reached in the window to get the keys out of the switch, the boy who was driving punched it and nearly side-swiped me as he hightailed it out of there. I called the law and told Millard that he had some young boys on the loose and that if they weren't drunk yet they would be soon. Then Dakota Blue and I had a long talk about drinking and driving and about how everything good and decent in the world can be gone in an instant and that saying I'm sorry doesn't mean a thing once it's all been thrown away. He rolled his eyes and we fussed a while and then I stayed up all night just to be sure that he didn't sneak out and try to go hook up with his buddies, because that's exactly what you and I would have done back in the day.

The next morning we got the news that those boys in that Camaro had run into some serious bad luck and they were dead. It turned out that they were hauling ass down Bankhead Hill doing about 100 or so—I told you that Camaros didn't run like they used to—when they hit that bad dip at the bottom of the hill and launched themselves right into the Cherokee Oak. You talk about history repeating itself! Dakota Blue walked around all day looking like he was going to throw up, and at the end of the day we had another talk. He knew he had come about this close to dying and he wanted me to know that he got it. As long as he doesn't backslide we'll be all right. But it's kind of like it was with your mama. Dakota Blue was on the house too, so I still owe Cheddar. Maybe I'll ease over to Asheville someday and collect that money from Harris for him.

It's a funny thing. I did seven years at Sweetwater prison and I spent three more taking care of your mama. So I did my full ten years for killing you. I wish you were still here and I had that time back, but that's not how it works. My life is not what I thought it would be but it could be a lot worse. I could be dead. I could still be in prison. I could be paralyzed. Instead, I run the junkyard and Dakota Blue works for me and Trenton stops by from time to time. I've started driving again and I've dated a couple of women, and most days I'm pretty content. I don't know what's next, but I know what's behind me, and pretty much anything will be better than that.

I used to think Kathleen was the lucky one because she couldn't remember, but I was wrong. I think we all need to remember every minute of it. The future isn't guaranteed and the present is gone as soon as it happens. The remembrances are all that we have.

THE END